RED BLOODED ROOKIE

CINDY STRAUCH

Cindy Strauch/Red Blooded Rookie
Printed in the United States of America

Publisher's Note: This is a work of fiction. Names, characters, places, and incidents are a product of the author's imagination. Locales and public names are sometimes used for atmospheric purposes. Any resemblance to actual people, living or dead, or to businesses, companies, events, institutions, or locales is completely coincidental.

Red Blooded Rookie/ Cindy Strauch. -- 1st ed.

ISBN 978-0-9981431-0-1 Print Edition
ISBN 978-0-9981431-1-8 Ebook Edition

This book took a long time coming to be. My goal was just to write a book, so I could say I had, but my husband had other ideas. The joke was - he always said you have to publish this book and make a lot of money so I can retire. Once I finished the book he made sure that we took the next step and got it published. So here you go Ken - this book would not have happened without your encouragement and support in every way. As far as retiring...... You better keep that job.

Acknowledgements

I would like to thank my husband and daughters Amber and Kelli for doing my first editing. Your help was deeply appreciated. And most of all a Huge Thanks to Eileen Cushing for her great editing. You did an awesome job guiding me through several re-writes. This book would not have happened without your help.

CHAPTER ONE

Brad and Ashley were finally alone, stealing away from Angelina while she jetted off to some faraway place. They both knew in their hearts that it was wrong, but they could not control their desires. They were in Ashley's bedroom, with the lights turned low and candles burning softly throughout the room, giving it a warm glow. They had just climbed from a romantic bubble bath, scented with their favorite aroma that Ashley could still smell as they moved further into the room. Their bodies were flushed with the heat of the water and the passion to come. They were standing a few yards apart, each of them giving the other a thorough look filled with promises of what they wanted to do to each other, when suddenly he gave her a smoldering smile and slowly began crossing the room in her direction. He never took his eyes from Ashley's as he inched his way closer to her. Ashley could feel her knees growing weak, and dampness was beginning to form between her legs. He stopped a few inches from where she stood, anticipating his slow approach, and looked into her eyes until she thought she would combust from the inside out. Ashley let out a soft moan filled with such desire they both sucked in startled breaths. Suddenly he grabbed her and spun her around, pulling her so that her body was tight against his. She could feel the muscles of his chest against her back and the beginning of his desire alongside her ass. He wrapped his arms around Ashley and pulled her so tight against him that she had no doubt of his feelings for her.

He reached around and wrapped one arm across her waist, and with the other he touched her face with a gentle caress of his fingers, running his hand along the side of her face and down her neck, sending shivers up and down her body. He could feel the way he was affecting Ashley and she heard a low chuckle escape from deep within his throat. He pulled her hair aside and placed gentle kisses along her neck, knowing that by doing so, he would send her into an instant orgasm. His hand had moved to within inches of her right breast and she moved so that his hand would touch her. Ashley could feel the heat as it engulfed her breast, and she was becoming impatient as he took his time, stroking her like he had never done before. When she didn't think she could take any more he spun her around and threw her onto the bed, gently falling on top of her, kissing her softly along her jawbone and down across her neck, his lips delicately caressing the erotic spots he found along the way. His hand moved up her thigh, inching ever closer to her throbbing womanhood, desire racing through both of them...

Bang! Bang! Bang!

"ASHLEY? Ashley, are you awake? Open up, you sleepyhead, it's me, Bill. It's time to go to work."

Turning over in bed, her pjs soaked with perspiration, she reached over for Brad, stroking her hand lovingly over his hair, smiling at the purring coming from his throat. She smiled a sexy little smile, opening her eyes slowly, only to discover she was stroking Miss Priss, her longhaired cat. She had one of her lazy green eyes open, giving Ashley one of her famous looks, making it clear that she had better not even think of disturbing her any more than she already had.

Groaning, Ashley let out a sigh of deep frustration, knowing her body was on the verge of something sweet, and that it was not going to be able to reach a climax made her more frustrated than she already was. Turning over and looking at her digital alarm clock blinking its glaring numbers at her, she realized she had been so into the hot dream with Brad Pitt, she must have slept right through the alarm. God, she hated Bill right now. That dream was the only sex she was getting nowadays, and her over-eager partner had to go and ruin even that.

Growling, she crawled out of bed, sending Miss Priss flying from the bed, and made her way into the living room. With no thought to what she was wearing, she jerked open the door and stood glaring at Bill. He gave her a puzzled look and then a frown stretched across his round face.

"Thanks a lot, Bill, I can't believe you ruined my sex life completely." Ashley turned away with a flourish and stomped into the bathroom to get ready, leaving Bill standing there with a dazed look on his face.

Entering the bathroom, she looked down and realized that she was only wearing a thin white baby-doll top and the matching boy underwear that went with it. Oh god, not only did she have her dream interrupted by Bill, but this was not exactly what she wanted her nerdy partner to see her in. Oh well, there was nothing she could do about it now. Deciding there was no time for a shower, the best she could do was wash up as far as possible and wash down as far as possible and she would wash *possible* when she got off work in the morning. Ashley stared into the mirror at some scary woman who looked like she had been rode hard and put away wet. She ran a brush through her hair and teeth and ran some mascara across her lashes. Ashley tossed her hair into a loose bun on the top of her head, put on her uniform, socks and clunky black shoes, and she was ready to go. Ashley grabbed her cap and threw it over her bun as she walked out her bedroom door. It was definitely not her best-looking day, but where Bill and Ashley were headed, the stiffs wouldn't care if she wasn't exactly Miss Hygiene. Any odors coming from them would make her smell like a powder puff.

As Ashley walked into the kitchen, she found Bill making coffee and going through her cupboards. He would open one cabinet, shake his head and move on to the next one. She knew what he was looking for but she was just bitchy enough to put him through the drill.

"What are you doing?" Ashley barked out.

Bill jumped and turned a raised brow at her, trying to decide if she was still in a psycho mood or if she had come around to being her typical happy self. "Well, from the abrupt way you answered the door, it sounded like you needed coffee, and I don't even want to ask how I ruined your sex life unless you have something going on with Miss Priss that I don't know about. Besides, it didn't look like you had your lunch fixed, so I was trying to find something for you to eat. Do you have any food in this apartment?" Bill said in his cheerful voice. He gave her a look that most men turned towards a woman when she wasn't Ms. Happy-ass, probably thinking it was because *it was that time of month.* Then he gave her a quick up and down look, which got her blushing. Ashley hated to think what was going through his mind right now. He may be on the nerdy side, but he was still a male. She could imagine he was wondering what kind of underwear she had on under her uniform. Ewww, gross.

Pushing that thought from her brain, she answered, "Yes there's, food...cat food, a hunk of brown stuff, something with green mold growing on it and a jar of pickles. You can't make a lunch out of that?" she answered in mock seriousness. Ashley reached into the cabinet, pulled two travel mugs down and filled the cups with coffee, adding sugar and enough cream to hers to make it look like chocolate milk. Handing Bill a cup, she headed for the door, leaving him standing there with his mouth open and no answer.

He reached over and clicked off the coffee maker, closed the refrigerator door and the few cabinets that were still open, and followed her through her small apartment, picking up the duty belt that had been lying across the back of the couch. "Are you going to take your duty belt tonight?" he asked, holding it out to her.

Turning, Ashley stopped and gave Bill a questioning look. "Why? Do you think Mr. Phillips, with the bullet hole in his head, is going to be on the prowl tonight? Or maybe I need to stop old Mrs. Schafer from crawling over to Mr. Smith's box and doing the Mumbo Jumbo with him?" She opened the door and walked through it without reaching for the belt; she knew Bill would bring it.

Bill shook his head and just chuckled, tucking the belt under his arm on the way out the door. Ashley reached back, turned the lock on the doorknob and pulled the door closed behind them.

Sipping her too-hot coffee, "You really like doing the night shift, don't you?" she asked him as they headed down the apartment hallway to the entrance of her building. She lived in an apartment complex that contained sixteen apartments, eight on the second floor and eight on the bottom. She lived in the corner apartment on the bottom floor. The Ramirez family was across the hall and the newlywed Johnsons on her other side. Other than a few very intense headboard-banging sessions from them, it was a fairly quiet building. It was mostly older couples and a few singles like her, who kept to themselves. Ashley wasn't sure who had moved into the apartment above her last month, but there were some strange odors that drifted down through the vents every once in a while.

Ashley and Bill were both recent police academy graduates, and were starting their police careers assigned to checking in bodies at the morgue. This was not the assignment that either Ashley or Bill had dreamed of when entering the academy twenty-one months ago.

5

They continued outside and made their way across the parking lot to where his 1967 Ford Galaxy sat. Looking at Bill's heap of a car, Ashley was amazed that the thing still got him where he was going. It was once white, but had faded to a mellow cream color with patches of rust starting to show around the fenders. The inside was still in pretty good shape, for as old as it was. It had belonged to Bill's mom, and when Bill had gone off to college he had inherited the classic, as his mom called it. She wasn't sure anyone else would consider it a *classic*, but Bill didn't seem to mind driving it, and that's all that mattered. She couldn't believe she had to be seen riding to work in this piece of rust, but beggars can't be choosy, and her Ford Bronco was in the shop getting a new muffler.

Jerking back to the present, Ashley realized Bill was answering her question. "Actually, I don't mind it. It's quiet and I don't have to worry about someone trying to shoot, stab or hit me. On slow nights I can sleep. Plus, someone has to check in the bodies," Bill offered as he got in and put his big black lunch box on the seat between them. He maneuvered his boat out onto the street, which was beginning to fill with cars, all of which were going somewhere a hell of lot more fun than where they were headed. She gave Bill a questioning look. "Bill, are you sure you want to be a cop?"

Laughing, he shot her a quick glance. "Yes, I was just joking about the shooting part. I can't wait to get on patrol so we can see some action."

Ashley gave him a dubious look, still not sure she could picture Bill in the middle of a robbery or breaking up a domestic call. He seemed more like the kind of guy who would take off running rather than get in the middle of a raging couple throwing punches at each other. But who could tell what someone would do, until you've seen him in action. Hell, she wasn't even sure how she would react when they actually got out on the street and saw some crime. He was about the same height she was, maybe an inch or so

6

taller depending on the shoes they both were wearing. He probably weighed somewhere in the one seventy range but she didn't think any of that weight was muscle. He was on the pale side, with a round-shaped baby face. He wore black-rimmed glasses that made his light blue eyes look twice as big as they were.

They pulled into the police station parking lot and eased into an available spot, parking beside a brand new red Jaguar, just as Big Tits Malone was getting out of the car. How she could afford a car like that on a rookie policeman's salary was beyond Ashley. Her guess was she made the payments from flat on her back.

The rumor was that she had to have her uniforms specially made, just to get her double Ds to fit. Not that Ashley was jealous of her overblown plastic balls, because she wasn't and she would take her firm natural Cs to her double Ds any day. She had always wondered: if she ever had to take off on foot, chasing a perp, would Malone kill herself with those plastic mounds of silicone? It was a sight she was sure everyone in the precinct wanted to see.

How she ever made it through the academy was also a wonder to more than half of them who had gone through it with her. Seeing as none of them had ever seen her even attempt to climb the wall or, God forbid, crawl under the wire, they assumed that she had slept her way around all the physical parts of the academy, and the classroom parts as well.

"Well, well, if it isn't the two stiffs from the morgue," Malone purred to Bill as she walked by, running her hand up and down his chest. She gave Bill's car a quick glance and then turned a satisfied smirk in Ashley's direction.

Bill stood with his mouth gaping open, staring at her hand as she slithered past him. He continued to stand there like he was in a daze for several seconds after she had turned and walked into the station. Her ass was swinging from side to side in such a way, Ashley wondered how she didn't throw her back out. Ashley looked over and Bill's mouth was still open, and she could have sworn she saw a little drool drip out. She walked around the car and slapped him on the arm. "What in the hell is wrong with you? You actually just drooled over Malone." He jumped and turned an embarrassed look her way. She almost felt sorry for him; she'd watched as Malone had made mincemeat out of him in a matter of seconds.

Bill gave Ashley a blank look. "I did not drool. But you have to admit, Ash, that woman is built like every man's fantasy."

With a look of disgust, Ashley asked, "You're kidding me, right? Men really prefer fake plastic to the real thing?"

Bill stood there, twisting his foot back and forth. "Well, maybe not prefer, but we do like to look, no matter if they are real or, like you say, plastic."

Ashley was not going to have any teeth left if she kept grinding them every time she came into contact with that woman. Malone had been a pain in Ashley's life from the time they were in grade school to the present, and sometimes more so than she wanted to admit.

After the academy, when she had first learned that she and Malone were going to the same precinct, she had tried bribing her brother Michael, who was a detective, into getting Malone transferred to another precinct where the crime rate was much higher than here in their suburb. They needed scent hounds down there, to sniff out gangs and drug dealers, more than they did. All they needed them for was the occasional lost cat or lost kid. Michael had claimed he had no control over transfers, but she thought he enjoyed watching the hair on the back of her neck rise whenever she was in the same room as Malone. Everyone who knew Ashley and Malone was aware that it was a constant battle between the two of them. Ashley had tried to be an adult and ignore Malone most of the time, but Malone made it her goal in life to constantly interfere with Ashley's, and it was never in her best interest, either.

Grabbing Bill's arm, Ashley turned him toward the building that housed their precinct. It was an old brick building that had stood in the center of town for over a hundred years. It had two stories and a full basement. Through the front doors was the booking desk and behind that was the area used for offices and the holding cell. Upstairs was filled with more offices and the evidence storage area. They had converted the basement into the morgue when the old morgue had burned to the ground years ago. Rumor had it that old Mr. Taylor had set the place on fire, after they had brought his wife in when she was found dead in their apartment. Some said he was trying to destroy any evidence that they might have found on his wife's body, but they had never been able to prove anything. Ashley remembered her parents talking about how the fire had lit up the whole block, it was so big.

Ashley entered the room and did a quick look around, noticing Malone had positioned herself right next to Phillip Kelly, the best-looking guy in the room. She was trying to engage him in conversation, but he was doing a fine job of ignoring her and talking to Jim Grant instead. Ashley couldn't help but smile, just knowing Malone did not have the power over every man alive. It made her feel good to know there were still a few guys out there who were not mesmerized by a woman with fake tits and an overblown ego.

The night shift had all assembled in the squad room to listen to the Division Chief give out the nightly duties. Ashley and the other new rookies were currently on a three-week rotating shift, only into the first shift by nine days. That meant Ashley had one week, seven hours and fifty-six minutes to go on this miserable assignment. Maybe Bill didn't mind it, but she was bored to death. Four nights in a row now, and they had not had to check in one new body, just watch over the ones left over from the day shift. They lived in Timberwood, a suburb of Denver, Colorado, and the police department did things a little differently than most cities.

Graduates were not all put on the patrol division right out of the academy. The Chief of Police thought all new fourth-grade officers coming straight out of the academy should be exposed to all the divisions of their city, so they would be more knowledgeable in all the positions of law enforcement. So, they were assigned to three-week shifts in morgue duty, traffic patrol, robbery/homicide or vice/narcotics to learn what they could, in a twelve-week period, before they assigned them to their permanent jobs.

They were only into the night roll call by a few minutes when Ashley looked over and caught Ryan Williams dropping little pieces of rolled-up paper down Scott Walsh's shirt. She may have only been on this job for nine days, but it was easy to pick up on some of the people's personalities already. Ryan was a jokester, and Walsh was a rookie trying to climb to the top, right up through the Lieutenant's ass.

Ryan noticed Ashley watching, and gave her a wink and a big ol' grin. Walsh was going to be very surprised when he took off his clothes tomorrow and all of those little balls of paper fell to the floor. Not that he didn't deserve that and more; he was one of those "yes" men, who thought that if he agreed to everything anyone with authority said, he would get further in the department. Unbeknownst to him, he was already the joke of the precinct. No one, especially cops, could stand a pansy-ass "yes" man. He was in for a rough twelve weeks. If it had been anyone else she might have given him a heads up, but the guy was such a jerk, he wouldn't take anything she told him seriously. He was also one of those men who thought women had no place being in the police department.

They finished up with roll call, with everyone else heading off to their assignments for the night, while Bill and Ashley milled around visiting with a few stragglers before they started for the dungeon.

While Ashley was busy talking to Bill, Officer Steve Merritt walked up beside her and put his arm around her, leaning over to whisper into her ear. "Hey baby, maybe I'll get lucky tonight and get a DOA so I can come pay you a visit. Then while ol' Bill is busy checking him in, we can sneak away and get to know each other a little better." He had taken the liberty to run his hand up her arm and gently stroke her neck above the collar of her uniform.

Ashley fought the urge to grab his hand, pull one of the defensive moves her brother Michael had taught her and break his damn thumb, but opted to just turn sideways so his hand would fall off her shoulder. She replied in the nicest voice she could muster, "I would rather get to know old man Smith down in the morgue than I would you, but I'm sure Malone would be glad to take you up on that offer. You two seem to be cut from the same cloth."

Ashley didn't stick around long enough for him to answer, but as she walked down the stairs, she turned back to see that he was still standing there, glaring at her. She decided right then and there, she would never turn her back on Steve Merritt again. The man was slime. He was a cocky, know-it-all prick who thought every woman should stop and lick his balls just for the sake of it. Some women might find that kind of man attractive, but she sure as hell didn't.

As Ashley was turning the corner of the stairs to head down into her prison, she almost bumped into Shaffer, another fellow graduate, and Malone, making their way back up the stairs with their heads together in a serious conversation. Wondering what the two rookies were doing in the basement ran through Ashley's mind, but since Malone was involved, she really didn't want to dwell on it too long. Malone gave her a cat-like smirk and leaned into Shaffer. Ashley really liked Shaffer; she hoped he wasn't falling for any of Malone's tricks and lies.

Bill checked the log-in sheet to see if they had any new clients, but the guests were still Mrs. Thorpe, waiting to be shipped to Iowa, and Mr. Smith, who was to be picked up first thing tomorrow by Franklin's Mortuary. Bill had a habit of always checking to make

11

sure the bodies were where they were supposed to be. Not Ashley, she was just as happy to assume they were where they needed to be. There were thirty metal compartments they kept the bodies in, stacked ten to a row, three deep. Why the city thought they would ever need that many was beyond her. It wasn't like they lived in a war zone or anything.

Ashley settled down into one of the two hard metal chairs that sat before the old scarred wooden table in the outer lobby of the morgue. She had brought a deck of cards to work, in the hopes of talking Bill into some gin rummy. She would rather have played poker, but felt like it would be taking someone's milk money if she had played poker with Bill. Bill did not look like the type to be into poker; he was more into the high-tech gizmo computer game stuff.

"What do you say, Bill, how about I beat your butt in a couple games of gin rummy? Winner gets to take the first nap after lunch," Ashley asked.

"Sounds good, but I have to warn you, I used to play with my crazy old grandma when I was a kid," he answered as he walked to the other chair.

"Hey, me too, except I'll bet yours didn't cheat like mine did. She would distract me with chocolate chip cookies and then go through the deck to get what she needed. I always knew what she was doing, but I didn't really care, because I was getting cookies and my brother and sister weren't. My parents never did understand why I was always so eager to go to Grandma's, and then just go off and play gin rummy with her," Ashley replied.

"Are you close to your grandparents? Mine lived in Florida, so I only saw them on some of the holidays," Bill asked as he picked up the cards and started shuffling them. Ashley could tell by the way he handled the cards that he was an experienced card player. Maybe she should rethink the poker idea.

Ashley sat there and thought about her grandparents for a while before answering his question. "My dad's parents are farmers and ranchers and live about two hours from us. He came from a huge family with a total of ten brothers and sisters. Although we spent a lot of time out on their farm when I was growing up, there were always so many people around, I wouldn't know if you would call us close. Grandpa always said he was going to have twenty-five kids so he could have a complete alphabet. His name was Adam; his first-born was a son so he named him Bruce. He made it all the way to the letter L before grandma threatened him that if he even thought of going on to the letter M, they would find him tied up in the barn, hanging from the rafters by his gonads."

Ashley watched Bill's face as she had started talking; people were always a little amazed when she started telling them how big her family was. "My grandparents have twenty-eight grandchildren and forty-eight great-grandchildren, so there was no way that they had time to be close to all of us. It was like a three-ring circus when we all got together. Grandpa turned the old red barn into a gathering place for his humongous family. He built a kitchen with four ovens and two range tops, along with two old commercial-sized refrigerators, and he filled it with tables and rows and rows of benches. He and my uncles had installed two pot-bellied stoves in the corners, so we could meet no matter what time of year it was. I remember it was one of my favorite times, when we were all gathered under the rafters of that old barn…still is. The hayloft was where all of us kids escaped to after our dinners and it was too cold to be outside. That's where I learned about the birds and the bees, from listening to my older cousins talk about their boyfriends and what they did with them. We younger kids would hide behind the hay bales while the older ones would talk, and one thing I learned about country kids is, they started experimenting with the birds and bees way earlier than us city kids."

Ashley sat there in thought for a few minutes, remembering all the good times. Bill and Ashley had stopped playing as they talked; both were caught up in their memories, so neither one of them really noticed. Pulling her thoughts together, she went on describing her family to him. "But one thing I can say about my grandparents is they knew every single one of our names. If things were a little hectic, it might take calling out three or four names before they eventually hit on the right one, but they would get to it sooner or later. And, yes, they cared for every single one of us. They may not have had the time to spend a lot of quality time with each and every one of us, but you could just feel the love when you were around them. I guess I take that for granted and don't realize not everyone comes from that kind of love and security."

Bill sat in amazement as she talked about her dad's family. She knew Bill was from a small family, so he probably couldn't even imagine what she was describing.

"And then there are my mom's parents, who are just the opposite of my dad's parents. They were one hundred percent city folk, belonging to the local country club and several other organizations around the city. But they were always pretty fun. Grandpa was a stuffy insurance salesman by day and liked to enjoy a toddy or two at night. He said his evening toddies were to unwind him from a long day of putting up with whining customers. Grandma Rogers never worked outside of the home; she was the quirky stay-at-home mom." Ashley couldn't help but start chuckling at this point, "But don't get me wrong, she was no June Cleaver; she was a lousy cook and a so-so housekeeper, but she was active in all of her volunteer work and women's clubs. She had a lady come in once a week and clean her house, so it would always look good in case someone stopped by unannounced. They lived only a few miles from where we did, so we spent a lot of weekends at their house. She was the grandma who liked to play gin rummy with me. It wasn't until I was a lot older that I realized the cookies were not homemade; she bought them at the bakery and came home and put them in the oven to warm them up. But hey, you didn't find me complaining, a cookie was a cookie."

"Sounds like you had it pretty lucky. I think it would be fun coming from a large family. It was just me and my little brother and my mom. Things were pretty quiet at our house."

Ashley could see the haunted look that passed in his eyes and knew some memories about his family caused him pain, but she also knew that if he wanted to talk about them, he would. She was not the type of person who dug into someone's private life without an invitation.

Thinking back to the times spent with all her wild cousins had her answering, "I don't know if lucky is the right word to use. You weren't the one always being chased around the yard with fifteen ornery boys flinging cow patties at you, or pushing you into the corral with Grandpa's mean old bull, Tex, and sitting there taking bets to see how long it took us girls to crawl through the fence rails, or fall down in a fresh cow pie scrabbling to get out of the corral. With that big of a family, you could always count on one of the boys to be thinking up new ways to annoy us silly girls. You have to remember, I was one of the sissified city girls and they loved to torment us first, before they set their sights on their country cousins. I could sit here all night and tell you stories of what they did to us over the years, but I'm sure you would be bored to tears with them."

Bill reassured her that he would love to hear them, that he came from such a quiet family that he considered it an honor to be part of her memories. Ashley couldn't help giving him a strange look, wondering what kind of childhood he had lived. He only mentioned his family on a rare occasion, and none of them had been there when they had graduated from the academy. He had said that both his mom and brother had been unable to get off work, but she still wondered if he had even told them about it. It made her a little sad to think that he had no one he was close to in his life. Ashley was constantly surrounded by either family or friends, and took that part of her life for granted. She could not imagine being in this world without the love and support she got each and every day. There had been times in her past that she felt smothered by all that affection, but as she looked back on it now, she realized how blessed she was.

Bill and Ashley sat through the first half of their shift, playing gin rummy and reminiscing about childhood memories, mostly hers, with Bill throwing in a comment or two every once in a while. So far they were pretty even on wins and losses, so she wasn't sure who was going to get to take the nap. Three o'clock rolled around and her stomach starting singing the *I want lasagna song*. Bill raised his eyes from his cards and gave her a smug look. She knew he was thinking about her empty cupboards at home as he listened to her stomach growl with hunger. It was their so-called supper break, but her body was still not used to eating a full meal at three in the morning, night after night. Everyone knew the only time you ate at three in the morning was after you had spent the night at the bar and were drunk, and then it was greasy fried food that you ate, not something thrown together or some stale piece of cardboard from the vending machine up in the break room.

Bill started chuckling as he listened to her stomach growl again, and said he figured her stomach was better than an alarm clock; he was going to go on ahead and get his lunch ready in the break room. Knowing she had nothing special waiting for her, she headed off to the ladies' room to get rid of the gallons of coffee she had consumed.

The restrooms in the basement were a scary thing at night. The rooms were painted a dull prison gray, were dimly lit and smelled like an old gym room in high school. Ashley put off coming in here until the last possible minute because the place really creeped her out. She didn't mind the morgue because the lights were blinding, plus the bodies were already in their nice little homes when they came to work.

Ashley pushed open the bathroom door while she struggled to unfasten her duty belt. She had waited too long to make the trip and had to cross her legs as she fought the buckle on the 20-pound belt around her hips. She finally managed the belt, laid it on the sink counter, and was just getting her pants unzipped when her eyes moved from her zipper to the stall door, where she noticed the door was closed. Usually the doors were kept open, an unspoken rule among all who worked in this part of the station. She grabbed her pants with both hands with her legs still crossed and leaned down, looking under the door, whispering, "Anyone in there?" No one responded and she really needed to go. She could smell a weird odor as she slowly pushed open the stall door. Her eyes were trying to adjust to the dim light and her heart was beating so loud she was sure Bill could hear it in the other room. It took a few seconds for her eyes to adjust, and when they did she dropped her pants in shock. There on the toilet was a guy. A dead one! She let out a blood-curdling scream, jumping back, tripping over the pants around her ankles and made a dash for the door, struggling to get her pants back up around her ass. As she came barreling out of the door, there stood Malone, Shaffer, Luchetta, another rookie, and a group of unknowns, laughing their fool heads off.

Luchetta was laughing so hard, Ashley thought he was going to piss his pants, but he managed to get out, "Nice pink thong, Ashley! Is that standard issue with the uniform?"

Ashley's heart was racing so fast she was sure it was already up the stairs, while her shaking, quivering body was still standing there in the hall as she clutched her pants up, trying to figure out what the *hell* had just happened. She was breathing fast and having a hard time slowing it down.

All she could do was stand there, gasping for breath with her heart racing at lightning speed. She was shaking from fear and shock, but when she looked around at the amused crowd she could feel anger replacing the fear. But still she managed to stutter, "Okay, which wise-ass put the stiff in the john?"

Shaffer finally took pity on her, and confessed to taking the cadaver that had been donated to the local university and propping it up on the toilet seat.

Everyone had moved into the restroom so they could witness the little pisspot's handiwork. Except Malone, of course, who stood over there grinning like a cat that had just licked up spilt milk. She gave Ashley the look she always did when she knew she had got the best of her. God she hated that bitch, and someday she was going to make sure Malone got what was coming to her. Ashley had played the nice girl long enough, but this crossed the line. Malone had tried to make her look like a fool in front of the people she had to work with every day for the rest of her life, and that was something she wouldn't stand for. Ashley and Malone stood there glaring at each other. Malone must have sensed she might have gone too far, because for a split second Ashley saw a flicker of fear in her eyes before it was replaced with her usual cockiness.

Buckling up her pants, she moved into the restroom to get a better look at Mr. Stiffy. They had dressed him up in old clothes taken from some previous dead guy, or at least she assumed they did since they were a little better quality than most homeless people who came through the morgue. They had pulled his pants down around his ankles, placed a Playboy in one hand and a cigarette in the other. He had no socks on and was wearing mismatched shoes. His hair was fairly long, and Malone must have used hair spray to get it to stand up on end. His mouth was open along with his eyes.

Rigor mortis must have been already starting when he came in, because they couldn't get him bent the whole way, so he was kind of just squatting over the toilet.

Ashley had to admit they had gotten her good. She had seen cadavers in training, but not in a dark bathroom as she was trying to take a piss.

People started slapping her on the back, telling her what a great sport she was, and that this had to be one of the best rookie pranks yet. Ashley laughed and smiled and played along with the fun, but leaning over, she whispered to Shaffer, "I can take a joke with the best of them, but be aware of my personal motto—paybacks are a bitch! Watch your back, because I'm good at giving back better than I got."

He gave her a nervous little smile, not sure if he should take her seriously or not. Maybe Ashley needed to have him talk to her brother and sister to testify to her famous paybacks. Throughout the years, being the middle child always found her at the brunt of her older brother's and little sister's shenanigans. They would gang up and play all kinds of pranks on her. But she was always a good sport. Then she would wait patiently for the right time and pay them back big time. Their parents never understood why they kept setting themselves up for such heartache, but they always did.

Ashley reached down, picked up her duty belt and fastened it on, deciding the need to use the restroom had come and gone. She joined everyone back out in the hall and they traipsed back up to the break room, to use the rest of the time to scarf up some food.

As they entered, Bill was sitting all by himself. "Hey, where was everyone? What was all that racket down in the morgue?"

Leave it to Bill to miss out on all the action. He was up here being the good friend, fixing his lunch while the other scumbags were downstairs playing havoc with her pride. Oh well, no real harm done, and her mind was already at work thinking of ways to get even.

Bill proceeded to unpack his lunch box. She swore it contained more than her whole apartment refrigerator on a good day. Two sandwiches, a bag of chips, potato salad, a container of pudding, Twinkies, cookies, a candy bar, a jar of apple juice, a can of soda and a bag of peanuts. Ashley walked to the vending machine and pulled out a tuna salad sandwich and a Snickers bar. Making her way over to their table, she was suddenly everyone's friend and received more comments on the stiff and her reaction to it. Several comments were thrown out about her lacy pink thong, and she could just imagine how long it would take for that to die down. She glanced over Malone's way and could tell this was not the result she had been after. She was hoping more for the hysterical-woman-throwing-a-fit-and-crying scene, and it had to be tearing her up that Ashley was suddenly the one in the spotlight and not her. She was trying to engage several men around her in conversation, but for the most part they were ignoring her. She shot Ashley a murderous look as she walked by, which she just answered with a huge smile and a wave.

Ashley went over to Bill's table and settled in for her gourmet supper. She watched in amazement as he shoveled one thing after another into his mouth. She felt like she was watching a science fiction movie in slow motion. She couldn't help smiling, wondering how Officer Bill Wynn made it through the physical part of the academy. Not that he was fat or anything, but he had the beginning of an extra tire around his waist. And unlike Malone, she didn't think sleeping around was how Bill had passed.

Bill reminded her of a kid at heart. In the months that she had known Bill, she had come to the conclusion that he didn't have a real desire to be on the police force. He had never really said as much, but she thought he would have been much happier being a computer programmer somewhere. He always just kind of meandered around, not really having a purpose to his actions. She wasn't sure how he would hack it out in the real world when they were done with this assignment, but she would keep an eye on him and help him where she could.

Ashley filled him in on the happenings in the downstairs restroom and watched as horror crossed his face. "Ashley, that's not right. That man was someone's family. That is disrespectful of the dead and I think those guys should be severely punished."

She had to agree with him on the punished part, but these homeless people who donated their bodies to science had no one to pay to have them buried, so there was a good chance that there was no family waiting in the wings, wanting to sue the city for the misuse of their loved one. It was a fact of life in the big cities; sad for those individuals, but it was still just a part of society. What they were going to do to that poor man's body next was a lot worse than being stuck in a women's john for a few hours.

After lunch, when Bill and Ashley were safely tucked back into their little hole, she decided she was a little too wound up to be taking a nap, so she told Bill to go for it. Plus, she didn't trust anyone now, and half expected that if she did take a nap, she would wake up with her arm around someone cold, clammy and stiff. Not that she hadn't done that before, but that was in college. She had been at a frat party and had drunk way too much. She passed out and woke up next to Jesse Frank, who had also passed out. Their friends thought it would be funny to move them out to the backyard and put them both in a hammock. Ashley woke up first, and looked into Jesse's face, and thought she had become a royal slut who slept with a pimple-faced freshman. She rolled over and tried to get up, sending them both flying to the ground. Jesse never did wake up, and she made a beeline out of there, promising herself that she would never drink that much again.

21

While Bill settled in for his nap, she filled her time with solitaire and watching the clock, ready for the night to be over.

As she sat there looking around the bleak morgue, she thought about why she was here in the first place. Which brought her to remember it had all started in high school.

She blamed it all on Jimmy Gleason, her "first love," who swept her off her feet their junior year of high school with his perfect smile and two huge dimples. He stole her heart and her virginity, in the back of his Blazer CRZ. It was okay because they were in love, and he had promised her the moon, the stars, and the happily ever after. It lasted one week and that's when she found him and Big Tits Malone under the bleachers after a home basketball game. There they were, going at it like a couple of rabbits, his basketball shorts down around his ankles and her hip-huggers flying in the air where they had got caught on her high-heeled shoe. His hairy white ass was bouncing up and down like the basketball he'd dribbled up and down the court earlier that night. Ashley swore off dimple-faced men right then and there, and that was the beginning of the adult hatred Malone and Ashley had for each other. They had crossed over from school-ground pranks to the real deal.

Ashley kept that promise, or at least until the summer after she graduated when she decided to spend the summer on her grand-parents' farm. That's when she met Brandon Swift, a Greek god, who was six feet of pure heart-stopping delight. There she was with her head stuck under old Betsy's stomach, pulling on her teats like there was no tomorrow, talking to her like she was her best friend when she heard a soft chuckle behind her. Figuring it could have been any one of her twenty-eight cousins, she took one of Betsy's teats and shot a stream of milk over her shoulder at the offending chuckler. Without turning around, she knew she had scored a di-rect hit by the sudden gasp of surprise. She turned around expect-ing to see a cousin, but instead stared into the face of someone right out of a male fashion ad. Realizing her mistake, she jumped up, knocking over the milk bucket and scaring Betsy, who swung her ass around, causing her to trip and fall right in a pile of fresh cow shit. That only brought on more laughter from the Greek god. She didn't know which was worse, being covered in everything a cow could produce or being laughed at by a complete stranger. But as she looked up into the greenest eyes she'd ever seen, all she could do was join in the laughter.

Looking at the fresh manure on her hand, he smiled. Out popped two gorgeous dimples, and she knew she was doomed. He gave a soft chuckle, reached out and wiped the milk from her cheek, and bent down and brushed a light kiss on the corner of her mouth.

That was the best and worst summer of her life. Brandon turned out to be her grandparents' summer help, and they spent the summer falling in love. He was a local boy home for the summer from college, trying to pick up some extra cash. Her heart would flop around in her chest every time she would see him, her thong would become wet and she couldn't help certain parts of her anatomy from humming and purring. They worked beside each other, took lazy walks down by the river, skinny-dipped down at the pond, and told each other they were meant to be. He was way different than old Jimmy Gleason ever was, so she didn't mind when her clothes started disappearing. That doesn't mean she didn't keep one eye on the farm's driveway at all times for any sign of Big Tits Malone's little red Jaguar. Not that she would ever stoop to coming way out here to a farm, but if she heard that there was a Greek god involved, Ashley wouldn't put anything past her. Ashley wasn't taking any chances, and kept a pitchfork handy. She actually hoped Malone would show up; the thought of chasing her down with a pitchfork brought a smile to her face. She could see her running away in her designer high-heeled shoes, her big tits flapping in her face, trying to avoid fresh cow pies the whole time and still trying to entice Brandon into some wild sex act.

Then the summer was gone and so was her heart. It was time for them both to head to college. Although she was only going an hour away from home, Brandon was clear across the country at some stupid college that offered a great program on construction management. They were not going to let that be a problem to them; they were going to beat the odds and make a long-distance romance work.

They called twice a week, and sent letters every day. He came for Ashley's college homecoming, and she went to see him over Thanksgiving break. But then they got busier with school, and the calls happened only when they got a free minute, and the letters came sporadically. She was doing the whole living-in-a-dorm thing, partying till dawn and going to class so she could get some sleep. He took a job in his college town over Christmas break to earn some fast cash, but she was so wrapped up with the whole holiday thing, she didn't have time to worry about it. They still loved each other, so everything was all right.

When Ashley returned to her dorm after the Christmas break, she decided it was a good time to try and call to see how he had survived the break without her.

"Hello," came this giggly little voice on the other end of the phone.

"I'm sorry, I was trying to reach Brandon's phone," Ashley said.

"You did," giggle, giggle.

Brandon was suddenly on the phone, with a "Hi babe, what's up?"

"What's up? I'll tell you what's up, you sneaky, lying son of a bitch. I'm not going to sit around and pine for you when you have some bimbo straddling your lap, playing Hoochie coochie with your loodle-la-dol." Click.

She sat there fuming, more at herself than at anyone else. How could she have been so stupid? She had trusted that man, and the first chance he got, he had some naïve girl in his room, flashing those good looks and dimples around, like she knew he could. She could have him, dimples and all.

That was the end of that love affair. She refused to take his calls, and he eventually stopped trying. There were days she was tempted to answer, just to see what he had to say, but she knew her heart was too fragile after the Jimmy/Malone ordeal and she would eventually fall for all his excuses. Right then and there, she decided that God must have made dimples as a sign of evil. And who was she to not trust God's signs?

She spent the rest of the year avoiding men at all costs. It seemed the more she tried to keep her distance, the more they chased her. She was sure she was considered the conquest of the campus. Whoever could nail her would go down in the campus history books for that year. Ashley was lucky to have made some good friends at the beginning of the year, and she kept to her group and ignored the rest of the idiots who were always trying to break into their circle.

Bang! She jumped about a foot out of her rickety chair, turning around sharply towards the noise. "Holy crap, what the hell was that?" Ashley really did hate that she had pulled the morgue shift. If she didn't stop sitting here, reminiscing about the evils of dimples and not paying more attention to what was going on around her, one of those dead guys could sneak up behind her and kill her. Looking around, she noticed that it was just Bill trying to turn over in his little slab bed. She personally thought trying to sleep on a cold steel slab in a three-foot by three-foot square next to a dead lady with blue hair was just a little creepy, but if Bill could do it, who was she to complain? She personally preferred to take her naps

25

in her hard metal chair, outside the room, completely away from all the deadness.

Once her heart slowed back to a normal rate, her mind went back to the memories of what had brought her to this dungeon. After the break-up with Brandon her college life settled into the normal up and downs, just like everyone else's. During that freshman year, she settled into classes and partying just like everyone else around her. Her sophomore year was filled with classes; she got a part-time job as a bartender down at a college hangout and picked up a few shifts at the steakhouse for extra cash. She spent that summer there instead of heading home like so many others. For the most part college was okay, classes sucked, but she had no real idea what she wanted to major in, like most other sophomores.

Ashley had always been blessed with lots of friends. Since she was a little girl she'd constantly had friends around her, except little crybaby Malone. *She* always caused trouble for everyone, especially Ashley. From the first day she met Malone in kindergarten, they were bitter rivals. Ashley had the friends and she didn't. Because of that, Malone made it her top priority to make her life a living hell, from glue in her hair, to notes telling everyone she had cooties, to trying to steal every boy she ever liked. They had kept the feud going to this day. She was a thorn in Ashley's side and that of everyone else she came into contact with. She was famous for using men to get what she wanted and then dropping them like hot potatoes. What Ashley couldn't understand was why they didn't seem to mind. This could only mean she must be one hot piece of ass. Her friends constantly joked that Malone had gone through every man on campus, and that she would have to start doing everyone twice or transfer to another college.

The fact that she had followed Ashley to college was unbelievable. There were thousands of colleges all over the United States, but no, she had to come to the same one Ashley had. She knew

Malone had waited until after Ashley had been accepted before she decided to follow her, just so she could continue to cause her headaches. Although she had been a pain all throughout Ashley's life, once they moved away and went to college, she became even nastier. She didn't play around with just stealing boyfriends and childish pranks, she moved on to more vicious ways to make her life hell. She slept with professors and then talked them into giving Ashley more homework than necessary, she hacked into the college computer and gave all Ashley's friends and her F's. The faculty figured someone had played with the grades and restored them to the correct grades, but they all knew who had done it. She talked frat boys into breaking into her dorm room and stealing all her and her roommate's underwear; they hung it all over the campus along with signs saying who it belonged to, and that they would give free blow jobs to anyone who brought the underwear back to them. It took weeks of stupid boys knocking on their door at all hours of the night trying to redeem their rewards before finally getting all their underwear back. Personally she threw hers away and bought new; no way was she wearing something that frat boys had had in their possession. She continued to cause havoc, and after two and a half years of boring classes, putting up with Hoochie Malone always invading her life, and the general funk of college life, Ashley wanted to quit college. She had been playing with the idea of quitting school, but could not get up the nerve to approach her parents with the idea. She was not up for the lecture about needing a college degree to go anywhere in this world. She had fallen into a funk and was feeling restless with her life. She hated the endless worthless classes that were a waste of time, and since she could not decide on a major, that was all she was taking.

All that changed the fall of her junior year, after one night at Johnny's, the local college bar where she worked part time. Ashley and a group of friends had decided to get into the holiday spirit by dressing up for Halloween and partaking in the local events at the bar. Johnny's was having a costume contest, so her group all decided to dress up as a group of pimps and hos. They had gone to the local secondhand store and picked up all kinds of things to use in their outfits. It was hard to believe that people actually wore these kinds of things in their daily lives, but they found some awesome stuff for just a few bucks. Ashley had chosen a white leather mini dress that was laced up the front. It showed more than it covered and was just long enough to cover her ass, but that's what Halloween was all about, wearing stuff you never would any other time. She had white hose and white hooker boots with her hair teased up into this wild just-slept-in look. Her makeup was piled on and her jewelry was wild and crazy. They had hot-glued pieces of boas around the big hats the guys had found. The guys had actually found flared polyester pants with wild animal prints. A few silk shirts and they were set. They all looked great and played their parts to a tee. There were nine of them in their group and they made quite an impression when they entered the bar. Everyone was hitting the pimps up for dates with their "ladies," men and women alike.

Everyone was buying them drinks and the night was going great until a real jerk, dressed up like Tarzan, decided that just because Ashley was dressed up as a hooker, she was one. She tried to politely brush the guy off, but he would not leave her alone. All night long he just kept pestering her, making rude comments, trying to grab her ass every time he got close. The bar was crazy with everyone in costumes, yelling and screaming. Her group tried to just stay out of the guy's way and ignore him. This worked for most of the night, but Ashley would look up every once in a while and catch this guy just staring at her. He scared the holy bajebees out of her, so she talked everyone into taking their party to a different bar.

Ashley and a friend needed to hit the ladies' room before they left, so they told everyone they would meet up with them by the front door. The place was all decked out in Halloween stuff, black lights, fog machines and decorations. Just trying to get to the back of the bar where the restrooms were was almost impossible. Somewhere along the way Ashley and her friend got separated, but figuring they would both eventually meet up at the restrooms, Ashley just kept heading to the back of the bar, pushing her way through Batmen, witches, and devils.

When she reached the hallway to the restrooms it was mass confusion, with everyone trying to maneuver their way against the wave of costumes both coming and going. Before she knew it, someone had grabbed her from behind and pulled her into a storage room across from the restrooms. There was only a small light on at the back of the room, but it was enough to see that it was Tarzan who had her pushed up against the wall.

He had an evil look in his eye that had her knees shaking and her heart pounding so hard she thought it was going to jump out of her chest. He started groping her and saying how he knew Ashley wanted it, that she was just acting tough in front of her friends. All she could do was stand there frozen with fear, her mind blank. It was all happening so fast; it was like her brain was frozen in a state of shock. He held her hands above her head, pinning her against the wall while he used his other hand to pinch and squeeze her tits. He was slobbering all over her face and then he pried her mouth open and stuck his tongue down her throat. Ashley thought she was going to gag as he continued to grind against her, drooling and licking her neck as he felt her up. But it was when he ripped off her underwear that her brain finally kicked in. One thing her brother Michael had taught her growing up was how to hit a guy where it counts. Before he knew what was happening her knee came up and connected with his loincloth, hard, dropping him to his knees in a split second. She stood over him, gasping and trying to catch her breath, watching him roll around in agony. After she had regained her senses, her fear turned to anger and she bent over him and screamed, "You asshole! Don't *ever* do that to another woman again," and kicked him in the loincloth again. She pulled herself together the best she could and made her way back to her waiting friends. After she left the bar and had calmed down enough, she realized that she never wanted to feel that helpless again.

She spent the next few days sorting out how she felt, but after what had happened at the bar, it was much easier to break the news of her desire to quit college to her parents. After hearing about what had happened to her, they wanted to move her back in with them to protect her from all the evils of the world. Although Ashley wasn't ready to take that drastic a step, she was ready to move back to her hometown. Her dad and brother Michael were both on the police force, and had talked about driving down to the college to find the guy and arrest him—after they beat the shit out of him. It took hours for her to make them realize that she had no idea who the guy was and that they would never be able to find him again.

After Ashley's run-in with Tarzan, carrying a gun was definitely becoming more appealing. It took her months to not walk around in fear. She would jump at every little noise and was afraid to walk around at night. She was pissed that the prick had made her afraid of her own shadow. She had been lucky that time, but next time she might not be so lucky, and she never wanted to feel that vulnerable again. There were way too many evil men running around the world trying to do evil things to innocent women.

She spent countless hours trying to decide what she wanted to do since she had left college. A part of her was ashamed that she had tucked tail and run the first time something serious happened. People were always telling her they understood why she felt the need to quit after what had happened to her, that she had a right to get herself together, she could always go back to college when she was ready. Ashley was torn between feeling sorry for herself and being royally pissed off. She had never been through anything she felt she couldn't handle before, and she was no fool, she knew she was lucky that night in the storage room. If the guy had not been such an amateur, and drunk, she would not have been able to pull that ball-breaking move so easily. Most guys anticipated and were ready for that move.

Ashley ended up spending the next few years going from one meaningless job to another, feeling like she had no purpose in life there either. She had no real idea what she wanted to do when she grew up, but she was pushing at the age when all the little old ladies in her mother's church group were beginning to ask those embarrassing questions, like "Is Ashley gay? What, is no man good enough for her? Do you want me to call my nephew? I'm sure he would be just right for her." Although she might own up to wanting to find Mr. Right someday, she was getting tired of having no purpose in life. She didn't really enjoy the idea of being the crazy old cat lady who worked for Taco Bell till she was sixty.

That's when she came up with the idea of joining the police academy. Her dad and her brother were both detectives in the homicide/vice division. Needless to say, neither of them was thrilled with the idea, and her mother went absolutely ballistic. It took six months to finally convince everyone that it was the perfect solution to her problem. She would have a career, she could legally carry a gun, and both her dad and her overly protective big brother could keep an eye on her at all times.

Ashley remembered that first day when they all showed up for the police training. There were about fifty cadets milling around, waiting for someone to come tell them what they were supposed to be doing. That's when she looked across the group and into the devil's very own eyes. There stood Big Tits Malone with a smirk on her overly made-up face. You would have thought she was headed for Hollywood instead of police training. Ashley was so consumed with Malone she failed to notice the man who had come to stand behind her. *"Everyone fall in!"* was bellowed in her ear, by a six-foot-tall by six-foot-wide man in uniform.

Ashley swore to God, she actually dribbled a little in her pants as he stood behind her shouting his orders.

His name was Dennis Spade, and he lined them up and told them they were there to complete a battery of tests, interviews and background checks. Anyone who had the balls or pussy (whichever the case may be) to get past that stage would be put on a police candidate eligibility list.

The whole time he was giving his "You're not tough enough to be a cop" speech, all Ashley could think of was *how the hell did Malone find out she was joining the police training?* That bitch was like a basset hound, which, Ashley guessed, if she did pass the training could become her specialty. They could retire all of the police dogs and just let Malone get down on all fours and sniff around.

That brought a smile to her face, but apparently the sergeant didn't find her smiling amusing at all. When he looked over and saw Ashley grinning like a baboon, he finished his speech one inch from her face, throwing spit all over the place. Made her realize from here on out, she was going to have to learn to keep those smiles to herself. She never even glanced Malone's way, knowing she would have taken great pride that she was the cause of her spit bath.

Once Ashley was through the interview and testing part and into the actual training program, she found that it really was not that difficult. Growing up in a house of cops like she had, she had listened to her dad talk about police work her whole life. And when her brother found out she was serious about joining the police force, he took it upon himself to make sure she was ready. He made it very clear no sister of his was going to fail out of the training; he would be the laughingstock of the squad. Every spare minute he had, he drilled all the information he could into her "pea-sized brain," as he referred to it. She loved her overprotective brother, and appreciated all the help he gave her.

If they weren't going through manuals, they were out at the shooting range. Ashley became excellent at target practice. If Michael was along, she would aim for the head and heart, but if she was on her own, the paper men would have nice holes where their penises would have been. She always liked to name her paper targets Jimmy, Brandon, or Tarzan.

She breezed through the academy without any difficulties. She was a natural at everything they threw at her. She was athletic, and Michael had put her through the toughest drills. He had set up a rope on an old brick wall in an abandoned lot, and made her practice over and over again until climbing it was second nature to her. They constructed an obstacle course in their parents' back yard, and any spare time she had, he made sure she was out running it. He took pleasure in sneaking out at night and switching things up, so she never knew what to expect when she went out to practice.

Ashley ranked highest in both the field and the classroom. It made her proud to know that she could excel at something. Having her brother pound everything into her brain all the time probably helped out a little, but he had nothing to do with her ability to hit the target at any range and ace all the tests. And for some reason she still had not figured out, Malone kept away from her, and as far as she knew, had not caused any problems for her. Actually, she did her best to stay as far away from Ashley as she could, maybe thinking, for once, the shoe would be on the other foot and Ashley could make her life hell here. So by some unspoken pact they kept their distance from each other.

Most of the instructors knew either Ashley's dad or her brother, so she was always considered the class favorite, but that had nothing to do with how well she did in her reviews. She worked as hard as anyone else in the class, even if a few like Malone thought she was a suck-up and getting special treatment.

There were very few positions open in the state for new cadets, so that meant that only a certain number of cadets could graduate. This meant it was an intense twenty weeks, with fifty men and women fighting for twenty-five positions throughout the state. Ashley felt bad for the ones who had done well, but were passed over because of the limited number of recruits that were needed. That meant they would have to wait for another year and then go all the way through the academy again, hope to pass and hope there was an opening somewhere in the area.

Throughout the training there were several of the men who were openly hostile about having to compete with two women. Both Malone and Ashley had received hate notes stuck on their lockers, and someone went so far as to flatten all the tires on Malone's car. Ashley had never received so many glares in her life. Some of the ones that were struggling with one area or another would pass by her and purposely bump into her, almost knocking her down. It was hard to turn the other cheek and not raise a fuss, but she put herself in their shoes and gave them the benefit of the doubt, the big pussies. It wasn't her fault she scored higher than they did, and if this was the way they handled themselves, maybe they weren't cut out to be cops anyway. She remembered one guy spitting on her shoes after she had scored higher on the shooting range than he had. She had been shocked and remembered looking up into hate-filled eyes as he glared at her, daring her to make something of it. The guy had been a jerk throughout the whole training, and she for one was glad he had failed. After he had spit on her shoes she had given him a "kiss my ass" smile and salute and kept right on walking. One of the other guys passed over had gone to her high school. He had been a couple of years older than she was, but she never really knew him then and never bothered to during the training either. He always was polite, but kept to himself most of the time.

Out of the graduating class there were six now doing their field training with Precinct 11: Thomas Shaffer, Luchetta, Tiffany Malone, better known as Hoochie/Big Tits Malone, Scott Walsh, Bill Wynn and Ashley Wright. How that basset hound bitch Malone pulled the same squad as Ashley still amazed her.

All new rookies had to spend time in each division of the precinct. When it came time to decide who got which division first, they had drawn straws to see who would pull the morgue shift first. Ashley would swear to her dying day that Malone must have slept with the guy holding the straws. When Ashley pulled the short straw and looked over at Malone's face to see her smug expression, she knew she had been had.

The city had just gone through budget cuts, so City Hall had decided that paying someone to cover the morgue twenty-four hours was a waste of the taxpayers' money, when they had new recruits who could take turns covering it for the next year at least.

Suddenly a hand reached out and touched Ashley on the shoulder. Screaming, she jumped up and drew her gun, and before she knew what was happening, she was pointing it in Officer Pillsbury Doughboy's face.

"Whoa, Jesus! Ashley, it's just me, it's almost time for our shift to end." He was quaking from his head to his toes. But she supposed it wasn't every day that your partner pulls her gun and puts it against your short round nose.

Once her heart returned to its normal pace, she returned her gun to her holster and muttered, "This place is going to be the death of me yet."

To which Bill replied with a muttered, "Or the death of me!"

About that time Detective Phillip Kelly stuck his head around the corner and gave Ashley a crooked little smile. "I heard they pulled a good one on you tonight?"

Thanking her lucky stars that he had not just witnessed her complete overreaction, she managed to reply: "Yeah...they proceeded to scare three years of my life off of me." That's all she needed, was for the squad's hottie to think that she was a quivering mass of rookie meat.

But she couldn't help thinking to herself that there stood one fine specimen of what she would call a one hundred percent prime hunk of man. He stood at least six feet three inches with what she decided was a solid mass of muscles, had beautiful brown hair and big brown eyes, and was more handsome than any man deserved to be. He was dressed in a pair of ironed Dockers and a linen shirt that all those glorious muscles were buried under. His blazer fit him perfectly and his thick hair had fallen across his forehead, giving him a relaxed look. His brown eyes had a gleam in them that promised a sense of humor along with maybe some orneriness. His nose was straight and he had a square chin that fit his face perfectly. She had only seen him around the station, and so far had not had any reason to talk to him, but that didn't stop her from drooling a little every time he walked by. He just had an allure that screamed he was all man; come take me if you dare.

Her brother had filled her in on most of the guys in the precinct. Kelly had become a detective after only three years on the force. Everyone liked him, and he was an all-around good guy. She was already dreaming about the time she would get to spend in his company doing her training. She could think of a lot of things that man could teach her that weren't in the police manual.

He gave her a big smile, and there on the left side of that gorgeous face was one very beautiful dimple.

Oh shit, she thought to herself. *He can't be evil; he only has one dimple.* God must have realized his mistake and stopped himself from giving him the sure sign of evil by placing two dimples on that face. She could only muster up a weak smile to return to him.

He tilted his head and gave her a strange look, taking a minute to look her up and down. "Are you sure you're okay? You look a little flustered. Was there more to the story than I heard?"

Shaking her head from side to side like a stupid schoolgirl, she managed to whisper, "No, really, I'm good."

Taking another minute to give her a searching look, he replied, "Hang in there," and took off to the squad room to get briefed on the night's happenings.

Ashley climbed the stairs a little bit *in love* and dreaming about how this man would make a perfect Mr. Wright to her Mrs. Kelly. She was feeling a little overwhelmed this morning between the she-nanigans in the restroom, and almost blowing poor Bill's nose off, to seeing that quick flash of dimple. As she walked into the squad room, all she could think of was that she was so glad this shift was over; she didn't think her over-stimulated body could take much more. She needed to take her tired self home and put it to bed. She looked around to see where Kelly had sat, thinking maybe she would find a chair somewhere close to him, but she was surprised when every chair in the place was full, which was odd because usually about half of the chairs were empty coming off of the night shift. Looking around, she noticed every eye in the place was on her. She was starting to get a really nervous feeling that this night was about to get a lot worse, when she noticed Mr. Stiffy, with a sign around his neck that read "Mr. Ashley Wright," in the seat where she usually sat.

Everyone had rushed in so they could see her reaction, so the room was ringing with laughter and off-the-wall comments. Taking a deep breath, she decided she wasn't going to let them get the best of her. Looking Malone right in the eye, she walked over and sat right down on Mr. Stiffy's lap, put her arm around his neck, took his cigarette out of his blue, slack-lipped mouth and pretended to take a puff.

The laughter in the room was loud enough to compete with a few frat parties she had attended, and she took immense pleasure in the look of hatred coming from Malone. Instead of making Ashley look like an idiot, Ashley had proved to be a levelheaded person who could take a good prank in stride, not some hysterical woman. She looked over and saw that her dad Harold and big brother had apparently heard about the now famous prank, and decided to show up and witness part two. Harold gave her a little smile and an ever so slight thumbs up gesture. No one would have noticed but her, but it made her feel proud to have his support.

You could tell he was proud that his rookie daughter had the good sense to not make a scene and had played along with the shenanigans. He knew how important it was to make a good first impression when working with a group of tough-as-nails men and women. If you made a mistake right out of the chute, it was hard to ever recover and gain a footing in their tight little circle of a select few. It made his chest swell a little, knowing she had passed the first test thrown at her, and came out with the respect of many veterans who had seen a lot in their years at the station.

Captain Freeman finally regained control of the room, taking the time to reprimand whoever had pulled this childish stunt, stating that they had too much time on their hands and if he found out who it was, he would make sure they found the time to clean every car in the squad inside and out, *with a toothbrush* and then he would personally watch them brush their teeth with that same toothbrush.

Ashley took a quick glance around the room and could see Shaffer was turning a little green around the gills. She bet it was a while before he let Malone talk him into any more gags around the station. Malone of course could talk her way out of anything, and besides she had no conscience.

She took a little longer to get out of the station than normal, having to stop and go over the details of the basement prank for the benefit of those who had missed it. Her dad and Michael gave her a hard time, but she could tell they were both proud of her, even if they were not going to show it. It was a good feeling knowing she could hold her own when thrown into a situation like she had been today. She had never had any doubt that she would make a good cop, but there was a lot more that went into this job than just arresting the bad guys. From day one she had to prove herself to the other cops, showing that they could trust her every day and know that she could be trusted in every situation that came at them, no matter what. If it took sitting on a corpse's lap to gain a little respect, she was glad to do it. Malone might be the poster woman of the department, but Ashley had serious doubts that most of the guys in their squad would want her as their partner, or even as their backup. Chalk one up for Ashley.

CHAPTER TWO

Walking out of the station, Ashley found Casey Carter leaning up against her Chevy Camaro, waiting for her. With everything that had happened tonight, she had forgotten they had made plans for breakfast and to catch up on all the latest gossip. It was something they had promised to do when both of their lives had taken such different directions. They had been friends since they were five, and they had promised each other that no matter what happened in their lives, they would work really hard to keep their friendship going strong. So they planned something at least once a week, whether it was a movie, shopping or just lunch.

She was dressed in a power suit, probably made by some big name designer, and some fancy three-inch pumps that made her five foot two frame look five five and not the six feet she hoped for. She might be a tiny thing but she had an air of power about her. Ashley had seen her make men six feet tall back off when she turned her influence on them.

She gave Ashley a quick once-over, starting with her dusty black clodhoppers, up over her very fashionable uniform and ending with her hat. Ashley could see her raising her perfectly tweezed eyebrow as she held in a chuckle.

Bill and Ashley walked over to where she was still leaning on her car.

"H...hi, Casey," Bill stammered out.

Ashley gave Bill a quick glance and noticed he had turned a bright shade of red. Well damn; her shy little partner had a crush on her best friend. She felt like she was in high school again, watching another guy fall for the petite little thing standing in front of them.

"Hi Bill. How have you been? Has my nasty-ass friend here been treating you well? If not, you just let me know and I will see to it personally that the captain kicks her ass out of the department," Casey answered.

Bill turned a horrified look Ashley's way. "Oh no, she's been fine, I assure you. No problems at all. She has been very pleasant..." His forehead suddenly wrinkled as a thought suddenly came to him. "Well, except when she pulled her gun on me tonight."

Casey raised both of her perfect eyebrows at that one.

Ashley patted Bill on the arm, telling him her car should be ready today. She thanked him for the ride, grabbed Casey by her arm, turned her towards her car door, and gave her a gentle push. Ashley waved at Bill, who was still watching them with a look of wonder on his face as Ashley walked around Casey's car and slid into the front seat.

"Hey officer, you better watch yourself, or I will have you arrested for police brutality," Casey said.

"You'll think police brutality after I get done with you, you pansy-assed white girl. And stop flirting with my poor partner, he's already a goner."

"Really?"

"You didn't notice him stammering around you like you were some Hollywood star?"

"Well, obviously the man has good taste."

"You are such a slut."

"You're just jealous because you look like you might be about ready to join those bodies down in that hole you just crawled out of."

Leave it to her best friend from grade school to be bluntly honest with her. Casey and Ashley had hooked up in kindergarten after crybaby Malone had pulled Casey's chair out from under her, causing her to crash to the floor with her dress up around her face, showing off her pretty pink and white flowered girlie panties. It took them the whole year to get people to stop calling her "Panties Carter." From that day on, they became inseparable; their main goal in life was to make Malone's life as miserable as she made theirs. They gave as good as she did. If she pulled a silly prank on one of them, they would gang up and pull an even nastier one on her. All through their school years, the three of them had become the school entertainment. The kids just stood back and watched and waited to see what the three would come up with next. They never let them down, spending more time in the principal's office than in their classrooms.

As they pulled out of the parking lot, Phillip Kelly was just walking to his car.

Casey suddenly slammed on her brakes, almost crushing Ashley's chest with the seat belt. "Holy, Mother of God...who the hell is that?"

Ashley chuckled. "I knew you, of all people, would appreciate the precinct's very own stud muffin."

"My God, that man is just too damn dreamy for his own good! Is he married?"

"I don't think so, but he's way out of my league. Plus he has one dimple. Wait—are you asking for my benefit or are you thinking of cheating on Dan?"

Casey chuckled, "Good lord, woman, some day you have to get over that dimple thing. And don't underestimate yourself, you know you're gorgeous. Of course dressed like you are now, with that ugly uniform, clumpy big old shoes, all that gorgeous hair tucked up under that stupid hat, and wearing hardly any makeup, I can see why you might be starting to have some doubts."

Ashley reached over and punched her in the arm, telling her to mind her own business. Besides, she told her, she thought her lace-up black army shoes were sexy.

They both sat and watched while Kelly got in his car, ran his hands through his hair and buckled up. You would have thought they were both love-starved the way they sat in complete silence, just enjoying the view. He pulled away from the parking space and they watched as he drove out of the parking lot and down the street. When they could no longer see his car they looked at each other and burst out laughing. "You are so pathetic."

"Me? At least I have a good reason to stare! I'm a love-starved lunatic, while you're in a long-term relationship with the man of your dreams. You have no reason to be drooling. As a matter of fact, I'm going to tell Dan you made a complete ass out of yourself over a man you don't even know."

"Go ahead, and I'll tell him you masturbate while looking at our old high school album and then I'll proceed to tell him whose picture you look at."

"Casey Carter, I DO NOT!"

"Yeah, but he doesn't know that, and he'll believe anything I tell him. So just remember that when you go around threatening me." She looked over and gave her the most innocent look imaginable.

She might only be a little bitty thing but she had a quick mind and was famous for her razor-sharp wit. She could fling a response to anything thrown at her. When she was in court, Ashley pitied the opposing counsel.

"You are so not my best friend; we are fighting."

"No we're not. You love me and you know it."

"You're right. I do." They headed over to the Hill's Café, the diner where Ashley's little sister, Shannon, was working during her summer break from college. It was just a little place that was open twenty-four hours a day, but people loved it because it had great food, and old Mr. and Mrs. Hill had owned it forever. They were the greatest old couple in the world. They looked the same as they did twenty years ago, never slowing down for a minute. No one had any idea how old they really were, and even if they were brave enough to ask, neither one of the Hills would give a straight answer. Everyone in their group from high school had worked there at some time in their lives. The diner was located smack dab in the middle of a bunch of fast food joints, but you could always count on having to wait for a table at Hill's because the food was so good.

They made their way into the restaurant and weaved their way through the bright chrome tables. A couple of walls were painted a bright red and the tables were all chrome with red tops. It was like something out of the 1950s. The booths around the edge of the diner were rich leather, kept gleaming with plenty of elbow grease and tender loving care. At each booth was an old-fashioned table-top jukebox. Not all of them worked but a few would still belt out a song or two. They had the same music in them as when they were first installed in the diner, but no one seemed to care. The big picture windows were sparkling clean and gave a good view of the city park across the street. The diner drew a diverse crowd, from business people grabbing a quick lunch, to college kids hanging out doing their homework, to families bringing their kids for a good old-fashioned hamburger and fries. Mrs. Hill still made all the desserts, and many came in just for a slice of her famous Dutch apple pie or her delicious triple-layered chocolate cake with rich chocolate frosting. No watching calories here; if you came to get some veggie plate, you came to the wrong place.

Shannon was behind the counter, serving a plate of bacon and eggs to an older gentleman who had sat in the same spot for the last thirty years and had the same breakfast every day. She waved at them as they slid into a booth at the back of the room. Alice, the diner's long-time waitress, came by and brought them their coffees and said Shannon would be coming over to help them as quick as she could. That was another thing they liked about coming here. The servers were free to wait on their families and friends no matter where they sat.

They sipped their coffee, waiting for Shannon to come take their order, talking about the small things that were going on in their lives. Casey belonged to a big law firm in downtown Denver, and didn't have to be there until nine. She was all bright and cheery, and all Ashley could think about was going home and crawling into her big comfy bed. These nights were starting to kill her. It was hard to get her body to adjust to being up all night and sleeping all day. Thank God the morgue had a huge coffee pot with an endless supply of coffee, or she wasn't sure she would make it through the boring quiet nights. Hopefully when she got out in the streets there would be enough excitement to keep her going. Not too much, mind you, just a few domestic calls to keep things hoppin'.

Casey and Ashley had attended the same college; the only difference was Casey went on to finish, while Ashley chose not to. She finished her college degree after three and a half years and then went on to law school for four years. Those four years were the longest they had ever been apart. They were more like sisters than best friends, except she had raven-black hair, which she kept cut in this flippy little style that always looked awesome on her. She was only five foot two, had jet-black eyes, and weighed a whopping one hundred five pounds sopping wet. Ashley was five seven, had long, thick, naturally wavy strawberry blonde hair and big blue eyes, and weighed closer to one hundred twenty-five pounds. All through school they were referred to as the Siamese twins, because you never saw one of them without the other close by. They had an amazing friendship that many could not understand. They never fought and understood each other's feelings without having to say a word. They had developed this silent language in high school so they could communicate across the room with just a certain head gesture or eye movement. They had been there for each other through countless boyfriends, broken hearts, joyous events and the never-ending Malone. Ashley loved her sister to death and considered them very close, but not as close as she and Casey were.

Shannon slid into their booth with her ever-present smile plastered on her face. "Hi ChickyPoos! What's up? Mr. Hill said I could take my break and sit with you two while you ate your breakfast. What did I miss? Did you say anything juicy? If you did, just start over, I don't want to miss a thing."

Chuckling at how fast the words flew out of her mouth, Ashley had to wait for a break before she could respond, "No, sis, we waited for you. We knew we would be in big trouble if we started without you."

Shannon had followed Casey and Ashley around all the time as they were all growing up, trying to be one of the big girls. She was five years younger than they were, but she was always such a happy little thing, they never did mind that she liked to hang around with them. Plus, they were sneaky and knew how to ditch her if they really wanted to.

Alice came back to take their orders, giving Shannon a playful tug on her hair as she told them the specials. After she left, Ashley proceeded to fill them in on the embarrassing events of last night. They both gasped at the dead guy part, but hooted with laughter when she mentioned sitting on his lap.

"Oh shit, sis...Mom is going to hit the roof when she hears you sat on some dead guy's lap. We have listened to all of Dad's and Michael's stories of the pranks that go on at the station, but this is her baby going through them now. She will probably be hunting Malone down herself and reading her the riot act." Raising her eyebrows in a devilish arch, she said, "Actually, that might be kind of funny... Maybe I should give her that idea."

"Shannon, don't you dare...and besides *you're* her baby, not me. Mom's used to this kind of crap from me. Now, if something like that happened to you, it might cause her to call in the National Guard to come to your defense. Besides, we need to concentrate on our revenge for Malone and how I'm going to get her back without the department being involved. I want to do it outside of work. If she is stupid enough to pull stuff at work, let her, but I'm not that dumb."

Casey had just been sitting there with this huge *I've got a secret* grin plastered on her face the whole time Shannon and Ashley were bantering back and forth. Finally, Ashley realized she had not said anything for several minutes, and it wasn't like her to not be right in the middle of things. Ashley sat back, crossed her arms over her chest and gave her the look.

"What's up with you, sitting there all happy assed? Did you get laid last night? I'm impressed if Dan can still make you grin like a silly high school girl, after all these years together."

Dan and Casey had started dating when she was a sophomore and he was a senior in high school. They had the fairytale romance and, yes, they had made the long-distance romance work. Ashley always teased them that they made her want to puke. She couldn't help but feel partly responsible for the success of their relationship; if it hadn't been for her smoothing all the rough spots they had encountered, they might not have made it. At least she liked to claim their success was partly due to her.

Casey denied any wild sex and sat there looking back and forth between Shannon and Ashley. She had her left hand on the table cocked at an odd angle, and just kept grinning.

Shannon and Ashley looked at each other, thinking maybe she had been indulging in a few Bloody Marys before she got there. Casey was not one to play games, so this was not like her.

Ashley looked her over, thinking maybe she had missed a new haircut, or a new pair of earrings, and she was waiting for Shannon or her to notice. Finally, she happened to glance at her hand and realized she had a huge diamond on her ring finger.

"You slut!" Ashley screamed at her, jumping across the table and giving her a big hug.

Everyone turned around and stared at them. Shannon just shrugged and mouthed, "It's okay, they're gay." Shannon started demanding to know what was going on in a semi-hushed whisper. "Okay you two, what the hell is going on? You can't keep me out of the loop."

Ashley settled back into her seat, giving Casey the happiest look. She could not believe that Dan had finally got up the nerve to pop the question. Everyone in their circle of friends knew that it would eventually happen, but when the years started slipping by, some of the gang thought otherwise. Casey and Ashley had never had a doubt. Dan was always someone who lived his life by his own standards, not anyone else's, so they sat back and waited. Ashley was going to kick his ass for not letting her in on the secret, but other than that, she was deliriously happy for them both. They finally settled down enough to fill Shannon in on what was going on, and then she erupted into her own set of shrieks. She bounded over the table and gave Casey her own set of hugs, laughing and giggling like a kid.

All of the commotion had brought Mr. and Mrs. Hill and Alice over to the table to find out what all the uproar was about. They soon had a whole group of well-wishers surrounding their table, oohing and aahing over Casey's ring, wishing her the best. Their group of friends had made this place their regular hangout over the years, so they were considered family by everyone who ever worked there, along with the customers who had made this their regular eating establishment.

After they finally settled down, they demanded Casey give them all the juicy details. Casey had never given up hope that Dan was going to propose marriage, and they had agreed to both get their degrees, which they had done. That time had come and gone and the subject of marriage had never been discussed again.

Casey settled back and started her tale. She said that she had arrived home from work last night, and there was a note on her door from Dan, telling her he had to work late and asking if she could meet him at his office building at seven so that they could go to dinner from there. She admitted to thinking that the whole thing was a little strange, that he was usually in the habit of calling if he was running late, but she figured it was no big deal.

She said as she looked back on it she should have guessed that he was up to something, but at the time she didn't think anything of it. She told them that at six-thirty she headed out the door, wondering if she should have changed into something sexier or if they were just going to grab a pizza at Frankie's. She tried Dan on his cell phone as she walked to her car, but only received his voice mail, so she decided her jeans would just have to do. When she got to Dan's office, she entered the lobby and walked to the elevator to go up to Dan's floor, but the doors wouldn't open. She wondered how she was supposed to get up to the thirty-fourth floor, because there was no way she was dragging her sorry ass up thirty-four flights of stairs after working all day. She had worn four-inch stilettos with her designer jeans and they were definitely not made to climb up stairs. She had stood at the elevator trying the button again and again, deciding she was just going to stand there and he was going to have to come find her. She tried him on his cell phone again, but she had no service in the building.

Their breakfast arrived and Ashley pushed hers aside, waiting for Casey to finish her story. Casey unwrapped her silverware and went about salting her eggs and putting jelly on her toast. Shannon and Ashley looked at each other in amazement, not believing she had the gall to even think about eating a bite of her breakfast before she finished her story. Ashley grabbed her plate and Shannon grabbed her fork, both of them glaring at her. She gave them an innocent look and made a play for her food.

"Do you want to die before the big day?"

She started giggling and explained that as she finished trying Dan on his cell phone, the elevator doors opened and Dan's boss stepped out of the elevator.

"Hi Casey, looking for Dan? He's up working in my office; take the elevator up to the fiftieth floor. He should be about ready to take off now. You kids have fun and enjoy your evening."

Casey had met Dan's boss several times at company functions, but he had never been so friendly before. He was always pleasant, but way too busy to know who she was, or at least that was how she had always perceived it. Casey said she took the now working elevator, went up to the fiftieth floor as instructed and took a look around. Everything was dark except the office at the end of the hall. As she stepped into Mr. Johnson's office, she noticed that Dan wasn't anywhere she could see. She was starting to get a little pissed off by this time. What the hell was going on? She was tired and hungry and a little peeved at all the runaround that Dan was putting her through. She had just turned and was headed out the door when the phone on Mr. Johnson's desk rang. She just looked at it. It was seven o'clock, and no one was around. The phone kept ringing and ringing, so she picked it up. It was Dan, telling her that a gentleman would be there shortly, and that he would bring her to him. Before she could even question him he had hung up.

"I have to tell you that by this time I was getting royally pissed off at the entire cloak and dagger shit. I was feeling strange about the whole thing, when about that time a man stepped into the office and asked me if I was ready."

Ashley had to give her a hard time at this point.

"What were you thinking, going off with a stranger? He could have been some serial killer. You know better than that."

Casey giggled and slapped her hand and asked her, "Do you want to hear this story or not?"

She said that by then she was feeling really freaked out about the whole deal, but went along with the guy, since she had just talked to Dan and he approved of her going with this guy. She followed him through a door and ended out on the roof. All she could see was a helicopter on the helipad. The guy smiled at her, walked over to the helicopter and climbed into the pilot's seat.

She had stood there with a dazed look on her face, wondering what the hell was going on. Unknown to her, Dan had come up behind her and was waiting for her to notice him. He took her hand, which scared the holy piss out of her. She jumped about a foot and screamed like a little girl.

Casey explained, "I really thought I was going to kill him, I was so scared. I slapped him on the shoulder and started yelling at him, but he just bent over and started kissing me to shut me up. When he had succeeded in getting me to shut up he leaned back and smiled and whispered 'I love you.' Then he led me to the helicopter and opened the door and helped me up into the seat."

She had never been in a helicopter before and was having serious doubts about taking this little adventure. She watched him as he went around to the other side, climbed in the helicopter, buckled up and gave the pilot a thumbs up, and they took off. She tried to ask Dan questions, but he would not let her ask any. Instead he told her to just enjoy the experience.

"Oh you guys, it was so wonderful. The lights were all on in the downtown area. We just circled around, taking in the sights, drinking champagne and eating chocolate-covered strawberries. It was so romantic."

Shannon and Ashley looked at each other, completely fascinated.

After about thirty minutes Dan told her it was time to head back, but reached over and gave her the most romantic kiss he had ever given her. As they came around to land on his building, she let out a gasp. On the side of the building, the office lights were turned on to spell out "MARRY ME CASEY"

Shannon and Ashley both sat there with tears streaming down their faces, sniffling like a couple of ninnies. "Casey, you've got to be kidding us! Dan did something that romantic? Our Dan! Are you sure it was really Dan?"

"How in the world did he pull that off?"

"I guess at the morning meeting, somehow the word got out that Dan was going to propose, so everyone was throwing out ideas, when out of the blue his boss piped up with this idea. He offered his own helicopter and arranged for all the lights to be turned on at seven-thirty."

"You're engaged! I can't believe it! It's about time. I'm in shock. I knew this day would come, but now that it's here, it's just too unbelievable," Ashley exclaimed.

"I know it's hard to believe after all this time. You should have heard my mom when we called. I'm not kidding, I thought she was going to faint for a minute or two. Now the big question…"

"What question?"

"Will you two jackasses be my maid of honor and my bridesmaid?"

"Hell no! You'll probably make us wear some frilly pink chiffon thing with lots of bows and ruffles," Ashley answered.

Shannon had to get back to work, so Casey and Ashley sat awhile longer, going over all the romantic details again, picking at their breakfast, eating the bacon and toast and foregoing the cold eggs.

They had to eventually break it up, since Casey had to get to work and Ashley needed to get home to bed. It took them awhile to work their way out of the diner, with everyone stopping them to congratulate Casey and give her their well wishes and words of advice.

She dropped Ashley off at the car repair shop, where she picked up her Bronco and then headed for home. She was suddenly exhausted. It had turned out to be quite an eventful day.

As she entered her apartment, she found Miss Priss lying in the exact spot that she had left her. She shed her uniform, crawled in beside her, and hoped she was lucky enough to pick up her dream of the day before, right where she had left off.

CHAPTER THREE

Ashley woke to a feather-light touch on her face, smiling sleep-ily, thinking that Brad was caressing her face. The touch gently moved back and forth, back and forth, softly brushing against her skin. She slowly opened her eyes to find that she was not being caressed by her lover, it was just Miss Priss's tail swishing back and forth across her face. Not a sensual lover, just her cat's ass in her face. That pretty well summed up her love life lately.

Ahhh…a day off. Boy, was she was ready after a boring week, then the excitement of last night, and Casey's exciting news this morning. She might only be 26, but her heart couldn't take that kind of excitement that close together. The Casey part was great; the dead body part wasn't her idea of fun. That Malone and Shaffer had pulled a fast one on her was still a sore spot where she was concerned. Ashley was great at giving out, but didn't relish the idea of being on the receiving end. She was surprised her mom hadn't called yet, to remind her that this was why she did not want her daughter going into police work. She was always worried about how the other officers would treat her daughter, and once she found out someone had put a dead person anywhere in the vicinity she would be livid. Of course she thought Ashley should have become a doc-tor, or a lawyer, or some other fancy-schmancy kind of work. But it hadn't taken Ashley long to figure out she wasn't cut out for office work, after endless desk jobs after dropping out of college.

Looking at the clock, Ashley realized it was six o'clock and she had promised Casey she would join her and Dan and the old gang down at her Uncle Irwin's bar, the Whistle Stop, to celebrate.

Uncle Irwin was one of her favorite uncles. He was a *tell it like it is* kind of guy, always in a good mood and willing to give a stranger his last dime. He had always been considered kind of the black sheep of the family as they were growing up, because he owned a bar and didn't have a *real* job. But that didn't stop him; he just ignored the whispers and went right on about his business, acting like none of it bothered him. Truth be known, it probably didn't.

Having an uncle own a local bar was exciting to Ashley and her brother and sister as they grew up, and their Dad was one of the few who always supported his brother no matter what the rest of the family thought. Uncle Irwin had been married and divorced three times that they knew of, but it wouldn't surprise any of them if there were a few more thrown in. His first wife was some psycho bitch who scared the hell out of everyone. She stood about a foot taller than Irwin, and had coal-black hair that she cut short and spiked up like some brassy dyke in a motorcycle bar. She never smiled that Ashley remembered, and had worn the pants during their whole marriage. She had absolutely no tolerance for kids and hated when her dad would bring them down after work while he had a cold beer. Ashley thought he had done it just to piss her off. Uncle Irwin would just chuckle under his breath at her rumblings, and fix them up with special Roy Rogers or Shirley Temples with extra grenadine and lots of cherries. No one really understood why he married her in the first place, except she had huge tits, and Uncle Irwin always was a sucker for a woman with big boobs. As a matter of fact, all of his wives could be put into that same category.

Harold always preached to Uncle Irwin that he could date them if he wanted to, but it didn't mean he had to marry them all. Uncle

Irwin would just laugh and explain he wanted to make an honest woman out of them, and swore that he loved them all.

His second wife was a sweetheart and gave him two great kids, but she couldn't take the bar life. She was this little bitty thing with a pair of Dolly Parton boobs, and Uncle Irwin was a goner from the first time he saw her. They were married for about ten years, but it was hard for her being home, raising the kids, when she never knew what was going on at her husband's bar. She knew what a flirt Irwin was and she let her imagination get the better of her. It was finally too much, so she packed up the kids and moved across the state.

Harold always swore that his brother had never been unfaithful to any of his wives, but you wouldn't know it by the way he flirted with every woman who came into the bar. It didn't matter if they were 21 or 99; he made them feel like they were worth a million bucks by the time they left the bar. He and his second wife still got along great; they just couldn't survive being married to each other. To this day Ashley thought he regretted that he let that one slip away from him.

His third wife was an empty-headed bimbo he fell for at the supermarket, and she was twenty-five years younger than him. She looked like Pamela Anderson's little sister and was not the brightest crayon in the box. It lasted six months, and then she took off with some biker dude she met at Taco Bell. Uncle Irwin wasn't too bitter about that one. He always just smiled and said it was the best six months of his life.

The Whistle Stop was the local cop hangout. Ashley had been going there since she was six, with her dad. He would stop by the house every once in a while and take one of them with him down to play a game of pool or shuffleboard. It was the highlight of their lives. They thought they were pretty cool, standing on a chair, taking on the local guys who hung out at the bar. Ashley's mom always insisted her dad had them out of there before six, when the bar started getting busy with the rowdier crowd. You could tell her mom didn't go to the bar much if she thought Uncle Irwin's place was rowdy. Oh, it had its moments, especially on the weekends when he would hire a band, but usually it was just a quiet group of people having a few drinks after work, and the regulars searching for God knows what.

Ashley found herself reaching over and petting Miss Priss. "What do you think? Should we gussy ourselves up and try and knock the socks off of some unsuspecting man tonight?"

Stretching her front paws out, Priss gave her famous look again, the expression in her eyes saying, "I don't care, just don't bring him home and let him think he gets my side of the bed." Ashley had discovered years ago that Miss Priss was not exactly fond of the male species. More than one of the dates she had brought home had left with scratch marks. With some of them, she actually had to lock the stupid cat in the bedroom. Maybe she should carry her around on her rare dates so if she started throwing a hissy fit, Ashley would know he was a loser and not bother with a second date. She could get one of those pet carriers and...geez, she really was going to become the old cat lady down the hall. She could see the kids teasing her about how she chased all the men away with her psycho cat that was so old she had to be hauled around in a carrier.

Deciding it was time to get up and go wash *possible*, she headed to the bathroom to get in the shower. That was one good thing about her apartment; all of the rooms were good sized, even her bathroom. She had painted it in rich creams and tans when she moved in, and it matched the marble-looking tile and countertops to a tee. Rich brown fluffy towels hung from the towel racks and the shower curtain was a pretty Victorian-looking material. She loved her apartment and was proud of the way she had decorated it. She had struggled to save up the money to fix it up nice, but it was worth every generic cookie she had ever eaten, to finally get it the way she wanted it. It was her own little Victorian home tucked inside an apartment building.

She stripped off her pajamas and crawled into the shower. She took the time to wash her hair twice and give it a good conditioning. She was lucky to have naturally thick hair that stayed in good condition with just a little effort on her part and good advice from her aunt Dixie, her favorite hairdresser, so it was basically care free. She stood there until the hot water was gone, trying to wash off any trace that might possibly be left after her experience with Mr. Stiffy's lap. Now that she thought back, she should have showered last night; who knows what might have been crawling on the corpse. Maybe if she was lucky, everything would have hopped onto Malone, being attracted to her dead soul when she helped set up the stiff in the john. Knowing her, though, she didn't do any of the actual work, just bossed Shaffer around while he did it all.

Throwing on an old flannel shirt, she headed to the kitchen to see if things were really as bad as Bill had indicated last night. She knew she hadn't been to the grocery store lately, but surely there was something to eat. Opening the refrigerator, she saw that he was right. There wasn't a decent thing in there; she chucked the green and brown things, and moved on to the cabinets.

Jackpot…peanut butter and honey, and there was a heel left in the bread bag. What more did Bill want? Gourmet dinner again!

After feeding Miss Priss and wiping down the counters, she decided she had better get her butt in gear or she would be late to the party.

Bending over and taking the hair dryer to her hair, she started running her clothing options through her mind, trying to remember what was clean and what wasn't, trying to decide if she had anything at all to wear tonight. She put her hair in electric rollers, put her makeup on, took the rollers out, ran her fingers through her hair and she was done with her beauty regimen. She was not one of those women who took hours to get ready. If they didn't like what they saw, oh well. If she was truthful with herself, that was not usually a problem. She would get her fair share of attention. Men seemed to be attracted to her looks, and they always made observations about how they loved her hair. The creeps always had to throw in asinine comments about what they wanted her to do with that hair, but most were just nice remarks that made a girl feel sexy. Her family had all been blessed with their fair share of good looks. Her mom was just as beautiful as the day her dad married her. She hardly ever wore makeup, but she had that natural beauty that didn't need makeup. Her dad always said he preferred her not to wear it because he got tired of arresting the string of men who always made a play for her when she did.

Ashley entered her walk-in closet and stared at all the empty hangers. She decided it was definitely time to hit the laundromat and the grocery store. She was going to be down to eating cat food and wearing her pjs all day. Lacking any choice, she decided on a cute little outfit she had picked up in her college days. So what if it showed more boob than she had shown in the last couple of years? Those babies needed some fresh air anyway, after being confined to a sports bra for the last six months.

After picking out a sexy pink Victoria's Secret lace bra and panties set, she wiggled into a tight little black skirt, black tank top, and a lacy sweater. They clung to her curves and accented her legs to their best advantage. She dabbed some perfume between her breasts, behind her ears and on her wrists, then put on her hooker heels and she was ready to go. Shannon had decided earlier she was going to pick her up so they didn't have two cars to worry about.

She was actually really looking forward to this night more than she thought. It had been a long time since the old gang from high school had been together. Everyone was so busy with their own lives; they didn't take the time to get together like they used to.

Ashley would occasionally see someone when she was out shopping or at the movies, but they had not been together as a group for a long time. She missed everyone and was glad they had a reason to get together. They always talked big and promised they would get together at least once a month, but it never seemed to work out that way.

Shannon called on her cell phone and said she was waiting in the parking lot. Ashley turned on the living room lamp, locked the door, and headed out to meet Shannon. She was parked in the handicap spot right in front of Ashley's apartment. Ashley gave her the *I'm a cop and I should give you a ticket look*, but she just smiled and waved.

It had been a long time since she had worn a skirt this short, and she had forgotten how hard it was to maneuver herself into a sitting position without giving a huge beaver shot to anyone who happened to be looking. Looking up, she noticed she had attracted several sets of eyes, giving her the once-over. You would think these people had never seen her dressed up, because she never got looks like this when she left the apartment wearing her uniform. Hell, half the people staring at her probably didn't even recognize her as the same plain Jane who walked out of this very same building every day.

Laughing at her ungraceful plop into her passenger seat, Shannon managed to spit out, "Geez sis...you look like a million bucks! I pity the poor guy you set your sights on tonight."

"I'm not looking for a guy tonight, just getting together with our friends the same as you are."

"Yeah, right. If that was true, you would have jeans and a t-shirt on."

"And this is coming from someone wearing a slinky red dress that hugs every curve you have and, if I'm not mistaken, Michael arrested a hooker last night wearing that same dress," she teased.

"A hooker! My dress covers up way more than that skanky little outfit you pulled out of the back of your closet."

Laughing in reply she said, "Okay, let's pity *both* the guys we set our sights on tonight. Because the Wright sisters are out on the prowl and those men don't stand a chance when we enter the Whistle Stop. Hell, why should we stop at just two? Let's gather a whole group and then work our way through them, one at a time. What do you think, little sis?"

"I think someone needs to get laid, is what I think."

"You are such a party pooper. Who else are you picking up?"

"Brent, Jen, and Mike. Everyone else is meeting us there. Can you believe that Casey and Dan are finally engaged? They have always been such a great couple."

"Is Michael coming?"

"You know our big brother, he always considered Casey his third sister. He wouldn't miss her big night for anything."

They drove through the quiet neighborhood, making their way to Grant Street, about twenty blocks from Ashley's apartment building, and pulled up in front of Mike and Jen's house, just as Brent was pulling into the driveway. He got out, gave them both a jaunty wave, ran and knocked on the door, then came over and jumped in the back seat. He leaned in between the bucket seats and gave each of them a complete up and down, whistling. "Damn, you two are looking fine. I'm going to have a hard time deciding which one of you lucky ladies gets to go home with me tonight."

Mike and Jen were just getting into the car and heard his last remark. Mike chuckled at his comment. "Brent, are you ever going to give up trying to snag one of the Wright sisters?"

"Are you nuts? No way! Have you seen these two? They have been breaking my heart for years, and after seeing them tonight, it's time I stepped up my chase to a lot faster speed."

"You men are all pigs," Jen said, punching Brent in the ribs.

"You married the biggest one of all," was Brent's reply, grunting and grabbing his ribs in

mock pain.

She smiled and agreed, reaching over to give Mike a huge kiss and a quick feel.

He grabbed her hand and peeked around his wife's head to see three sets of eyes enjoying the shot being performed in the back-seat. He instantly turned bright red, to the amusement of his wife. She pulled back, gave him a seductive grin and turned her attention to the rest of them, knowing full well she had left her husband with a raging hard-on. They were all used to their antics, having watched them all through high school.

They spent the ride to the bar in conversation about Casey and Dan and what they had all been up to since they had seen each other last. Before they knew it they had pulled up at Uncle Irwin's. Jen and Mike piled out of the car and made their way towards the door, looking back to wait for the rest of them. Brent stood back and watched as Shannon and Ashley both took a little more time maneuvering themselves out of the car, again trying to not to give Brent the show he was so eagerly waiting for. It was Friday night, so the place was hopping with cops, business men and women just getting off work, single guys on the prowl, and single women wanting to be prowled.

They stood at the door surveying the crowd, drawing their fair share of looks. The women would all glance at the door as it opened, but when they saw that it was not a man, they would turn their attention back to what they had been doing. The men did the same but held their stares, sizing them up to see if any of the women in the group were going to be available. They worked their way through the crowd, spying Dan waving from the table they had snagged. Actually they had pushed about three or four of the tables together, so it looked like the whole group from high school were going to make it for the party.

Michael, Steve, and Natalie joined them a few minutes later.

The table was already loud, everyone talking at once, congratulating the happy couple, and greeting all the newcomers to the table. Shannon and Ashley snagged a seat near the wall, so they could have a full view of the bar with hopes of maybe meeting Mr. Wonderful tonight, just like Casey had.

Gladys, Uncle Irwin's cocktail waitress, came to take their drink orders, giving hugs all around. She had worked here for as long as Ashley could remember. She was anywhere from sixty to eighty, had bleached blonde hair she wore in a beehive with a whole bunch of curls at the top of her head, and clothes straight out of the seventies. Tight leopard-print capris were her choice tonight, along with a sequined red halter top, letting more of her boobs hang out than it held in. She wore huge gold earrings that hung down to her shoulders and her makeup would have made Lady Gaga proud.

After she made her way back to the bar, the group couldn't help but razz the happy couple. "So Dan, what's this crap I hear about you being all sappy and trying to make all us real men look bad?" Michael yelled down to the other end of the table. "You know, we confirmed bachelors don't stand a chance now that you went above and beyond what was expected from any one man. We should be out stringing you up instead of here celebrating the show you performed."

"Yep, you got that right. But that's Mr. Sap to you." Dan and Casey took the teasing in stride, knowing that there wasn't one single person here at these tables who wasn't extremely happy for them both.

A lot of soul searching was going on among those of them who had made it this far in life and had not found the person they wanted to spend the rest of their lives with. Everyone except Shannon had been out of school for years, and none of them who weren't married were in a serious relationship. Ashley didn't know about anyone else, but it made her downright sad to think that she might never find the one person in this world she was meant to be with. She took a good look around at the bar, and she could see that they were not the only ones who were feeling time slip away. From the desperate looks on many of the women's faces, they were feeling the same as she did right now. The look on the men's faces was the same as always...were they going to get lucky tonight?

Ashley was not going to let her moment of sadness get to her. They were here to celebrate and that's what she was going to do. Besides, who knew if her Mr. Right was right here tonight?

Ashley's uncle Irwin helped Gladys bring the drinks over to the table. "What's this I hear that some lucky girl finally lassoed this fine young man?" He patted Dan on the shoulder and reached down and gave Casey a big hug and a kiss. "When you two are ready, just come by and see me, so I can give you all my marriage advice."

"Um, I think we'll pass on that offer, if you don't mind, Uncle Irwin," Casey giggled, leaning over and laying her head on Dan's shoulder.

"Girl, you cut me to the quick, but I'll forgive you and just to show you there's no hard feelings, the first round's on me."

There were cheers from around the table. Uncle Irwin raised his glass and said, "Let me be the first to raise a toast to two very special people."

They all stood, raised their glasses, looked at the two love birds, and waited for Uncle Irwin's words of wisdom.

"First rule to remember: there are no rules. If there are rules, they only get broken and then someone gets hurt. Second: no matter what, always listen, even when no words are spoken. Sometimes the most important things ever said are never put into words. And third, never put your dirty underwear on the floor. If you two follow those simple guidelines, you should live happily ever after. As you probably have guessed by now, I was forever leaving my underwear on the floor."

Everyone drank to the couple, and Ashley wasn't surprised to see a few watery eyes as she looked from one friend to the other.

Wow. She had to admit she was secretly impressed with what Uncle Irwin had said. She didn't even have a boyfriend, but could see how all those things could make for a strong marriage. Looking at Dan and Casey talking with all their friends, she knew deep down these two would beat the odds and be together forever. The noise around the table was loud as Dan and Casey explained the big event to everyone who had not heard the details yet. Ashley sat back and just enjoyed watching their faces as the story was told, and it never failed, each and every one of them would turn and give Dan a look of disbelief. It was so out of character for him to do something so elaborate. He was more the type of guy who would just pass her the ring while they watched TV and say, "Ya wanna?"

It was fun being with all the people she had grown to care for deeply. They were friends she'd had since their high school days and in today's society, that was a rare thing. She decided she was starting to get really sappy; it must be time for another drink. She worked her way over to the bar and squeezed between Mr. Cizik and some lady she didn't know. Mr. Cizik was a regular who made his nightly stop come rain or shine. The Wright kids had always considered him an adopted uncle. The lady to his right was probably in her seventies, and looked like she should be in a library instead of perched on a barstool.

Ashley waited for the bartender to make his way to her, but really did not mind the wait, because with the view she was getting of his backside she was really in no hurry. He was tall, had shoulders like a linebacker, a slim waist, and a firm ass stuffed into jeans that caressed thighs made to rub up against hers.

"I see you're enjoying the eye candy."

Ashley tore her eyes away, and turning to the librarian said, "Excuse me?"

"Honey, I saw where those eyes were going. Why do you think I'm sitting here?"

Smiling at her, Ashley returned her gaze to where she was looking. "Who is he?"

"His name is Derek. He started working here about six weeks ago. You don't think all these bimbos are in here for Irwin, do you?"

Tearing her eyes away again, she actually looked around the bar at the large number of women who were surrounding the bar. There were a *lot* of women there, and where there are women there are men. Explained why the place was extra busy.

"So what's his story?"

The lady smiled. "No one really knows much. He's fairly quiet, really nice, keeps to himself, makes a great margarita and looks better than anything these old eyes have seen in a long time. I come here on the weekends just to watch the show. The way these women throw themselves at him is just way too much fun. Some are just downright blunt, some are coy and others are sneaky. Last week, one of them had her friend pretend he was giving her a hard time, hoping he would come over and be her knight in shining armor. He just sent one of the off-duty cops over to calm things down. He didn't even look up to see if things had been taken care of. I've seen more numbers passed over this bar, more eyelashes batted and more sultry looks thrown his way than I care to think about, and one gal just reached across the bar and gave him a big wet one."

"Really? It's sad that women are that desperate. I mean, don't get me wrong, that man could make a sane woman do some strange things, but kissing a man across a sticky bar is crossing the line. What did he do?"

Laughing, she replied, "Nothing, that's what was so funny. He didn't miss a beat. She only got a quick peck in before he could pull back. He didn't even acknowledge her, just pulled away and went back to mixing the drink he had been working on. I laughed for a good minute over the expression on the poor woman's face. I don't know if she thought she had the pucker power of Superwoman or what, but you could tell she thought with that one kiss he would give her his undying love, and when she got squat, it was priceless."

About that time, he came up to Ashley. "What will it be?"

"Margarita on the rocks, please."

As he moved down the bar, she looked at the lady and said, "Oh my! I almost said, 'you over ice at my place.'"

She laughed, "See, I told you."

"But I'm not some desperate bimbo. I may be having a dry spell, but I still wouldn't throw myself at a man."

"You've got a libido, don't you? When that man looks at you, the brain shuts off and ol' Miss Libido kicks in. If I was twenty years younger, that's not saying if he turned those hazel eyes on me now, that I wouldn't jump at the chance."

She was right. Ashley thought Phillip Kelly was gorgeous, but this guy was someone women dreamed about meeting, knowing it would never happen.

He brought her drink, she paid, and he moved down the bar. Just like that, no, "Hey baby, how are you"...nothing.

Wow, a girl could get her ego bruised big time. She was actually beginning to feel sorry for the poor lady who tried the kissing stunt. Ashley was not some drop-dead gorgeous model type, but she was used to getting a little more attention than that.

She was still playing it over in her mind when she looked up and caught his eye. He smiled a little grin, and went back to waiting on some brunette.

Ashley turned to the lady who said, "I'll be damned! Girl, that's the first time I've seen that happen. Are you some kind of witch or something?"

"Not that I know of. Beats me, but I see what you mean about those hazel eyes. I could spend a lifetime staring into those puppies." She glanced down the bar at him again, but didn't want to be caught staring, so saying goodbye to the nice lady, Ashley headed back to their table. She felt like she was walking on air. If he could make her feel like this with just a look, what would happen if he actually talked to her? She was afraid she would turn into a quivering mass of Jell-O.

When she sat down at the table, Shannon leaned over and asked what had her face so flushed. Not wanting to share her hot little bartender, she just said it was warm in there. She gave Ashley a look that said she didn't believe a word of it, and she would get the truth later.

It was hard to stay focused on the events at their table. One, because twelve people were all talking at once, and two, because she just wanted to stare at the bar and, more importantly, what was standing behind the bar. It was the hardest thing she had ever done, but she forced herself not to even look that way. When she was ready for another drink, she would wait for Gladys or have one of the guys get it for her.

Michael and Ashley challenged Mike and Jen to a game of darts, kicking their butts, and they accused Uncle Irwin of having a rigged dartboard. That led to new challengers, and Michael and Ashley ended up spending over an hour defending their title. They finally lost to Uncle Irwin and Mr. Cizik.

The crowd had thinned out a lot by this time, heading home to families or on to clubs where the chances of hooking up were better, and they were left with a much quieter place. This was the Uncle Irwin's she loved, where you could actually hear what the person beside you was saying, and didn't have to shout in their ear to be heard.

As Ashley looked around, she noticed several hopeful women that she was sure would still be here at closing time, a handful of off-duty cops, lonely singles, several guys watching the big screen in the corner, and tables filled with people like them, just partying with friends. They were the largest group still left in the bar and definitely the loudest. As the night wore on and the drinks kept coming they were all starting to feel the effects. It was a good thing that Shannon was the D.D. for their group, because Ashley sure couldn't drive. She had not been this buzzed since before she joined the academy.

No one had left and a few others had joined their group. Ashley looked around at them and had to smile. Dan and Casey, Mike and Jen, Michael, Steve, Natalie, Brent, Shannon, Brian, Tom, and Ashley. They had all gone to the same school throughout their school days, some a few years older, some younger, and a few her age, but it never seemed to matter what particular grade they were in, they all just clicked for whatever reason and it stuck. They had all hung out together, partied together, and got into trouble together.

They were a wild mix of different careers. Dan and Casey were in the law and business world, Mike was a mechanic, and Jen was teaching history at their old junior high. Steve owned a computer store; Natalie was a dancer at a theater, Brent was a disc jockey at a radio station, Brian was a high school football coach, Tom was a salesman, Shannon was in college, and Michael and Ashley were the local fuzz. Ashley thought Michael was the only one of them who was actually doing what he had set out to do after high school. It felt good to catch up on everyone's lives; she hadn't realized how much she missed everyone.

All of a sudden Brent grabbed her hand and jerked her to her feet, dragging her to the little dance floor in the corner. "Come on, sweet cheeks, I've waited long enough to hold you in my arms." He put a dollar in the jukebox and punched some numbers while never letting go of her hand. He began spinning her around when the music started, all to hoots and hollers from their table.

Brent was a good dancer and they were swinging around like they were on Dancing with the Stars. Ashley had to be a little more conservative than she normally would have been, due to the shortness of her skirt. It was one thing to put on a show with their dancing, but she didn't want to put one on because her ass was showing. Before long everyone had joined them, laughing and joking, trying to outdo each other. The song ended and a slow song came on, and Steve cut in. She didn't think Brent was going to let him for a minute, but he just smiled and grabbed Shannon. Steve was a really great guy, and Ashley was probably the only one there who knew how hard it was for him to be there.

"How are you holding up?" Ashley asked.

He pulled back, looked her in the eyes, and gave her a sad little smile. "I'm okay, and my heart has finally stopped doing that painful little squeeze when I see them together."

Steve had secretly been in love with Casey since high school. He never acted on his feelings out of respect for both Dan and Casey, but Ashley had picked up on the looks he couldn't always hide. One night after they both had way too many beers, he had finally confessed it all to her and then swore her to secrecy.

She gave him a hug, and they just kept dancing because they both knew there was nothing they could say or do to change the situation.

The dance floor was now packed with other couples joining in the fun. The song ended and Ashley turned to receive her next partner, and was pulled into a set of very strong, unfamiliar arms.

"Oh my," she breathed, looking up at her partner's face.

"'Oh my' is a strange way to say hello," the bartender replied.

Her heart had jumped into her throat, her palms instantly start-ed sweating, and she hoped to God he could not tell. "You took me by surprise. Why aren't you working? Besides, are you trying to get me killed?"

"I'm on break and I'm not that bad of a dancer."

Smiling she said, "We'll see about that after the dance ends, but I was referring to all those women standing outside of the dance floor staring daggers through my back."

"What women? I only see one woman," he answered, gazing down into her eyes and making her knees go weak. His arm around her waist tightened a little when he felt her sag. She was making a complete fool of herself over this man. She needed to get her act together and not let him have such an effect on her. Surely he was used to women swooning in his arms, but she did not want to be one.

Looking up into hazel eyes twinkling with amusement, she real-ized he knew exactly what she was talking about.

He was holding her way too close for someone he didn't even know. His leg was between hers and his left hand was on her lower back, on the verge of being damn close to being on her ass. But it was a nice feeling, not like being held by some dirty old man trying to cop a quick feel. They moved around the dance floor like they had been dancing together for years. Everything around her disap-peared, except the man holding her. God, she didn't want this song to end and have to leave the circle of his arms. It had not felt this good being in a man's arms for a very long time.

Tilting her head back, she looked into those mesmerizing hazel eyes. "You know that when this song ends, you are going to be ripe pickings for that mob over there, don't you?"

"Then we'll just have to work our way to the edge of the dance floor closest to the bar, so I can make a mad dash behind it for pro-tection when the dance ends."

"You're a big fat chicken!"

"You got that right! Have you seen the look in those women's eyes? They scare the hell out of me, the way they look at me like I am a piece of meat."

"Then why did you take the chance and dance with me? You could have kept them all at arm's length if you would have stayed safely behind the bar."

"And miss out on the only chance I might have had to speak to you? You were avoiding the bar like it had the plague or something."

His fingers were slowly moving along her back, sending shivers throughout her body. Ashley was not even sure he was aware that he was doing it. It seemed like a natural thing to do.

"I was not, and how do you even know that, unless you wanted me to come up there?"

She hadn't realized it, but the song was almost over. He had danced her over to the edge just like he said he was going to, where he suddenly spun her around, leaned down and kissed her ear and was gone in a flash.

Ashley just stood frozen on the spot. Her ear was on fire, her heart was beating a hundred miles an hour, her knees were shaking like crazy and she was sure she had a dazed look on her face.

Before she could recover, Casey and Shannon were there, each grabbing an elbow and whisking her to the restroom. When several other women tried coming in after them, Shannon locked the door and yelled at them that it was full.

"Who the hell was that, and what the hell just happened out there on that dance floor?" Casey asked.

"That man is pure heaven! Where did he come from, and why did you let him get away?" Shannon piped in.

Ashley just stood there and smiled, trying to sort out what just happened. So if the lady at the bar was right and this guy *never* came on to women, then what the hell was he doing kissing her ear?

Shannon gave her arm a vicious pinch.

"Ouch…stop that! What did you do that for?" Looking around, Ashley realized where they were and that other ladies were banging on the door. She gave Shannon a curious look, suddenly feeling silly that a man could make her lose complete awareness of her surroundings.

Casey screamed through the closed door, "Use the men's, this one is full."

"So…"

"I don't remember his name but he started bartending for Uncle Irwin about six weeks ago, he keeps to himself, and I got all that from some stranger at the bar earlier tonight."

"You call that keeping to himself? You two were practically glued to each other and I saw him lean in and whisper something in your ear."

"He didn't whisper anything."

"Then what the hell was he doing?"

"Kissing it!"

"Oh my God, this is amazing. So are you going to see him again?"

"Not that I know of. You know everything I know."

Shannon put her hand on her hip, and had that meddling look in her eye.

"Oh no you don't! You are not going to get involved."

"But sis, maybe he's just shy and needs a little help."

"Shy my ass! I don't think there's a shy bone in that man's body. Shy guys don't go around kissing strange girls on their ears."

"You are kind of strange," Shannon said.

"I know, but don't tell him that." They all started giggling, used the restroom and headed out and back to their table.

Several women were still standing outside the restroom glaring at her. Ashley wasn't sure if it was because she had danced with Mr.

Hottie or that they had tied up the restroom for so long. But right then, she really didn't care. They waltzed back to their table, their heads together, giggling like they were back in high school.

Once they were seated, Ashley looked over and caught her big brother's eye, saw his little frown, and knew she was in for a lecture on the evils of strange men. That she needed to be careful, this was a crazy world, and men were only out to get one thing from women. She remembered the first time he gave her that speech, she had asked him, "You're a guy, is that the only thing you're after when you talk to girls?" He had boxed her ear and told her to pay attention.

For the most part, she had taken his advice, learning that lesson the hard way in college, but she was still human and liked men, enjoyed dating, and even liked the occasional love affair. Not that she let that take place too often, and she never told her big brother about her lustful longings. Maybe she should tease him sometime, and start going into detail about how horny she could get, but she could see his reaction now. Any guy she looked at longer than five seconds, Michael would beat to a pulp. To save all mankind, she decided she had better keep her mouth shut.

It was getting close to two and Uncle Irwin had already called last call for drinks, so they all made a plan to head to Hill's Cafe for breakfast. They gathered up their stuff, and made their way to the bar to settle up their bar tab.

Ashley was both excited and dreading the idea of being close to Mr. Bartender again, because she had no idea what to think about his little escapade on the dance floor. He had left her feeling hot as hell, and she knew for a fact he was definitely interested, if the rise in his jeans had been any indication. But the story from the lady at the bar kept running through her head; this guy was not a player, so what had happened tonight? Was there a chance that they would get together in the future, or was she just a diversion for the night?

The guys were all throwing money out to cover the bill, so Ashley took the chance to peek and see if he even noticed her. He was busy collecting the money and squaring up their tab, so she just turned and started talking to Jen.

Uncle Irwin came over to wish the happy couple well again, telling them if they needed the bar for anything at all, it was theirs for the taking. He had an arm around both Shannon and Ashley and gave them each huge hugs, making them promise to come back more often. They gave their promises, telling him he would have to join their family for one of their Sunday night dinners. He made sure everyone had D.D.s or cabs lined up before he went on to the next set of customers.

Ashley had turned her back and was talking to Brent and Mike when she heard Shannon saying in a very loud voice, "Our group is headed to Hill's Café, and if any of the bar staff wants to join us they are more than welcome." Ashley turned around suddenly and glared at Shannon down the bar, where she was standing with a satisfied smirk on her face. Ashley knew she should have kept her on a tight leash, knowing the matchmaker in her would not wait to come out and do its magic.

Mr. Bartender never even looked Ashley's way, and she was going to kill her sister. She knew it and made a beeline to the car. She was already in the driver's seat, buckled up, ready to go, before the others even got to the bar door. Casey was laughing the whole way to the car. "You should have expected that from her. You knew it was too much temptation for her."

Ashley climbed into the front seat, reached over and pulled Shannon's red hair, and said, "Paybacks, little sis, when and where is yet to be determined!"

"Come on, Ash, what if he shows up, and you guys fall in love and get married and have lots of hunky little boys and obnoxious little girls just like you. Then paybacks are null and void."

"That would be determined by a lot of ifs, don't you think?"

"Never underestimate the power of the almighty Shannon in her quest to find true love for her spinster sister."

By this time everyone else had made their way to the car, and Shannon knew that she had better shut up before Brent and Mike heard and started giving her the third degree. All she needed was for them to know what had happened between her and the bartender.

Going to Hill's Café at two thirty in the morning was just asking to be engulfed by weirdos and drunks. They pulled tables together to make room for all of them. Shannon and Ashley helped Michelle, the evening waitress, with their table, getting menus and drinks and silverware for everyone.

Ashley couldn't stop her eyes from straying to the door, not sure if he would show up or not. By the time their food arrived, she had relaxed and knew there was no way he would come this late. She was starved anyway and was scarfing down her breakfast burrito like there was no tomorrow, so she was glad he didn't show up. Ashley was not one of those women who only picked at her food when a man was around, but that didn't mean she wanted Mr. Hottie to see her wolfing down food like she hadn't eaten in three days. She should have expected that he wouldn't show up. It always took at least a half hour to get the bar cleaned and packed up for the night. She knew that, but had held out a little hope anyway.

They all agreed that they were not going to let so much time go by before they got together again, or worse yet, wait till someone else got engaged. Laughing and joking, they all headed out the door to their cars, headed to their own homes and back to their own lives.

CHAPTER FOUR

The next morning, Ashley woke dreamless and rested from the night before. She was glad that there was no headache to go along with all the margaritas she had put down. In her younger days, a hangover would never have even been in question, but as she had gotten older, she was not always so lucky. She lay in her big comfy bed and thought about all that had happened in the last forty-eight hours. For leading a fairly quiet and boring life, she'd suddenly had a rush of excitement. Ah, and Mr. Hottie Bartender was the best excitement of all. Just thinking about that man made her want to reach for Big Daddy in her nightstand drawer. A girl who had not had a decent date in months had to rely on sexual satisfaction wherever she could, and for her it was her favorite toy instead of a string of one-night stands that meant nothing the next morning. Today was shopping day, laundry day, run errands day and supper with her parents, and she really didn't have time to indulge in self-pleasure.

There were just not enough days off in the work week for her to get everything done she needed to and have any *her* time. She thought about writing letters to her congressman, suggesting they all get paid more, so they could invent the three-day weekend for all those hard-working Americans.

Ashley took a quick shower, threw her hair up into a clip, put on some makeup, pulled on a pair of old cutoff jeans, a worn out AC/

DC t-shirt, and a pair of flip-flops, and she was ready to tackle the day.

While she gathered up all her dirty clothes, she mentally made up a grocery list to get her through the week without Bill having to feed her or resorting to the vending machine every night.

She headed to her car, arms loaded with her laundry basket filled with a week's worth of laundry. She piled everything into the back seat, climbed into the front and started it up. That's when she noticed the rose stuck under her windshield. Aw…someone left her a rose. Ashley got out and removed it, noticing that it was dead. She wasn't sure if it had been dead when placed on her windshield, but it sure was now. It had been years since someone had done something romantic like that. As a matter of fact, she used to get this kind of thing all the time in high school. Never did figure out who had done it. She had no idea who had put this one on her car, either. She had no men in her life at this time. Suddenly she had a crazy thought that it might be her bartender. Then she came crashing back to earth. First of all, he didn't seem the sappy type. Plus, he had no idea where she lived. She was disappointed that the rose was dead but, oh well, it was a good beginning to her day.

Her first stop was the bank, so she could deposit her check and get some cash. It didn't take her long working the night shift to realize she needed cash so she could feed the vending machine in the break room at the station. If she wasn't careful, she would gain ten pounds by the time she got off the graveyard shift. She loved all the food that was wrong for her, of course. Give her a bag of M&Ms over carrot sticks any day.

Pulling up in front of the bank, she noticed Mrs. Hazel Steffen, her parents' next-door neighbor, was just coming out the door. She was the neatest old lady she knew. She looked the same as she did when Ashley was five, with her snow-white hair, always worn in a French twist. She was a friend and a confidante throughout her youth and her adulthood. She was always there for Ashley on the many occasions when she had attempted to run away from home, and always knew when she was either down in the dumps, in trouble, or just needed ideas on how to put up with crybaby Malone.

Mrs. Steffen always had fresh chocolate chip cookies and a kind word or bit of advice for her. Ashley's mom, Laura, always knew if she couldn't find her, she would be sitting at Mrs. Hazel's kitchen table. She was the one who had taught Shannon and Ashley how to bake her yummy desserts and make home-cooked meals to tempt any man they ever set their sights on.

Laura was a nurse at the hospital and worked twelve-hour shifts, so she wasn't always home to do those kinds of things. And truth be known, Laura wasn't the best cook in the world. She took after her own mom and was more the Ragu kind of woman.

Mrs. Hazel always made Ashley all warm and fuzzy on the inside. Ashley grew up wanting to be just like her, married to the same man for sixty-four years, blissfully happy and content with whatever life sent her.

Ashley stopped and took the time to talk to her for a few minutes. Mrs. Hazel was always interested in what was going on in their lives and the Wright kids had all considered her their third grandma. Listening to her now made Ashley a little sad. She realized her biological clock was moving into desperate mode with no happily ever after in sight.

Ashley hugged her close as they separated and pulled herself out of the pity-party mode. She was just making sure she didn't settle for anything less than her Mr. Perfect, she told herself. Ashley promised to stop by and try Mrs. Hazel's new strudel recipe that she had found in one of her cooking magazines, and told her to give Mr. Steffen a kiss for her.

Finishing up at the bank, Ashley headed to the cleaners to pick up her extra uniforms that she had dropped off last week. She had decided right away that having the cleaners do her uniforms was worth the few extra dollars it cost her every week. This is where she took after her mom; they didn't own anything that needed ironing. The Wright women had decided long ago that ironing was way overrated. If she was going to get all hot and sweaty, it wasn't going to be over an iron.

Next stop was Dixie's Spa, her aunt Dixie's beauty shop. Her salon had originally been a two-station building that had relocated to a large full-fledged, pamper-yourself-silly spa. Ashley loved coming here, with all the soft warm colors Dixie had used when moving. Walking into her place was like walking into pure luxury. Aunt Dixie had five kids and between them and her husband John, who was an electrician, they had used their talent and a lot of hard work to make a salon that could fit right in on Rodeo Drive. It was decorated in rich earth tones with gold accents, and marble-like desks and stations. When she had decided her business was growing so fast that she either needed to start turning people away or do a major expansion, the whole family got behind her, giving her the encouragement to expand and helping make it what it was today. Ashley's aunts and mom would scour garage sales and estate sales watching for items that she could use. The younger generation did the same on the Internet, checking E-Bay and other sites, finding all kinds of bargains. With all the talent in their family they would refinish the items they found, painting, staining, reupholstering, or whatever the item needed to look like it had just come out of some high-priced store. Every time one of them would walk into her salon and see what great work they had done, it made them all feel good about how they had all pulled together as a family. Dixie's shop had blossomed into a thriving business, and with all the money they had saved her, she saw a profit right away.

The only difference between Dixie's and some expensive salon was that it was still a two-station beauty shop at heart. Dixie's wasn't staffed with a bunch of snotty hairdressers who only cared about the almighty dollar, but local girl-next-door types, who made you feel welcome whether you wanted a fancy highlight or just a quick trim. She had added a massage therapist last year, along with a pedicurist and a line of the new high-tech tanning beds to complete her list of services.

She had hired Troy Hughes, a walking enigma to them all. He was about 5'9" and built like a wrestler. Muscles in all the right places, but not Hulk Hogan-like. He had longer blond hair that just brushed his shoulders, with just the right amount of highlights to make most women envious of him. He would not be classified as downright handsome on the whole, but he had the brightest blue eyes and his teeth were perfectly straight and brilliantly white, a smile that could knock the socks off most women. The question was, did he want to? No one really knew whose socks Troy wanted to knock off. He was a very private person who never talked about his personal life. Actually he didn't talk much at all. He respected that when you entered his massage room, you did not want to have a deep conversation, but instead wanted the peace and quiet needed to enjoy his massages to the max. No one had ever seen Troy out with anyone, male or female, at least not anyone Ashley was acquainted with. But everyone respected Troy and he had hands that would melt the tension out of anyone, so they all left his private life to him and enjoyed the fifty or ninety minutes of pure bliss he could give your body while wrapped in a sheet on his massage table. She would classify him as good looking with a mysterious air that drove many women to distraction.

Dixie's other staff were Leanne, Heidi, Brianne, Faith, Candi and Sue Lynn. Ashley's aunt Dixie considered them all her second family, and made sure they were very happy in her shop so that none of them were ever tempted to stray to a different shop. She knew how important it was to keep a content shop, and in today's society the young women just coming out of beauty school were pretty fickle. She prided herself on keeping the same women for years.

"Well, look what the cat dragged in. Our own little Miss Officer Wright. We haven't seen you in what seems like months, girl. You know, just because you're some hotshot policewoman now doesn't mean you can't come in here and visit us poor old lonesome gals, now does it?" yelled Candi as she bent over some lady in the shampoo bowl.

"Ahhh, did you all miss me?"

Aunt Dixie was trying to cut a little boy's hair, but he was doing more squirming than sitting still. She gave Ashley a big smile but kept her eyes on her client. The boy's mother was talking away, not even aware that her child was making Aunt Dixie's job twice as hard as it needed to be. If the mother would stop talking long enough to help distract her son for just a few minutes, they could be done and out of there.

"Well, of course we did! We were just wondering how we were going to get all the juicy details about some poor stiff doing his duty down in the morgue restroom."

Ashley heard several ladies let out gasps of horror, several small snickers and some hoots of laughter.

"It didn't take long for that little bit of news to make it around the community. Who do I have to thank for spreading my humiliation to everyone?"

Chuckling, Faith answered, "Officer Shirley Miller was in getting her eyebrows waxed and told us what she knew, which wasn't a whole lot, so we need all the juicy details from you."

Deciding she had better fill everyone in on the truth before things got completely blown out of proportion, Ashley settled down in Faith's chair and started recalling the events of the now famous night. Faith worked her magic on Ashley's hair, trimming her split ends that were way out of control. It had been months since she had made it in to get her monthly trim, and it felt so good to get her hair back in shape again. Ashley looked in the mirror as Faith was finishing up, and decided her own eyebrows could probably use a wax. Her eyebrows were a light shade so she could get away without waxing for a lot longer than Casey, who came in almost weekly to keep her Frankenstein brow under control. Ashley remembered Shannon teasing her their freshman year about how she was getting one huge brow, and ever since, Casey had kept them plucked and waxed to perfection. So now they teased her that if she wasn't careful, she wouldn't have any left and she would have to draw them in like the little old ladies at her grandma's bingo parlor.

"Well, I hope you have spent the last twenty-four hours coming up with some devious plan to get back at those two," exclaimed Brianne in a huff. She was a pretty straight-laced woman who had no patience for the shenanigans of people who played practical jokes, and she always requested April Fool's Day off, so that she would not be the victim of some customer or one of her fellow beauticians' jokes.

"To be honest, I really haven't thought about it again since we heard Casey and Dan's big news." Ashley knew she was baiting them to see if they had heard the latest. It was hard to get one up on the ladies who worked there. They knew all the latest gossip and kept everyone informed of any tragedies or events that someone might have missed. Women were known to make appointments for haircuts the minute they got back from vacation so they could get caught up on anything they might have missed while they were gone. The women who worked there didn't really do any of the talking; they left that up to the customers in their chairs. They made sure not to spread idle gossip, because it could cause them to lose a customer if it proved to be false. If no other customers were in the shop and one of the family was getting her hair done, then it was a different story. You could count on the juicier stuff being told, not having to worry about it being spread to untrustworthy sources.

One by one, everyone working in the shop stopped what they were doing and turned their heads to stare at Ashley, their mouths open wide. Then everyone started talking at once.

"What news?"

"Girl, what do you know?"

"Spill it, girlfriend. What are you keeping from us?"

Troy came out of the massage room just in time to hear the uproar. Looking around at the scene of women in desperate gossip mode, he came to the conclusion that Ashley must be the cause of it, since everyone was talking to her. He looked over Faith's shoulder into the mirror at her. "Ashley, you do know how to get these girls in a tizzy. Knowing something these women don't is enough to send some of them into heart failure."

SPLAT! A wet towel came flying through the air and smacked him in the back of the head. He reached back and grabbed the offending towel and turned to give each woman a severe look. It suddenly turned deathly quiet as he surveyed the room, trying to decipher who the guilty party was.

"Tsk, tsk. Childish behavior will get you nowhere. Just for that, don't tell them anything, Ash. They don't deserve to know anything now. Let's go for coffee next door so you can fill me in on all your news." He spun the chair around, grabbed her hand and started leading her to the front door, with Ashley laughing so hard at the looks on their faces that she was about ready to pee her pants. She still had the cape tied around her neck and a clip holding a section of her hair up. He never missed a beat, just kept walking toward the door. Ashley had never seen so many women move so fast as they did once they realized he wasn't going to stop, no matter what. Grabbing them both, they pushed Ashley back down into Faith's chair, surrounded Troy so he could not make a play for her again, and waited for whatever news she was about to enlighten them with.

Ashley's idea of running in and getting a quick haircut turned into a two-hour ordeal. After she filled everyone in on Casey's news, Troy talked her into a massage, saying anyone who had sat on a dead guy's lap deserved an hour of relaxation. And boy was he right; it felt good to let him work the kinks out of her shoulders from sitting at that stupid wooden table for five days straight. He always worked the outer edges of her butt muscles, which she needed after sitting on those hard chairs for the same amount of time.

Telling everyone at Dixie's goodbye, and promising to get in more often, she headed to her car to finish up her errands.

So, who cared if she didn't make it to the grocery store today? She had cash, and the vending machine had lots of gourmet delights, like tuna salad surprise, yummy cup of soup, and mega bean burritos.

Thinking of all this food reminded her she hadn't eaten anything all day, so she whipped into the closest fast food joint and grabbed a burger to gobble down on her way to the pharmacy to pick up her three-month supply of birth control. Why? She wasn't really sure. It wasn't like her bed was a happening kind of place. That's not saying a little romp with Officer Phillip Kelly, Mr. Hottie Bartender, or even a little *extra* massage with Troy wasn't something that hadn't run through her horny little mind. As she made her way to the back of the pharmacy, she actually thought about her love life, and she realized it was a pretty bleak story. She had not had a meaningful relationship since Brandon. A couple of flings in the last six years were downright depressing. Not that she wanted to turn into someone like Hoochie Malone, but she was craving a little male attention. She was a smart, modern woman; surely she could indulge in some wild flings, enjoy some crazy sex and go on about her life.

The pharmacist looked up and caught her with a goofy grin on her face, regarded the pills in his hand and gave her a peculiar look. Ashley did not even want to venture a guess at what he was thinking. And she knew he went to her parents' church, so thankfully a pharmacist was sworn to patient client privilege, or was that just doctors?

Oh Lord, she was dead meat. Grabbing the pills, she made a bee-line to her car. Maybe she wasn't cut out for a footloose and fancy-free lifestyle after all. If she couldn't even think about it without getting caught, how was she ever going to pull off a few one-night stands in this godforsaken town?

Sitting in her car, she looked at her watch, trying to decide if she had enough time to go to the grocery store, then go home and un-pack the groceries and be at her parents' house by six, when there was a rap on her driver's side window.

Letting out a squeal like a little girl, she turned to find Michael standing there waiting for her to roll down her window.

"Jesus, Ash. You're not going to do that when you get out on patrol, are you?"

"No, Michael, I won't, but I'm off duty right now so I'm allowed to be scared out of my wits by some nitwit banging on my window."

He reached in the window and made a grab for her head, but she had anticipated his move and leaned out of his way.

Laughing, he leaned in and said, "I had a great time last night, how about you?"

"Yeah, it was great seeing everyone; I missed them more than I had realized, plus did you see how happy Casey and Dan were? It was great sharing their celebration with everyone."

"So you want to tell me what the bartender was doing kissing your ear?"

"Michael!"

"You didn't answer the question."

"I'm not going to, and what are you doing spying on me?"

"I'm a cop and it's my job to be aware of what's going on around me."

"Not when it's your sister."

"Especially when it's one of my sisters. So, I have Smith doing a background check on Mr. Dimple Butt right now."

"Michael, you wouldn't dare."

"Maybe not, but if I see him anywhere close to your ear again, I just might do that."

"I'm not some sixteen-year-old schoolgirl, Michael. I can let any guy I want do anything he wants to my ear, anytime I want."

He raised his eyebrow and gave her the look that used to scare her silly. But she was an adult now and he couldn't bully her around anymore. Okay…maybe he could a little bit.

Changing the subject, Ashley asked him if he was going to their dad and mom's for supper.

He took a minute to answer "Yes," still giving her the evil eye.

Ashley plastered on her fake smile, put her Bronco in reverse, rolled up her window and eased out of the parking space, giving a big wave as she drove away.

Phew, I need to get that guy a girlfriend!

Since her brother had taken up any extra time she had left, she decided to just head to her parents' house early, and take the extra time to do her laundry there. Her mom was used to her using her house instead of going to the laundromat. She preferred that Ashley come to her house anyway; they both knew what kind of creeps hung out at laundromats. There was a time in college when Ashley had done a load of laundry, put that load in the dryer, went next door to get a cup of coffee, and came back to find a guy wearing a pair of her panties and one of her bras. It was enough to make her swear off laundromats if at all possible.

Ashley pulled up to the curb, noting that neither of her parents' cars was home, but Shannon's was parked in the driveway. Making her way into the house, lugging her basket of dirty clothes in, she headed to the back porch where the washer and dryer were located. Looking out the back door, she noticed Shannon was in the back yard reclining in a chaise lounge, soaking up some sun and talking on her cell phone.

Remembering her little stunt last night, Ashley saw her opportunity for a payback. She went back into the kitchen, found a plastic pitcher, filled it with ice water and snuck out the back door. Luckily, Shannon had her chair turned so her back was to her, making it easy for Ashley to sneak up behind her. She waited for her to put her phone down, and *splash* she dumped the whole thing over her head.

Shrieking, she jumped up. Ashley made a fast dash back to the house and had the door locked before Shannon even realized it was Ashley who had dumped the water on her head.

She came running back to the house, screaming the whole way. Ashley was laughing hysterically, yelling through the door, "Paybacks, little sis, paybacks." She was laughing so hard she had to cross her legs because she was afraid she was going to piss herself.

Laura had come in while Ashley was out delivering the bath, and now stood behind her, asking what her sister had done this time to deserve a famous payback from her big sister.

Waiting to make sure her sister realized it was a payback and that they were even, Ashley unlocked the door, stepped back so Shannon could grab a towel, and turned to fill her mom in on the censored version of what happened last night.

Laughing, she muttered something about her children being the death of her. She told Shannon to put something dry on and come help with supper.

They chit-chatted while she started laundry and Laura un-packed the groceries she had picked up for supper. Their grandpa and grandma Rogers were coming over to join them, so she was going to have barbecued chicken, potato salad, coleslaw, deviled eggs, and cheesecake for dessert.

Shannon came back into the kitchen dressed in a cute little summer dress that accented her red hair. She came over and gave Ashley a hug while Laura was watching, and then when she turned away, she reached around and pinched her ass, hard. She made a beeline for their mom, standing beside her, while Ashley rubbed her ass and mouthed that she was dead.

Laura started cleaning the chicken while Ashley put eggs on to boil, and Shannon gathered up the plastic tablecloth to put on the picnic table in the back yard. It felt good to sit in her mom's kitchen and fill her in on all the news of their lives. She had heard about Casey's engagement at the grocery store, and chewed both of their butts out for not calling her and telling her the news themselves. They both knew they were guilty and felt bad that they sometimes got so busy with their own lives that they left their mom out of the loop. She considered Casey one of the family, since she had spent more time at their house as they were growing up than she did at her own house. They got so they didn't even ask if she could stay for supper, knowing it was expected. Casey's mom was single and working two jobs at the time, to support Casey and her older brother, Nicolas.

Ashley had a crush on Casey's brother from the very first time she had seen him. She had been in kindergarten and he was in the third grade. He was out playing in the backyard with his friends one day when she came over to play at Casey's. He wore a Superman cape, had a patch over his right eye and was swinging from tree to tree on a rope. He was her superhero from that day forward. He always teased her and called her his very own sidekick beetle bug.

Ashley would follow him around, trying to be the best sidekick any superhero had ever seen. He was always nice to Casey and her, and had put up with her crush throughout the years. As they grew to middle school age, her fascination turned into full-fledged love, but she kept that from both Nicolas and Casey. Just being in the same room with him made her stomach do nervous little flutters and her heart race. He moved on to high school and girls with boobs, and Ashley hated him then. Well not really, but at that age it felt like hate. She was so jealous, she stuffed her bra with Michael's tube socks one day and was going to go over to Casey's and see if Nicolas noticed her then. Michael had been standing in the kitchen when she came out of her bedroom, had burst out laughing, sending her back to her room in embarrassment. From that day forward she put her love on the back burner and idolized Nicolas from afar until he went off to college.

She had only seen Nicolas a few times since he had left, but he had grown into a gorgeous man with rich brown hair and blue eyes, the combination startling. His only drawback was that he possessed two tiny little dimples that only showed when he had a big smile on his face.

Casey kept her informed about his life, not knowing that to this day she craved information on her superhero. He had graduated college and gone into business, working his way up through his company, and was now the CEO. He was living in L.A. and hardly ever came home anymore. Casey and her mom would travel to see him, going there and enjoying the warm weather and the beach, versus him coming here and freezing his butt off most months.

The rare times she did see him, he still set her stomach to fluttering and her heart racing when he turned those serious blue eyes on her. The last time he had been home was last year, and she could have sworn when he looked at her he was not seeing his little sister's friend, but the woman she had grown into. She caught him staring several times with a look of interest in his eyes, but before she could get the chance to investigate what she thought she had seen, he got an emergency phone call and had to catch a plane to L.A. to solve some company crisis. Ashley had spent the next several months trying to decide whether she should just call him up with some lame excuse and see if he was interested, or if she had imagined it. She never did make the call.

While she was peeling the hard-boiled eggs, her dad Harold and Michael came through the door discussing the pros and cons of their district attorney.

The women all looked at each other, rolling their eyes, and went to break up the conversation before things got heated. Not that they ever let things get out of hand, but they had learned years ago, if they wanted a quiet peaceful dinner, to steer things away from politics right away. Laura grabbed Harold and started talking to him about the leak in the bathroom sink, and Shannon asked Michael about the upcoming festival their town held every summer.

It felt good to have the whole family together for a change. When Shannon had gone off to college, their family had felt a huge void. There was no way you could stay in a bad mood when she was around; she was just that kind of person. When Ashley was younger, she would try her hardest to not let Shannon turn a perfectly grouchy mood around, but she gave up, it was just impossible. The funny thing was Shannon didn't even know she had the ability to make everyone smile, it was just natural for her. The man who finally snagged her heart was a lucky man indeed.

While the chicken was marinating, Ashley fixed a pitcher of margaritas and they all gathered around the patio set in the back yard. Harold and Laura had lived here in this quiet little neighborhood their whole lives. It was a neighborhood filled with families, with kids riding their bikes down the middle of the street or writing on the sidewalks with chalk or playing football across two front yards. Their house was a standard three-bedroom ranch with a finished basement. Shannon and Ashley had bedrooms on the main floor while Michael's had been in the basement. He had always wanted to be as far away as possible from the raging hormones, as he put it. When they were young Harold had turned the garage into a woodworking shop, to make his escape. He made beautiful pieces of furniture. She had been gifted with several pieces so far. She was still waiting for the lovely Victorian house to put them in, but for now her apartment would just have to do.

After all the kids had moved out, Laura had turned Ashley's bedroom into a quilting room. She had learned how to quilt from Grandma Wright when she was first married to Harold. She told stories about how all her dad's sisters, sisters-in-law and Grandma would get together on Sunday afternoons after church and have an old-fashioned quilting bee. They did that for years until everyone started having kids, and then it was just too hard to try and quilt with thirty-one little kids running around.

Laura had continued to quilt through the years and Ashley's apartment was filled with the warmth of the beautiful quilts she had made her. The only quilt that she was still waiting to give Ashley was her wedding ring quilt. She had made wedding ring quilts for Michael and Ashley after they graduated from high school with the anticipation that they would be marrying and starting their own families. Needless to say, they were still wrapped up and stored on the upper shelves in the quilting room, waiting for the day she could lovingly pass them into their hands. She was currently working on Shannon's, and never missed a chance to tell Michael and Ashley that she would probably be giving Shannon hers before she ever got to give them theirs. They never argued the point because they both knew she was probably right. Neither of them had the time to put into a relationship; not that Ashley wouldn't like the chance, but Michael never seemed to hang on to a woman long.

He was kind of a love 'em and leave 'em kind of guy, but the women never seemed to mind. He always swore they knew what they were getting into when they dated him; he was always upfront with them on his dating practices.

Ashley's grandpa Donald and grandma Liz arrived around six to hugs and kisses all around. Don carried his drink caddy into the kitchen, and her grandma had made a Jell-O salad that they put into the refrigerator.

Don never went anywhere without his toddy fixings. He didn't want to take a chance that wherever he might go, he wouldn't be able to have his favorite bourbon and a can of 7-Up. He went to work mixing a drink for Liz and himself and then joined them in the back yard.

Liz was a chain-smoker, so everyone had learned years ago to always sit upwind of her. They had all given up hope of ever talking her into stopping. She said she had been smoking for sixty-six years and there was no way anyone was going to make her quit now. She was a courteous smoker and always kept her cigarette smoke out of everyone's eyes if she could help it, and she always smoked outside now. When they were young her house always smelled like stale smoke and everything had a yellow tinge, but after they had remodeled about ten years ago, she changed and never smoked in the house again, choosing to go outside or to the garage from that day on.

Sitting around the picnic table, they filled their grandparents in on what they had missed, and then the men moved to start up the charcoal grill. That's one thing Harold insisted on keeping, his charcoal grill. He said those new gas grills made the food taste like rubber. They all agreed with him, so it was a family tradition that was here to stay.

They had a great meal, enjoyed the lovely evening and the chance to spend time with the family they loved deeply. It was so relaxing to be in her mom and dad's back yard again like they had done just about every weekend as they were growing up. They watched the sun make its descent behind the neighbor's garage and Michael lit the lamps that were situated around the patio, giving it a tropical feel even if they were nowhere near the tropics.

About nine, they finally got up the energy to clean up the dinner mess. Michael began picking up the paper plates and Liz emptied her ashtray onto her plate before he put it into the garbage sack. He gave her a look like that was the nastiest thing she could do, but she was totally unaware of it. Shannon made a finger down the throat gesture and went into the kitchen.

Michael carried the trash out and put it into the shed at the back of the yard. Dad had turned their old playhouse into a storage shed for his lawnmower and the week's worth of garbage. He had gotten tired of the neighborhood dogs and cats getting into his trash and stringing it around the yard. Ashley always teased him that he had to promise to turn it back into a playhouse when Shannon and Michael started having kids. His three kids, plus Casey, had spent countless hours out there, playing anything from house to school to police station. Michael was always the cop, and arrested the three girls and locked them up in a makeshift jail he had made in the corner with an old chain link gate. He would feed them bread and water and tell them they could not go home until they paid for their crimes. Sometimes if they were really good, he would let them out into the yard on work release, and make them hoe the weeds he was supposed to have hoed. That only worked for a few years till they were old enough to realize what he was pulling. They even played doctor with the neighborhood boys; that's where Ashley actually saw her first little penis. She remembered all the boys had lined up and dropped their pants in front of the three girls, strutting around like their penises were amazing. The girls all laughed at them and told them they looked like little worms to them. Shannon had been younger than the other three were, and sometimes they wanted to play more grown-up games, so they invented a way to communicate to each other without talking so that they could sneak away without Shannon understanding. They would use their eyes and hand signals to relay what they wanted to do. They spent hours on their own special signals, perfecting them over the years. Eventually they had let Shannon in on it so that she could use them as they had all gotten older.

Laura had brought out a pot of coffee, along with the cheesecake. That's when the fight was on. They all loved cheesecake, so they always tried to get the biggest piece. Laura made her kids all stand back from the table, where there was a lot of pushing and shoving going on, while she cut up four pieces of cheesecake. She passed out the pieces to Harold, her parents and herself. She then divided the remainder of the cheesecake into three huge pieces, finally allowing the three of them to come to the table.

Smiling at how well their mom knew them, they dived into their dessert. She always went out of her way to Tillman's Bakery, to get their to-die-for desserts. They made everything fresh and took pride in being the best bakery in the area. This cheesecake was a turtle with lots of gooey caramel. They ate every bite, not caring that they would have to waddle out of the back yard and pry themselves into their cars, their stomachs were so full.

Donald and Liz decided it was getting late and that they had better head home. Everyone was giving goodbye hugs and kisses when Shannon started screaming, "Fire, oh my God! The shed's on fire!"

Everyone turned to stare, mouths hanging open in shock. About that time Harold realized that the lawnmower and extra gas can were in there.

"Laura, call 911! Everyone else get back, it may blow up!"

Everyone took a minute to absorb that bit of information before pandemonium broke out, Harold running for the garden hose,

Laura running to call 911, Michael grabbing the fire extinguisher out of the kitchen, and Don and Liz staring in shock, while Shannon and Ashley went to help their dad unroll the garden hose. They tried frantically to get the stupid hose untangled, but before they even got it off the rack, they heard a huge explosion.

They all looked up as a huge fireball lit up the night sky. Ashley felt a whoosh of hot air and reached up to see if she still had her eyebrows.

Harold dropped the hose and Michael, who had been on his way to the shed with the fire extinguisher, was now sitting flat on his ass. The force of the explosion had knocked him back and he sat with a dazed look on his face. They all rushed to him, helping him up and out of the way of the flying debris. They came back to stand up by the house where Laura was talking into the phone like crazy, and Ashley looked over to see that her grandma was flat on her butt also, with her grandpa trying to help her up.

Garbage was everywhere. Looking around, you would have thought they were in a war zone.

Shannon and Ashley went to help their grandma up. She sat with last week's spaghetti on her lap and a chicken bone stuck in her hair. Don's face was covered with soot and he had coffee grounds all over the front of his shirt. They must have been in the direct line of fire of one of the garbage bags. Shannon and Ashley looked at each other over their grandma's head and burst out laughing. She swatted at their hands as they tried to help her and mumbled something about ungrateful kids as Don finally got her to her feet. They proceeded to brush most of the garbage off of each other, but Ashley was afraid her grandma's white pantsuit would forever be stained with the spaghetti. They had missed the chicken bone in grandma's hair and Shannon and Ashley started laughing hysterically again.

About that time a squad car rolled up in the alley with a fire truck right behind it. The shed was completely engulfed in flames. Pieces of wood were flung across the yard and some of the debris had even landed in Mrs. Hazel's yard. Little pieces of paper on fire kept floating around the yard and landing on the grass, and then dying out. Down the row of back yards, all the neighbors were gathering around to see what had just rocked their quiet little neighborhood.

It took the fire department less than half an hour to get things under control. Ashley's family started picking up the mess while Harold talked to the fire chief.

"So Harold, what in the world happened?"

Giving a quick scowl over his shoulder in the general direction of his mother-in-law, he said, "I believe my lovely mother-in-law failed to get one of her cigarette butts put completely out before it went into the evening's trash."

"What did you have in there, C-4?"

"A lawnmower full of gas and an extra gas can I had just filled."

Slapping Harold on the back, he asked, "Are you sure it wasn't rocket fuel?"

Ashley had made her way up to the shed and was peering into the blackened pile of rubble.

Suddenly she heard a voice above her left shoulder. "Doesn't look like much is worth saving."

"Yeah, Dad's lawnmower is toast." Taking a look over her shoulder to see who she was talking to, she let out a gasp as she looked up at the fireman who was talking to her.

"What's the matter? Do I have a piece of lettuce hanging from my helmet?"

"Umm no...you just surprised me is all."

He grinned and said, "I usually have that effect on people."

He stood at least six feet six inches and had shoulders as wide as the shed had been. Ashley's eyes moved down and appreciated the sight of a slim waist, then on down to legs that could have been tree trunks. Her eyes traveled back up to try and see behind his fireman's mask.

"How do they get you to fit in the fire truck?"

Laughing, he reached up and removed his helmet. "They don't, they make me hang onto the back."

Whoosh! Ashley felt like all the air was sucked out of her lungs in one swoop. She started gasping for breath.

He started whacking her on the back. "Did you inhale some smoke? Do I need to get you some oxygen?"

All she could think as she was trying to suck some air into her lungs was, *No, I want you to throw me to the ground and give me mouth to mouth for the next hour.*

This man was drop-dead gorgeous. He had curly blond hair, eyes the deepest blue she had ever seen, a straight, perfectly shaped nose, gorgeous mouth and a strong square chin. Ashley's eyes went back to his mouth, thinking that this was a mouth meant for kissing.

He was so concerned with her not being able to breathe, he never noticed her reaction to him. After catching her breath, she gave him a smile and assured him she was fine. But she really wasn't. She wouldn't be, until they were married and he had given her a dozen kids.

Ashley had met a lot of good-looking men in her life, but none of them had ever given her an instant orgasm by just looking at him. The lady at the bar was right, Ashley's libido was kicking into full gear.

"Are you sure you're okay? You look a little flushed. Why don't you come over to the truck and sit for a while?"

Ashley was ready to follow this man to the ends of the earth if he asked her.

She made her way to the back of the truck and took a seat on the bumper, letting him fuss over her for as long as she could milk it.

The rest of the family had made their way to the back of the yard, standing around the smoldering pile of rubble.

Shannon caught her eye and gave her a questioning look. Ashley looked her in the eyes and then turned her head slightly toward the fireman. Shannon followed her gaze and her eyes got huge. Right then he turned and faced Shannon and Ashley almost laughed out loud at her expression.

Michael had made his way over to them. "Hey Nick, glad you could join our weenie roast. And why is my sister sitting here?"

"She must have inhaled some smoke. She was having some trouble catching her breath."

"Oh really? Wow! That must have been some wild smoke that reached just her and none of the rest of us in the family," he commented, staring at Ashley as though trying to decide if she was really in need of help or just being a stupid female.

Realizing Michael was going to blow her charade wide open, Ashley jumped up and informed them she was feeling much better.

"Nick, let me introduce you to my apparently very fragile sister, Ashley. Ashley, this is a friend of mine, Nick Owens."

"Hi. Nice to meet you. Thanks for the help," Ashley said as she reached out her hand for him to shake, any reason for this man to keep touching her.

He grasped her hand and gave it a firm but gentle handshake. "No problem. I'm just glad no one was hurt."

"Well there is Dad's pride and, of course, he hasn't got Grandma alone yet."

"Well, I think we're done here, so I will leave you to play referee with your family. It was nice meeting you, Ashley; maybe we'll run into each other again." He took a few extra seconds to look straight into her eyes when he said that. Ashley's toes curled and she leaned into him without even a conscious thought and replied, "That would be nice, but let's hope it's under better circumstances."

He gave her a look that in another time and place would have said *Oh babe, you and I are going to have so much fun together*, then smiled and walked back to the truck, jumped onto the back and it took off down the alley. Ashley did not take her eyes off of him or the truck until it was out of sight.

"You are pathetic. I think I actually see some drool running down your chin," Michael grumbled.

"I know, but my God, Michael, that man is unbelievable. I could be in love, or at least I'm definitely in lust."

"Stop it! I don't want to hear that kind of stuff. Come on, we better go make sure Dad is not beating Grandma with a rubber hose." They walked back across the lawn, shaking their heads at the mess still left scattered around the yard. Harold was going to have to spend a few hours out here just raking and picking up the scattered pieces of debris.

As Michael and Ashley entered the back door the family was all gathered in the kitchen, with Liz sitting at the counter, big crocodile tears streaming down her face. Laura was patting her back and trying to console her, while Shannon stood leaning against the sink with a worried look on her face.

"I am so, so sorry! I can't believe this is all entirely my fault. I could have sworn all my cigarette butts were out," Liz sputtered between sobs. "I am so careful about that. Donald, write Harold a check right now for the damage."

Laura leaned over to comfort her, Shannon and Ashley got all teary eyed, and Harold and Michael stood shuffling their feet around, uncomfortable with the whole female crying thing. Ashley thought her grandpa was still in shock, because he was just staring off into space.

Liz wore herself down to a sniffle and then five sets of eyes turned expectantly to Harold.

He glanced around at the worried faces staring at him. You could tell he would rather face a whole week's worth of homicide cases than a roomful of upset women. He sat down beside Liz, put his arm around her and said, "Liz, if you were cold, you should have said something, I would have gotten you a sweater."

She just looked at him blankly. Michael turned his back and his shoulders started shaking. Shannon's eyebrows formed a big arch, and Laura stared at Harold like he had lost his mind. It took everyone a few minutes to realize Harold was not upset, and was trying to put Liz at ease the only way he knew how, with his humor. Liz finally understood what he had said, and gave his shoulder a playful slap. Then she reached over to grab a cigarette and started to light one up. The look of horror that passed over everyone's faces was priceless. Liz realized what she had done and nervously put her cigarette back into the case. It still took about fifteen minutes to reassure her and Don that it was an accident, it was no one's fault, and that the insurance company would take care of everything.

Michael decided it might be a good idea if he drove them home, with Shannon following so she could give him a ride back to get his car. Ashley grabbed her laundry, gave her dad and mom hugs and kisses, and headed home.

She headed her Bronco down the street while going over the events of the night, stopping and giving the time spent with Nick a little extra thought, smiling the whole time. She could only shake her head in wonder, thinking that only in her family could this kind of thing happen.

CHAPTER FIVE

Ashley's alarm was set for nine with the thought that she would get up, finally make it to the grocery store, come home, clean her apartment, take an extremely long nap, and then go to work.

When she heard the alarm buzzing on the nightstand, she wasn't exactly thrilled to jump up and get her game plan going. Turning over, she lay there and watched the green display flash nine and wondered how much she would regret it if she turned the alarm off, rolled over and went back to sleep again. She reached over Miss Priss, turned the alarm off and rolled over and snuggled deeper into the covers. Her mind was on that edge of sleeping and being awake. She wasn't ready to give up her peaceful bliss and face what the day would bring, or better yet, what the night would bring. But it didn't work, her mind started going over all that she really needed to do today and there was no way she was ever going to be able to go back to sleep. This would have been a great day to stay in bed with a lover, make sweet love all day long... Oh yeah, you had to *have* a lover for that to happen. Wow...it really must be time for her to get a man in her life. It had been a long time. Maybe her goal today would be to check into that prospect rather than get groceries. No, groceries had to be her top priority, lover second.

Finally, she crawled out of bed, almost tripping over Miss Priss on her way to the bathroom. Deciding she would wait and take a shower tonight before work, she pulled on a pair of jeans with the knees out of them, then a tank top, threw on a little makeup, brushed her hair and she was set to go. She loved days off when she could just run around in her grunge. Having to wear a stiff uniform five days out of the week made her really enjoy the time she could just throw on jeans and a t-shirt and not fuss with how she looked. Her mom would be appalled at how she went out in public, but she was hoping she would not run into anyone she knew who would tell her.

She changed the sheets on her bed, realizing she should have done that yesterday before she had done her laundry. Oh well, it had been awhile since she had changed them, so she couldn't put it off another week. Plus, if she did find the man of her dreams today and she brought him home, she did not want him to think she was a slob. Ashley pulled the rose-colored sheets up into place and then put the beautiful quilt her mom had made her back on the bed. It made her smile to think how cozy the quilt always made her feel when she crawled underneath it. She had told her mom that she wanted her to teach her to how to quilt so that she could hopefully make a quilt someday. She liked the thought of someone getting the same comfy feeling she did under her handmade quilt.

Next, she tackled the bathroom...yuck! It was the worst. She hated to clean the toilet and the tub. She needed to hire a housekeeper just to do those two things. The rest of the housecleaning was fine, but the bathroom she could pass on. The whole time she was scrubbing out the tub, Miss Priss sat on the toilet and watched her, licking her paw and occasionally giving Ashley a green-eyed look of disgust. Just to be mean she stuck her hand under the running water and flung it on the cat. She jumped down and sat in the doorway and started licking the wet spots. It wasn't much, but it made Ashley feel better to know that maybe next time she would not have to deal with her cat's attitude when she cleaned the bathroom. She was lucky that Ashley kept her litter box clean and her dish full of food.

Ashley ran the vacuum and dusted the living room, mopped the kitchen floor and she was done. It didn't take long to do it; it was just the thought that she could be doing something way more exciting like reading or shopping, or actually anything else but housecleaning.

Taking a minute to run the brush through her hair again, she grabbed her purse and headed to the grocery store. Mr. Ramirez, her neighbor across the hall, was just coming out of his apartment.

"Señorita, you are good?"

"I'm good and your family, are they all well?"

"Si, si, they are all well." Patting his stomach, he said, "Rosa is about to pop."

"She's due any day now, isn't she? You'll be a papa for the fifth time, right?"

"Si...I am very proud papa."

"Would you give her my best and let me know if I can do anything at all?"

"Thank you, you are too kind. Have a good day, Señorita."

The Ramirez family were the nicest neighbors, always bringing her fresh tamales or homemade tortillas. Ashley wasn't sure exactly how many were actually living in their two-bedroom apartment, but she knew there were at least Jose, Rosa, their four kids, Jose's mother and maybe a few others she had seen coming and going, but she had no idea who was just visiting and who lived there. They were quiet and besides, they fed her, so who could ask for better neighbors?

Jumping into her Bronco, she once again noticed something under her windshield. Getting out, she found a note folded in half. Opening it, she read *someone's watching*. No signature. Something two days in a row. She was either very impressed or a little scared.

She laid the note on her seat and looked around the deserted parking lot. She could not see anyone lurking around and no suspicious cars either, so she pulled out of the parking lot and headed to a coffee shop, where she could pick up a muffin and a cup of coffee to get her through her shopping experience. Going to the store hungry was never a good idea. She bought enough junk food as it was without a growling stomach helping to make her decisions.

She ate the muffin and drank her coffee, and arriving at the supermarket she grabbed a cart and headed down the vegetable aisle. Lettuce, tomatoes, peppers, onions, potatoes; turning to the fruits, she grabbed a few bananas and ignored the rest. She had never been a big fruit eater and melons were not in season yet, so she stuck to her occasional banana.

Ashley made her way up and down the aisles, throwing in things that were easy to fix for one person. No use buying something that took a lot of prep time, because it just wouldn't happen. God, her life sucked.

Her cart was filled with stuff to make her lunches and her solitary meals for one, chips, dips, cookies, cereal, lunch meat, snack crackers, bacon, eggs, bread, butter, mac and cheese, canned chili, spaghetti and sauce, frozen pizzas, frozen entrees—or as she preferred to call them, nuke and puke items—cheese, yogurt, ice cream, soda, juice and whatever else looked good as she walked by. Her basket was full, and since she hated carrying in all the sacks, she thought about putting some of the stuff back, but knew it would be weeks before she got back here, so she headed for the checkout instead.

As she turned the corner, she almost bumped into Mr. Bartender, pushing a cart filled with what looked like an ad for some health-food store. He had vegetables, all kinds of fruit, meat, chicken and some whole wheat stuff that looked like it would take two glasses of milk to wash down.

Looking into her cart, he shook his head. "Ash, we need to talk about your food choices."

"I'll have you know I think I make great food choices. My body thinks I feed it very well, and how do you know my name? We were not even introduced the other night," Ashley answered.

Looking her up and down with his hazel eyes, he nodded his head. "Well I have to agree with your body, it does seem to be doing just fine. Damn fine as a matter of fact, and besides I work for your uncle, and he is very fond of you and your family and loves to fill in the quiet times with stories about his whole family. You have no secrets with me, babe."

"Oh God…that's just too scary. I need to talk to Uncle Irwin and tell him people are just not interested in our boring family history." Ashley had to admit that she was a little bit in shock standing here talking to this man again. That he seemed to know quite a bit about her was a little scary, but then she shouldn't be surprised, knowing he worked for her uncle Irwin. They all knew he liked to brag about his family.

He stared at her like he wanted to dig deeper into whatever he found. "That's where you're wrong; I find the stories about you especially interesting. I understand you have a thing for guys with dimples." He flashed a huge grin and his face lit up with the two most beautiful dimples she had ever seen.

Ashley groaned and covered her eyes. "You have it all wrong. I avoid dimples like the plague. They are a sign of pure evil; believe me, I know firsthand." Peeking out between her fingers she checked to see if he had stopped smiling. He hadn't, but she saw no way out of being around those two beautiful dimples.

He reached out and gently peeled her hands away from her eyes. He never let go of them as he continued to smile at her like a big buffoon.

"You know, the lady at the bar had you all wrong," she told him as she pulled her hands from inside his warm touch.

"What lady and what did she have wrong?"

"This is the second time I have talked to you, and you do not come across as the aloof, 'I'm not interested in women' kind of guy you portray at the bar."

"Is that what you think?"

"I heard that was the vibe you gave everyone at the bar, and then when you kissed my ear the other night I began to have my doubts. I decided she had to be mistaken and I came to the conclusion that you were just some pervert who went around molesting strangers' ears."

She thought she actually hurt his feelings. He gave her a surprised look, took a second to think about that, got a wolfish grin on his face, and leaned down and kissed her square on the mouth.

Amazing, just when she thought she had the upper hand, he pulled the rug out from under her again. She just stood there like an idiot, hanging onto her cart like it was her lifeline. Holy crap, this guy could kiss, his lips were teasing hers with the gentlest touch but it was enough to make her insides quiver all the way down to her toes. As he pulled away he barely touched her lips with the tip of his tongue. He pulled back just a few inches and stared at her lips. He reached up and gently brushed his fingertips across her lower lip.

Some old lady, who had witnessed the whole thing, gave them a dirty look and told them they needed to get a room. She bumped into his butt as she walked by, muttering the whole way about the kids nowadays and how they had no morals.

Ashley had forgotten they were standing in the middle of the grocery store, although the thought of dragging his hunky ass to a motel was not such a bad idea. She had never had a guy approach her with this kind of come-on, so she was a little out of her element.

She considered herself a pretty good flirt, keeping her head above water with the best of them, but this guy was playing a whole different game.

"You are unbelievable. Do you always just go around kissing women you don't know?"

"Just gorgeous strawberry blonde women who bring out the animal in me and accuse me of being a pervert," he answered her with that wolfish grin back on his face.

Although his kiss had been fantastic, and she would love it if she were brave enough to act on the desire he had created in her, she just wasn't able to make herself do it. So instead she found herself saying, "I haven't brought out anything in you. I haven't said more than fifty words to you since I met you. You know, I would love to stand here all day and give the old ladies a show, but my ice cream is melting, so I'll leave you to prowl around looking for some other strawberry blonde woman."

She gave him a saucy smile and pushed her cart around his, and headed to the front of the store. Afraid to turn around and see what he was doing, she headed to the nearest checkout and started unloading her items. After a few minutes she got up the nerve to take a quick glance around, but saw no sign of him lurking. She didn't know if she was relieved or disappointed that he hadn't followed her and proceeded to tease her. Ashley wrote a check for an ungodly amount, then planned to take her very nutritious food home to fix herself a very large bowl of ice cream, pop a movie in and just veg for a while. After this experience, she was in no mood to do anything constructive.

As she made her way to her car, there leaning against her Bronco was the man himself. Pushing away from the car, he reached out his hand and stood there looking at her.

Ashley gave his hand a look and asked, "Now what?"

"Hi. I'm Derek Laws. I think we started off our relationship a little on the weird side."

"A *little* on the weird side?"

"I should apologize; I don't know what it is about you."

"Me? What did I do? And by the way there is no relationship." She stood there with her eyebrows scrunched down into a V, trying to decide if this guy was for real, or some complete maniac.

"That's where you're wrong. We have something, we just need time to see what it is."

"Does this line work with other women?"

"It's not a line. It's the truth, and you just need more time to realize it. Do you need me to kiss you again?"

"No more kissing, are you crazy? And my ice cream is really melting now."

"How about I make you a deal? We load your groceries up, I follow you home and help you carry them in, and I'll even help put them away."

"I don't think I want you following me. You're kind of scary."

"I already know where you live; I looked it up in the phone book."

"See, that's just scary."

"No it's not. I was going to call you later to apologize for not coming to the restaurant the other night after your sister invited me so nicely, but I ran into you here instead."

Ashley just looked at him, her mind going in a thousand different directions. On one hand, here was a gorgeous guy who wanted to get together, and she had to admit her body was definitely interested, but her cop brain was sending out all kinds of warning signs. Was this a nice guy who just happened to shop at the same grocery store she did, or was this Jack the Ripper's great-great-great-grandson? He patiently waited, leaning on her car with this devilish little smile.

Finally he chuckled, bringing her out of her fog. Turning bright red, she let her body win. "Okay, it's a deal. You can follow me home and help with my groceries, but just remember I'm only allowing this because you owe me for molesting me in front of that little old lady. She will probably have nightmares tonight."

"Or her poor husband will be attacked when she gets home."

That brought a chuckle to her lips and helped her relax a little.

After putting her groceries in the back of the Bronco, she watched Derek walk over to a crotch rocket and put his small bag of fruits (and what looked like stuff Ashley wouldn't feed to Miss Priss) in a cooler strapped to his seat. Damn, but that man looked good, straddling that bright blue hunk of metal. He was wearing 501 jeans, a faded University of California t-shirt that was too tight around his biceps, and hiking boots. He put a helmet on and fired up his motorcycle. He looked over, gave her one of those dimpled grins and waited for her to pull out. God, she must be crazy to allow this.

In the last three days she had encountered three absolutely magnificent guys who made her insides quiver. For months she had absolutely nobody showing her any interest, and all of a sudden she had met a fellow officer, a hunky bartender, and now a fireman who was going to father her children. Although, to be fair, only one out of those three had actually showed her any interest, but she held out hope that the other two would soon.

As she drove home, she became more and more nervous. She didn't know why this guy rattled her so much, but he did. He had this quiet intense vibe about him that made her feel like a schoolgirl again. He seemed very worldly, while she was just a rookie cop trying to act all grown up.

Ashley pulled up in front of her apartment, easing into a parking space. She looked in her rearview mirror and watched as Derek came around the corner and pulled up beside her Bronco. Taking a deep breath, she climbed out of the car and went to the back to grab as many bags as she could. Before she could turn around, Derek was there, taking some of the bags from her hands.

"The deal was for me to carry your bags in and help put them away, remember?"

Smiling at the macho antics, she turned and headed for her apartment.

They were heading down the hall when Rosa came out of her apartment with a bag of trash. "Ah, Señorita Ashley, you have a new man? That is good. You pretty girl, need big strong man to take care of you."

"*Rosa*, this is not my *new* man. He is just..." Looking up at Derek, Ashley was at a loss for words.

He threw back his head and let out a huge laugh. "Rosa, you are so right! She does need a big strong man like me."

"I do not need a strong man. Rosa, this is just a *friend*, and I use the term loosely, helping me with my groceries. How are you feeling today?"

"Like a big ripe watermelon ready to pop, Señorita. The bebé is ready to meet his Papa."

"You take care of yourself and let me know if you need anything at all."

"You are so sweet. A good catch for some nice young man, no?" she said, giving Derek a big smile and wink.

"Okay, I think I'm going to go in now. You two have a nice time out here plotting against me."

Derek was telling Rosa goodbye as Ashley unlocked her door. He followed her into the apartment, taking the bags into the kitchen. By the time she had set down her keys and purse, he was already unpacking the bags and putting things in the cupboards and the refrigerator.

"Make yourself at home."

He turned around and gave her a look. "All part of the deal."

"Remind me to be very careful when I make deals with you in the future."

"So, you are admitting we have a future? Maybe Rosa was right."

"I did not insinuate we had a future. I was just…" She noticed his shoulders were shaking with laughter as he still went about putting away her groceries.

Ashley threw a bag of shredded cheese at him. "You think you're really funny, don't you? Are you always this aggravating?"

"Aggravating? Most people think I'm fascinating."

"Maybe those bimbos at the bar," she muttered under her breath as she started helping put things where they actually went.

They finished with the groceries and there was that awkward moment of not knowing what to do next.

"Are you hungry? I could make us a late lunch, and then I hate to be rude, but I need to get some sleep before I go to work tonight."

"Food and a nap sound great. I have to work tonight too."

"You can have the food; you're on your own for the nap. Napping wasn't in the deal."

"Remind *me* to make better deals in the future."

Deciding on omelets, they both went to work cutting up peppers and onions. It was nice working together while having a regular conversation. Boy, this was not how she thought her day would end up when she headed to the store. Maybe shopping wasn't so bad after all. She wished she had taken a little more time with her appearance and put on something a little more flattering. If she had known she would actually have a chance to bring a man home with her, she would have. Thankfully, she had taken the time to clean her apartment before she left to shop.

They sat around her dining room table enjoying their omelets, keeping the conversation light, mostly talking about her uncle Irwin and the bar. Neither one of them seemed to want to get into anything personal. Miss Priss had come out of the bedroom when she smelled the food cooking. She made her way into the dining room and gave Derek a good once-over, decided he was okay, and then settled down to wait for anything that might hit the floor.

As they lingered over their coffees, Ashley couldn't help but admire the way he fit so comfortably into her kitchen chair. He had one foot stretched out before him and the other one bent and crossed over that knee, which caused Miss Priss to jump up into his lap, a very unusual thing because she usually shied away from strangers, especially men. He was absently scratching behind her ears as they talked, so she purred and settled in for the duration. Just watching Derek become fast friends with her man-hating cat did funny things to her heart. Miss Priss had a great sense of who was good and who was bad, and making herself right at home with this man, who had basically pushed his way into their lives, should mean something.

Looking at his watch, he set Miss Priss on the floor and stood up. He carried the dishes to the sink and helped Ashley get the kitchen cleaned up, even rinsing the plates before he loaded them into the dishwasher. When the kitchen was all cleaned up he turned to her. "Well, I guess I had better leave you to your nap, unless you've changed your mind and decided you want some company."

Chuckling, she reassured him that she wanted to nap alone.

"Thanks for the help with the groceries. I always put off going to the store because I hate carrying them in and putting them away. Your help was greatly appreciated."

They walked to the door and he paused as he reached for the handle. "Believe me, it was my pleasure. You just let me know when you go shopping again and I will be happy to come help you, especially if I get such a wonderful lunch out of the deal. I'm so used to a quick salad or fast food; I think I forgot what real food tastes like."

As they talked he had reached out and wrapped a piece of her hair around his finger.

Ashley's insides turned to jelly and she was beginning to reconsider the nap thing. "Thanks again…" She licked her lips in sudden nervousness.

He gave a low chuckle and let her hair go. "Bye, Ash. You do that again and there won't be a question of whether you would be napping alone. Maybe if we're both lucky we'll bump into each other again soon." He stepped through the doorway and stood on the other side, making no move to go down the hall.

She gave him one last smile and as she started to close her door, she couldn't help giving him one last shot: "It's more than likely, since I really think you were stalking me today."

She stood at the door and listened as he finally made his way down the hall. She ran to her window and peeked out, watching him walk to his motorcycle. She didn't know what had just happened, but she definitely had a smile on her face and a very warm feeling in the pit of her stomach.

She headed to the bedroom, stripping clothes off as she went. She crawled into bed wearing just her thong, snuggling with her extra pillow and wishing it was Derek. Miss Priss jumped up, curled up in a ball and within a few minutes they were both sound asleep.

CHAPTER SIX

The week flew by fairly smoothly. There were no more dead bodies in the restrooms, no scary bodies with parts missing, no interfering Malone, just quiet boring shifts, which was really okay with her. They had the occasional body to check in, but only a few of those, and Ashley had to admit she was still a little on the jumpy side since the body in the john episode. She was just waiting for the other shoe to drop and for someone else to try and play a practical joke on her. She half expected someone to play dead and be brought into the morgue under a covered sheet, then scare the holy crap out of her. So without anyone else knowing, she had brought a straight pin to work with her and kept it pinned to the cuff of her uniform. Then when the bodies were brought in, while everyone was busy with the paperwork, she gave the bodies just a little prick. Yeah, she knew it went against everything humane, and her mom would kill her if she knew, but it gave Ashley piece of mind that they *were* dead after all. So far none of the stiffs had jumped up screaming. God forbid one of them would, because the pandemonium that would surely break out in the morgue would be talked about for years. That was not something she wanted to be a part of, since it was going to be hard enough to live down the stiff in the john episode.

She had received another note on her car the night Derek helped her with her groceries, and this one was not as polite as the last ones had been. This one had asked *who was the stud on the motor-cycle and why was he in your apartment so long?* She had received two more since that night, all demanding information, asking *who do you think you are, Super Woman?* Another said *overly confident women have no place on the police force.* They had her scared and she was going to talk to her dad about them today when she got off work.

She had not seen Derek since the day at the grocery store, which if she were honest with herself, was *not* okay. She liked him, a lot. He was nice and guys like that were hard to find nowadays. And, if she admitted it, he turned her on like no other guy ever had. There was just something about that smoldering, quiet passion he had. His wasn't a fast, hot lust that burned out of control and then cooled down just as fast as it had started, but a slow-burning kind of intensity that made a girl ache for him all the time. And, unfortunately, most of the guys she had run into in the last year or so fit into the "married asshole" or "just wants a piece of ass" category. It was nice to maybe have met someone with something actually going for him.

Ashley had spent the week hoping they would run into each other or that he might even call her up and ask her out. It was a little difficult since they both worked nights, but they could have had breakfast or something. But as the week came to a close without him contacting her, she knew she had to put him on the back burner. Leave it to her to get her hopes up for nothing. She should have known nothing would come of it.

It was her Friday and she was supposed to meet Shannon and Casey for breakfast after she got off work. She had not told either one of them about her encounter with Derek, and she was really glad she hadn't made a big deal out of it, since he hadn't bothered to get in touch this whole week. Shannon would have instantly gone into matchmaking mode and Casey would have just been pissed at him for not calling.

Bill and Ashley had spent the last half of their shift playing Texas Hold 'em. They played for pretzels since Bill was already broke and they still had a week to go till their next paycheck. He spent all of his money on high-tech computer stuff. Yep, the more she knew him the more she decided he was definitely a computer geek, but a really nice geek. She was glad she had pulled this assignment with him. She couldn't imagine what would have happened if she had gotten stuck with Steve Merritt or Malone. This was the only time two rookies were working together; everyone else was taking their rotations with the senior officers. There was no need to have a seasoned cop down here holding their hands, when all there was to do was watch over dead people.

Bill looked over his cards. "Hey Ash, you're awfully quiet, something wrong?"

"No, just concentrating on my cards, I want to make sure I get the rest of your pretzels."

"I may be a loner and something of a geek, but I think I can tell when a woman has something heavy weighing on her mind. You haven't been your usual perky self this week."

"Perky! You're calling me perky? You do know I carry a gun, don't you?"

Bill couldn't help laughing. "Now there's the Ashley I'm used to."

She realized that she *had* been pretty quiet this week, with all the thinking she had been doing about Derek and what might have been, along with the creepy notes she had started getting. That's it! She wasn't going to waste any more time worrying about him. It apparently wasn't meant to be.

"Sorry, Bill, I guess I have been a little off this week. Nothing big, just a little lonely in the personal life, didn't mean to bring it to work."

"No biggie. Just wanted to make sure you were okay, and I understand how you feel about being lonely. Between being stuck down here and spending the last few months training, none of us have had the time for dating."

Ashley knew her eyebrows shot up at that remark, surprised that Bill had mentioned dating. She guessed that was mean of her, thinking Bill wasn't into the dating thing much, when she really didn't know that much about his personal life at all. He didn't do much of the talking when they were working together, instead always asking her questions about her life and family.

Ashley, for one, was glad this week was over. That meant she only had one more week left of the morgue duty. They were supposed to receive their next assignments Monday when they came in to work. Being stuck down here in the tomb, she had not really had a chance to talk to any of the other rookies to see how their rotations were going. Maybe she would make an effort to get together with Shaffer and see how his last two weeks had been going.

Bill and Ashley finished up their game and spent the last few minutes of their shift cleaning up their mess. They had learned their first day that the daytime mortician did not take well to crumbs left all over the table. When their shift was finally over they headed up to the squad room, ready to begin their two days off. They were met by a pretty somber group of officers. Several of the rookies looked a little green around the gills. Malone was sitting in a chair all by herself, and the fact that she wasn't hanging on some poor man gave Ashley pause.

Officer Shirley Miller was standing by the door, looking pretty glum. "Hey Shirley. What's going on?"

"You haven't heard? They found a woman murdered in the alley off of Kennedy."

Ashley's stomach instantly started forming a knot. This was the part of the job she feared. Their community was pretty quiet, so this kind of thing was big news.

"What do they know so far?"

"Not much. They just found her about an hour ago and most of the squad is still out at the crime scene. A woman who looks to be about twenty-five, was raped and then brutally beaten, mutilated and stabbed."

Ashley knew her dad would be out on this one and how hard it would be for him. He always took murders hard, and this one sounded like it could be one of the worst he had ever had to work.

The captain filled all of them in on the details that he knew, and then he wrapped it up and headed out. Ashley climbed into her Bronco and just sat there. She was numb from her toes all the way up to her head. Her thoughts were in turmoil. How could something like this happen?

She looked up and caught Malone's eye as she was walking past her Bronco. For the first time in their lives, there was no hostility, jealousy or resentment, just pure fear. She stood there for a few minutes looking into Ashley's eyes, and then she turned and walked on. She knew it wouldn't last but she was relieved that she at least respected the moment.

Ashley drove to Hill's Café, thinking maybe she should just call and cancel. She wasn't in the mood for idle gossip but knew the girls would never forgive her if she bailed on them now. No doubt those two had already heard and were waiting for her to fill them in.

The café was buzzing when she walked in, so she knew the news was out. Casey and Shannon were already sitting in a booth waiting for her.

Ashley slid in beside Shannon and they all just sat looking at each other.

Shannon laid her head on Ashley's shoulder. "Are you okay?"

"I don't know. It hasn't sunk in yet. Really I just found out. I take it that the news has already been on TV."

"Yes. It started running about half an hour ago. Have you seen Dad yet?"

"No. He must have been still out at the scene because he wasn't in the squad room for the morning briefing. I'm sure everyone was called in for this one. Before you even ask, I absolutely have no information. Not that I could talk about it anyway. So, let's talk about something else. What's new with you two?"

Shannon said she was going on a date with a guy she met at the gym, and Casey said she had been busy at work all week and trying to pry information out of Dan about what he wanted for the wedding.

They drilled Shannon for more information on the guy from the gym, and learned he was a construction worker and they had been making eyes at each other for the past few weeks. Yesterday he got up the nerve to come help spot her when she was bench-pressing. She was pretty excited, even with the news of the murder.

"Hey, since Shannon is busy tonight, let's go have a few beers at Uncle Irwin's," Casey suggested.

The first thought that popped into her head was *DEREK*. She was not in any mood to play the flirting game tonight. And besides, he hadn't contacted her all week and she didn't want to be the one who looked like she was chasing him.

"Thanks, Casey, but I don't think I really want to go to the bar tonight. It will be filled with a bunch of people all talking about the same thing. I don't think that would put us in the happy mood we would be after, do you?"

"Yeah, you're probably right. We could just go to my place? Have a few beers and watch a movie."

"That sounds great. I'm going to go home and put my head under my pillow and try to get some sleep. I'll call you when I get up and we can make a plan."

Their food was brought to them but they all just picked at their breakfasts, none of them really having any appetite.

They finished up and Casey took off for work. Shannon and Ashley sat in their booth, both caught up in their own thoughts. Ashley's were racing between the poor dead woman and thoughts of her dad and Michael, and what they would be going through… secret thoughts of how she was glad she was stuck down in the morgue and not up on patrol while this was going on. She was not some gung-ho police officer, wanting to jump into the middle of a case like this. If the truth was known she was hoping to go through her career with nothing more exciting than maybe a peeping-tom case or a runaway, mild things like that. She knew she was being selfish, but this news had put a damper on her day off. Not that she had any big plans or anything. Nor did she have any hot date like Shannon did, which really made her depressed. It wasn't that she didn't deserve a hot date, but Ashley couldn't help wondering if maybe the guy had a hot older brother who had a thing for policewomen.

They walked out of the restaurant, with Shannon promising to stop by tomorrow to fill her in on all of the details of her date.

Ashley climbed into her Bronco and headed for home. She stopped by the grocery store and picked up a few fresh things, like milk and juice, to get her through the weekend and the rest of the week. As she was going down the aisles, she secretly hoped she would run into a tall bartender with a basket full of healthy stuff. Of course she had no such luck. Middle-aged women with shopping carts full of crying kids, single men wandering aimlessly, and older couples with cat food and generic items were all she ran into.

When she came out of the grocery store, she noticed a note under her windshield. She grabbed the note, put her bags in the back and settled into the driver's seat. She unfolded the note and gave a little gasp. It read *It's nice to see you frowning; you don't deserve to be happy.* This was getting out of hand and the note was scary. Someone *knew* she was frowning. That meant someone was watching her. This was not funny and she gave a nervous look around, hit her lock button and headed for home.

Ashley trudged into her apartment, throwing all of the notes that had been left on her windshield on the counter. She put the few groceries away, sat down in front of the tube and ran the local channels. Of course all the local channels covered the death of that poor woman and the rest were soap operas, game shows, old movies and shopping networks. Deciding the TV was only making her more depressed, she clicked it off and headed for her computer.

She checked her e-mail and found she had one hundred sixty-four unread messages. She decided she should check her e-mail on a more regular basis. Ignoring the jokes, she read messages from her mom and both grandmas, telling her she should come and see them on her days off, invites from Mike and Jen from a week ago and a few from Bill and some of the other rookies. She responded to the ones that needed a response, played a few games of solitaire and decided she had bored herself enough to finally go to bed.

Miss Priss let it be known that her bowl was empty, so she fed her, grabbed a Twinkie and a glass of milk for herself, and headed off to bed.

Her dreams were nightmares with strange sightings of all the men in her life. Jimmy, Brandon, Tarzan, Derek, Phillip and Nick, even though Phillip and Nick weren't really in her life except in her fantasies. And, if she was truthful to herself, Derek wasn't *really* involved either.

She tossed and turned all afternoon, finally giving up around five and crawling out of bed. She didn't really feel like going over to Casey's but she didn't want to stay home alone either. She made her way to the bathroom, stripped out of her wrinkled uniform and stepped into the shower. She stood under the hot water till it ran cold, enjoying the relaxing water. Stepping out and toweling off, she wrapped her hair up in a towel and headed to the bedroom to find something to wear to Casey's. Just then someone knocked on her door. Figuring it was Shannon looking to borrow something to wear tonight, she threw on an old flannel shirt, grasped the front closed, and headed to the door.

To her utter horror, it was not Shannon but Derek. Ashley was shocked.

He was leaning against the doorframe with a pizza in one hand and a twelve-pack of beer in the other.

"Oh baby, I see I came at just the right time."

"And exactly what time would that be? And why are you here, anyway?"

"I thought maybe you needed some company."

"And what makes you think I don't already have company?"

"I don't. I was just hoping. And by the looks of things you are just getting ready for something."

That's when she remembered her state of undress. Looking down she realized her shirt was not hiding much, and as a matter of fact it was showing more than Mr. Bartender had a right to see. Looking back up into Derek's eyes, she realized he was appreciating the view just a little too much. He had the biggest grin on his face, and his eyes were sparkling with something she would have to describe as the beginning of desire.

Reaching up with the hand not desperately holding her shirt together, she punched his arm. "You could have reminded me I was standing here half-naked instead of distracting me with all those questions."

"My momma never raised a stupid man, or maybe she did, since I was the one who *did* make you finally look down."

"Come in out of the hallway before Rosa or José comes out to investigate all the noise and I have to try explaining why I'm standing here half-dressed with a *friend*."

Derek's grin grew even bigger as he waltzed into the kitchen.

"You stay out here and I'll go get dressed."

"Please don't change on my account. I think you look great just the way you are."

"Yeah, I'll bet you do." Ashley made a mad dash to the bedroom, grabbing up her cell phone along the way, and went into the bathroom to call Casey.

Casey picked up on the fifth ring, all out of breath. "Hi there, are you headed over?"

"What are you doing? You're all out of breath."

She gave a little chuckle. "Dan stopped by, but he's leaving, really."

"You know if he wants to stay, that's okay, something has come up and I'm not sure I'm going to get over there anyway."

"Oh really? And do you want to go into detail about why you are standing me up?"

"I'm not standing you up, just postponing to a later date, and besides it's not like you don't want to get back to humping Dan anyway."

"I'll have you know we do not hump. We fuck."

"Casey! I'm going to tell your mother you said that."

"Go ahead. She will just shake her head and mutter something like 'her kids will be the death of her yet.' So what's up with you not coming over?"

"I'll call you tomorrow and fill you in."

"That's bullshit, Ash! Maybe Dan and I will just pop on over and see for ourselves."

"*NO!* Really, that would not be a good idea. I promise I'll fill you in tomorrow."

"Wow. Must be some hunky guy?"

About that time Derek knocked on the bedroom door, "Do you need some help in there? The pizza is getting cold."

"Oh my God, Ashley Wright! Who was that man?"

"Casey, I'll call you tomorrow, I promise. Bye!" She hung up and dropped the towel, threw on some mascara, and yelled, "No, that's fine, I'll be right out, but thank you so much for the kind offer." She picked through her hair, ran into the bedroom and pulled on a pair of jeans and a top. She threw open the door and ran right into Derek.

He caught her in his arms and held on.

"What are you doing? I thought you would have moved away from the door by now," she said.

"I wanted to be close, in case you changed your mind."

He was still holding on to her arms and pulled her close so that their bodies were touching. Her breathing started getting a lot heavier and her knees were getting weak. She wanted nothing more than for him to lean in and kiss her, and take her right back into the bedroom and remove all the clothes she had just put on.

Pulling away instead, she said, "Pizza is getting cold, remember! And even though I'm going to eat your pizza, because I'm hungry and it smells so good, why *are* you here? Do you always just go around inviting yourself to dinner at some strange woman's house?"

"Well, now that you mention it, you are kind of strange."

"I am not! Have you been talking to my sister? And you never answered my question. Maybe a phone call first would have been a nice idea. You already informed me you know it, since you looked it up the day you were stalking me."

"I was not stalking you *that day*, and I did try to call you earlier but you never answered. So I decided to take the chance that you were sleeping."

A chill ran through her. Was *he* the person leaving the items on her windshield?

"You must think I have no life at all. That I'm just sitting around waiting for some guy to bring me pizza and beer. Which by the way, you still have not answered my question."

"Okay, Miss Impatient, here's the story. I've been out of town the past week, and when I got back today, I heard on the news about the woman found dead and figured you were having a bad day and maybe, just maybe you needed a pizza and a lot of beers. But it sounds like maybe I was assuming too much and that I had better just get the pizza and beer and go." He leaned over the table and made a grab for the pizza, but she was faster. Never come between a Wright and her food.

"Wow. I may be Miss Impatient, but you are definitely Mr. Touchy. You're right, I did have a bad day, and my sleep was filled with nightmares, so I'm thankful for your thoughtfulness, so stop wasting my time with small talk and pass me a beer."

Things with this man were definitely on the bizarre side. How was it that he knew she was going to be alone? Okay, so everyone at the bar knows she's not dating anyone at the present time, but there was always the chance she could get lucky and get asked out on a date. Truth was she got asked out a lot, she had just become pickier about who she accepted dates with. She had to admit no one she was slightly interested in had asked lately, until now. She grabbed some paper plates, napkins and Parmesan cheese and took them over to the table. Derek had opened a couple of beers and she put pizza on their plates. She looked up at him and just started laughing.

"I'm glad I can amuse you." He raised those gorgeous eyebrows in a question, probably wondering if she was some kind of crazed female.

"Sorry. I just realized that the last time I saw you, you were sitting in the exact same place. Apparently we at least have eating in common and I apologize for the way I acted earlier. You surprised me, I guess."

"Oh we have more in common than that, as we discussed this last time, remember? We just need to see what those things are. I have my ideas, but I'm not sure you're ready to hear them yet."

"Maybe you don't know me as well as you think you do."

Chuckling, he said, "Okay, Miss Flirt, let's just see." He slowly rose out of his chair and leaned over hers.

Ashley put a hand to his chest, and a mighty fine chest it was. She could feel the strength and muscle all the way through his shirt. She asked in a shaky voice, "Can I get you another piece of pizza?"

He chuckled and took his seat again, reaching for another slice.

"So you've been out of town all week?"

"Did you miss me? Were you by the phone waiting for me to call?"

Frowning, she answered, "Do I look seventeen? I don't have to wait by the phone to see if some guy is going to call me." Although that is exactly what she had been doing all week, but she would go to her grave before she would ever tell Mr. Smarty-pants that information.

"I had to go to L.A. and take care of some things. I'm sorry to hear about the murder though. Were you on duty when she was found?"

"Yes, but I have morgue duty for another week, so I only heard about it when we went up for the briefing. I tried calling my dad and Michael, but they were either still out investigating or home in bed. What kind of sick bastard would do something like that?"

"The news report I heard went into some of the details, but it would have to be someone with no morals whatsoever to murder a woman so brutally. I would like to spend ten minutes behind Irwin's bar with him and a baseball bat."

"I think everyone in town would help you out there. One of the officers said she was a waitress walking to her car after her shift."

"Someone who would rape a young woman and then do the things he did has to be one sick bastard."

This caught her by surprise; he seemed to have more knowledge than the public was aware of yet. Was he just an average guy, a cop or some sicko who was too familiar with this kind of thing?

She mulled this over in her mind quietly.

Derek looked at her oddly. "No, Ash, I'm not some serial killer who knows this kind of thing, it's just common sense."

"That's not what I was thinking." How the hell did this guy always know what she was thinking? She had better be careful, or her lusty thoughts about ravishing his hunky body could get her into trouble.

They finished up their supper and he helped her pick up the mess. She liked how he just automatically helped, never having to be asked.

"So what do you want to do now? Would you like to go out somewhere? We could go grab a beer at Irwin's or catch a movie, or we could just stay here and see what's on TV."

She wanted to do it all, anything to be with him. She wasn't too hip on going to Uncle Irwin's and taking the chance of getting attacked by all of those hopeful women waiting for their chance at him. Not only that, but the place would be filled with off-duty cops and she wasn't really up to all the razzing she would get from them. But she did want to get out of the apartment for a while.

"Did you ride your motorcycle over?"

"Yes."

"How about taking a ride to the Red Box and picking up a DVD there? Then we can come back here and watch it."

"See, you are definitely my kind of woman."

"Oh really, and exactly what kind is that?"

He calmly walked over to her, took her in his arms and kissed her, really *kissed* her. This man knew how to push a woman's buttons. He took his time, his lips moving over hers, with just the right pressure, and he didn't shove his tongue down her throat and try to touch the back of her esophagus either. He gently nibbled her lips and barely touched her mouth with the tip of his tongue, one hand was in her hair and gently massaging her neck and ear. The other hand was on her upper waist doing some serious damage to her insides.

She was enjoying this more than she cared to admit. Who needed a ride or a movie? She just wanted to do this all night long.

She had gotten over her surprise and was really getting into the kiss. He had moved from her mouth to her neck and was placing gentle kisses along the side of her neck up to her ear. She had one hand in his hair, hanging on for dear life, and the other was moving sensually up and down the planes of his muscled back.

They were standing beside the kitchen wall, and as the kiss progressed they had moved up against it and were pressed together as tightly as two bodies could get. She was having a hard time keeping her thoughts in one place; she was just enjoying the most passionate kiss she had experienced in a long time. His leg was between hers and she could feel the muscle of his thigh as it pressed between her legs, close to where she really wanted it, but not quite.

He whispered in her ear along with the kisses, "A woman who knows what she wants and doesn't play silly games. Someone who takes charge of her life and isn't afraid to do and say what she feels. Someone who is comfortable with herself and isn't afraid to let everyone know it."

Wow. She had no idea if she was really that type of woman, but who was she to argue with him at this point?

He put his forehead up against hers and gently rubbed her lips with the tip of his finger.

"Are you ready for that ride?"

Lordy, she hoped he was talking about his motorcycle because one of them had to be strong. And she knew it wasn't her. She wanted to suck his finger into her mouth and continue kissing.

"Let me grab a jacket and I'll be ready."

How she had the courage to say anything at all, let alone walk into the bedroom, was a wonder considering every bone in her body had turned to mush. She felt like she was having one of those out-of-body experiences. Her legs were shaking and her insides were humming in a warm sensual way. She put on some socks and boots, grabbed up her leather jacket and walked back into the living room.

"Are you okay to drive? We did have a beer. I would hate to have to arrest you for a DWI."

"We only had one, and I think my adrenaline just evaporated anything I might have still had in me."

She gave him a saucy look, letting him know she was glad she had the power to get his adrenaline in such a state.

It was almost eight, with about a half hour left of daylight, a perfect time for a ride. They walked to his bike and he took off an extra helmet strapped to the seat. "I may be a prude by insisting we wear helmets, but I don't want anything to happen to that beautiful head of yours."

"Thanks, I appreciate that fact. I really don't want anything to happen to it either. Besides I think it's great that you're responsible enough to wear one and not have to be all macho."

They took off down her street, and all of the neighborhood kids were whistling and hollering for them to do a wheelie. It felt good to be out in the fresh night air. It felt even better to have her arms wrapped around someone nice enough to see to her welfare on a night that could have turned out way more depressing. They drove to the Red Box so they could get their video. Ashley kept teasing him that she wanted to watch a chick flick, but they settled on the newest action release instead. They decided to continue their ride, going nowhere in particular, just cruising around. It felt good to have her arms wrapped around someone so completely male. She could feel the vibration of the motorcycle between her legs, which were spread around the tightest male ass she had encountered in a very long time. The combination of the two was enough to give her an orgasm. She laid her cheek against his back and just enjoyed the sensations. They pulled up to the stoplight on Elm, and she glanced over into the car beside them and looked right into the eyes of her sister.

Shannon's mouth fell open in shock, as she looked at her with complete astonishment. Ashley could see the wheels in her sister's brain going in a thousand different directions. Just as she realized that she had no idea who Ashley was with and started to look at the driver, the light changed and Derek took off. She never got the chance to see Derek, not that she could have seen who he was with his helmet on. This would drive her crazy all night long and probably ruin her date. Her sister was the nosiest person, and the idea of Ashley sitting on the back of a motorcycle with someone she didn't recognize would cause her to have a sleepless night. Ashley realized she had better remember to turn her phone off or she would be getting a phone call as soon as her sister's date was over, if she could even wait that long. As a matter of fact, her phone was probably ringing right now, but she could not hear it over the noise of the motorcycle.

The whole idea caused Ashley to chuckle, making Derek look over his shoulder with a raised eyebrow. She mouthed "later" to him, and wrapped her arms around him just a little tighter.

They rode around for another fifteen minutes or so and then headed back to her place. They parked and Derek helped her take off the helmet, then re-strapped it to the back of the seat. As she reached up to smooth out her hair, his hand came up and joined hers, pulling his fingers through her hair. Ashley's hands fell away and let his take over. She raised her eyes and stared into those hazel eyes that had turned into a liquid fire. The ride had already put her halfway to an orgasm as it was; just looking into those eyes was enough to send her over the edge.

"I love your hair. So soft and inviting, makes a man want to run his hands through it."

She swallowed the lump in her throat, grabbed him by the lapels of his jacket and pulled him in close. When he was up against her, she reached up and kissed him. Not a make your toes curl in your boots kind of kiss, but just a simple comfortable kiss.

"See, my kind of woman."

"Let's go watch that movie before we give some other old lady her own private X-rated show."

He raised his eyebrows at the suggestion, and then wrapped his arm around her and they walked to her apartment.

Ashley could not believe how right it felt being in his arms. They did not have to play the silly flirting game you usually had to when you first met someone. It was like they had known each other forever, knowing what the other wanted without asking. Or at least he seemed to know what she needed or wanted. Which could be the problem in itself? What did she really want from this man? Was she hoping for something like Dan and Casey had, or did she simply want some companionship and maybe some no-strings-attached sex? Not that she was usually that kind of woman, but for the first time in her life, she thought with this man she would be happy with at least that. She was tired of being alone and they were both adults. She decided right then and there that she was just going to let whatever happened happen. No worrying about whether he would call tomorrow or if he was only here to get laid. She didn't really think that was the only thing he was after, and even if it was, she bet she would have no regrets if they did have sex.

They made it to her apartment without running into any of her neighbors, and as she tried to unlock the door, Derek stood behind her and moved in close, pulling her ass right up against the front of those tight Levi's that were stretching a little tighter, if the feel of his erection was any indication. She was having a hard time finding the hole to the lock on her door, her hands were shaking so much. His hands were on her hips, with his fingers inching their way under the edge of her t-shirt. The minute his fingers hit bare flesh, she felt shock waves to every nerve of her body. She gave up all pretense of trying to unlock the door and just let her body lean into the door with his hands circling her waist. Ashley's hands were above her head flat against the door; his fingers had moved up to caress her stomach and she found herself thankful for all the physical training the academy had them do, which had given her a washboard stomach. It was the one time in her life she could claim a little sexy six-pack of her own. He had placed his other hand over both of hers on the back of the door, holding her in place while he began kissing the side of her neck, which caused her to let out a little purr. She could feel his erection as he pressed it into her ass, and oh my, the man was rock hard and she could tell he was not only gifted with good looks and a great body, but God had made sure he was a complete package of male wonder. Her head was tilted back, giving him full access to her neck, and his hands were circling around her stomach, inching higher and higher, just barely brushing the underside of her breasts. Every time he came close to her breasts her breath would hitch with anticipation, but he would only barely graze them and then move back down to her stomach. They were both starting to breathe heavily and she gave herself up to the wonders of how, with just a simple touch, this man could send her body into a state of complete meltdown.

"My, my, Ashley, I do believe you are having way more fun than I have been on this lovely evening, and I'm the newlywed."

Ashley jerked her head around to see Jasper Johnson standing there, with sacks of groceries in her hands and a very pleased smile plastered all over her face.

Ashley peeled herself away from the door, her face flaming with embarrassment. Derek had turned with her and now his back was to the door, with Ashley covering the very noticeable erection he still had pressed to her hip.

"Hi Jasper. Um, I didn't hear you coming down the hall, sorry," Ashley sputtered around the mortification she felt at being caught in a very embarrassing position by her neighbor.

"Oh I'm sure you didn't. I think the tongue in your ear probably had something to do with it." She smiled up at Derek, and Ashley turned to look over her shoulder just in time to see him give Jasper a *yep that was my tongue and damn proud of it* look.

"Well. I will leave you two to finish what I so rudely interrupted; I'm going to go attack my unsuspecting husband. For some strange reason I'm suddenly horny as hell." She waved as she rushed by. As she opened her door, they could hear her yell, "Gary, where are you? Get those pants off, honey."

Ashley leaned her head back to rest on Derek's chest. "Well, that was just embarrassing as hell."

"Look at it this way, five more minutes and it could have been a lot more embarrassing."

Laughing at the thought she said, "When you put it that way, I guess it could have been worse." She turned and shoved him out from the front of the door, unlocking it to the sound of his chuck-ling in her ear. He followed her in and then reached behind him and locked the door, giving her a wolfish grin the whole time. Ashley put some distance between them and shed her jacket and boots. She carried the movie over to the DVD player and Derek stood leaning against her front door the whole time. He watched her as she went about all this with a knowing smile on his face, fi-nally walking into the kitchen and asking her if she wanted a beer. She could hear the amusement in his voice when he asked her, but she was too flustered now to even think about starting up where they had left off. She could not believe she got so carried away that she almost let Derek feel her up right out in her hallway. She could never look Jasper in the eyes again. At least if someone was go-ing to catch her in an act of complete insanity, she was glad it was one of her newlywed neighbors and not widowed Mrs. Randall, or even poor Rosa. The shock could have sent her into early labor. She could hear it now, "Oh José, your birth was due to our nasty neigh-bor humping her boyfriend in the hall. She did not mean for you to be born early and have so many health problems because of it."

He brought them each a beer, settling on the couch while she set up the video. Miss Priss ventured up onto the couch beside Derek, curling up into a ball beside him before Ashley could even make it back to the couch. He reached over and gently started stroking her head, and she could hear her starting to purr at his touch, just like Ashley had been doing out in the hall. The man had a way with women whether it was of the feline or human form. She could feel her cheeks turning pink just thinking of how he made her lose complete control.

Deciding she needed to bring this back to a more casual state, she turned from the TV. "Well, I can see that I have already been replaced. I guess I'll just watch the movie from the loveseat over here all by myself." She walked past him on the way to the loveseat,

139

and he reached up and grabbed her arm as she passed, pulling her onto his lap.

Ashley gave a squeal of surprise and landed with a flop. "There is plenty of room for all of us," he said, tickling her. She was laughing and squirming, trying to get away. Miss Priss decided she didn't want to be in the middle of all the romping and moved to the loveseat, giving them a bored look before settling down.

"All this giggling reminds me, what were you laughing about during our ride?"

Trying to catch her breath, she said, "I almost forgot about that. While we were stopped at the stoplight, I noticed my sister was in the car beside us, having a small heart attack when she looked over and saw that it was me on the back of a crotch rocket with a guy that she didn't know."

Derek started chuckling. "Boy, are you going to have some explaining to do tomorrow."

"Not to just her, but if I know my sister she will have already informed my mother, my best friend and anyone else she happens to run into. I can just imagine what her date had to listen to, the poor guy."

"So what are you going to tell her?"

Looking into his eyes for several seconds she replied, "I don't exactly know. Any suggestions?"

"Nope, you're on your own. Depends on if you want to play with her a little and tell her you were walking the streets and some stranger asked you if you wanted a ride, or if you just want to be honest with her and tell her it was a *friend* who was spending the evening with you, watching a movie."

"The idea of playing with her does sound appealing."

To his disappointment she had moved off his lap and they were both sitting on the couch with about a foot of space between them. It was awkward not knowing how close to sit, not wanting to seem like a slut but not wanting to seem like a cold fish, either. They were already past the not knowing each other stage when it came to physical attraction, but on the other hand, they knew absolutely nothing about each other's personal lives. He knew more about her from working for her uncle, and she wasn't even sure how much that was. All she knew about him was that he worked as a bartender at nights, drove a pretty blue motorcycle, ate a lot of healthy stuff and an occasional pizza, and had been out of town for a week for who knows what. That and the fact that he was well endowed, but she couldn't really count that as knowing someone.

"So is it too much to ask a little about you? Or would you think I was some desperate woman needing to know your every deep dark secret?"

"You can ask and I'll see if I want to answer."

"Oh really? So you do have deep dark secrets you don't want me to know about."

"I didn't say that, you just assumed that."

"You are slick with your answers. I have a sneaky feeling that bartending is not your career choice."

"You are correct. Do you always interrogate all of the people who come over to watch a movie?"

"Only the ones who invite themselves, who accost me in the hall and the grocery store, and kiss my ear on a dance floor and then run."

Laughing, he said, "Okay, so you may have a point there. I told you, there is something about you that makes me do things that I have never done before."

She didn't know whether to take that as a compliment or not. "So what *is* it about me exactly that makes you do all of these strange things?"

"I told you, I have no idea. I get around you and I don't think things through. I just react to what seems right at the time."

141

"So kissing me whenever you run into me seems right to you?"

"Oh yeah, babe. That and a lot more."

Slapping him on the arm, she asked, "So have you always lived in our happy little suburb? Or are you a transplant from some other place?"

"I moved here a couple of months ago from Boston."

"Job or woman?"

"You like this, don't you? Do you have a rubber hose between the couch cushions in case you don't like my answers?"

"Maybe. So job or woman?"

"This time, job."

"Boy, you don't give anything more than you have to, do you?"

"Sorry, I feel like I'm in a Bruce Willis movie and this is how I'm supposed to answer. So is this a two-way interrogation?"

"You can ask and I'll see if I want to answer."

"Why did you decide to become a cop?"

"I wanted to carry a gun."

He seemed surprised by that and a little taken aback. "So why didn't you just buy one?"

"They have all these rules and regulations. Plus, my dad and brother thought I would probably end up shooting some innocent bystander."

"What made you so very angry that you wanted to carry a gun?"

"A man."

"He must have really pissed you off."

"He did."

"Want to share with me?"

"No. So do you come from a big family? Do they all live in Boston?"

"Big enough and they are spread all over the United States. I understand from Uncle Irwin that you have a huge family. What's that like?"

"It has its moments. For the most part it's great, a little crowded at holidays, but I wouldn't trade it for the world. I love them all, some more than others, just like in any family. You said this time was the job, so I take it some other time a woman must have been involved?" She watched the emotions flash in his eyes, and for a moment she thought maybe she had crossed the line on that question. He sat there for a few minutes, looking off into some other time.

"It's not what you think."

"Want to share with me?"

"No. Have you ever been married?"

"No, have you?"

"No, came close once. I let my heart rule my head but swore I would never make that mistake again."

"That's kind of sad and a little boring. What's life without the joy of romance?"

"I have romance."

"There is a difference between romance and lust."

"Not really."

"I'm sorry."

"Sorry? Sorry for what?"

"That you were hurt so bad that you have that outlook on love," she said softly.

"Love can be overrated."

"It can also be wonderful."

She decided she didn't want to venture any deeper into this area; she might not like what she heard. She didn't truly believe he felt the way he talked. His actions proved that, even if he didn't realize it. But when a man's head believed what he said, sometimes there was no way of getting through to him. Besides, she wasn't sure she really wanted to try and fix his beliefs. She would admit to a physical attraction to him, but she wasn't sure about anything else.

143

"So do I dare ask if you plan on bartending for a career or is this just a between-things kind of job?"

"No, this is what I want to do. I went to bartending school and everything."

This was not the answer she had expected to hear. She had a hard time believing this man really was content to bartend the rest of his life. She was a little ashamed to admit that she was disappointed. She thought she was a better person than to judge someone by his occupation, but she guessed she just discovered something about herself that she was not too happy with.

She had been staring off at the television, and when she looked back to Derek, he was giving her that famous grin of his that meant he had just put her in her place again.

"You're an asshole."

"No I'm not! You're mad at yourself, not me."

"That's true, but you're still an asshole for making me feel that way."

"So the real answer to your question is that bartending is just helping me pass some down time I found myself in."

"And what field of work are you really in?"

"Circus clown."

Giving him a look of disgust, she got up and sat at the far end of the couch.

"You can't be mad at me. You think I'm irresistible."

"I do not find you irresistible, you do. I can just see that I'm not going to be able to have an intelligent conversation with you, so we'll just watch the movie."

"Are you going to sit all the way down there just because we can't have an intelligent conversation?"

"I hadn't put any real thought into where I sit, but apparently you did."

He gave her an evil smile and started sliding down the couch towards her.

"What do you think you are doing?"

"Playing nice."

"Who says I want to play nice with you anyway?"

"Would you rather play naughty?"

"Stop that! Are you ever serious?"

"Yes, I am. How about if we call a truce and you meet me half-way, then we can sit beside each other to watch the movie? That way I can put my arm around you and play with your hair without you noticing. Then maybe I can lightly trace up and down your neck when you are engrossed in the movie. Maybe reach over and place my hand…"

"Okay, okay… I'll move over closer, but none of that funny stuff. We're just going to watch the movie."

"Oh believe me, it would not be funny."

"I know…that's what I'm afraid of."

They both moved to the center of the couch and she pushed play on the remote. She looked at him out of the corner of her eye and could tell he was watching the TV, so she relaxed and decided to enjoy the movie.

They were about a half hour into the movie before she realized he had put his arm along the back of the couch. She acted like she hadn't noticed. Besides, she really was hoping he would do all of those things he had described.

Another fifteen minutes later and she felt the slight pull on a strand of her hair as he gently played with a curl that had fallen over his hand. She had curled her legs up beside her, which only brought her closer to him. She had totally lost track of what was happening in the movie, as she was more concerned with what his hand was going to do next.

Five minutes later, his hand had made it to her neck and was stroking gently up and down the side with feathery light strokes. She looked at him again out of the corner of her eye and as far as she could tell, it looked like he was watching the movie, giving it his whole attention. Not her, she was completely unnerved. This man had a way about him that made her body do crazy things. She had men do the exact same thing to her before, but none had ever made her body respond like he did.

Without even realizing it, she had leaned into him, and was snuggling into his arm as he drew her even closer. She never protested. He had stopped pretending to watch the movie and was watching her. She was terrified to turn and look into his eyes because if she did, she knew she would be lost. She knew without a doubt that sex with this man would be something that she could write in to *Penthouse* about. She just didn't know if she was ready to do that. All her talk was just that: talk. She was not the kind of girl who could just have casual sex and think nothing of it. She was a relationship kind of girl.

Derek must have been reading her thoughts through her eyes, because he placed a finger under her chin and turned her head toward him.

Neither of them said anything, just looked into each other's eyes for what seemed like an eternity.

He had never removed his hand from her face and it was now stroking her cheek. He never looked away from her eyes. She wished she could read his thoughts as easily as he seemed to be able to read hers.

"Ash...?"

Oh wow, what did that mean? Was that asking permission to take it to the next level? She still had no idea where this man was coming from or where he was headed.

She reached up and placed her hand on his chest. His heart was racing, which brought a smile to her lips and made her realize he was just as nervous as she was.

"I already told you that you affect me like no other woman ever has, but I didn't think my traitorous heart would confirm it. *I want you*...God how I want you, but for the first time in a very long time, I don't just want sex."

Hope filled her heart. Was this guy a dream come true, or was he just a really smooth operator? But it did help her decide what she wanted. She wanted the *happily ever after*, not just a one-night stand.

"I think we both have some battle scars from previous relationships and I'll be the first to admit it. And as much as my body is telling me what a fool I am, I don't want to make a mistake I will regret in the morning. I..."

He placed his fingers over her mouth and stopped whatever she was going to say. "It's okay, I agree."

He got up and pulled her to her feet, and then he lay down on the couch with his back against the cushion, took her hand and patted the couch beside him.

It took her only a second to accept his invitation. She lay down beside him with her back to his chest, and her checks flushed remembering the last time she found herself in this position. He had his head on the arm of the couch, and she placed her head on the arm he provided for a pillow, facing the TV. He grabbed the remote and hit the rewind button to a spot where they both agreed they remembered stopping. Then he pulled her close.

She felt like she was in heaven. It had been a long time since a man had just held her in his arms, offering comfort and not expecting a reward at the end of it.

They both relaxed and enjoyed the movie. She didn't know exactly how long she lasted before she fell asleep.

147

CHAPTER SEVEN

Ashley woke up alone in her bed, not on the couch. She sat straight up and looked down to see if she was dressed or if this had all been a dream. She was still wearing the same pair of jeans and t-shirt. Miss Priss was lying beside her, curled up in a ball with not a care in the world.

Ashley lay back down and tried to make some sense of what happened. She knew that she fell asleep beside Derek watching a movie, but she didn't know how she ended up in her own bed. She suddenly had a wild thought...what if Derek was still here? She did not want him to find her with raccoon eyes from smeared makeup, morning breath and hair that surely looked like a rat's nest.

She jumped up and ran into the bathroom, stripped off her clothes and jumped into the shower. It was the fastest shower she thought she had ever taken. She toweled off and peeked out into her bedroom to make sure there wasn't a man lounging on her bed. The coast was clear, so she raced in and pulled on a pair of shorts and a tank top, picked out her hair and opened her bedroom door.

Nothing...no sign of Derek anywhere. The movie case was still sitting on the coffee table, empty beer bottles were also there. So at least she knew she was not dreaming the whole thing.

Ashley had to admit that she was disappointed. Not surprised though. She headed to the kitchen to make coffee and throw a bagel into the toaster. That's when she saw the note. It was leaning up against the toaster beside a bag of bakery muffins.

It read *Good Morning...had to take off. Thanks for letting me snuggle with the hottest rookie on the force. Talk to you soon... D.*

Not exactly a declaration of love, but at least he took the time to leave a note, plus he brought her muffins. To a lonely single girl, that was good enough. She turned to make coffee and noticed for the first time that it was already made, and a long-stemmed rose was stuck into the handle of the pot.

Smiling, she decided he may not be a poet, but his actions were way more romantic than mere words could ever be. She opened up the refrigerator to get out the creamer and found another rose. Okay, so her day was not starting off so badly after all.

Someone knocked on her door. She smiled and her heart started beating like crazy, sure he had come back to share the muffins and coffee. She hurried to the door, opened it and said, "Did you come back to join me?"

Shannon and Casey stood there. They looked at each other and shoved their way into the apartment. Casey stood against the door, blocking it in case Ashley had some wild-hair idea of escaping.

Oh brother, Ashley knew she was in for it now. Shannon didn't waste any time. She must have woken Casey up at the crack of dawn.

Casey walked over to the couch and took inventory of the movie and beer bottles. She picked up a beer bottle and turned and raised an eyebrow at Ashley.

Meanwhile Shannon had gone into the kitchen and found the note, muffins and roses. She carried the note and rose out into the living room, and she and Casey stood there, each holding evidence of the night before and the confirmation that someone had been there this morning, at least to bring muffins. Ashley knew she was going to have to explain in great detail what had happened before either one of them would give her a minute of peace.

They both started talking at once.

"Who were you with last night when I saw you on that motorcycle?"

"So, you blew me off for some guy."

"Who is D?"

Ashley just smiled and walked into the kitchen, calmly got out coffee mugs, spoons and plates, and put them on the table. She was enjoying this. She still had not said a word and she knew it was driving them crazy. She proceeded to set the table with the muffins and butter and filled the mugs with coffee.

They had both moved back into the kitchen, asking questions the whole time.

Ashley sat at the table sipping her coffee and buttering her muffin, all the while listening to those two talking to each other, speculating about who her mystery date was. It was several minutes before they realized that they were the only two doing the talking. They suddenly stopped, turned to her and attacked. Casey came at Ashley with a knife covered in butter and Shannon held a muffin.

Ashley let out a squeal, holding her hands up in defeat. "Okay, okay! I'll tell. Just put down the muffin and butter or I may have to arrest you two for assaulting a police officer with deadly weapons. Do you guys remember the night we celebrated Casey's big news at the bar?"

They both shook their heads yes.

"Do you remember the hot bartender kissing my ear?"

Again they both shook their heads yes.

Ashley just sat there waiting for them to put two and two together. It didn't take but a few seconds before Casey got it.

"You're shitting me! You mean that gorgeous hunk of man-flesh is who you blew me off for?"

Shannon just sat there with a dazed look on her face. "You were on the back of *his* motorcycle? How in the world did that happen?"

151

They drank their coffee and ate the delicious muffins while Ashley filled them in on the details, or at least most of the details. She chose to leave out some of the juicier events. She wasn't ready to share those moments just yet. She wanted to keep those and enjoy them in the comfort of her big bed on lonely nights.

They giggled like they used to when they were schoolgirls with crushes on the older boys. Casey and Shannon were planning her wedding by the time they had finished their muffins.

Ashley suddenly got serious and told them something else had happened to her that she needed to run by them.

Shannon looked at her and said, "If you're going to tell me you have a date with that giant fireman tonight, I just might go ahead and attack you with the muffin."

Casey chimed in with, "Or that stud muffin from the station we ogled the other day."

"No, it's nothing good, or at least I don't think it is." Ashley went on to explain the dead rose and the notes on her windshield.

Casey looked over at the roses Ashley had placed in a vase and the note that Shannon had laid on the table.

Following her gaze, Ashley got up and retrieved the note, went to her counter where she had thrown the other ones left on her windshield. They set them on the table and proceeded to compare them.

Ashley realized she had been holding her breath. After looking at them, she let it out with a big swoosh. "They're not even close. Either he did a really good job of making them look different or someone else wrote them."

Shannon gave her a worried look. "I think we need to tell Dad and Michael."

A part of her did too, and she had even thought that she would, but she was a cop now. She did not want to run to her daddy and her big brother every time something happened to upset her. "I think we're making more out of this than we need to. It was probably some jackass from the precinct."

"Malone," Shannon and Casey said at the same time.

"I don't think she would care if I was frowning or not. As a matter of fact she would probably prefer if I was."

"Still, I think you should tell someone."

"I just did…you two are my confidantes. Tell you what: if I get anything else I'll go to Dad."

About that time the morning news came on with an update on the murder. They flashed a picture of the poor woman and everyone at the table went still. Shannon looked at Ashley with huge eyes and asked, "Had you seen a picture of her yet?"

"No. Remember this happened right when I was getting off work and now it's my days off."

"Ash, did you look at that picture?"

She was hoping no one else had noticed.

Casey and Shannon gave each other *the look*.

"You two stop that. She may resemble me a little, but that's just a coincidence."

"Coincidence, my ass…that girl could be your twin sister. You are so going to tell your dad about the notes and rose on your car."

"Do you really think that Dad is going to think they have anything to do with each other? And it wasn't like the notes were a death threat or anything. You two are just spooked, so stop spooking me too. Let's get out of here and go do something girlie, like shopping!"

They both sat there for a few seconds and then shrugged their shoulders in agreement.

"I'll agree to go shopping with you, but I refuse to be seen in public with you unless you put on some decent clothes and some makeup. And curl your hair for God's sake. I don't want anyone to think my sister is a frump."

Ashley sent the napkin flying across the table and hit her square in the face. Her look was priceless. It took her just a few seconds before she was out of her chair and sailing around the table after her. Casey had anticipated the move and calmly picked up her coffee cup so it would not be spilled in the ensuing fight. Ashley was already out of her chair and headed to her bedroom, slamming the door and locking it a split second before Shannon reached it.

"You better lock that door, you skanky-ass. I may be younger but I can kick your ass any day of the week."

Shannon turned and gave Casey a big smile, not expecting Ashley to open the door back up. She had eased the door open and waited till Shannon wasn't looking, then did a flying leap and landed on her back. She staggered under the assault, trying to shake Ashley from her back. They were whirling around, giggling and trying to get the best of each other. Casey played referee, moving things out of their way so nothing would get broken.

"You two stop it; you're going to hurt each other. Plus you look like a couple of grade-school girls on the playground. Or even worse, you remind me of Malone."

That got their attention, so Ashley reached over and whispered in Shannon's ear.

They played around a second longer, placing themselves closer to Casey, and then before she realized what was going on, they attacked.

Casey had been standing beside the chair and they both leaped on her before she knew what hit her. They all three landed on the chair, knocking it over, and taking them along with it. Three sets of legs and arms became entangled along with black, red and blonde hair. They wrestled around on the floor, with Ashley finally getting both of them under her. She sat straddling them both, squeezing with her legs.

"Holy shit, Ash! Stop that or I am going to piss my pants. I drank too much coffee."

"Are you two going to be nice to me?"

"Yes, at least to your face."

"That's right, but we are going to tell everyone at the precinct that you and Bill were looking at the stiff's privates."

"Were you guys spying on us?" Ashley squeezed a little harder, before finally relenting and letting them up.

Casey raced to the restroom, with her legs squeezed together and her hand between her legs. Shannon and Ashley burst out laughing.

She had run into the restroom without bothering to shut any of the doors. "I can hear you jackasses laughing."

Ashley went into her bedroom, wiggled into her Wonderbra that made her firm Cs pop, shimmied into a black tank top, then changed into a pair of white capris. Her thong was visible so she shucked them and decided to go commando. By that time Casey was finished in the restroom, so Ashley curled her hair and put on her mall-shopping, looking-for-hot guys makeup. Slipping on her sexy white sandals, she was ready to go.

They decided to take Ashley's car; it had more storage space in case they hit some really good sales.

As she was driving to the mall she couldn't help feeling like someone was following her, but could not make out any cars in her rearview mirror. Ashley was just spooked from their earlier talk and the recent murder. She had to shake the negative feeling she had about the notes. Maybe the last one was just that someone was deeply in love with her and *really* did not want to see her frown.

They made a game plan for what stores they wanted to hit first. Shannon and Casey wanted clothes and Ashley wanted to find a new necklace to go with her little black dress. She circled the parking lot till she found a space close to the entrance doors. She wasn't going to do any more walking than she had to.

They walked in strutting their stuff, even if it was to a bunch of fourteen-year-olds. Hey, a wolf whistle was good to hear, no matter who it came from. Shannon gave some silly kid the precinct's phone number when he asked if he could have her number. Ashley gave her a hard time about traumatizing a fragile youth, and she gave it right back to her in the form of, "He just wants a piece of ass anyway, so that's what he gets."

Casey walked into the first clothes shop they came to, and within a matter of minutes she had her arms full and was headed back to the dressing room. Ashley wandered around, looking for something that would catch her eye, with no luck. Shannon and Ashley wandered around the store waiting for Casey to finish trying her clothes on. Shannon would hold up the ugliest thing she could find and tell Ashley that she thought Derek would love seeing her in it. They had seen no sign of Casey for fifteen or twenty minutes, so they finally headed to the dressing rooms to see what was keeping her. Shannon got down on all fours, looking under the dressing room doors to see if she could figure out which room Casey was in. Ashley could not believe she was actually looking under the doors. She had made it to the third door when it opened and a very large woman came out and tripped over Shannon as she was crawling by. They went down in a pile with Shannon on the bottom, a very pissed-off woman next, and then a pile of extra-large clothes on top of her. Ashley heard an "Ommmfff" from Shannon and saw arms and legs flying around, or at least the legs on top were; she didn't think Shannon was even moving.

She bent over laughing at the spectacle Shannon had created with her ridiculous stealth spy moves. The lady could not get up; she was tangled in all the clothes. Every time she would just about get so she could maneuver herself up, Shannon would move wrong and send them both tumbling back down. Other shoppers had begun sticking their heads out of the dressing rooms to see what all the commotion was about. Shannon finally got turned so she could see Ashley leaning against the wall, holding her stomach and laughing so hard she was trying not to pee her pants. Shannon gave Ashley a look that would scare Charles Manson, and barked out, "For the love of God, Ash, would you please help us?"

Pointing to her chest she asked, "ME? You want *me* to get in there? Well, I don't know, I could get hurt, and then my old man would be pissed when we couldn't have sex tonight. He's real particular when it comes to sex."

Ashley thought Shannon was going to have a heart attack right then and there. She knew the payback on this would be a big one, but she just couldn't pass up the opportunity.

One of the women who had been peeking out of her room gave Ashley the dirtiest look, walked out of her dressing room in her bra and underwear, and started tugging on the lady on top of Shannon.

"What kind of person would be more worried about her sex life than helping two poor ladies in trouble?"

Ashley gave a little sob and acted like she was going to cry. She pretended to start trembling. "Oh please, you wouldn't ask me that if you knew my old man. If he doesn't get sex every night at least once, he will beat me and the kids."

Everyone stopped what they were doing and just stared at her in shock. Ashley kept mumbling things about how bad her husband's anger was and how she just couldn't take another beating because he didn't get sex, that the kids were tired of hiding in the closet when he got mad.

The woman who had been helping Shannon dropped the fat lady's arm and walked over to her. Several of the other shoppers started comforting her, giving numbers and names of agencies, priests and women's shelters she could call for help.

157

In the meantime, Shannon and the other lady had finally managed to get themselves untangled and up off the floor.

Shannon walked over to her, put her hands on her hips and remarked, "Well, if you weren't out screwing every other guy in town, then you wouldn't be too tired to have sex with your husband. I've seen you around, and you would screw anything with a dick. Man, horse or dog, it wouldn't matter to you. I've even heard tell that you like women."

Several women took a quick step back, looking between Shannon and Ashley. It took her a minute to ripen to the challenge, but she did.

"For your information, I do not like horses and dogs. They smell and have you ever seen the size of a horse's dick? Why, that could damage a poor small woman like me. Now someone your size could probably handle a horse's dick."

By this time, they had scared most of the women back to their dressing rooms or they had made a mad dash out of there. All except one woman, who was standing back with an evil smile on her lips. She purred, "If either of you *really* want to get kinky, you should call me." She handed Shannon a business card and left.

They looked at each other for a shocked second and then burst out laughing.

During this whole episode they still had not seen hide nor hair of Casey.

"Casey, where are you?"

They heard a muffled voice in the fifth dressing room, so they opened the door. There stood Casey, or at least it looked like her. She was standing with her hands above her head, her body engulfed in some very tight latex/spandex kind of dress. The tops of her arms were visible, and from her waist down. She had either been trying to get the dress on or off over her head and had become stuck. Her arms were caught in the too-tight dress and she couldn't go up or down with the dress.

Ashley didn't think she could laugh any harder than she had earlier, but she did. Shannon and Ashley were both doing good belly laughs, tears streaming out of their eyes. Casey stamped her foot and mumbled something that sounded like she was going to kill them, but they couldn't be sure.

They both got themselves under control, and agreed to help, but first they took out their cameras, Ashley's digital and Shannon's camera phone. Shannon snapped a picture and forwarded it to Dan. Ashley proceeded to take pictures in all the various stages of Shannon peeling her out of her dress. They were lucky the dressing room was as big as it was. Shannon grabbed the top of the dress and pulled while Casey tried to hunch her shoulders to help.

"Geez, Casey, did you try on a dress from the infants section? I know you only weigh about a hundred pounds, but I think you still need something bigger than a toddler's size four."

Casey tried kicking Shannon but she couldn't see where she was aiming and kicked the wall.

Ashley was playing Ms. Shutterbug and snapping pictures like crazy. She wasn't sure how well they would turn out, since she was laughing so hard.

Dan sent a text message saying, "That has to be my fiancée. I would recognize that thong anywhere. I won't even ask what the hell you three are doing!"

Shannon finally gave one mighty tug and out popped Casey. She fell back onto the dressing room bench with a few choice words her mother would be shocked to hear come out of her mouth.

"I cannot believe you two took pictures of me like that. Who the hell did you send it to?"

"Everyone in my address book."

"Shannon, you didn't!"

"Sure did. Your face wasn't showing, so no one knows who it is."

"How the hell did you get stuck in that, anyway?"

"Don't ask, and by the way, Shannon, the dress was an *adult's* size two, thank you very much. What in the hell happened outside the dressing rooms and what took you two so long to come back and check on me?"

Shannon and Ashley both started laughing hysterically again and informed her it was a story best told over a cold beer.

They left everything right where it had landed, since Casey said she never wanted to see anything in that pile ever again.

They headed out into the mall, doing a lot of window-shopping now since Casey said she would probably have nightmares every time she thought about trying clothes on again.

The mall was pretty busy for this early in the day. That could only mean one thing: sales. Shannon and Casey had stepped into the Hallmark store to look at wedding stuff, so Ashley told them she was going next door to look in the jewelry store.

She was looking at the jewelry showcases and had told the saleslady she was just browsing. She loved looking at all the gold and the diamonds. Especially the diamonds! A girl could drool all she wanted when no one was around.

She was so intent on looking that she did not notice someone had come up behind her and was looking over her shoulder. When she started to move to the next showcase, she accidentally bumped into him. "Oh excuse...what the hell are you doing standing so close to me?"

Steve Merritt was standing there with an evil grin on his face. "Just enjoying the view, honey."

"Well, don't let me get in your way. I was just leaving."

As she tried to walk past him, he reached out and grabbed her arm. "What's your hurry? Why don't we go have a cup of coffee? I think you and I need to get to know each other a little better."

"No thanks, I'm with friends." Again she tried to move on, but he gave her arm a tighter squeeze, and when she looked down at her arm and then back up at him again, he finally let go. She was not going to give him the satisfaction of seeing her rubbing her arm.

"Don't ever grab me like that again, Merritt."

"Or what? Is the big bad girlie cop going to bust my chops?"

"You really are the dick everyone says you are."

The look that came across his face scared the piss out of her, but she wasn't going to let him know it. This guy was psycho.

She pushed past him and went back into the store where Casey and Shannon were. She was shaking like a leaf, whether from anger or fear, she didn't know. She took several deep breaths and tried to calm her nerves. Casey and Shannon were finished ringing up their purchases and were headed her way.

"Geez sis, you're as white as a ghost. We didn't take that long."

Ashley smiled and they headed out into the mall. She glanced around and spotted Merritt lounging against a wall behind them. He never took his eyes off her. Now him, she would mention to her dad. If this guy had a problem with her, she could not let it affect her job. Her dad would know how she should handle him and the situation. She could never tell Michael, he would just get in the guy's face and then there would be trouble for all of them.

They had all had enough of the mall and decided to go grab some lunch and a beer. Ashley noticed right off there was something on her windshield. She was hoping she could get it off before either of the other two spotted it.

No such luck. Casey spotted it right off the bat. "Hey, what's that?"

Ashley reached up and took out the hunk of strawberry blonde hair that had been placed under her windshield wipers.

"Oh my God! *What the hell is that?*"

CHAPTER EIGHT

Ashley stood with the wad of hair, her hand shaking violently. Who would do something like this? And more importantly, what did it mean?

Shannon and Casey were both freaking out. Shannon was calling Michael on her cell phone before Ashley even realized what she was doing. But even if she had been aware, she didn't think she would have stopped her. This had gone past the cute stage and was now just full-blown creepy. Casey was trying to talk over Shannon to Michael about the notes and the rose while Shannon was talking about the hair. Ashley was sure he was loving this call, two hysterical women both talking to him at the same time, and he probably couldn't hear what either one of them was saying to him.

Ashley kept her head down, pretending to study the lock of hair, but she actually started casually looking at the scene around her, checking her car to see if there was anything else on it and taking notice of cars in her vision that looked suspicious, and mentally remembering the people who just seemed to be loitering around. She did not see anything suspicious, but that didn't make her feel any better. She had a sinking feeling in her guts that this was going to turn out really ugly.

Shannon hung up the phone, and screamed at her, "Oh shit! Michael is pissed off." She had this really scared look on her face.

The sound of her voice and the fear in her face brought Ashley right out of cop mode. "What do you mean he's pissed off?"

"He wanted to know why he wasn't informed when the first note was found."

"And what did you tell him?"

"I told him you thought it was just some weirdo and didn't think it was a big deal. Umm…he didn't agree."

"Great. That's just great. Now I not only have some sicko leaving stuff on my windshield, but now my macho vice cop brother is on the warpath."

Casey had been standing by quietly, listening to everything going on. She had a frightened look on her face, like she might take off at a dead run in a split second. Ashley thought she must have been in shock, because Casey was usually the feisty one who took the bull by the horns and met things head-on. Ashley looked from one to the other and tried plastering on a reassuring smile, but she was sure it was pretty wobbly. It was hard to calm others down when her whole insides were a mass of jumbled nerves racing around at top speed.

Ashley was leaning against the car when she happened to look up and right into the eyes of a guy sitting across the parking lot in a rusted-out, piece of shit car. Or should she say into the pair of binoculars he was holding up to his eyes.

Ashley could tell he knew he had been caught because he threw down the binoculars, pulled his hat down lower and took off. He raced out of the parking spot, ran the stop sign at the corner, and made a turn onto the interstate that ran alongside the mall.

Ashley pushed Casey out of the way, jumped into her Bronco and took off after him. It wasn't till she was at the stop sign that she realized she had left Casey and Shannon standing in the middle of the parking lot. She gave a quick glance in her rearview mirror and witnessed them both just staring after her. Casey looked like maybe the shock had run its course, and if the fist on her hip was any indication, either the guy who had left the hair was in big trouble or she was.

Ashley could see the guy's rusted-out piece of crap about ten cars in front of her. She had not even had a chance to get a make or model; he had been too far away. She was trying to weave in and out of traffic to catch up with him, but it was Saturday and everyone and his dog were out today.

She had a fleeting thought that she had not taken the time to put on her seat belt, and the way they were both driving, there was a good chance that one of them would hit the median or a side rail at the least. She had moved up to within six cars, when he must have glanced in his rearview mirror and realized she was following him, because all of a sudden he was driving like a bat out of hell. He was cutting people off and changing lanes with only inches to spare. Horns were honking and people were slamming on their brakes as he whipped by them, cutting them off. Ashley floored the Bronco and was suddenly whizzing through the early afternoon traffic at speeds hitting ninety. She had gotten within two cars of him and, as she tried to get closer, he changed lanes and the car he cut off spun out of control and slid into the guardrail. Thankfully, most of the drivers had reduced their speeds and had been trying to get out of their way, so a quick glance reassured her that probably no one was seriously injured. As she turned her attention forward again, she noticed that he was once again pulling away from her and she was afraid someone was really going to get hurt with his reckless driving. All of a sudden he cut across two lanes of traffic and took the first off-ramp he came to. Ashley was caught in traffic and could not cut across to follow, the cars had blocked her in when they had slowed and moved to the outer lanes. She drew even with him just as he made his way down the ramp, still going an ungodly speed, and she could see that he turned to give her a satisfied smile know-ing he had outdone her.

Ashley could not make out any of his features with the ball cap covering his face in shadow, and with the dim light in his car. There was no way she would be able to make out any features for a future line-up. She didn't try to get over to follow, knowing there was no way she could get to him now. For just a split second she thought about doing a Dirty Harry move and just cranking it to the edge and going after him, but first, she couldn't get there, second it was a re-ally steep embankment and third, she was already about to piss her pants at the rate of speed she had been driving. She slowed down to the speed limit and took the next off-ramp. She came to a stop at the sign and gulped in huge amounts of air. She rested her hands on the steering wheel and laid her head down on them, trying to get her adrenaline back to normal. She could see how rookies made mistakes. When the action starts you just react, with no thought put into place. Looking back, she realized maybe she should have used her cell phone to call in some backup, but while the chase was on she never once thought of it. Now that she was sitting here feeling like an idiot, the thought crossed her mind like a huge neon sign in front of a strip joint.

People behind her were honking their fool heads off, some even going around her and giving her the finger as they went by. Taking a deep breath to get her shit together, knowing there was no way she would ever find him now, she crossed under the overpass and re-entered the interstate, going the opposite direction to head back to the mall. Traffic had resumed to normal in the opposite lanes and the car was gone from against the rail, so she assumed no one had been hurt.

Her cell phone had been ringing off the hook, but she hadn't taken the time to answer it. Now she just didn't want to. It was Casey, Shannon or Michael. She knew she would be seeing them in just a few minutes in person so she just let it ring. She had adrenaline pumping through her veins at warp speeds and her hands were shaking on the steering wheel. Thankfully she had not been on duty during her first high-speed chase, if this was the way she was going to respond each time. She was amazed at how her body reacted to the situation and her brain tried to play catch-up somewhere in the race. She had to admire the men and women who always kept a calm head in times like she had just gone through, and maybe with this behind her, the next episode would go a little better and she would stay a little calmer throughout the chase. She could only hope so, because she was not impressed with her actions after the fact. She had held her own in the actual pursuit, but her emotions got the best of her when it was over. Typical rookie nerves, but coming from a houseful of cops, she had thought when the chips were down she would handle herself better. Guess not.

What had that guy been doing? It was obvious that he had been watching them, but why? Was he the guy leaving the notes and roses on her car? Or was he a P.I. staking one of them out for some reason? God, what if he was the killer and she had just chased him down the interstate. What was she going to do if she had caught him, pursue him in her killer heeled sandals and whack him with her purse? She had not brought her gun or badge, leaving them home on her dresser for Miss Priss to play with, she guessed. From this day on, she would be sure and carry them both with her, no matter where she went. Maybe she would get one of those sexy thigh straps to hold a pistol in, but that would mean she would have to wear dresses or skirts and she couldn't see that happening. She didn't think dropping her pants to get to the thigh strap was exactly what the precinct would have in mind.

She pulled into the parking lot and noticed Casey and Shannon were sitting in Michael's unmarked police car with his partner. She could see from here that everyone was still talking at the same time.

Michael was leaning onto the back door trying to take it all in, but she was sure he was about ready to kill them both. No one had seen her yet, and she was tempted to turn around and just go home and call Michael on the phone. She knew it was the chicken-shit way to handle things, but she was really not in the mood to handle her big brother's holier-than-thou attitude. She could already hear the lecture she knew was coming. Sitting in her car, she debated the pros and cons of her plan and decided that if she did go home, Michael would just be more pissed. So she pulled alongside them, put the Bronco in park, and just sat there. She knew it would only take Michael a few seconds to be in her vehicle.

She was right.

He opened the front door, climbed in and told her to roll up the window. She did as he asked.

"Can I see the hair?"

She still had the clump clutched in her hand. She had left in such a hurry, she had just grabbed the steering wheel with it still in her hand. She slowly opened her hand.

He reached out with a clear plastic bag and had her drop it in. He closed it and then took a few minutes turning it over and over, just looking at it.

She had expected that he would immediately start ranting and raving at her about not filling him in on the notes, but he just sat there all quiet-like. This scared her more than if he would have screamed at her.

"Tell me about the other items, from the beginning."

She told him when and where she had been when she had found all of the items. He had taken out a notebook and was writing everything down.

"Michael, you're beginning to scare me. What's with the serious attitude?"

He turned and gave her a very grave look. "Where did you just take off to?"

She filled him in on the man in the rusted-out car and the binoculars.

"Ashley, I think you're in serious danger."

"DANGER? What kind of danger?"

"We didn't release this to the public, but the young woman who was murdered the other night had a chunk of her hair cut off, and it was not found at the murder scene."

Ashley's insides turned to a quivering mass of Jell-O. She felt like her throat was closing shut. She was starting to see little black dots in front of her eyes.

"Jesus, Ash, are you going to pass out? Put your head between your legs."

He must have realized there was no way she could do that sitting behind the steering wheel of her car. He jumped out and ran around to her side of the car, waving everyone else to stay put, then yanked open her door, spun her around and grabbed her head and shoved it between her knees.

The black dancing stars finally receded to the back of her brain, waiting for another chance to spring forward. And she had a sneaky feeling that there was a good chance that it might just happen again in the near future.

She raised her head and looked into Michael's eyes. "Are you thinking that the hair left on my windshield belongs to the poor dead girl?"

"I can't say until I get it back to the lab to process, but *it is* the same color. Ash, this has to be taken seriously. Did you see the woman's face on the news?'

"Are you asking if I noticed that she could be my twin?"

He raised an eyebrow. "Umm, yeah."

"Has anyone else made the connection yet?"

169

"Dad and I noticed right away. As a matter of fact, I think poor Dad had ten years of his life scared off of him when we responded to the crime scene. At the time we just thought it was a coincidence, but now I'm not so sure."

"Michael, do you really think this guy is connected to me somehow?"

"I just don't know, Ash, but one thing's for sure, even if it's not, we are going to proceed like it is."

"How much of the precinct has to be made aware of this? I really don't want to inform everyone."

"I agree we have to keep this on the need to know basis. We will go get the notes from your house, and then I think we need to call Dad and go in and see the captain."

"This is not how I planned on spending my day off."

"Sorry, sis, I hope we're just being paranoid."

He gave her shoulder a reassuring squeeze and went to talk to the others for a few minutes, and then came over and had her trade places with him.

"What about Casey and Shannon?"

"Dave's going to take them back to your place and get their cars."

Dave pulled out and Ashley couldn't help but smile. There sat her two best friends in the world, sitting in the back of a police car. If things had been a little different, she would have gotten great pleasure at that sight.

They both gave her very worried, anxious looks as they passed them. She knew this had to be scaring them to death. They had no idea where she had rushed off to, why Michael was sending them on their way without her, and no idea a killer could be stalking her.

Michael called their dad and asked him to meet them at the station, not giving any details. Then he called the captain to make sure he was going to be in his office, and they drove to her apartment in silence, both of them lost in their own thoughts.

Michael insisted on coming up to her apartment with her, not wanting to take any chances. He unlocked the door, searched the apartment and gave her the okay to come in and get the notes.

He was really starting to get her spooked. This was not the Michael she had expected. This was the no-nonsense vice cop she had never seen in action. That it pertained to her was downright shitty, but her chest puffed up with pride at how he handled everything so professionally.

Harold was waiting for them when they reached the station. He gave them an odd look and followed them into Captain Freeman's office without asking a single question.

"Well, what brings the whole Wright family into my office?" The captain looked from one face to the other, moved a stack of papers he had been working on, and leaned forward onto his desk, sensing the significance of the visit.

They all took a chair and Michael proceeded to fill Harold and the captain in on what had been happening. During the conversation Ashley's dad turned to her, and she saw real fear in his eyes for the first time in her life. She knew he had seen some really bad things in his years on the force, but they had never involved his daughter before. She tried giving him a reassuring smile but with her lips quivering and the hint of tears shining in her eyes, she didn't think she pulled it off too well.

"Michael, run the items to the lab so we can start getting them processed. Ashley, we need to get you into a safe house right away."

Ashley whipped her head around from looking at her dad. "You cannot be serious! We don't even know if this is connected yet. I'm not going to go running into hiding. Plus if it is connected, I want to help flush him out. How else are we going to know what the connection is between me and the killer?"

"What do you think, Harold? You have a personal say in this," the captain asked.

He gave her a long hard look. "I agree with Ashley. I don't think putting her in a safe house is the answer. I think we need to set up some surveillance on her car and apartment, and maybe take some precautions for her safety, and see what happens when the lab finishes with their tests."

They continued discussing their options, and when Michael came back into the room, he threw in his two cents. Which was a little on the extreme side for her.

Ashley happened to glance up and catch Malone standing in front of the window of the captain's office. She was standing to the side so no one could see her but Ashley. She made a point to look at each person in the room, raise an eyebrow, and then walked off. Great, just great. Just what she needed, Malone sniffing around, sticking her nose where it didn't belong.

They agreed on installing more secure locks on her door and windows and installing an alarm system on her car, and then they came to her being alone. That's where they could not agree on a solution. Harold wanted her to move back in with him and her mom, Michael thought she should either move in with him or he in with her, and the captain thought she should ask a friend to stay with her.

She told them she would not do any of those things. She would not put anyone else in danger. She was a cop, for God's sake. She had been trained for this kind of thing, just not with her being the victim. She agreed to be more cautious, not go out at night by herself, park in well-lit areas, etc. etc.

They agreed to keep this among the four of them for the time being, at least until the lab reports were in, and then they would go from there. She could tell her dad and Michael had more to say on the matter, but she was happy they chose to wait until they were in private before they voiced their demands.

She really just wanted to be alone. Her head had started to pound somewhere in the middle of all the drama. She still felt like she was going to pass out; the little black stars were dancing in front of her eyes every once in a while, and her stomach was doing a very nervous roll. Overall, if she didn't know better, she would have thought she had one hell of a hangover.

As they walked out of the captain's office, Harold gently but firmly grabbed her elbow and guided her through the station. Michael followed, but he kept back a few feet so they didn't make quite such a spectacle of themselves as they left. As Ashley was walking she couldn't help thinking and wishing that she was still fast asleep in her nice comfy bed and this was all just a bad dream.

Harold and Ashley walked to Harold's car without uttering a single word. They headed out of the station parking lot with Michael following behind in Ashley's Bronco. Harold had still not said a word. Feeling totally depressed, Ashley laid her head back on the seat rest and closed her eyes. Her dad reached over and gently took her hand. His big strong hand engulfed hers and that's when the tears started rolling. She had tried to put on a brave face, but one gentle touch from her tough father was all it took. Who was she kidding, anyway? Everyone knew she was a softie playing at being a big bad cop.

She felt the car slow and make a turn, opened her eyes enough to see they were at the city park. Ashley guessed this was as good a place as any to talk without fear of being interrupted. She hated to break the contact with her dad, but she knew she needed to pull herself together if she was going to make it through the next inter-rogation. She really hated that Michael would be able to tell she'd been crying. She didn't want him to see her tears; he was already worried enough about her.

Harold looked over and gave her hand a reassuring squeeze, and then got out to meet Michael as he pulled up beside them.

Ashley flipped down the visor and took a look at her tear-streaked face, wiping away the tears along with the smeared mascara. As she sat there looking at her reflection, she couldn't help but see the poor murdered woman's face looking back at her. How could this be happening? Could the killer really be someone that she knew, or at least knew her?

Harold and Michael were waiting for her in front of the car; she flipped the visor back up, took a deep breath and opened the door. Ashley walked with her shoulders thrown back and her head held high, giving them each a firm look as they made their way to a remote picnic bench away from any prying eyes and ears.

Harold took over the questioning, which she was thankful for. She knew the questions would be hard, but she had a feeling Michael's would have been much more personal. He would have wanted to know every little private thing going on in her life, whereas Dad kept the questions to what needed to be known concerning the case.

They went over the details again. This time they asked more detailed questions than they had in the captain's office. They sat there hoping to grasp some insight into a situation she really didn't understand. She was stalling, not wanting to divulge any information on Derek. It was too new and too private to share with her Dad and big brother, but she knew there was no way around it. They had to know. She gave minimal details, saying that they had gone on a date last night and that was all. She left out the part about the grocery store; Michael would jump on that little bit of information with both feet. She could already see him interrogating Derek like the macho cop he was, and she didn't want him coming down too hard on this guy. She was afraid all this would scare him off as it was, let alone if Michael came on too strong. Ashley noticed Michael was giving her a strange look. It was like he could see into her brain and read what she wasn't saying. She raised her chin and looked him square in the eye without blinking. The corner of his mouth went up just a notch, but he didn't say a word.

None of them acknowledged that this was linked to the murder, but without saying a word, deep down they all knew that it was. Ashley may have made a fuss in the captain's office, but she was really okay with a little extra protection. Harold and Michael had filled her in on the grisly details of the woman's murder, feeling that she needed to know, and she was fast coming to the conclusion that they were dealing with one sick puppy. Not only had he chopped off a hunk of her hair, but after raping her repeatedly, he cut off her pubic hair also. He had carved *whore* into her stomach and beaten her after she was already dead. Then the sicko shoved a bullet up the woman's vagina. The rage this man must be feeling, to do something so brutal to an innocent woman, was mind-boggling.

Her dad made a call to the captain to find out where she was going to be assigned after her one week left on morgue duty. Hanging up, he informed them that they decided the best place for her would be with an experienced partner. They had also decided that the best person to put her with was Detective Phillip Kelly.

Ashley's heart hit her toes. The very thought of spending three weeks riding shotgun with the station's stud muffin was a little more than she thought she could handle right now. Michael must have seen the fear in her eyes, because he reached over and put his hand over hers. "It's okay, sis, I think this is the right time to put you with Phillip. It will be safer for him now."

It took her a few seconds to realize what he had said. "What do you mean, safer for *him*? I thought we were worried about my safety?"

"Well, the way I see it, you will be so worried about the psycho out there you won't have any time to jump poor Phillip's bones when he's not looking."

Harold started a coughing fit and she just sat there surprised. At first she couldn't believe Michael had said such a nasty thing at such a serious time. Then she realized he said it at the most appropriate time.

"Oh yeah? Well what makes you think I'll be that consumed with my stalker? Nothing could take up that much brain power when cooped up in a car for eight hours with the hottest man on the force."

"What do you mean, the hottest man on the force? I happen to hold that particular title."

"Oh yeah, only in your mind."

"*Enough!* I see you two are apparently finished discussing this situation. But we still have a few things to work out, like how are we going to tell your mother and sister about this?"

CHAPTER NINE

Ashley pulled up to her apartment and noticed both Casey's and Shannon's cars were still in the parking lot. She guessed she shouldn't have been surprised they were waiting for her. She knew if things had been the other way around, she would have had her happy ass planted in their places, waiting to hear all the details.

She could not believe how emotionally and physically drained she felt. It was only two in the afternoon, but it felt like she had been running uphill for twelve straight hours. She had started this day with such happy thoughts about how maybe her life was finally headed in a positive direction. A nice, good-looking, no, make that a *very* good-looking man was showing an interest in her, her job was going well, and Big Tits had not interfered in her life for a few weeks. As she sat in her car, her mind kept going over how fast things could take a downward slide.

Dad, Michael and Ashley had decided it was best if they informed her mom and Shannon about the situation that had turned her world upside down. They had agreed to meet at her parents' house at five when her mom got off work. Ashley was not up to telling the story more than once, so she dialed Shannon's cell phone and waited for her to pick up. It took half a ring before she heard Shannon's voice asking, "Where are you? And what the hell is going on? Casey and I have been worried sick. Why didn't you call us before now?"

Ashley took a deep breath, waiting for Shannon to shut up long enough for her to reply, "I'm in the parking lot, but I think I'm going to take a drive. Can you and Casey meet me at Dad and Mom's at five?"

"You're not coming in?"

"Shannon, some pretty serious things are happening and I only want to explain it once, so please just understand."

She must have grasped the seriousness of the situation by the tone of Ashley's voice. "Sis, you're scaring the shit out of me. Are you sure you don't want to come up and let us help you?"

"No, that's okay; I just need some time to collect my thoughts. I'll see you both at five, and sis…make sure you lock my place up tight, okay?'

Ashley hung up, started her car and slowly pulled out of the parking lot of her apartment complex. She really had nowhere to go, nervously glancing around, half expecting to see a beat-up, rusted-out piece of shit car sitting in the far corner of the parking lot. Not seeing anything that would send alarms off in her mushy brain, she decided to head over to Dixie's place to see if maybe Tony had an opening for a massage. She thought if anyone deserved a little relaxation it was her.

As she drove down the street she ran through all the details of the day, trying to sort out this mess. Was this last windshield incident really tied to the recent murder and rape of that woman? And why *her*? How was she connected to this psycho?

Her cell phone suddenly started going off, just about sending her through the roof of her car. Holy crap, was she ever jumpy. The caller ID showed it was Bill; she decided to let it go straight to voicemail.

Who knew how many in the precinct knew what was going on, but she definitely was not up to talking about it with anyone. Not even her sweet partner. She wanted to wait until the forensic evidence came back from the hair left on her windshield before she had to start trying to explain things. Not that she could really explain them anyway. She knew absolutely nothing. God, she needed a beer.

She got to her aunt Dixie's place and there was not a parking spot to be had in front of the shop, but there was no way she was going to park on some side street and have Mr. Psycho jump out, and hack all her hair off after he raped and killed her.

Ashley circled the block until a spot opened up right in front of the big picture window of the shop. She pulled in and looked around, aware of her surroundings, and took note of the people and cars in the area. She got out and locked her car and then checked to see if it was really locked. Glancing up, she noticed Dixie was standing in the window with a frown on her face. She gave her a sheepish smile and wave and made her way through the front door.

"What's with the James Bond act? I've seen you circling the block for the last five minutes. Are you getting lazy in your old age?" Dixie's voice had gone from being fairly loud to barely a whisper. "Girl, you look like you've seen a ghost. Are you okay?"

"It's been a rather long, trying day. What are the chances of Troy having an opening?"

Dixie grabbed her hand without saying a word and led Ashley back to her private office. She pushed her down into the chair facing the desk. "Sit here and don't move. I'll be right back."

Ashley leaned her head back, closed her eyes and just enjoyed the quiet.

Within a few minutes Dixie was back, closing the door behind her. She sat behind her desk and reached into her bottom drawer, pulling out a bottle of Ashley's favorite man, Jack Daniels. She grabbed two paper cups from the water cooler and proceeded to pour a generous amount into each cup. She handed Ashley one, gave her a silent salute with her cup, and they both downed the shot in one fluid motion.

"Honey, are you okay? I've seen some pretty haggard-looking women come through my shop, but you are looking a little worse for wear."

"Nothing that Troy's hands can't fix."

"He's just finishing up with a client and will come get you when he's ready for you."

They made small talk. Dixie seemed to come to the conclusion that Ashley was not going to go into any details about what was bothering her, and respected her privacy.

"Another shot of Jack?"

Letting out a soft chuckle she answered, "No I don't have much besides a muffin in my stomach from this morning, so I think I'd better pass. I may not be able to walk out of here as it is."

Troy knocked and stuck his head in the door. "Hey, Ash…are you ready?"

He gave the bottle on the desk a quick eyebrow raise, looking from Dixie to her and back again.

Giving her aunt a quick hug, she let Troy lead her back to his massage room. He opened the door and let her enter before him.

Ashley took a step in and let out a gasp of surprise. Troy's room was always a comforting place to be, but today he had gone a little further than normal. He had placed lit candles around the room and had turned off the soft overhead light that was normally on. The white sheets on the massage table were replaced with soft pale mauve ones. He had incense burning and the music was soft love songs, not the typical instrumental stuff he usually played. She turned and gave *him* the raised eyebrow look.

"Dixie said you were pretty stressed out today. I was told that when you walked out of here, there better not be a line of worry anywhere on your face or I was fired."

Smiling, Ashley said, "Well, thank God for Aunt Dixie."

He left, giving her the time to slip out of her clothes. Ashley stripped down and hung her clothes on the hook behind the door. She hurried up onto the table, not wanting to be caught naked by Troy. Slipping under the sheets, she knew instantly that these were high thread count sheets, not the cheaper regular ones usually found at a massage place. She lay down and turned her head to the side and let out a gasp. When she had hung her clothes up, she had hung her lacy bra on the outside of her clothes. She usually was very careful about putting it under her clothes, but today she was so flustered she never even noticed. She was just starting to get off the table to move it when Troy walked in.

"Babe, are you that anxious that you were going to come look for me?"

Ashley grabbed the sheet, making sure she was covered, and gave him a look. He just chuckled and told her to put her face in the hole, buckle up and enjoy.

Troy fiddled over by his table for what seemed like forever. She could hear him opening drawers and could hear bottles clinking. She was beginning to wonder what in the world he was doing. She started to lift her head up and she felt him reach for the sheet. He moved it down from her back, folding it and tucking it around her hips. It seemed to be a little lower than she remembered in previous massages. Also when he did the tucking it seemed like he took extra effort and time, making sure it was well tucked.

The first touch of his hands was like heaven. She could smell the scent of the oil. "Is that something new? I don't ever remember smelling this one before."

"Umm...it's my private stock, only used at special times."

She did a little gulp and wondered what was so special about this time, but was a little afraid of what his answer might be.

He stood to the left of the table and his hands were working the length of her back. He made sure solid strokes, rubbing the oil into her bunched-up muscles.

"I don't know who or what caused you to be this tense, but I'd like to spend ten minutes out behind the shop with *him*."

Troy had said more in the first five minutes of this massage than he usually did in the hour and a half she was usually in his presence. Ashley had to wonder what Dixie told him, but she could feel the tension leave her body as he did his magic, so decided that whatever it was, it was worth it.

She was lost in the bliss of Troy's hands. He was slowly working the kinks out of her back and shoulders. As his hands worked their magic, the stress of the day slowly receded to the back of her over-worked brain. How being under the hands of a strong talented man could make everything just seem unimportant was beyond her, but she was grateful nonetheless.

He took his time and paid special attention across her shoulders where her stress always seemed to settle. As the minutes went by she noticed his hands had begun to work their way down to her lower back, and if she wasn't mistaken they were doing a lot more caressing than they were massaging. Although it felt like heaven, she must have tensed unknowingly, because he moved to stand above her head. As he resumed working on her shoulders and neck, she was acutely aware that her head was at the same level as his crotch. When he stretched to reach the lower part of her back, she could feel him brush across the top of her head. Good thing her face was stuck in the little hole in the table, because she knew it had to be beet red. Every time he would brush across the top of her head it felt like her hair was on fire, and sent the most delicious feelings coursing throughout her body.

This massage had taken on a whole new life. She could feel it and she was pretty sure he did too. He moved around to the foot of the table and rolled up the sheet by her feet. Normally during her massage when he finished with an area, he would cover that area with the sheet. He did not do that this time. He left her back uncovered and instead of just moving the sheet to expose the leg he was working on, he rolled the sheet up and tucked it in so that all that was covered was her ass, and she wasn't sure it was covered like it should be. She lay there on his table feeling like a Greek goddess with just her butt covered. She had shaved her legs last night, along with more private areas, and she didn't think she would have felt nearly as glamorous if she knew that he would find hair on her legs that was longer than the hair on his arms.

He started working on her left foot, sending electric shocks up her leg. He was finding spots that were doing strange things to areas of her body that were not normally affected by a massage. As he slowly rubbed his thumbs across the pad of her foot, she squirmed a little. She could have sworn she heard him give a low chuckle. He took his own sweet time and she noticed a growing dampness between her legs. He slowly moved up her leg, his fingers moving in small circles. She could feel his hands moving dangerously close to her crotch. He would move his hands between the back of her knee, up along the back of her thigh. It was really getting hard to relax and enjoy what was supposed to be a massage. All she could think of was that she wanted to turn over, grab him around the neck and pull him down on top of her.

He moved to stand at the foot of the table again to work on her right foot. This man was good, damn good. She had enjoyed his massages before but this was nothing like those times. He had always been professional before, and no way in hell was this what he had been taught in his massage class.

As he stretched up to reach her thigh, his crotch was pressed against the bottom of her foot. It took everything she had to act like nothing was different. She was not going to give him reason to chuckle again. She knew he had to be aware of it, and if he wasn't going to move, neither was she. Ashley wasn't sure what kind of game they were playing, but she was going to play it out till the end. As he continued to work on her right leg, she could have sworn she could feel his crotch growing a little firmer against her foot. Oh sweet Jesus. Thank God he moved to stand beside the table; otherwise she thought her foot might burst into flames.

"Okay, Ash, you can turn over now."

She was so distracted, she flipped over at the sound of his voice. As she lay there, she realized she felt cool air along her body. Ashley opened her eyes and looked straight into Troy's stunned eyes. It was then that she realized that she was lying there completely exposed except for the sheet that barely covered her crotch. She had been so engrossed with the thought of his dick being pressed against her foot that she had not waited for Troy to pull the sheet back up to cover her torso.

She felt a moment of panic. Her brain was in complete shutdown.

Troy recovered faster than she did and moved to take hold of the sheet, gently unrolled it and pulled it up and over her breasts. She could have sworn his hands brushed across her already aroused nipples.

She felt like she needed to say something, but what in the world could she say? It was then that her eyes fell on her bra, hanging in all its glory.

Ashley dared take a glance at Troy. She noticed he had followed her glance and was staring at her underwear.

"Umm…"

"Nice, very nice. I always liked a woman who was comfortable enough to wear sexy lingerie."

"I didn't mean to."

"What, leave it hanging there so it was the first thing I noticed as I started my massage?"

184

"Sorry about that. I guess I was not paying enough attention when I hung it up."

"I'm not. I enjoyed looking at it and imagining you wearing such a sexy thing." He had started massaging her arm as he was talking. She closed her eyes and tried to relax. This might be the strangest massage she had ever had, but damn if she wasn't going to do her best to get her money's worth. She might never be able to look Troy in the eye again, but oh well.

He moved on to her other arm, making sure to spend equal time on each area. Before she knew it she was starting to relax again. He was working on her hand and it felt like heaven. He would gently rub his thumbs across her palm and gently massage each finger, making small gentle circles as he worked to the tip of each one.

He once again moved to the head of the table and began massaging her head and shoulders. He worked his fingers through her hair, rubbing her head in the most delicious way. He had the most talented hands of anyone she had ever known. If this man could make her almost have an orgasm by giving her a massage, what could he do with those hands in the bedroom?

Ashley was beginning to look at Troy in a whole new light.

This had been quite a day. Talk about riding a rollercoaster of emotions. And it was still only four in the afternoon. She still had six to eight hours left to get through. Her guess was that by the time she got through the meeting with her family, she would have covered every emotion there was.

Troy had moved to her shoulders and was working out the last of the knots. His fingers again were working magic. She also noticed that when he stretched those magical fingers, the tips brushed the tops of her breasts under the sheet. They would edge under the sheet to gently brush against the swell of her ta-tas.

Ashley wondered if Dixie would object if she had wild passionate sex with her massage therapist.

"Ash?"

"Yeah...?"

"Our time is up and I'm afraid if we don't come out soon Dixie will come in looking for us."

"That may be a little embarrassing, don't you think?"

Chuckling he said, "I think it could be. I'll need a few extra minutes before I'll be able to take on the next appointment."

Her eyes flew open and looked at his crotch. Yep, there was definite evidence to that fact. When she looked up to meet his eyes he reached out and took her by her arms, pulling her to a sitting position. She made a fast grab for the sheet.

"A little late for that. I've already enjoyed them today."

He gently moved her legs apart, stepping into the V. Ashley stared up into his eyes, just a little taken aback by his actions. Not that she wasn't enjoying it, just surprised was all.

"I don't know what or who caused my favorite client to be so stressed today, but I don't like it."

He gently took her face in his hands and gave her a mind-blowing kiss. His lips started out just barely brushing across hers. If she didn't know for sure he was doing it, she would have not been sure, his touch was so light. His hands were entangled in her hair, holding her head prisoner. His teeth and tongue joined in the onslaught. He nibbled her lower lip, pulling it into his mouth as his tongue did a dance with hers.

Ashley sat on the edge of his table, her hands clutching the sheet, trapping them between their bodies. Her mind and body were totally into the moment. It had been a long time since someone had cared about her like this. She could definitely get used to this kind of treatment.

Troy's kiss was unbelievable. Slowly going from soft and gentle to hot and demanding. He ravished her mouth, sending hot desire racing throughout her body. On their own accord her arms encircled his neck, her hands taking on a mind of their own. She was giving as good as she got. She didn't care if this was way inappropriate for either of them. It felt good, damn it, and she deserved a little pleasure after the day she'd had.

Troy's hands had moved from her head to caress up and down her back. Her hands had somehow found their way under his white polo shirt. They were enjoying the hard planes of his well-muscled chest.

Suddenly there was a knock on the door. "Troy, your four o'clock is here."

Leave it to her aunt Dixie to be the splash of cold water they both needed.

Taking a deep stuttering breath, Troy responded through a rather shaky voice, "Thanks, we are just finishing up in here."

He rested his forehead against hers, taking a few deep breaths. "Ash...?"

She gently placed her fingers against his lips. "Troy, please don't say anything. Let me just thank you for an unbelievable afternoon. It may have been a little more than either of us had planned on, but it was just what the doctor ordered."

He pulled back and gave her a soul-searching look. "Okay, I'll leave you to get dressed."

He stepped back and did a slow look at her from head to toe and back up again, taking extra time at her breasts where the sheet had slipped down to her waist as they had kissed. She made no effort to try and cover herself. She basked in his appreciative stare.

His lips curved up into a very sexy lazy smile, as his eyes finally made their way up to hers. "You're an amazing woman, Ash, and I mean that in more ways than one." He turned, re-tucking his shirt in, and made his way out the door

Ashley sat for several minutes enjoying the warm glow flowing through her body. She didn't think she could have moved if she had wanted to. Her body and mind were completely relaxed. She finally decided she had better move if she didn't want her aunt Dixie sticking her head in to check on her and find her naked, glowing in what could be called a sex-satisfied stupor.

Ashley slipped on the white robe Troy had left for her and gathered up her clothes, smiling as she grabbed her sexy bra. She didn't think she would ever wear any boring old plain bras again. She was going to have to save up for a trip to Victoria's Secret.

She opened the door and started down the hall to the shower room, thankfully not seeing any sign of Troy. She knew if she happened to see him, she would probably either turn red from head to toe or pull him into the laundry room, lock the door and finish what they had started.

As she turned the corner she was greeted by the sight of her aunt standing in the doorway of her office. She had her head tilted and was giving Ashley a strange look.

Ashley smiled and blew her a kiss and walked on to the shower. She could feel her eyes on her back and knew that she was dying to know what had happened behind Troy's closed door, but was too professional to ask. It's a good thing, because Ashley didn't think Dixie would have handled it very well if she found out her favorite niece and her employee had crossed over the line of what would be considered inappropriate behavior for her shop.

Ashley was so glad the shower room was empty. Dixie had thought of everything when she relocated. It was all marble and glass. The showers were equipped with the shampoos, crème rinses, and body lotions that matched the oils that Troy used in his massages.

Ashley didn't think Dixie had the scents he had used on her today, but that was okay. Dixie had equipped the room with everything you would need to get ready. Hairdryers, curling irons, razors, lotions, you name it, it was there. Ashley hustled up and took her shower, coming back to earth. She still had a very hard night ahead of her.

When she was finished getting ready, she couldn't help pausing at Troy's door, wondering what was happening behind it. Was her experience a one of a kind, or did he do this kind of thing for all of his really stressed-out clients? She secretly hoped not. It would take away from the magic if she knew he was that intense with anyone but her.

Her aunt Dixie was waiting by the front desk. "Well, you sure look a hell of a lot better."

"I feel a lot better." Ashley reached for her debit card and she stopped her.

"Don't bother, this one is on us. Even if I wasn't going to already do it, Troy let me know there was no charge. I have never seen him quite so flustered."

She paused, waiting to see if Ashley would supply any information, but she was not going to get anything from her. This was one experience that she was going to savor to herself.

Realizing she was waiting in vain, she handed Ashley a sealed envelope. "Troy said to give this to you."

"Really?"

Giving her a big hug, thanking her and promising to come see her soon, Ashley headed out the front door, taking the time to check out the area before she pushed open the door and headed to her car.

After locking the door, she proceeded to rip open the envelope to see what Troy had sent her. *Ash...I wanted to tell you that today was very special for me and that nothing has ever happened in my massage room like it did today. I will not apologize for my behavior because I think we both enjoyed it too much for that. I know something was really bothering you today and I want to give you my cell number in case you ever need to reach me. You can call me day or night no matter what. And please feel free to call me anytime if you decide you need another special massage; for you I would make a house call. Troy*

Just when she thought her body had settled down, he sent her a note to get it purring again.

Wow, this had her thinking in a whole new way about Troy. Was he her knight in shining armor? Had she ignored something that had been right in front of her for a long time? This was something she had to mull over in the privacy of her big lonely bed as she remembered what he had said and done. She had never gone for the silent types before, but Troy had her thinking in a whole new direction.

Ashley looked up and noticed Dixie standing at the big bay window, giving her a very strange look. Ashley smiled and waved and eased out of the parking spot. Great, she could see a call to her mother in that look. Hopefully it would be before their little talk tonight, otherwise her mother would have a hard time not telling her sister-in-law all the scary details, and the last thing Ashley needed was for the salon to have those facts.

CHAPTER TEN

Ashley turned onto her mom and dad's street a little before five. She could see that her dad's car was in the driveway behind her mom's, and Michael's was blocking their dad's. Shannon's and Casey's were parked out front on the street. So much for the tragic victim getting any special treatment. She went to the end of the block, flipped a U-turn and parked across the street. How could such a quiet, peaceful neighborhood cause so much anxiety in her? Her heart rate had accelerated just seeing all the vehicles parked in front of her parents' house. She knew that this was going to be one of the hardest things she had ever had to do. She could just imagine the look of concern that would become a permanent fixture on her mother's beautiful face. She hated to be the cause of so much worry.

Harold and Michael were waiting out front for her, leaning against the porch railings, and Shannon was standing looking out the door. Poor Casey was stuck in the house with her mom, which had to be weird since neither of them knew what the hell was going on. Ashley could see that her dad and Michael were tense and still worried, probably pissed at her, now that they had heard from Shannon that she had not gone home and they had no idea where she was. So much for following their plan to try and stay safe. She was so rattled by everything that in her mind she *knew* that by going to Dixie's she was safe, but she was sure they wouldn't see it that way. She had been cautious and that was the most she could do at this point. She wasn't used to having to think about her actions or how what she might do would risk her life.

She had no idea how they were going to lay this out for everyone. Laura would freak out and insist she move in with her and her dad. She would want her to quit the police force and get a job making doughnuts at the bakery, something safe and away from all the crazy people in the world. She would go through Ashley's closet and throw away everything that was not made out of jersey or thick wool. She would confiscate all her curling irons, makeup, sexy underwear, and do anything else she thought would keep her safe. Ashley's mom had always tried to give her daughters the freedom to live their lives as they wanted, but no one had ever before seriously threatened one of them to the point that her life might be endangered.

She would make Shannon quit school and move home, so she could keep them both safe. She would have her get a job at the bakery also.

Casey would be Casey. She would want to join the force so she could help find the guy and kick some royal ass, all five feet of her. She would volunteer for stake-out duty and she would make Dan take a turn watching out for Ashley too. She would insist on driving her everywhere. She would help install every kind of alarm system to be found in Ashley's house and car. She would make sure there was some kind of weapon within easy reach, no matter where Ashley was.

Shannon would cry. Then get pissed and rant and rave. Then she would get scared. Then she would sit by and let Michael and their dad take over.

Ashley's cell phone rang, and caller ID showed that it was Derek. Great, her coochie was still gently purring from another guy and he has to call.

"Hi, good looking."

"Hey, Ash. How was your day?"

"Well, let's just say it started out fantastic and went to hell in a hurry."

"That's not good. What happened to turn it around?"

Michael was glaring at her from his side of the street, and he pushed off the porch and started her way. Motioning for him to give her a sec, she told Derek, "It's a long story and my parents are waiting for me." Michael frowned at her but turned around and went back to talking to Harold.

"Are you at their house?"

"Yep, the whole family is gathered for a meeting."

"Sounds scary. Hopefully I'm not the subject."

"Ha-ha, not this time, stud, but if Michael gets wind that you stayed over, you may be the topic at the next one."

"Protective big brother syndrome?"

"You have no idea. He still thinks of me as if I was sixteen."

"Can't say I blame him. If I had a sister who was as hot as you are, I would be on brotherly patrol full time."

"Saying stuff like that will get you far."

"Like how far?"

"Listen, I would love to sit here and flirt with you, but they are seriously waiting on me. I'll try and call you later."

"I have to work tonight, so maybe I can catch up with you later on."

"Let's see how I make it through this, okay?"

"You could always leave the door unlocked and I could sneak in after my shift is over and do a little cuddling."

Laughing, she answered, "No unlocked doors for this girl, and what makes you think you deserve some cuddling?"

"Wow! Roses, muffins and notes aren't enough, huh? You drive a hard bargain, Wright. What does it take? A steak dinner, maybe a grocery basket full of junk food?"

"No, the muffins were enough for at least a hug."

"Damn, woman, what do I have to do for a kiss?"

"I can't tell you that. That's something you'll have to discover on your own."

After hanging up with Derek, she dragged herself out of the car and started crossing over to where Michael was. She could tell by the sour look on his face, the night was going to be a real ball of fun. She was dragging her feet, she knew, but so what?

After the afternoon on Troy's massage table, the whole thing seemed like some bad dream she'd had last night. Maybe they were blowing this way out of proportion. Maybe this was some gang-related initiation and she was just in the wrong place at the wrong time. Because this kind of thing only happened in Clint Eastwood movies.

Ashley would be really glad when the labs came back tomorrow and showed the hair was from a golden retriever. Then they could all relax, enjoy the practical joke someone played on them, and go back to living their normal boring lives.

She glanced at the house and noticed Shannon had come out and was talking to Mrs. Steffen. She had a plate of cookies in her hand, and Ashley could tell Shannon was trying to gently get rid of her so that she could get back to the house and not miss a thing. But Mrs. Steffen had other ideas. Once she got you cornered, it was hard to get away. Usually it was not a big deal, she was such a sweet old lady, and her visits were enjoyable. Ashley could tell that Shannon was trying to be nice but wanted to wrap things up fast. She would look at Ashley, then glance at their dad, look back at Mrs. Steffen, nod and smile, and start the circle again.

Ashley had been watching Shannon and not paying any attention to her surroundings. She was just slowly crossing the street, dreading the upcoming conversation. If she thought she could get away with it, she would seriously turn around and just let her dad and Michael fill everyone in. She actually paused in the middle of the street and looked back over her shoulder, wondering if she could make it back to her car before Michael could reach her.

It was becoming more and more appealing. She glanced back to where Michael and Harold stood by the cars, and back to her car. Michael must have read her mind because he yelled out, "Don't you even think about it, sis, or I'll just bring them all with me and we will track you down, and then I'll leave them all with you while I go get drunk."

Ashley flipped him the bird and received her dad's scowl for the effort. She didn't care; it was worth it to see the look on Michael's face. At first there was a look of shock. None of them had ever done anything like that in front of one of their parents before. They knew better. They would have been carrying around that particular finger in a splint if they had. Then his face turned into a glare. That man could give out the scariest looks. He might be one of the handsomest men she knew, but when he leveled those eyebrows over those intense eyes of his, they could make the hardest criminals quake in their boots.

He took a step towards her and that's when she heard her dad scream, and all of a sudden she saw Michael start running toward her, yelling for her to run. She looked around in alarm and couldn't figure out why flipping her grouchy-ass brother the finger would cause so much excitement. Geez, were they both going to spank her for it? Shannon was staring down the street and that's when Ashley looked over and saw a beat-up, rusted-out piece of shit barreling towards her as she crossed the street. She was frozen in place, watching him get closer, everything happening in slow motion.

She could see every detail of the approaching car. It was an old Chevy Impala. There were no license plates on the front, and the grill was broken out. The windshield was cracked all the way across the front and it had a huge dent in the left front quarter panel. As it got closer and closer she could tell it used to be some shade of blue, but there wasn't much of the original color left. It seemed like hours passed as she took all this in, when in actuality it was a mere few seconds.

She stood there taking in all those details; her mind was telling her feet to move, but it was like she was watching from across the street in a second body, because the one standing in the middle of the street was not listening.

Michael dove for her, knocking her off her feet, just as the car flew by.

Ashley lay on the ground and as the car passed, she looked right into the driver's eyes. He was wearing a ski mask, but his eyes bored right into hers.

He flew around the corner and was gone.

Michael and Ashley lay in a tangle of arms and legs as everyone else came running toward them.

Michael had landed on top of her and knocked the wind out of her, and she could not catch her breath. She felt like her lungs were going to explode. She must have hit her head on the pavement, because she was seeing her fair share of stars. Everyone was hovering over them, but Ashley couldn't seem to focus. She knew they were all talking, but all she could hear was a loud roar in her ears.

Slowly the air started to get to her crushed lungs and the voices were starting to penetrate her fog. She turned to look at Michael and she noticed he was clutching his arm at an odd angle. She tried to get up to help, and that's when everything went black.

CHAPTER ELEVEN

"She looks like shit."

"Michael!"

"Well, she does."

"I don't care; you don't talk about your unconscious sister like that."

"Dad, do you think she's going to wake up?"

"Shannon, the doctors said she should wake up any time."

"Harold, when are you going to tell us what's going on and why you insisted we all get together before this tragic accident happened?"

"This was no accident," Ashley heard Michael mutter.

"Harold, what does he mean, this was no accident?"

Ashley could hear the voices around her, but as hard as she tried she could not force her eyes open. *What the hell did Michael mean, I looked like shit? And where am I? And why is everyone talking about me like I wasn't in the room?*

"I'm going to kill that son of a bitch!"

Who was Michael going to kill now? Why is everything so fuzzy? She felt like she was floating above her body, looking down, but not able to see anything. If she asked, would they turn the lights on? Why was everyone standing around in the dark, anyway?

"Did you get a good look at the guy?"

"Nope, I was trying not to pass out from the pain."

"We called in the license plate, it was a stolen plate."

"I didn't see a plate on the front, and who would steal a plate and put it on a piece of shit car like that?"

"Michael, please."

"Sorry, Mom."

Ashley heard other voices, but she could not identify them, they were too far away. Maybe Casey and someone else; his voice sounded familiar but she could not place it. She tried again to open her eyes, but to no avail. *What the hell is going on?* The voices grew fainter and then everything was quiet again.

"Why don't you all go get something to eat? I'll sit here with her."

This from the strange voice.

"Oh, I couldn't ask you to do that. What if she wakes up?"

Ashley could hear the worry in her mom's voice.

"I'll call Michael's cell phone, right away if something changes. You have all been here for hours. At least go have a cup of coffee, you all look like you're about to drop."

Ashley could hear chairs scraping, voices murmuring and the sound of a door opening, and then quiet again. She tried again to open her eyes.

"Ashley?"

Who the hell is that?

She felt someone take hold of her hand, and an electric shock ran up her arm and straight to her brain. Her eyes flew open and she was staring straight into the deepest blue eyes. She knew those eyes, but from where? She couldn't seem to focus on anything, just those gorgeous eyes, staring at her with concern.

She tried to talk, ask why he was there and what had happened. But nothing would come out. She tried to turn her head, and wham, it exploded in pain, and she instantly closed her eyes again to try and block the pain.

She heard him reach for his cell phone and listened as he placed a call to Michael. She could hear him fill Michael in on what had just happened, and then he shut his phone down.

He reached out and stroked the side of her head, being careful to avoid the huge bump on the right rear side of her skull.

"Do you know what happened?"

Without opening her eyes, she answered, "No."

"I was at the fire station when the 911 call came in, saying there was a pedestrian hit by a car at your parents' address. When we arrived we found that Michael had been bumped by the car that tried to run you down, breaking his arm in the process. Michael had pushed you out of harm's way, but you hit your head hard on the pavement when Michael landed on you. It's never easy answering calls when you know the victims, but since I met you at the back-yard fire I had been hoping to run into you again. This wasn't exactly the way I hoped to see you though."

It was her baby daddy, what was his name? She couldn't remember it.

She could hear the door open and steps as someone approached the bed, but she was still afraid to open her eyes and face the pain she knew waited for her.

"Who the hell are you?"

"Nick, and I can ask the same of you."

"Derek Laws. Is there a reason you are stroking my girl's hair?"

"Your girl?"

Derek seemed to think about this for a few seconds before answering, "Well, maybe not technically, but that doesn't give you the right to be here stroking her like she was *your* girl. Who are you, anyway?"

"You're kind of nosy, aren't you?"

"You're kind of evasive with your answers."

She lay there with her eyes still closed in amazement.

She could tell Derek had moved to the opposite side of the hospital bed from Nick. They were leaning over the bed, doing their little male territorial dance, and all she could do was listen. She knew she had to force her eyes open again, or there could be bloodshed if these two didn't back off.

She managed to open her eyes and was fascinated by the male testosterone flying above her bed. If her head weren't about to explode, she would be really enjoying this. Two absolutely gorgeous guys acting like jealous lovers fighting over their woman. Except neither one was a lover, and one of them had no right to be even acting like one. Not that she minded. The idea of these two fighting over her was damn exciting. Certain parts of her body were starting to do some crazy things without her even putting any effort into it. Did she have no shame? How could her heart start beating in double time by just listening to these two hunks bicker back and forth?

"Gentlemen, what the hell is going on in here?"

Ashley watched as their family doctor pushed Nick out of the way to get to her. Derek gave Nick a gloating look and a satisfied smirk. Nick glared back and moved to the foot of the bed, never taking his eyes from Derek. She closed her eyes again, chuckling, and all eyes flew to her face.

"So you have finally decided to rejoin us?"

"Umm, I guess so."

"Do you know these two?"

"I'm pleading the fifth, until I know what the hell happened and why they are standing over me like I'm some piece of meat."

They both looked at the doctor, a little sheepish.

"Gentlemen, give me a few minutes to examine my patient. Ashley, can you keep your eyes open while you talk to me?"

"Hell no! I tried that once and have no desire to do that again."

Derek and Nick both moved to the far side of the room, and she assumed Nick was making a call to her brother again. She bet in a few minutes her room would be invaded by a very concerned group of family and friends.

While the doctor did his exam, she tried to put the pieces together in her fuzzy brain.

She remembered being at her mom and dad's, talking to Derek, and then things became real blurry. She couldn't seem to remember why she was here lying in this hospital bed. Nick had mentioned Michael being hit by a car, but she was having a hard time focusing.

"Ashley, how do you feel?

"Like I've been run over by a Mack truck."

The room suddenly got very quiet. She slowly opened her eyes just a little and looked around very carefully, making sure she did not move her head. It still hurt to even move her eyes, let alone anything else. Derek was giving her a scowl, Nick looked like he wanted to kill somebody, and the doctor looked concerned.

"What did I say?"

"Do you remember anything at all, Ashley?"

"I remember being at Dad and Mom's, but things are a little fuzzy after that. Nick said Michael was hit by a car?" About that time the room erupted in total madness. Harold, Laura, Michael, Shannon, Casey and Dan all rushed in. Added with Derek, Nick and the doctor, the room was filled to overflowing.

Everyone started talking at once. Her mom and Shannon were crying. Harold was standing beside the bed holding her hand. Michael was talking to Nick, and Casey and Dan were standing off to the side by Derek.

"Okay, everyone out!" shouted the doctor.

Laura gave him a look that would have made a lesser man shake in his boots, her dad was scowling at him like he was ready to arrest him, and she thought Shannon was going to go psycho on him. Michael whispered something in Harold's ear, and he gave her a worried look, took his wife's and Shannon's hands, and led them and everyone else from the room.

That was way too simple. That's when she became worried. Her family did not give up that easily. Something must be terribly wrong for them to give up that effortlessly. She started to reach down and make sure she had all of her body parts, but just moving that much caused her head to explode in pain.

The doctor stilled her hands. "Everything is still intact, Ashley. How does your head feel?"

"It hurts like hell."

"Well I'm not surprised, with the size of the knot on your head. Let's take a look at your eyes. Follow my pen light."

Ashley did as he asked, fairly certain she was in one piece.

"Well, everything looks pretty good, Ashley. You're going to have one hell of a headache for a while."

"I think that's an understatement."

"I'm going to keep you overnight just to make sure everything is okay. I'll be back first thing in the morning. I need you to take it easy and get plenty of rest. No more circus side shows tonight. I'm going to let your dad and mom in for a few minutes, but everyone else is going to have to wait till you are home before they can see you. I want you to have complete rest tonight."

"You mean I can't have those two sexy guys back in here doing their mating dance?"

"No, you may not, young lady."

"Ah, come on doc, you sure know how to take the fun out of a lady's misery."

"I'm glad to see you still have your sense of humor. Now get some rest."

After the doctor left, she tried to put all the pieces together, but could not for the life of her remember the details of what had happened. She should have asked the doctor if that was normal, but she was too busy teasing him about the two males fighting over her.

Laura and Harold entered her room, coming to stand beside her bed. She had closed her eyes the minute the doctor left and had no desire to open them now.

"Hi, you two. Do you mind if I keep my eyes closed? It really hurts when I open them."

She heard her mom give a sharp intake of breath and could just imagine her dad putting his arm around her shoulders, giving her his silent comfort like he had for the past thirty-four years.

"Yes, dear, that's fine. How are you feeling?"

"My head hurts really bad, and I'm sensitive to light, and when I move my head I feel like I am going to puke, but I think after a little more rest I will be just fine."

"Is there anything I can get for you? Are you hungry? Would you like a drink of water?"

"Yes, that would be nice." Ashley slowly lifted her head a few inches off the bed as Laura fitted the straw into her mouth. The water felt so good, but the few seconds it took her to get that drink sent her head spinning like she had just gotten off the Tilt-O-Whirl at Elitch's. She lay back down, and she was sure she had broken out into a small sweat with just that little bit of movement. Oh holy hell, she was worse off than she had thought, but she could not let her parents realize that fact. She could tell they were worried enough without knowing that little bit of information.

"So Dad, how about a game of golf tomorrow morning when they release me from this prison?"

"Ashley Elizabeth, don't you even joke about something like that. You'll be coming straight to our house. I've already called work and told them I would be taking some personal time."

"Now Mom, I'll be fine at my house, there is no need for you to do that."

"Listen to your mother, Ashley."

Ashley knew she was doomed when her dad spoke in that no-nonsense tone of voice. She really wasn't up to arguing with them when, if the truth was told, she would probably need the help if just lifting her head caused her to be totally wiped out. But she didn't want them to worry about her.

"Okay, fine. Whatever you two think is best. Dad, can you explain what happened? I still don't remember what happened to put me here. My mind is so fuzzy, I feel like I have been on a three-day drunk."

"Young lady, you better not even know what that would feel like." This coming from her saintly mother who, thank God, had lived hundreds of miles away from Ashley's college life.

"Just kidding, Mom. I was only going by what Shannon told me."

"I'm sure your sister has never behaved in that manner..."

"Laura, she's only teasing you."

"Oh."

Ashley's head was starting to pound harder. She just wanted to sleep for a while, or for a really long time if she admitted it.

"Are you ready to get some sleep, honey?"

"Yeah, I think I am."

"Okay, the doctor told us we could only stay a few minutes anyway. I love you, sweetie. You have them call if you need anything at all. They won't let me stay here, I already asked. I've worked here for over twenty years and do you think that matters?"

"I will, Mom, I promise. Give everyone a hug for me and tell them I'm fine."

"Bye, honey, you take care."

"I will, Dad, no need to worry. I'll be up before you know it, causing more havoc at the station than you can even imagine."

She heard him mutter very faintly under his breath, "That's what I'm afraid of."

They both reached down and gave her gentle kisses on her forehead, and made their way out of the room. Ashley couldn't help but give a sigh of relief and she wasn't even sure why. She just knew that something heavy was going on, but for the life of her, she couldn't remember what it was.

Her eyes flew open. "Damn! Dad got away without answering my question." She instantly regretted her action and let out a huge groan filled with pain.

About that time a nurse came in and heard her agony. "It looks like I got here at just the right time. Here is some pain medicine and a sleeping pill the doctor ordered for you." She moved to her I.V. and injected two syringes into it. The nurse fiddled around with the I.V., took her blood pressure, checked her other stats, and then thankfully turned off the light and left. Ashley lay there enjoying the quiet, letting her body absorb the medication, praying that it was strong stuff and would work fast.

CHAPTER TWELVE

Ashley came slowly awake, lying still and listening for any sounds, trying to gather what time of day or night it was. Those must have been some really good happy drugs, because she thought she had fallen asleep in a matter of seconds. She slowly opened her eyes to see how things felt after some good rest. All she could see was the faint light coming from the crack in the bathroom door someone had left partially open; otherwise the room was in shadow. Her head was still throbbing, but not nearly as intensely as it had earlier.

She was starving. She had no idea what time it was, but she was sure she had missed several meal times. She looked down at her watch, but it was not on her wrist. Not that she could have seen it in the dark anyway. She swore she could smell coffee and cinnamon. She needed to go to the bathroom too, but was afraid to try and sit up by herself. Where the hell was the nurse who brought her all those yummy drugs?

Suddenly, she was aware of someone breathing in the room. She knew immediate fear, not really sure why, but it was there just the same. She was in a private room so she knew no one was in a bed beside her; someone who wasn't supposed to be here, according to the doctor, was.

Ashley moved her hand slowly along the bed, trying to find the call button without drawing any attention to herself. Whoever was in her room must be sleeping, by the sound of the even breathing. Her mind raced with possibilities as she slowly searched for the stupid button, which was probably lying clear over on the nightstand where it did absolutely no good to anyone, especially her; she was going to pass out from fear or the need to go to the bathroom, she wasn't sure which. Her hand bumped the hospital tray that was partially over her bed, and whatever was on it rolled off the tray and landed on the floor, sounding like a bomb went off. Well, maybe not a bomb, but to her over-sensitive ears it was.

She heard a rustle on the side of the bed where the boogeyman was sitting. Oh God, she woke it up. She could make out the shadow of a man stirring in the chair as he stretched out. Whoever it was, he was tall, so that ruled out her dad, and it couldn't be Michael because he snored like a freight train and would have kept the whole hospital up, so it had to be someone else.

She sensed he was fully awake now and waiting to see if she was awake or if something else had woken him up. She lay perfectly still, not moving or breathing, hoping whoever it was would just go away. She needed to breathe, but she had held her breath for so long she knew it would be a huge gasp for air. Her cop brain went into overload looking for a way to defend herself. She could just make out the tray, and the only things on it were the water pitcher and a plastic cup with a straw in it. So her choices were drowning him with the few inches of water in the pitcher or poking his Cyclops eye out with the straw. She went with the Cyclops eye plan. At the same time, she took a huge breath and made a grab for the straw. "Get the hell out of my room or you'll be sorry."

"Or what, you're going to hit me with that straw?"

"Derek?"

She heard a soft chuckle and watched as the boogeyman ambled out of the chair and made his way to the side of the bed. She still could not see any details, but could tell he was reaching up toward her head. She raised her hand with the mighty straw in it and made a jab at his head.

"Ouch, dammit, what are you trying to do, put my eye out with that thing?" The overhead nightlight suddenly came on and she got a glimpse of Derek, looking very grouchy, holding his hand up to his left eye.

Her heart was pounding about a thousand beats a minute and she didn't think that was exactly healthy. It was a good thing she wasn't hooked up to a heart monitor, or she was sure they would have been calling a code blue into her room.

She reached up and smacked him really hard on the hand that was covering his watering left eye. "What the hell are you doing here? It's not good enough that someone tried to kill me today, you thought you should come in here and scare the shit out of me?"

They both looked at each other in complete shock, on her part because she suddenly remembered exactly why she was lying here in this bed; his she wasn't so sure of.

"Someone tried to kill you?" The look on his face was very intense. Ashley suddenly realized that her dad and Michael had kept her little drama a secret, at least from all the outsiders who had been here earlier.

She decided Derek wasn't in the right frame of mind to hear anything about her masked Jeff Gordon. Nervously she sputtered, "Well, maybe I over-exaggerated a little."

"Ash, don't lie to me. What happened to you yesterday? Does this have something to do with the family meeting you were going to?"

She really didn't want to get into this; her head was starting to hurt again now that her body's adrenaline was getting back to normal. "Derek, could you please help me up so I could use the bathroom?"

He stared at her like he was going to refuse her, but he must have seen the urgency in her eyes, because very gently he took hold of her arm, helping her sit up on the side of the bed. Her head felt like it was spinning right off her shoulders and she felt like she was going to throw up. *Oh please don't let me get sick in front of this very sexy man.* Even if she still had no idea why he was in her room in the middle of the night.

"Are you sure I don't need to go get the nurse? You're looking a little green around the gills."

"Thanks for the observation. That really helps." Things slowly started to feel better, or the urge to use the bathroom just overcame all the other factors. "No, I'll be fine, thank you."

With his help she slid her feet to the floor and stood for a few minutes with his warm solid arms wrapped around her, giving her the comfort she had seen her dad give her mom earlier. Ashley was suddenly hit with a wave of sadness. She wanted someone in her life she could always count on to be there to give her that silent show of comfort. She could feel her eyes start to burn and knew that one way or another, she was going to make a fool of herself in front of this man. Crying or making a puddle on the floor were not things she really wanted to do. She moved out from underneath the comfort of his arm and made a quick swipe of her eyes, hoping he didn't notice the sudden tears that had come. But somehow she didn't think this man missed much with those too-intense hazel eyes of his.

With as much dignity as she could muster under the circumstances, she grabbed the I.V. pole, made her way to the bathroom before he could even offer to help her. She closed the door and plopped down on the toilet, barely making it there before a tidal wave broke loose. Jesus, you would have thought she had not gone in days, but the reality was she really had no idea how long it had been. She felt like her whole world was crashing down around her.

The severity of the situation she was in must have suddenly hit her, because she could not stop the tears from coming. Apparently it must be getting close to her time of the month if such a thing as almost peeing on the floor, in front of one of the nicest guys she had been around in years, could bother her. She took care of finishing up with her bathroom duties, but she couldn't find the energy to get up off the toilet. The rush of adrenaline, the walk to the bathroom and then the crying jag must have used all the energy she had left. How humiliating to be stuck on a hospital toilet, wishing for anyone to be on the other side of the door but Derek. Well, not Nick or Troy or even Officer Phillip Kelly, either. Where the hell was her sister or Casey when she needed them the most?

"Ashley, are you all right?'

Putting her head in her hands, she mumbled, "Hell no! I'm stuck on this goddamn toilet, wishing when I had flushed it the stupid thing had taken me with it."

Again she heard a soft chuckle and realized he had heard her. Could this night get any worse?

"Are you decent? I'm opening the door."

"If by decent you mean sitting on a toilet in an ugly hospital gown with a huge lump on my head and messy hair and makeup and no strength to get my sorry ass up off the toilet, then yeah, I'm decent."

Ashley reached up quickly and switched off the light just as he opened the door and peeked in at her.

Chuckling he said, "Do you think shutting off the light is going to help?"

"Well, it sure as hell can't hurt."

He bent over and picked her right up off the toilet in those muscle-bound arms of his. She barely had time to grab the I.V. pole before he was carrying her back to her bed. She let out a gasp of surprise, because she had expected him to help her up like he had before. "What are you doing?" She was frantically trying to reach back and pull down her hospital gown because she could feel the cold draft on her ass as he walked towards the bed.

"Ash, stop it before I drop you."

"But, my gown..."

"It's a little late to worry about that."

"What's that supposed to mean?"

He gently laid her on the bed, grabbed the blankets and pulled them up over her, tucked her in all nice and comfy; reached behind the bed and plugged the I.V. back into the wall. He had this little half-smile on his face as he was doing all this.

"Derek...?"

"I don't know why you're suddenly so modest."

"Modest? What do you expect? It's not like I want my ass hanging out so everyone can see it."

"No one else is here but me."

"Exactly my point."

"But I've already seen your cute little ass with the two little dimples."

Her mouth fell open and her mind raced. When the hell had he seen her ass? When he put her to bed yesterday? Was it yesterday? Hell, she didn't know. Did he take a quick peek at her privates? Or was he just referring to it in general, like through her clothes? But then how did he know that she had dimples?

Derek watched as she struggled with his comment. He loved to rile her up and then watch the emotions fly across her face.

"Ashley, you can stop fretting over when I saw your cute rear end. I never molested you when you fell asleep, either tonight or last night. You're the one who proudly showed it to me."

"I did not."

"Yes you did, and I have to say I was damn glad you did. I haven't seen anything so hot since..."

212

"Derek, stop it. I did not show you my ass."

That grin of his was driving her nuts.

"You know if you weren't so stubborn and had let me help you to the bathroom, we wouldn't be having this conversation."

"What does that have to do with it?" But as she said that it dawned on her what he was talking about. She had been so worried about him seeing her cry that she hadn't even realized that her gown was open in the back, and he had enjoyed the view of her walking to the bathroom in all her glory.

"Oh hell…"

"I've always enjoyed a strong-willed, stubborn woman and today just proved that theory."

"You're such an ass. You enjoy humiliating me, don't you?"

He suddenly got a serious look on his face and she could tell the joking was over. He sat down on the side of the bed, which had her scrambling to move over to make room for him or he would have sat on her. He reached out a hand and gently cupped her face, and just stared into her eyes.

He didn't say anything at all, just sat there. At first she was enthralled, and then she just became nervous. What did he mean by looking at her like that? Did he not see that she was a fragile wreck and was still capable of bursting into tears at any moment?

Ashley didn't have to worry long because he leaned in and gave her a heart-stopping kiss. It was filled with gentleness and caring. This didn't help her emotional state. Desire she could have handled right now, but caring was another story. This man had her going in circles; there was no way she could read him. He wasn't the normal, boasting macho guy she was used to being around; this guy kept his life behind a closed door. She still knew nothing about him, but he had wormed his way into her heart in the short span of a few days.

Suddenly uncertain, she pulled back and gave a nervous laugh. "How did you get in here, anyway? The doctor left strict instructions that I was to have no visitors till tomorrow."

"It is tomorrow."

"It's dark outside."

"It's still tomorrow."

"You're the most annoying man. You never answer my questions."

"Yes, I did."

Laughing despite herself, she said, "Okay, does the nurse know you're in here?"

"Yes."

"And did you have to bribe her or did you seduce her into letting you get in here?"

She realized she really didn't want to know the answer to that, but Derek just wiggled his eyebrows and smiled. Somehow she knew that he didn't do any seducing tonight. She was surprised how relieved she was to know that.

"So now that we have all the urgent items taken care of, how are you feeling?" He gently rubbed the goose egg on the side of her head.

"Better."

"Do you still have a headache?"

"Yes, a slight one."

"Do you need medication?"

"No."

"Are you being stubborn again?"

"Yes."

"Why?"

"To see how you like short answers."

He sat back with a look of wonder on his face and burst out laughing.

"Derek, stop it! You are going to get us in trouble."

"You're amazing."

"I am? Why?"

"You are. I never know where you're coming from. You're not like most predictable females."

"Well, for all other females I should take offense to that, but being the independent female that I am, thank you. Do I smell cinnamon?"

"Jesus, woman, you change subjects faster than I drive. What would you give me if I told you I had a big fat juicy cinnamon roll from Hill's Café?"

Ashley's mouth had an orgasm at just the mention of one of those famous cinnamon rolls. It took her brain a few seconds to catch what Derek had said.

"You'd play hardball with an invalid woman lying helpless in her hospital bed? Now that would be totally uncouth, even from a bad-ass like you!" She gave him her most pitiful face, sticking her lower lip out.

His eyes went to her lip and she instantly realized her mistake. He got this hot sexy look in his eyes and ran a finger along her lower lip. "Damn straight, woman. I want a kiss for a bite of that cinnamon roll."

"For one bite?"

"We'll negotiate after that."

"Why would I give up one of my mind-blowing kisses when I can just hit the call button and get food?"

Looking way too confident, he answered, "Go ahead, you can get some runny hospital oatmeal and I'll sit beside you and eat the cinnamon roll." He leaned over to the chair, grabbed a bag and proceeded to pull out two cinnamon rolls and two cups of coffee. He picked up the call button. "Here, I'll do it for you."

Reacting faster than either of them expected, Ashley yanked the call button out of his hand. "No, that's okay. I think I'll take you up on your offer. I would hate to disturb the nurse and I'm sure there is no one in the kitchen yet."

"Yeah, okay, you go with that story. You know we both know that it's not about the cinnamon roll. You just want to kiss me."

The truth was he was half right. Her body could still remember the passion they had experienced in her hallway the other night. But at that exact moment her stomach gave a huge growl, giving him the proof that she was really hungry.

He inched his way up so he was only inches from her face, looking at her lips the whole way. Just watching him caused her heart rate to accelerate, and they hadn't even kissed yet. His eyes flicked up to look into hers and he gave her a little half-smile, like he knew exactly what she had just thought.

She grabbed the back of his head and pulled it down, and she gave him a kiss that he would not be forgetting anytime soon. She put a little magic into the kiss. He sat in a state of shock for a few seconds before he became the dominating one and pushed her back into her pillow, deepening the kiss. His left hand came to rest at the base of her throat, where she knew he could feel her heartbeat racing. He trailed his hand down over the top of her hospital gown, coming to rest on her over-sensitive left tit. She gave out a throaty little groan and arched her back so that his hand was pressed firmly over her breast. He brushed his thumb over her nipple in slow circles, causing both of them to start breathing a lot harder. Her hands were making their way under his shirt, melting over his rock-hard solid muscles. My, this man was built. She could feel his six-pack as she ran her hands up and down his chest.

Again her stomach let out a protest, causing them both to pull apart and smile.

He looked at her with amazement.

"For that much action, I get the whole cinnamon roll and half of yours, right?"

"Deal!" He opened the cinnamon roll container, drew out a fork and knife from the sack, then cut the cinnamon roll into bite-size pieces. As she reached for the fork he brushed her hand away, stabbed a piece and brought it to her mouth. "I wouldn't want a helpless woman in her hospital bed to overdo herself, now would I?"

He took the piece of cinnamon roll and gently swept it along her lower lip, spreading the sticky icing along her lip before he placed it in her mouth. As she chewed he watched her lips, and just as she started to lick the icing from her lips he beat her to the task. His tongue reached out and licked off the icing, taking a little more time than was necessary.

Eating cinnamon rolls took on a whole new meaning. He followed the same pattern for each bite he gave her, the icing covering a little more of her lips each time, and him taking a little more time with each bite to clean it off. Before they even realized it he had fed her both of the cinnamon rolls. They looked at each other with disappointment on their faces, before they started chuckling.

"Looks like you ate my half, so you have a whole lot of making up to do. The way I see it, your punishment should be severe."

"The way I see it, you're the one who should be punished. You were in control of food rations, and due to your lack of supervision and total disregard of the contract agreement, your supply was depleted. I will ponder the circumstances and will decide on your punishment in the next few days."

"Oh really! I'll await your decision with great anticipation. But you must take in the facts when making your decision. One, I brought the cinnamon rolls to feed your starving self. Two, I cut them up into bite-size pieces so you would not choke. And three, I was your human napkin, making sure that you were cleaned up after each bite."

"True, but I must also take into account the fact that I still do not know why you're here, and how you got in here to begin with."

"Okay, that's only fair, since it affects the outcome of my punishment. I'm here because I was concerned about you. We were pushed out of here last night so fast I never even got a chance to talk to you, and your family was being pretty tight lipped about what had happened. Plus the Neanderthal was being way too familiar with you. Who is he, anyway?"

"Nick Owens. He's a firefighter and a friend of my brother's."

"And a friend of yours?" he asked with concern in his voice.

"I met him the night my grandma blew up our storage shed. He was one of the firefighters who answered our 911 call. Plus, he answered the 911 call last night."

He gave her a skeptical look. "I got in here because I promised the nurse I wouldn't disturb you, I just wanted to make sure you were okay. It took a little extra persuading before she agreed, since they have a cop posted outside your door."

"*They have a cop outside?*"

"I thought you knew that."

She shoved him off the bed, climbed out and opened the door. There, sitting in a chair sound asleep, was Thomas Shaffer. She felt like kicking his chair and telling him to go home, but she knew he was only doing what the captain told him to do. Shutting the door and turning around, she found Derek standing beside the bed with a huge-ass grin on his face.

"Babe, I love when you get all riled up and go strutting around in that hospital gown."

Mortified, she reached around and closed her gown with one hand while she made it back to her bed. Her legs were shaking and her head started spinning and throbbing again. She turned so she faced him and backed into the bed, making sure when she got in that the gown stayed closed. Her rash actions made her queasy again, and she was afraid that the delicious cinnamon rolls were going to come right back up.

"Babe, as much as I like to watch your cute little ass sashaying around the room, you are going to have to take it easy. You are as pale as a ghost and that's even with the blush you got going."

"I think you're right. I just forget that I am as weak as a kitten still."

"So are you saying that I could take advantage of you in your weakened state?"

"Who are you kidding? I think you already did that when you fed me my breakfast. What time is it, anyway?"

Looking at his watch he replied, "It's a little after five a.m."

"Good God, why am I awake? When did you get here?"

"When I got done with my shift at the bar, I stopped by Hill's and then headed over here."

"You must be exhausted."

"I can sleep later. I wanted to see you. Can you tell me what happened to you now?"

Ashley tried to decide what to do. She didn't really even know this guy, and although they had decided not to tell anyone at the precinct, she assumed that since Thomas was sitting in the hall it probably wasn't a secret anymore. So she filled Derek in on the notes, the rose, the hair, and then the guy in the ski mask who had tried to run her over.

As she told her story, his expression turned from one of mild interest into one that looked like a dark storm cloud.

"You mean to tell me you have a psycho following you and you never said anything?"

"This has all happened within the last few days, and I had no idea it was anything serious. The hair and the attempt to run me over happened in a matter of hours. Besides, why would I run and tell you something like that anyway? We are waiting for forensics to finish up on testing to see if the DNA matches that of the murdered waitress."

"You think there's a connection?"

"The captain thinks so. He said since the murder victim and I could be identical twins, that it was more than likely."

Derek's face was turning serious, and that had Ashley wondering, why so much concern?

"Did you get a look at the person who tried to run you over?"

"No, he was wearing a stocking mask that covered his whole face. I thought that was a little strange. At the speed he was going there wasn't much chance we would have been able to identify him."

"Maybe you know him and he was afraid you would recognize him."

"I never thought of that. What if it's someone I see all the time? I could be standing right beside him having a conversation, and the whole time he's thinking about how he's going to kill me." That thought sent her into a near panic. She had really not taken it seriously up until now.

"Ash, I want you to come stay with me when they release you."

"Are you kidding me? I don't think that's necessary. Plus my mom already laid dibs to that right. She probably stayed up all night making the house into some fortress. Whose idea do you think it was to put the guard at the door? My mom may be a little tiny thing, but you threaten her kids and she becomes a little dynamo. If Dad and Michael have filled her in on the rest of what's going on she will really be in protective mode."

"That may be, but I really think you should stay with me."

"Not going to happen, sorry. Between Dad, Michael, Shannon and Mom I'll always have someone with me, you can count on it. And that's not counting all the people at the precinct and all my friends who will be volunteering to help out."

"I thought we just covered that, you should *not* trust anyone right now but your family and those really close friends."

"So where does that leave you?"

"What the hell does that mean?"

"You just said it yourself, trust no one."

"Well that doesn't mean me, dammit."

"Don't get huffy with me; you're the one who brought this up."

"I'm not huffy..."

They glared at each other for several seconds. Ashley wasn't really sure why this guy was so emotional about this. They had only known each other for a few weeks, so it wasn't like they were a couple or anything. Something just didn't add up. She'd admit they had a great sexual attraction but that didn't explain the overprotective attitude. The cop in her wondered what his ulterior motive was.

The door swung open and this cute little nurse came bustling into the room. Not once did she look at Ashley, but had her eyes on Derek the whole time.

"Well, hello there, I had no idea you were still in here." She came around to the opposite side of the bed from where Derek was sitting. She fidgeted with Ashley's chart, not really even looking at it.

Derek only gave her a brief glance and then focused back on glaring at Ashley. Seeing that she was not going to get any attention from Derek, the nurse turned her attention on her.

"How are you feeling this morning?"

"Much better, thank you," Ashley answered, never taking her eyes off Derek.

The nurse proceeded to take her vitals and then fussed with her bed sheets. She gave Ashley her morning medication and made sure she took it. Ashley didn't think she was really interested in making sure she was comfortable, but instead hoping Derek would turn his sexy hazel eyes on her again. Giving up any hope of that, she finally turned and left the room.

Derek was still giving Ashley a death look. She was really too tired to worry about it right now. The rollercoaster of emotions since he had entered her room was taking a toll on her; either that or the medicine was taking the edge off.

A nurse's aide brought in her breakfast tray and put it onto her hospital stand, gave Derek a sly look and left the room. Ashley looked at Derek in amazement. Did every woman from age 15 to 80 look at him like that? Of course they did, who was *she* kidding; she looked at him like that.

Ashley lifted the lid off the covered dish and looked at a bowl of runny oatmeal, and then up into Derek's twinkling eyes. They both burst out laughing and then became sober, remembering the cinnamon roll he had fed her just a short time ago and the passion that had gone along with it. He reached up and stroked her hair, with his hand coming to rest on the side of her face. It felt so comforting, and again made the ache in the pit of her stomach grow into that tight ball she didn't want to think about.

Derek must have realized the fight had gone out of her, because he gathered her up into his arms, laying her head on his shoulder, and then just held her. She was going to start crying again. She gently pushed away from his comforting shoulder and gave him a smile of gratitude. She did not want to argue with him, she just wanted to feel safe again.

"Do you want me to feed you your oatmeal?" He gave the gray slimy goo a repulsed look and she had to smile. If the stuff didn't make her want to puke, she would make him, just to be mean.

"No, but the hot tea would be great since we never got the chance to drink the coffee you brought."

He got the tea ready for her and when he moved the bowl away, he found a folded piece of paper stuck under the edge of the dish. Giving it a suspicious look, his eyes then met hers.

"What is it?"

"I'm not sure." He took the napkin, picked it up by the corners and shook it out.

Ashley watched him in confusion, wondering about the whole napkin thing. A cop would know to do that, but would a bartender? The feeling that this man was not who he claimed to be grew even stronger.

He was reading the note and she could see the anger starting to radiate from his body. "What does it say?"

"Just some hogwash. I'll just get the officer out in the hall and have him take care of it."

"Derek! *Let me see it!*"

"I don't want to upset you; you've been through enough in the last twenty-four hours."

"Upset would be if you don't show me that note right this minute. This is my life and this affects me. Now give me the damn note."

She could tell he was seriously thinking about refusing, and then looked into her eyes and must have decided she was right, because he turned the note and held it in front of her face.

She read what was scrawled across the note in bright red marker and felt the color drain from her face.

You are so lucky your brother was there when I tried to run you over. It really pissed me off. He should mind his own business. Next time I'll be more careful. Did you enjoy your present yesterday? I wanted to share her death with you. Today's gift should bring you more joy. It's your fault you know...

Ashley asked, "What present is he talking about, 'today'?"

Derek had gone to get Thomas in the hall.

Ashley started moving stuff around on the tray, looking to see if she could find what he was referring to. She had just picked up the bowl of oatmeal when Derek and Thomas walked into the room. She dropped the bowl and it fell to the floor and broke, oatmeal flying everywhere.

Derek and Thomas rushed to the bed, each looking down onto the tray where she was still staring.

CHAPTER THIRTEEN

Curled up in a neat circle was a length of strawberry blonde hair. Although it was a bit darker than either Ashley's or the hunk that had been left on her windshield, it was still pretty close to her hair color. Revulsion filled her body, and she leaned over the bed and vomited all over Thomas and Derek's shoes.

Dancing out of the way, Thomas growled at her, "Geez, Wright, you could have warned us."

Ashley leaned over the bed, emptying her stomach of the last of what was once a great cinnamon roll, the contents mixing with the already spilled oatmeal. Man, if she wasn't sick before, the sight of that mess would have made her sick all over again.

Derek didn't say a word, just stepped out into the hall and signaled to the nurse at the desk. She watched him with a growing sense of doom. She felt like she was outside her body watching all of this happen to someone else again. She could hear Shaffer swearing as he grabbed a towel from the bathroom and wiped off his shoes, but it seemed like his voice was coming from far away. She was vaguely aware of a maintenance guy coming in with a mop and bucket and cleaning up the huge mess she had made, and of Derek standing in the corner talking on his cell phone. Now, who could he be calling at this hour? More than likely the station, but for some silly reason she thought maybe it was someone else. He would sneak looks at her every once in a while with a concerned expression on his face.

Ashley looked away from Derek and turned her stare to the coil of hair on her breakfast tray. This couldn't be happening to her. Why someone would involve her in his murders was something her very fuzzy brain could not grasp. Some psycho was killing women who looked like her and then sending his trophies to Ashley. She was a nice girl, really she was. She didn't deserve this. She minded her own business, didn't steal other women's men, didn't have a gambling debt that she owed to the mob, and didn't steal from the department stores. Her very short list of exes all left on good terms. Or at least she thought they did. She ran through the list, trying to remember if one of them was a secret basket case.

She had that fling with Jimmy in high school, but you couldn't even count that. She had not seen him since they graduated, and she heard he was a car salesman in California somewhere. Then there was Brandon. Even today after all those years her heart would do a little flip-flop when she thought of him. She was embarrassed at how she had handled that situation. She had acted like she was 15 when she had heard that other woman's voice on his phone. She had treated him badly when he tried calling all those times, and maybe he carried a grudge, but more than likely he was probably relieved to get rid of her and her childish behavior. She remembered her grandma telling her a few years after that experience that Brandon had graduated and gone on to get his master's. She had seen him every summer for a few years when he came home to visit, and said he always asked about her. That didn't sound like someone who held a grudge and wanted to kill her.

Ashley had dated a few guys throughout college but none longer than a few weeks, and all were the typical college guy trying to get into a girl's pants. Once they found out she wasn't an easy lay, they usually moved on to their next victim without any fuss. She'd dated off and on again leading up to joining the academy, but nothing serious. Not one name popped into her head as someone who would be doing this. Maybe she was looking at this all wrong, maybe it wasn't someone she dated, but someone else. Oh shit, how was she supposed to figure out who she pissed off enough to start killing women who looked like her? She closed her eyes to get the sight of that lock of hair out of her mind, but it didn't work. Her hands were shaking and she still felt like she was going to get sick again. Shaffer better watch his shoes; there was no guarantee she was done making a mess on the floor. She guessed she'd paid him back for his little stunt in the morgue restroom without even trying.

Ashley could sense that Derek was done with his call and had come back to the side of her bed. He took her hand, but she still didn't open her eyes. She just wanted it all to go away. She wanted to go back to being a piss-ant rookie with nothing to worry about except what Malone was going to do to her today.

Her eyes flew open...MALONE! No, it couldn't be her. What was the connection? She hated her, but not enough to kill women. Plus, she was sure that the person in the car who tried to run her over was a man. The eyes that turned such hatred on her were definitely a man's. Plus, they said the first victim was raped, and she was pretty sure that ruled out Malone.

Michael walked into the room just then and made a beeline to her bed. He gave Derek a strange look and then turned his attention to her.

"Sis...?"

"Hey, big bro...how's your day so far? Mine is kind of sucking."

Whoa! She forgot how her brother couldn't take a joke, the big grouch; no one was leaving locks of hair on his breakfast tray.

"Are you okay?"

Ashley snapped, "No, you idiot. I'm not. I would appreciate it if someone would stop leaving locks of hair for me to find."

"I have forensics coming. Did anyone touch anything else?"

Derek filled him in on what had happened since they discovered the note. Again, listening to him talk to Michael gave Ashley a funny feeling this man wasn't who he claimed to be. He was just a little too cop-ish for her. He not only acted like a cop but he talked like one. The first thing she was going to do when she got him alone was demand he come clean with her. Well, maybe not the first thing. She was kind of fond of his kisses, so maybe she would...

"Ash, are you even listening to me?" grumbled Michael as he glared at her.

"Hell no, you grouch-ass. Why are you yelling at me? If anyone should be doing any yelling it should be me. Neither one of you has some psycho playing with your life and trying to kill you." She tried her hardest not to cry as she pulled her tough act. She didn't think either one of the macho jerks standing beside her bed believed her, the jerks. Shaffer stood back and was giving her a big smile. Ashley thought he liked the idea of her yelling at someone besides him.

"Sorry, sis, I'm just worried about you. We got the results back from the first lock of hair, and it *was* from our murder victim. Now I have to alert the station that we should be on the lookout for another victim, if this lock of hair is any indication." He rubbed his arm through his sling, making her feel like a total horse's ass. It was because of her that her brother was standing beside her with his arm in a full cast from just below his shoulder to over his hand.

Ashley reached over and touched his arm. "I haven't had a chance to thank you yet."

"No need, I just wish I had been a few seconds faster. Then maybe neither one of us would be laid up like this. Plus, if you weren't such a lard-ass, I might have been able to get you out of the way sooner."

Her eyes swung to Derek and Thomas to see them smiling. She turned back to Michael. "*Lard* ass? I will have you know my ass is not lard, but a firm round delicious piece of me—" Michael growled and looked up to see that both Derek and Thomas were listening with rapt attention to their exchange. "That's quite enough, little sis. How are you feeling, anyway?"

"Better. I only want to puke when I open my eyes, or move, or breathe, but other than that, great!"

"That's the sis I know and love. Someone who never bitches and takes things like a man."

She started to open her mouth to give him hell, and realized that he was only joking and really wasn't trying to pick a fight. "You're an ass."

By this time her room was filled with all kinds of cops. Several forensic guys, and then her dad and Captain Freeman came in.

Harold gave Derek a look. "Why is it every time I come into my daughter's room you're here?"

"Just keeping a watch on her, sir," Derek answered.

It looked like her dad was getting ready to question that but at the last minute decided against it. It was silently conveyed to Derek that he was not done with him yet, and Derek gave him a look right back that said *Fine with me, I can take whatever you throw at me.*

The amount of testosterone that could fly around a hospital room was amazing. Just trying to keep up with it all was wearing her out.

Ashley watched as they collected the hair, and started finger-printing the breakfast tray and everything else they thought might have a connection. As they continued going about their business she felt so helpless. She wasn't used to being on the other end of the police work. She may only be a rookie, but she still felt like she should be up helping gather evidence. Michael was talking to Shaffer, and her dad was talking to the captain. She could tell that she was not going to like what they were discussing by the expression on their faces. It didn't take a rocket scientist to know they were plotting to stick her away in some safe house somewhere. Well, they could plot all they wanted but it wasn't going to happen.

"Why is it every time I walk into my patient's room there is total chaos?" Doc asked as he entered her room. He took a look around and scowled at everyone who was in there. "What part of 'no company' do you all not understand?"

"Sorry Doc, it was out of our control. Someone threatened our patient here," Harold explained. "We're almost through in here, and then we'll be out of your way. If you could just give us a few more minutes, it would be greatly appreciated."

Doc studied Ashley's face.

"I'm fine, I promise to chase them all out of here just as soon as I can." She gave him a weak smile and she had to admit she was ready for them all to be gone. She had been up since before five and she was starting to fade fast. Her head had started to pound again and her stomach was still doing flips. She really wanted to scream at everyone to just get out. Looking around the room, everyone was going about their own business, totally ignoring her. This was a good thing. She knew it wouldn't last before they would turn all their questions toward her. The sad thing was she had absolutely no answers for them. She was just as confused as they were. She just wanted everything to go back to the way it was a few days ago.

God, I promise if you make this all go away, I'll never complain about my totally boring life again. Ashley was not big into prayer, but if there was any chance that He was listening today, it was definitely worth a shot. She wasn't Catholic, but if doing twenty Hail Marys would help make this all go away, she was ready to do them right this minute.

Forensics finished up and left, taking several prints with them. Ashley already knew they were not going to lead anywhere. The guy was too smart. He had already proved that, by the way he had acted when she spotted him at the mall and the way he had stolen plates and put them on another car. This guy was no amateur, that was for sure. Shaffer said his goodbyes and left also. That left her dad, Michael, the captain and Derek. Four men she really wasn't up to dealing with for very different reasons.

As those thoughts ran through her head, her door opened and Doc entered her room. "Everyone out. No ands, ifs or buts." Harold started to protest, but he must have realized the doctor was right. If she looked anything like she felt, she was sure she looked like death warmed over. Her head was pounding and the rest of her body ached.

Her dad hustled everyone out, even though she could tell Derek wanted to complain. She was glad to see them all go, even Derek. She didn't think she was up to dealing with his intensity, and she still had her doubts about who he really was.

The doctor ran through his exam. Now that everyone was gone, she was having a hard time keeping the tears at bay. The shock must be wearing off and fear was fast invading her body.

"Ashley, how are you feeling? Is your head still giving you any problems?"

"A little, but nothing too serious. I'm ready to get out of here."

"I'm not sure you're ready. I would like to keep you one more day just to make sure there are no complications."

"What if I promised to go to my parents' house? You know my mom is a nurse and I can guarantee you she will take very good care of me. She will be Nurse Nazi where I'm concerned."

Chuckling under his breath he said, "I'm sure you're right. Your mom is one of the best nurses I've ever worked with, and I'm sure where one of her kids is concerned she will make sure you do as the doctor orders."

"You can be sure of that. I remember when I got the chicken pox, she made me stay in the house for over a week, not letting me have any friends over. She wouldn't even let me go outside and play in the back yard with my brother and sister."

"All right, young lady, if you promise to stay at your parents' and follow all of my orders, I'll let you go home later this afternoon. That means complete bed rest for a few days at least. That is a nasty concussion you sustained and not to be taken lightly. Do I make myself clear?"

"Yes sir. Believe me, I have no desire to do anything except crawl into bed and sleep for a week. I promise I'll leave all the cop stuff to my dad and brother."

"Okay, I'm going to prescribe something for any headaches you may have and something for the nausea, and you have to promise me you'll come see me immediately if you have any other problems. I will stop by later this afternoon and take care of all the paperwork. And until then I want absolutely no visitors, is that understood?"

"That's fine with me; I think I've had enough in here to last me for quite a while."

He left her room and she was suddenly overcome by the quiet. After all the hoopla of the morning she was a little shell-shocked by the sudden calm. She glanced at the clock on the bare white hospital wall and realized it was only nine thirty in the morning. It felt like it was midnight. How could so much excitement happen in such a short time? She was astonished at the gamut of emotions she had endured in the last forty-eight hours. From fun relaxed time, to anger, to sexual flirtation, to sexual amazement (she was still buzzing over the whole Troy episode), to fear, to complete bafflement, to sexual tension, to absolute terror and ending with mind-boggling exhaustion.

Her body was ready to give in to the latter emotion, but she knew she had to come up with some sort of game plan. She couldn't let things keep happening to her without getting involved somehow. First thing she needed to do once she was free from here was have a one-on-one with Mr. Sexy Bartender. That man had some secrets that she was going to find out one way or another. If he didn't come clean, then she thought it was time to involve Mr. Big Brother. Second, she needed to make a list of everyone she could think of who would want to do her harm. The funny thing about that was she still couldn't think of anyone to put on that list. Maybe Shannon and Casey could help her with that one. Maybe they could remember someone in her past that she had royally pissed off and she had totally forgotten about. And finally, she needed to brush up on her self-defense, and maybe spend a few hours at the shooting range.

CHAPTER FOURTEEN

Getting released from the hospital was like a day at the zoo. By the time the doctor got back and signed all the paperwork to send her on her way, she thought everyone in town had heard what happened, came to offer to help and try to get the lowdown on what was really going on.

Through her open door, she could see her dad, mom, Michael and Shannon along with her grandma and grandpa Rogers. She knew if there were any way possible, her grandma and grandpa Wright would have been here too. Knowing them, they were at her parents' house getting everything ready for her arrival. Besides her family, there were Casey, Troy (that was weird all by itself), Derek, Bill, and Nick, along with a few fellow officers. They were all crowded around the nurses' desk trying to hear everything the doctor was saying to Harold and Laura.

Ashley had to smile at the racket they were making. And they thought she would get some rest by going to her parents' house. It would be a revolving door of well-wishers. It was a good thing she got a few hours of good sleep earlier; it would be the last she would get in some time.

She watched as Michael broke away from the pack and headed into her room. She couldn't help but feel guilty, watching the way he held his arm when he turned and closed the door, and then stood in front of it and blocked it. Oh shit, that was not a good sign. All traces of guilt went flying out the window and were replaced by apprehension.

"Michael, you're starting to scare me."

"Sorry, sis, I needed a few minutes alone with you to fill you in on the latest developments before the mob out there whisks you away to Mom's infirmary, and I never get you alone again for days."

"Please tell me it won't be that bad."

He gave her the look. "Are you kidding me? Dad has already installed an alarm system, thanks to the help of your friendly neighborhood bartender, who by the way, we need to talk about, too."

"I know, something doesn't add up where he's involved, but I don't think that's what you came in here to discuss with me."

His face was as serious as she could ever remember. She knew it wasn't something she wanted to hear. Her brother took delight in butting into her life, but she could tell this was one time when he would rather be anywhere but here.

"Another woman was found murdered."

Ashley could feel all the blood drain from her face. After the lock of hair was found on her tray, she had expected as much, but still, that news wasn't what she wanted to hear. Without even asking, she knew it was another strawberry blonde roughly her age.

"Where?" she asked.

"She was found behind the dumpster at your apartment complex."

"Oh God, Michael. Who found her? Please tell me it wasn't one of my neighbors."

"No, thank God. She was found by the guy who delivered the morning papers."

"Was she...?"

"Yes. Same as the last one, but this time he left a note."

"I don't think I want to know what was in it."

"Sorry, I know this has to be hard on you. I don't understand who's doing this. Do you have any ideas?"

"None. I've been thinking of nothing but that. I can't come up with anything. Michael, why is this happening to me?"

He moved away from the door and made his way to the side of her bed. Her brother was not the type to show any real emotion and sure wasn't known to show his affection to either of his sisters, but now she saw a side of her brother she had never seen before. A lone tear escaped from the corner of his eye and slowly traveled down the side of his face. He made no move to wipe it away.

"I don't know, but you can be sure we'll catch the son of a bitch. The captain had no choice but to inform the precinct of the connection between the murders and you. You should have been there. I've never seen such loyal devotion among police personnel before. Everyone was volunteering their days off and much more to help find this guy before he strikes again, even Malone."

She couldn't stop the tears this time. Not because she just discovered Malone actually had a heart, but that so many people were willing to help. She was touched and deeply worried that someone might get hurt trying to either catch this guy or defend her, just like Michael had.

"What did the note say?"

"I'm sorry sis, I wish I didn't have to be the one to tell you this, but it said, *Tell Ashley she's to blame.*"

"Sweet Jesus! What the hell did I do to make someone hate me so much that he's willing to kill because of me?"

"That's the thing; it could have been something so small that you didn't even realize it. If someone's crazy enough to kill in the first place, who knows what it takes to set them off."

Ashley knew he was right, but when it was happening to her personally all that bullshit was just that—bullshit.

"So, do we have any idea how we're going to handle this?"

"The captain has a few ideas and we've collected a few clues. We found the stolen car and collected a few smudged fingerprints, and hopefully they will turn up in AFIS. This guy is good, but we're better. He's bound to make a mistake and then we'll have him."

"How many other innocent women will have to die before that happens, Michael?"

She could tell he had no answer, just like she had none.

Laura poked her head in the door. "Hi baby, how are you holding up?"

Ashley was impressed that her mom was doing as well as she was. She had expected a little more drama from her. She assumed her dad had filled everyone in by now, so the fact that her mom was neither crying nor ranting and raving was a small miracle.

She came in carrying a set of clothes for Ashley to change into. Hers had been cut off of her, which was really sad. She had looked really hot in that outfit.

"Hi Mom, thanks for bringing me some clothes. I think I've had my butt hanging out long enough."

"Ashley Wright! I don't think we need to discuss your butt with your brother in the room."

"You know that Michael likes to discuss butt, well, maybe not my butt, but word around the station is that he is definitely a butt man. As a matter of fact..."

"*Ashley!*" came from both Michael and Laura. Ashley smiled; it was so easy to get them flustered. It took a lot to put her in a bad mood, and she was going to try her best not to let that murdering psychopath destroy her life.

Before she could tease them anymore, the doctor came in to give them all the instructions that he wanted them to follow for the next few days. Other than a few days of bed rest and peace and quiet, he didn't demand too much. If the peace and quiet was achieved it would be a miracle, but Ashley thought she could handle the sleep.

"Ashley, I swear you're a crowd magnet. There are more people out in that hall now than during a normal week around here. But I already gave them the speech and rules that they were allowed to wave goodbye as you're wheeled down the hall, but that's the extent of their visiting."

"Aye, aye, captain. Sounds good to me, except I still think the hotties should get a free pass."

"You're crazy, girl. No hotties, doctor's orders, at least for two days. Then you're on your own with your so-called hotties."

As the doctor and Michael left, Ashley felt her mom's eyes on her. "I'm fine, Mom, really."

"You can tell everyone else that story, but I know my little girl and *you're not okay.* This whole mess has to be causing you pain. You can pretend that you're some big tough cop while you're with others, but you don't have to pretend when you're with me."

Ashley's chin started quivering, and she knew that if she didn't get herself busy, she would break down and become a blubbering idiot. She still had to walk through all of her visitors out there in the hall and she didn't want to do it with red-rimmed eyes and a runny nose. "You're right, Mom. This is tearing me up inside and I want it all to just go away, but it's not, so I have no choice but to pull myself together and get on with my life. This involves a lot of people, and if I fall apart then it will only make it worse. You know this has to be really bothering Dad and Michael, having this happen to someone in our family and not being able to do anything about it."

Ashley could tell her mom wanted to break down herself, but she took a big deep breath, pulled her into a bear hug, just about squeezed the stuffin' out of her, pushed her away and proceeded to get her clothes ready for her to change into. "Mom, I really want to take a shower and I think it would be easier here than at home."

"Let me get the water ready. Give me just a few minutes."

While she waited for her mom to get the shower ready, she took the time to ponder the hotties that were out in the hall. She wasn't surprised by Derek's presence, but she was a little surprised by Nick's and a lot surprised by Troy's. At any other time, she would be in her heyday with so much male hunkiness vying for her attention, but today it was a little intimidating. She could play the flirt with the best of them, but when it came right down to it, she was a one-man woman. She knew there was no way she could juggle the attention of three men, although the thought of those three men fighting for her attention was very flattering. Shannon and Casey had to be going crazy out there, not knowing what was going on. Hell, who was she kidding? She didn't know what was going on, but it put a small secretive smile on her face just thinking about it.

"Ashley, I am afraid to ask what you're smiling about."

"Oh, Mom. Did you not see all those hot male bodies out there in the hall?"

"Well, of course I noticed your brother and dad."

"Mom!"

"Yes dear, I did notice the extra three hot ones out there. I was going to ask you about them later. Does your Aunt Dixie know that one of her employees is hanging around her niece's hospital room? Or, for that matter does your Uncle Irwin?"

Chuckling she said, "I seriously don't think Troy is the type of person who fills his employer in on his off-duty habits, do you?"

"No, you're right. I'm sure that man answers to no one, but you still haven't told me why they're all three out there."

"I have no idea. I had what you would kind of call a date with Derek the night before this happened, and a massage with Troy earlier that day, but I haven't seen Nick since the shed fire and his visit after the 911 call. I think Nick and Troy are just being polite and checking in on me."

240

"You only say that because you haven't been out there watching them. It's quite comical to see them preening around like a bunch of strutting cocks."

"Mom, I can't believe you said cock."

"I may be older than you, but I'm not dead, and if you tell your dad I said it, I will bake laxative into your brownies later."

"My lips are sealed. I have enough problems without the added bathroom dilemma. Now how about helping this weak daughter of yours take a shower."

Between the two of them they had Ashley cleaned up and dressed in a matter of fifteen minutes. Not too bad, considering she had to stop every few minutes and rest.

"Mom, could you have Shannon come in here before we leave, please?"

"I thought the doctor said no visitors?"

"Mom, do you really think I'm going to go out in that hallway without any makeup on? I can take the wet hair, but no makeup?"

She chuckled but went to the door and motioned for Shannon to come in.

The minute Shannon hit the door, Ashley could tell she was about to explode with questions. Holding her hand up Ashley said, "Makeup first, questions later."

She stopped dead in her tracks and Ashley could tell she was getting ready to argue, but she pointed to the hall and Ashley saw that it all clicked into place.

"Oh yeah, totally understandable. I have no idea why it is that the three most gorgeous guys I've seen in a long time are all standing out in the hall right now, but as a single woman I want to thank you. I'm not too proud to stake my claim on any leftovers you leave lying around when the smoke clears. There is enough testosterone out there to make a nun weak in the knees. It's so funny to watch Michael stand back and glare at all of them. It's even funnier to watch them stare right back. It's a good thing you're just about ready to blow this Popsicle stand; much more and it could get ugly out there, because no one is going to back off. I don't think Dad could have handled things if they would've got out of control and there was no way Casey and I were going to interfere. Grandma is out there drooling, and Grandpa just keeps grunting at her that she wouldn't know what to do with it if they offered it to her."

"Shannon, stop it. I'm sure your grandma is doing no such thing. Just because the rest of us enjoy looking at the three of them doesn't mean your grandma is doing the same thing."

Shannon and Ashley stopped applying makeup to her bruised and cut-up face and stared at their mom. "Well, I'm not dead yet, you two."

They finished putting on Ashley's makeup; they did the best they could to hide the bruises but the cuts and scrapes were there for all to see. She felt a whole lot better just having mascara on. Shannon felt she should play up the sympathy card and leave it all uncovered, but Ashley felt she had plenty of sympathy coming her way as it was. The nurse had brought in the wheelchair, and was waiting for them to finish up so she could wheel her out of there. Ashley gave her mom and Shannon a brave smile, got into the chair, and told the nurse she was ready to face the pack.

As Shannon opened the door, Ashley's heart and stomach started doing a nervous roll. Maybe she wasn't ready to face the world just yet, and if she thought she could get away with it, she would have had the nurse turn the wheelchair around and head in the opposite direction. She took a quick survey of everyone looking at her at once, no one saying a word. Some had sympathy on their faces, others curiosity and a few even had scowls. She wasn't sure if they were directing the scowls at her or just the situation, but it was a little intimidating either way.

Pandemonium broke out. Derek made the first move toward her and once he did that, it was like everyone moved at once. Ashley had to give it to the nurse, she might have been a tiny little thing but she was not faint of heart. "Everyone stand back. You heard the doctor earlier. Our patient is going home to some peace and quiet and you are all going to respect those orders, correct?"

Derek stopped mid-stride and gave Ashley a quirky little smile with a promise that he was not going to abide by any doctor's rules. Troy was standing by the nurses' station and as he caught Ashley's eye, she could feel his unspoken words. *If you need me...* She gave him a small smile and a shy nod of her head and then turned her attention to the rest. Nick was standing by Michael with a worried look on his face. He would look at Ashley, then give Derek and Troy quick glances. She thought he was trying to see if he even stood a chance with all of the attention she was getting from the others. He gave her a reassuring smile and stepped back as the nurse wheeled her by the group in a no-nonsense manner. It was like watching the Red Sea part. Ashley got a few pats on the back and even a few well wishes.

Her brave little nurse never slowed for a minute, just pushed her along at a fast clip. They left the group and moved into the elevator with Laura and Shannon accompanying them. Harold had already gone ahead to pull the car around front so they could leave. She had to wonder what was going on back up on the fourth floor. She was sure Troy slipped quietly away and her grandma was probably trying to talk Derek and Nick into a nice friendly game of gin rummy. Casey and Dan were following them to the house and the guys from the station were headed back to whatever they were doing before they had come to the hospital. She really appreciated that they all came to see her, but was relieved that she hadn't had to talk to them one on one. She was at a loss for words and knew it would have been awkward for everyone involved.

243

Ashley sat in the back of Dad's car and watched as the world raced by. She could see kids riding their bikes with not a care in the world. As they pulled up to a stop sign, she watched a little boy carrying a slimy frog chase a poor girl around the front yard where they were playing. Was this the kind of boy who turned into a cold-blooded killer, or was it a boy like the one sitting on the front steps, just watching but doing nothing to help the little girl fend off the bully? The little girl fell and the boy held the frog to her face. She could hear her screaming in fright and before Ashley even realized what she was doing, she had yanked open the door and was charging over to the boy and yanking him away from the little girl.

Ashley held his arm and got in his face, yelling at him that it was not nice to pick on girls, and that he should treat her with respect and not kill her. Ashley froze the minute the words were out of her mouth. All three of the kids stared at her like she was a madwoman, which had her coming to the same conclusion. She let go of the boy, muttered how sorry she was, and turned to see her family staring at her in shock. Laura had jumped out of the car to follow her. Shannon and her dad were just getting out of the car when they heard her words. They all were giving her a look of horror. Hell, she could see a visit to a shrink in those looks, and maybe going by her actions, it wasn't a bad idea. Laura came and took her hand and apologized to the kids, and dragged her back to the car. Harold's and Shannon's expressions had changed from horror to pity, and she wasn't sure which was worse.

She was so ashamed of the way she acted that she didn't want to look any of them in the face. She let her mom put her into the back seat and she laid her head back and closed her eyes. "I'm sorry. I don't know what got into me." She could feel the worried looks they exchanged among themselves. Ashley turned her head toward the window as they pulled away from the stop sign. All three kids were looking at them, but she noticed the one boy had dropped the frog and the boy on the step had put his arm around the little girl, which made Ashley smile. Who knows, maybe she just prevented a serial killer in the making. She closed her eyes again, not wanting to deal with her worried family. A tear made its way down her cheek.

Her little dash out of the car had made her head hurt and she was breathing hard. She was in worse shape than she wanted to let anyone know, but she noticed her mom turn around with a look of concern on her face.

Ashley looked back through the rear window, glad there was no sign of Casey and Dan. She would have died of embarrassment if they had witnessed her outburst.

They traveled through the neighborhood in silence, no one knowing what to say to ease the tension. The car was as quiet as the morgue. She knew she had her family worried and felt terrible for it. "Hey Dad, how much would I have to bribe you to stop and get me a Frappuccino?" Harold swung around and gave her a relieved smile. He knew that if she was well enough to ask for her favorite drink, things could not be too bad

"You bet, sis."

"Hey, that sounds good. How about a white chocolate mocha to go along with that?" Shannon asked.

"Shannon, you'll ruin your appetite. You know Grandma has been at the house cooking all day. You would ruin her meal if you drank that this close to supper." Laura turned and gave Shannon the evil eye as she said this.

"She gets a frappe and you're saying I will get too full with coffee?"

Ashley poked Shannon, mouthing, "*So there, fatty.*"

She slapped Ashley hard on the arm and the war was on.

"Girls, stop it! Shannon, your sister's hurt."

"She started it."

"That's no excuse for you to hit her."

Ashley gave Shannon the most innocent look and mouthed, "*Sucker.*"

Shannon gave her a look of pure evil. Ashley saw Dad watching them in the rearview mirror. Giving him a bright smile, she turned to the front and knew she was busted. But her dad would never tell their mom, not today anyway. She was being treated with kid gloves by everyone…well, maybe not Shannon, after she got her in trouble.

They settled into a comfortable conversation with Ashley, asking why her mom lied to her doctor about no company being at the house, about what their grandma was fixing for supper, which at least got them past the awkward stage. Harold turned the corner of their block and she burst out laughing…so much for peace and quiet.

CHAPTER FIFTEEN

It was a three-ring circus at her parents' house. Grandma and Grandpa Wright were there and they must have been babysitting a couple of the great-grandkids, because four kids were playing tag in the front yard. They looked like some of her cousin Travis's six kids. Michael, Dan and Casey were just pulling up. Mrs. Steffen was standing at the front door with a plate in her hands, waiting for someone to answer the door. Derek was just coming around the corner on his crotch rocket. Across the street she could see her aunt Dixie and uncle John's car parked along with her grandma and grandpa Rogers'.

"Harold..."

"Don't Harold me. Just as many of your family are here as mine."

"But the doctor said—"

"Mom, it's okay, I'm fine. And the fact is I'd rather have a houseful than the quiet. In the quiet I think too much."

Laura turned around in the seat and gave her a soul-searching look. Ashley could feel the concern, and the fear she must be feeling for her. Laura turned her gaze to Shannon, who just shrugged her shoulders. "She's a big girl, Mom, and she knows what's best for her." She then turned her look onto Harold, who was concentrating on getting the car into the driveway without running over any kids, toys or cars.

"I promise if I get tired I'll excuse myself and go into Shannon's room and lay down."

"Sis, did you see that Mr. Hottie just pulled up?"

Harold's head whipped around at that and gave Derek a quick look, but instead of the irritation Ashley figured would cross his face, she could have sworn she saw relief. Whoa! Something was definitely going on that she had no clue about, and she thought it was about time she put an end to that. She looked out the window and watched as Derek pulled in between a couple of cars and parked, then watched as the kids all made a beeline to him, screaming for rides. Whose kids were these, asking a stranger for a ride? He got off, taking off his helmet, and she felt her insides start to quiver just looking at him. The man positively had some mega sex appeal going for him. Today he wore a pair of faded jeans so worn out that they were starting to get holes in the knees and fit snug around that gorgeous ass of his. He wore a black t-shirt that was stretched across his chest, defining those glorious muscles she wanted to run her hands across. He looked tired, and she wondered if he got any sleep after he left her hospital room this morning. He reached out and tousled little Eric's hair as he walked by.

They all climbed out of the car and she heard Eric ask, "Please, Derek? You said I could have a ride later."

Ashley looked up with a question in her eyes, but remembered someone saying Derek had helped her dad install an alarm system earlier. The kids must have already been here by that time, and met him then. She watched as he tried to make his way through the throng that had suddenly surrounded him on his way to them. She loved how he stopped to talk to the kids rather than just push them aside like some men would have. Her heart gave an extra little flutter, knowing that about him.

Now that everyone at the station knew the situation it was time to fill in all her family; they had to be worried sick. She knew that some details were out, but they needed to know everything that was happening with the murders and how they affected her. She motioned for everyone to follow her into the house. Glancing around at the sober faces, she knew it was going to be hard on everyone. Hugs and kisses were given by all, except Derek; he stood back and just watched. Ashley glanced over Aunt Dixie's shoulder as she gave her a hug and looked into his eyes. She could see a range of emotions flash in his eyes as he looked at her. Worry, frustration, lust and maybe a little something she couldn't put her finger on. The last one had her furrowing her eyebrows at him, causing him to give her that sexy little grin of his, but the moment was lost as her grandma rushed in from the kitchen.

Ashley wasn't sure how much her family knew, so she figured she had better start at the beginning. Her head was already throbbing and she must have put her hand to her head without realizing it, because her mom and both grandmothers were suddenly at her side, trying to get her to go lie down.

"Wait, please. Would everyone please just sit down for a minute so we can discuss what's going on?" Ashley shouted over the noise that had escalated to a fairly large roar in the few minutes since they had all traipsed into the house.

All noise instantly stopped, with nineteen sets of eyes swinging in her direction. "Grandma, would you mind taking the kids into the kitchen and give them a snack and then please come back and join us?"

She and Laura hustled the kids out of the room and everyone else found a place to sit. Harold and her uncle John brought in kitchen chairs, and Michael grabbed some folding chairs from the closet. Derek helped him set them up and then gently lowered her into one.

"Just who the hell are you, young man?" shouted Grandpa Wright. "Does anyone know this man who's all over our Ashley?"

Ashley could feel his gaze burning into the top of her head, but she was afraid to acknowledge it, because she was just as interested in his answer as everyone else in the room.

Harold answered, "That's not important right now, let's get into that later." He glanced at Derek and that's when Ashley witnessed what had passed between them. Now she knew that there was more to Derek, and her dad knew what it was. She looked between them and gave them a scowl, and noticed Michael was doing the same. It must be driving him crazy to not know what was going on any more than she did.

Everyone found a place to sit, and Ashley took a deep breath but had no idea where to start. She didn't know how much everyone knew and what the police were keeping private.

"Dad?" She looked at him and then Michael.

Michael must have sensed her dilemma and took over the story. He filled everyone in on the murder, leaving out all the grisly details but informing them how Ashley had been brought into it, by the notes and then the attempt on her life. He left out the part about the hair, and she could see both Casey and Shannon glance at each other but they kept that information to themselves. There were several gasps of shock and a few tears as Michael finished up his story. He didn't even mention the episode this morning or the second murder victim, which she was grateful for. The family did not need to know how involved she really was in this mess. She doubted Shannon or Casey even knew about the second murder victim or that she had been found at Ashley's apartment complex. The family only needed to know the basics so that they would understand what all the excitement was about.

"But I don't understand why they tried to kill Ashley," Dixie muttered.

Ashley gave her a teary-eyed smile. "Neither do we, Aunt Dixie, neither do we."

"Harold, what are the police doing to stop this madman?"

"Michael, you need to catch this nut," came from each grandmother.

"I know, Grandma. We're doing everything that we can."

"Well, it's not enough. Someone tried to *kill* my granddaughter, dammit."

There were several gasps of shock at her words. Not because she yelled at Michael, but because none of them had ever heard a cuss word come out of her mouth in all the years they were growing up. There were plenty of occasions over the years to utter a few swear words, especially when there were tons of people causing havoc at her house, but she had refrained, until now.

Ashley took her hand. "It's not their fault, Grandma. This has all happened in just a few short days and they're still gathering evidence and analyzing it. We'll find this madman and then everything will be okay."

She gave her the most dreadful look. "What do you mean *we*?"

Ashley gave her a puzzled look. "I mean us, the police force."

"Young lady, you are going to do no such thing. Adam and I have discussed this and we think the best thing would be for you to come to the farm with us. Get away from all this danger, somewhere where there is no crazy person trying to kill you."

Pandemonium broke loose as everyone started putting in their two cents at that idea. Her grandma and grandpa Rogers were not going to stand by and let one set of grandparents steal away their granddaughter without a fight. Her dad and mom were stating that she was not going anywhere but right here. The rest were talking among themselves, discussing the murder and the accident. Ashley sat back in her chair frustrated, watching as everyone discussed this like she was a snot-nosed kid of twelve with no say in the matter at all.

She felt a comforting hand on her shoulder and she didn't even have to turn around to see whose it was. She could feel the strength in the touch, and suddenly she felt like everything would be okay. It didn't matter what everyone else thought, she'd take comfort in his touch, and relaxed, knowing that she was not in this alone. She might be confused about what was going on between him and her dad, but she couldn't deny that she felt relieved having him there.

She gave another look around and shook her head in wonder. She stood up and Derek followed her into the kitchen, where they sat down with the kids at the counter and talked to them while they ate their peanut butter and celery. Ashley needed their innocence and laughter to keep her from falling into a funk. She was trying to keep her head above water and all the drama in the other room was not helping.

"Are you okay?"

"I will be." She gave him a searching look and he had the decency to look guilty. "I think you and I have some things to discuss."

"You're right, but I was hoping to do it in private without the sideshow getting involved."

"I agree. Maybe after supper we can sneak away, and then you can tell me what you have been keeping from me."

He looked up sharply, with a frown on his face. "I don't think I would necessarily call it keeping something from you."

"You have secrets that apparently my dad knows and I don't, so what would you call it?"

"Not secrets. These notes and now this attempt on your life have changed things. I can't explain this in front of the kids, things have happened and I haven't gotten the chance to tell you yet, for your own safety."

"My own safety! What the hell does that mean? Maybe we should find time to talk *now*." She could feel the anger beginning to bubble to the surface.

Ashley noticed the kids looking at them in alarm. "Sorry, kids. Derek and I were just playing around. Now who wants to get Grandma in here so we can have some of that delicious lasagna I smell baking?"

"I do! I do!" rang out from four faces covered in peanut butter. She looked up at Derek and could tell he was not happy about the way things were going, but that was just too damn bad. She wasn't going to get into a screaming match around her mother's kitchen island.

"Ashley, is everything okay in here?" Laura asked as she entered the kitchen. "Where did you disappear to? We all noticed you had left the room."

"I came to the conclusion that you all didn't need me in there, you were all doing just fine without me." Ashley couldn't help showing a little irritation. She didn't want to take it out on her mom but she just happened to be the one who came in first. Not that she wanted to take it out on anyone in her family, but she was just sick of the whole mess. Derek was scowling at her and her head hurt like hell, but she didn't want to be banished to her room like a little kid. "Sorry, Mom."

"It's okay, honey. I think after what you've been through you are entitled to be a little grumpy. Are you ready for some supper?" She stood behind Ashley and put her arms around her neck, giving her a gentle hug. Ashley put her arms over hers and soaked in the warmth those arms gave her. She didn't realize how much she had just needed to be held. Leave it to her mom to know exactly what she needed. She felt a tear starting to escape her left eye and she reached up to brush it away before anyone noticed. She was trying so hard to keep it together and be an adult that she had not let herself deal with her emotions. But this was not the time or place to let go. She still had several hard hours ahead of her. She could see the concern in Derek's eyes as he watched her, but she ignored him. It figured he would be the one to witness her moment of weakness.

The kids all answered Laura before Ashley could even open her mouth. One by one the kitchen started filling with all the women, everyone just going to work without anyone saying anything at all about her having left the living room.

"Okay, ladies, unless you need some help from me, I think this is my cue to join the men in the other room."

"Oh no, Derek, we have it all under control. If you could go tell Harold I need him to take the chairs out back and put them around all the tables so we can eat, that would be great. Everything should be ready in just a few minutes, if you wouldn't mind."

"Not at all, Mrs. Wright," Derek answered on his way into the other room.

"Please call me Laura. Mrs. Wright is way too formal. You can call my mother-in-law that if she'll let you, but I doubt it."

Ashley turned to help her grandma put in the garlic bread she had made earlier. She could feel his eyes still on her and she was sure he was trying to figure out where he stood right now, but the truth was she had no idea. She was so confused about everything else and he was only making things worse. On one hand she was so attracted to the man it made her dizzy just being around him, and on the other hand he made her nervous. He gave off this vibe that he was way more than he was pretending to be, and that pissed her off. Maybe a few days ago she would have just thought he was mysterious, but now she thought he was hiding stuff and that just wasn't cutting it. Come to think of it, she wasn't even sure why he was here acting like he was part of the family. And the weird thing was no one was even questioning him except good old Grandpa, and then he just got brushed aside when he asked about it.

The women got the food ready and carried it out to where the men had gathered outside in the back yard. They had set up card tables and long tables to accommodate all of them in a long row. It was the first time she had been in the back yard since the night the shed had caught fire. Harold and Michael had cleared away all the burnt debris and trash that remained after the firemen had put out the fire. She thought the yard looked so bare without their old play-house taking up the back corner. Just one more thing to erase her childhood. She thought the idea of the playhouse being gone both-ered her more than anything. She had always thought once they all started having kids, her dad would turn it back into a playhouse again. Now none of the kids would get that chance.

Ashley was standing there looking at the back of the yard and realized everyone had sat down to eat; they were all watching her, waiting to see what she was going to do. She gave a small smile and took a seat by Uncle John, glad the only empty seat was not by Derek. He was down at the other end stuck between Grandma Rogers and Aunt Dixie. In a way she almost felt sorry for him. But in another way, she was hoping Grandma drove him crazy with her gin rummy stories or tried talking him into volunteering for one of her organizations.

Her stomach was still not settled after all the excitement of the day, but Grandma's lasagna smelled fantastic, along with the garlic bread and tossed salad. She should be in seventh heaven. She had no idea how Grandma knew earlier how many people would be here for supper, or if she was just so used to cooking for a crowd that this was the norm for her. Everyone settled into a comfortable routine, passing the food and making conversation that steered away from Ashley's drama. She could hear Mrs. Steffens telling Shannon about some new recipe she wanted to show them how to make, Dan was talking baseball with Michael, and Grandpa was telling her dad that the garbage disposal at his house was stuck.

Ashley was content to just sit and listen, not having to worry about trying to come up with some idle small-talk. She enjoyed her supper after all and even took seconds on lasagna. Her uncle John, bless his heart, steered the conversation to him if someone sent a comment their way. Under the table she gave his knee a light pat as he answered Laura when she asked them a question. He got a slight smile on his face that no one else would have even noticed but her and maybe eagle-eyes Derek down at the other end of the table. He pretended to be paying attention to her grandma, but his eyes never left Ashley's face during the whole meal. Not that she was watching him or anything, but it was hard to miss when every time she looked up to glance around the table his eyes would be glued to her. Every time it happened she felt a little flicker of something in the pit of her stomach.

They finished up with their meal and sat around enjoying the cool breeze that had come with the evening. It was nice to be secluded in the safety of her parents' back yard, away from all the craziness of the outside world.

Dixie and Laura cleared the table, insisting that the rest sit and enjoy the evening. That was the great thing about the modern world they lived in today versus the days when they were growing up. Today they cooked in aluminum pans and used paper plates, not like when they were little and would have been doing dishes for what seemed like hours. The fact that Grandma had already cleaned up all the dishes she had used to make the lasagna earlier in the afternoon helped.

Casey and Shannon brought out coffee for the women while most of the men had a beer. Ashley made a cup of coffee, adding French vanilla creamer, leaned back in her chair, closed her eyes, and just let the evening soak into her muddled brain. Some of the men had moved away from the table and were standing back where the shed used to be, discussing plans for how Dad was going to rebuild a storage shed when things got back to normal.

Several of the other ladies were over looking at her mom's flower garden, admiring how her peonies were in full bloom. That left Shannon, Casey and Ashley still sitting around the table enjoying their coffees.

"How are you holding up, sis?"

"My heads hurts and I'm tired as hell, but the rest is just like it's a dream and not real. I don't think it's sunk in yet."

"Are you scared?" Casey asked as she stirred her coffee over and over again.

"Shitless."

"Jesus, Ash, this is nuts."

"Tell me about it. Have you two heard about the second murder?"

"Yeah, Dad and Michael told us and Mom before we came over to the hospital and picked you up. They say the second woman looked like you, too."

"That's what Michael said. Can you guys think of anyone who would be doing this and why it's happening to me?"

"Fuck no!"

"Casey and I talked while we were waiting for them to release you, and we could not think of one person in your past who would want to do this to you. Have you thought of anyone?"

"Not a soul. I keep going over and over in my mind everyone I've ever pissed off in my life, and I still can't think of one person who would hold a bad enough grudge against me to commit murder."

"And rape."

"I don't want to even think of what those women went through. And if this man did this all because of me, I don't know if I will ever be able to handle that."

She hadn't realized it but Derek had come up to stand behind her and heard her last comment. "Ashley, this is not your fault and you cannot let this get personal."

Turning to glare at him she said, "Not let it get personal? I don't see how this could be any more personal. When you have a madman sending you his murdered, raped victims' hair as a souvenir and leaving notes stating that it's entirely my fault, you don't expect me to take it personally?" She had sat up in her chair as she had been talking to him and didn't realize that her voice had risen a little louder than she had wanted.

"I know that it's personal in that he is involving you in his sordid acts, but you cannot let yourself believe that that this is your fault in any way. This man is sick and for some reason he has involved you. You have to concentrate on that fact and not dwell on anything else. THIS. MAN. IS. SICK."

Derek's voice had been even louder than hers. Shannon and Casey sat quietly, not knowing what to say. Ashley glared up at Derek and he stared down at her, glaring right back. Her chin started to quiver and she could tell that this little outburst was going to send her over the edge. She could feel the tears beginning to form at the back of her eyes and she did not want everyone to see her break down. "I'm really tired and my head is killing me so I'm going to go lay down. Shannon, will you tell everyone goodbye for me?" She pushed her chair back, bumping into Derek's legs as she did so. Hearing him grunt in pain gave her a little bit of satisfaction for his little tirade.

As she made her way down the length of the table, there was a sudden flash of light racing over her head and then an explosion in the middle of the yard. Everyone screamed at once and she was being pushed to the ground and covered by a hard male body. There was a second explosion a few seconds later, but she could not see anything because of the huge body that was covering hers. She could barely breathe from the dead weight that was covering her from the top of her head to the bottom of her feet.

258

Pandemonium broke out as everyone raced for cover. She could see that Shannon and Casey had crawled under the table and were looking at her with such complete panic on their faces that she knew, right then and there, that she had to remove herself from her family and friends before someone got hurt, if they weren't already.

After a few seconds without any more explosions, Derek jumped up off her, reached around to his back and pulled out a Glock that had been tucked underneath his t-shirt. Giving her a quick look to make sure she was all right, he was off racing around the side of the house, Harold and Michael right behind him with their guns pulled also.

CHAPTER SIXTEEN

She lay where she had been pressed into the grass by a man who carried a gun. A gun. Why was their friendly neighborhood bartender carrying a gun? They weren't supposed to have guns, only swizzle sticks and olives and maybe an occasional maraschino cherry or two. She was starting to see the little black stars again, since she had bumped her head when Derek had shoved her to the ground. They were so pretty dancing above her head. They would float in front of her vision and then dance away again, like they were playing a peek-a-boo game with her. She looked up into the sky and could see the elm tree that grew beside the house, and the sky that was starting to turn a darker shade of blue as the day became dusk. The leaves were gently moving above her head and seemed to be playing the peek-a-boo game with the stars too. First she would see the stars and then pretty green leaves would drift into her view. Then the stars floated around in front of her eyes and the leaves kind of disappeared. She didn't know what had just happened, but right now she really didn't care. The way she felt, the world could be coming to an end and she was just going to lie here and let it. She couldn't do anything to stop it, so she might just as well rest here and enjoy the evening while it lasted. Her body felt like it was made from cement. She knew she needed to move but just couldn't seem to find the energy.

"*ASHLEY? ASHLEY!* Oh my God! I think Ashley's dead," came screeching from her grandma Rogers somewhere to her left. Oh great. So much for just lying here and enjoying what was left of the world. Leave it to her grandma to think she was dead. *Was she?* Maybe that was why she couldn't move. Was she really dead? But if that were true, wouldn't she be looking down on everything instead of looking up? Leave it to her to get it all ass-backwards.

Suddenly several heads were blocking her view of the sky, which really irritated her. Couldn't they tell what they were doing? Geez the nerve of some people! It was a beautiful night for stargazing and they were standing in her way. Were they looking at the dead person lying in her dad and mom's back yard? People were so morbid that way, no respect for the dearly departed. She felt a toe nudge her. How rude! Just because she took a pin to work and poked the stiffs who came into the morgue didn't give them the right to nudge her. She bet it was Shannon, making sure she was really dead, before she went over and raided Ashley's apartment, stealing her blind. Hey wait, if she could feel the nudge, was she really dead? She was so confused.

From somewhere off in the distance she heard, "Ashley, honey, are you okay?" Her mom was kneeling beside her, taking her hand in hers, patting it like she had just fainted. She hadn't fainted. She was shoved to the ground like some kind of defensive end on some damn football team. She didn't even blink, afraid if she did the stars would take over and her world would go black. She could hear the excited voices of Dixie and her grandma Wright as they were screaming for John to get the garden hose. They sounded so far away, and why they wanted to water the garden right now was beyond her, but oh well. Casey was yelling at Dan to do something. What, she didn't know, and neither did he apparently, because she didn't let up, telling him to call 911 at least.

"Is she alive?"

"Of course, she's alive, Mom."

"Well, why isn't she moving then?"

"Ash honey...you're scaring your grandma. Can you answer me?"

No I don't want to. I want you all to go away and leave me alone. Ashley blinked and the images were still there and the black stars became bigger. Damn it! She knew that would happen.

"I saw her eyes blink. She's not dead."

"Mom you're not helping," Laura muttered.

"Well, she did. Why is she just staring off into space?"

"Honey, is it your head? Did you bump it again?"

Ashley squeezed her mom's hand and did not blink again. The train that was starting to roar through her brain was all she could handle right now.

"I think we should call 911 again," Shannon threw in from above her left shoulder.

"That was already done, dear, when the bombs were thrown in the yard," Mrs. Steffens informed her, her voice calm in the chaos surrounding Ashley. She did not turn her head to investigate what was happening around her. Instead she kept her eyes focused on the sky above her.

Bombs. There were bombs. What bombs? Why didn't I remember any bomb? Has Mrs. Steffens been into the cooking sherry again?

Ashley could hear the sirens blaring somewhere off in the distance and they made her think of Nick, which made her smile.

"Why is she smiling like an idiot? Make her blink, Laura. She's scary, staring off into God knows what."

"Mom! Why don't you go into the house and get me a cold washrag to put on her head? Everyone else, please could you just give her a little breathing room?"

Ashley could hear the aggravation and worry in her mom's voice as she threw out instructions to several people who were milling around.

The faces moved away from her view of the sky and she let out a sigh of happiness.

"*Ashley Elizabeth!* I want you to focus on me right this minute."

Geez Mom, no reason to yell, I'm lying right here. She blinked several times and focused on her mom's worried face. She was leaning over her, looking into her eyes.

"Are you with me now? I need you to concentrate on staying with me."

"Yes, Mom," Ashley whispered, afraid if she spoke any louder her head would explode. *Where did she think I was going to go anyway?* She didn't think her body was ready to do any marathons any time soon.

"We need to get you back to the hospital. This last blow to your head could have caused some serious damage."

"No. Please, Mom, I don't want to go back there. I'm okay now. I was just dazed for a minute."

Laura took Ashley's pulse and had her follow her finger as she passed it in front of her face. "Concussions are nothing to be taken lightly. You could have internal bleeding, Ash. You need a new CAT scan to make sure there was no further damage." She was turning her head gently to look at the bump on the back.

"Oh gross! That's really ugly and there's blood! Ewww."

"Shannon, stop it. You sound like your grandmother."

"Mom, that was mean. I don't sound like her."

Ashley lay there as they bickered back and forth, wondering how ugly it really was. "Blood? How much blood?"

"Honey, it's nothing to worry about. You just have a small cut. Your sister is being melodramatic, but I still think it would be a good idea if you went back to the hospital and had them check you over again."

"Oh, Mom, really? They'll want me to spend another night and I don't know if I can take that. Can't you just keep a close eye on me? I promise if you think anything is wrong, I'll go then." A lone tear escaped down her cheek to disappear into her hair. She knew she was hanging on by a thread as it was, and spending another night in the hospital was not going to help the situation.

Before she could respond, the back yard broke out in total chaos. The fire department was dragging hoses over to put out the small fires that were burning in a couple of places in the middle of the yard, knocking chairs over as they went. Ashley was glad she was out of the way or she might have been caught in the crossfire. The picture that brought to her mind made her chuckle inside her head, because she knew if she chuckled out loud, her mom would definitely send her to the hospital. What else could go wrong in her life? She might as well be drenched by the water squirting out of their hoses. So far she had seen no sign of her giant fireman. That's what he was, *my giant*. The thought of climbing up that gorgeous body of his, just like Jack and the Beanstalk, made her blush and giggle at the same time. She could start at those big feet of his, climb up those strong calves and up onto those magnificent thighs. Then after those thighs came...

"Ashley, are you all right? You are turning a bright shade of red and starting to perspire."

God, Mom, I'm more than all right or at least I would have been if you'd let me finish climbing up my very own personal giant.

Several police officers were questioning the rest of the family, and Derek, Dad and Michael came back into the yard. Ashley could hear them talking to someone whose voice she did not recognize, so she went back to climbing up Nick's giant limbs.

"Laura, what happened to Ashley? Was she hit?" came Harold's frantic cry when he noticed Ashley still lying flat on her back in the same position as when he left. Not that he probably even noticed that Derek had made her a "sandwich" between him and the grass when all the excitement had happened. Suddenly three different faces were blocking her view of the darkening sky. Make that four faces. She could see that the captain had joined their little circle. He had a scowl on his face, which if she were in his office would have scared the crap out of her. Why was he scowling at her, anyway? She had done nothing to deserve that look. Now, Malone, she was another story. She could hear her voice somewhere. Please, oh please, let it just be in her imagination. She could not deal with her right now.

"She's not dead, Harold," answered Grandma as she brought the cold rag Laura had asked for.

Dad glanced up at his mother-in-law like he was going to kill her, growling, "What the hell does that mean, Laura?"

"Ashley gave us quite a little scare earlier, didn't you, babe?"

Suddenly Malone had joined the circle. "My my, what have we here? Did Ashley pass out from fear with all the excitement?"

Ashley looked into her gloating face, but Malone was not even looking at her. She only had eyes for Derek. A flash of her bell-bottoms flying around her ankles flew through Ashley's mind. The lust pouring out of her eyes while she ogled Derek was frightening. Ashley was sure at any moment she was going to tackle him, and once she did, he was dead meat. She didn't think any man could ward off the she-devil once she attacked.

Ashley looked between her and Derek, who had not even spared Malone a glance. His eyes were on Ashley, staring at her with a look of complete shock as she muttered, "And you two will have beautiful kids."

Everyone looked at Ashley like she had lost her mind. Harold's eyebrows made a deep V over his eyes as he looked from her to Derek and then back again. Ashley noticed Malone had moved from in between the captain and her dad to stand by Derek, who had still not looked her way. Deep down it gave Ashley a satisfied feeling that he had not noticed her thirty-six double Ds resting on his arm. She was practically rubbing them up and down his arm, and he just moved away to squat down and get closer to Ashley.

Ha! Take that, bitch.

At the look of horror that crossed Mom's face, Ashley realized she had spoken that last thought out loud and not kept it in her fuzzy head. Oh great, now they really had reason to think she had lost it.

Malone was glaring down at her and giving Derek a look of confusion. She was not used to being ignored. Men flocked to her huge chest and bleached blonde hair like flies to honey. This might be one of the best days of Ashley's life, watching Malone flounce around trying to get his attention to no avail. Well, maybe not the *best* day, all things considered.

"Is she okay? She's acting pretty weird," Michael asked as he watched her with another scowl.

"I wish people would stop scowling at me. And yes, Michael, I'm fine. I just had the wind knocked out of me when some big oaf tackled me."

"Big oaf?" Looking at Harold in confusion, Michael asked, "What the hell happened to her anyway?"

Ashley looked up at Derek; everyone followed her gaze and stood staring at him, waiting for him to fill them in.

"Um. Well, I kind of panicked when I saw the firebombs flying over the roof, and kind of tackled Ashley to the ground. I may have been a little too zealous in my rush to get her out of harm's way."

"Gee, you think so, genius? Do I look like I have pads and a helmet on, ready to play for the Broncos?"

Her head was still fighting off a daze and the extra effort it took to speak was a little too much for her. She felt her eyes cross and the buzzing in her ears was growing louder by the minute. She groaned and put a hand to her stomach, with a real fear that her grandma's lasagna was going to be all over someone's shoes in a second or two.

Derek gave her an apologetic look that she could tell he really meant, but she was still mad at him. He was carrying a gun, for God's sake. What the hell was going on?

"Hey Malone, could you come stand closer to me?"

She gave Ashley a dubious look and moved back into the circle that was still formed around her prone body.

Ashley turned her head very slowly in the direction of Malone's shoes and felt her stomach give a sudden lurch.

"Ashley, I don't think that's a very nice thing to be doing."

"Michael, I got Shaffer back this morning. I still have one to go to be even."

"Now what the hell is she talking about? What did she do to Shaffer?" Malone barked out, giving her a curios look and stepping back.

Ashley smiled up at her dad and ignored Malone. She reached out for Harold's hand. "Help me sit up, would you, Dad? Slowly, please."

"I don't think that's a good idea. She has a head injury and needs to stay down," Mom insisted as she moved in to stop her from getting up.

Harold started to grab her hand and gently raise her to a sitting position at the same time. Ashley only got a few inches off the grass when her world suddenly swam before her and she felt like she was going to get sick for sure. The blackness was doing a good job of taking over. She took a couple of deep breaths and tried to keep everything at bay.

"The ambulance is here." Michael jumped up to usher them over to where she was semi-lying and sitting.

Laura gave her a questioning look at his statement, knowing how Ashley felt about going to the hospital, but Ashley wasn't going to argue about going. Her head felt like it was about the size of a watermelon and no matter how hard she concentrated, the blackness just kept trying to take over.

Harold lowered her back down and she went without a fight. The voices were starting to come from a distance, and that's when she knew she was a goner.

CHAPTER SEVENTEEN

Ashley slowly awoke as they were strapping her onto the gurney, pulling the straps tight across her upper body. She felt like she was being given a mammogram in her back yard. They had the white strap right across her chest and were cinching it down like she was being transferred to the mental ward. She could feel where they had already strapped her down across her midsection, right across her already full bladder. Thankfully they had not cinched that one any tighter, or she might have embarrassed not only herself but everyone else there as well.

The yard was still a beehive of activity. The fires were out but the firemen were still milling around, talking and collecting their gear. As she let her eyes roam the area she could see about thirty people: family, friends, firemen, cops and the EMTs. No one was really paying any attention to her; they were all involved in doing different things around the yard. Derek was standing a few feet away, trying to dislodge Malone from his arm. Malone had a death grip and was not going to let go. She was batting those fake eyelashes at him and rubbing her chest against his arm, trying to keep his attention. Every time he would start to look Ashley's way, she would tug at his sleeve and move to block his view. Ashley would have felt sorry for him, but she remembered him running to the front yard, pulling a gun out of his pants, and all her sympathies went right out the door.

In the fantasies she had of him pulling something out of his pants, a gun was the last thing she had in mind.

Laura was instructing the EMTs how to do their jobs and Grandma was telling some poor fireman about the fire she had started in this very back yard. He would glance at his fellow firemen, but they would all just chuckle and stay far away. He was going to have to save himself from the clutches of her grandma. Harold and the chief were huddled together over by the fence, and that worried Ashley more than anything. She could see her freedom flying right out of the picture. She caught Michael's eyes and he did not look very happy. He made his way over to her side. "Nice nap?"

"Dickhead."

"It's nice to know that you still love me."

Ashley's eyes moved to where Derek was standing, and Michael's eyes followed hers. "So, what's his real story? I don't think he's some sissified bartender."

"No, I think you're right."

Michael turned back and gave her an intense look. "You don't know any more than that? But the guy is stuck to you like glue and when the firebombs came hurtling over the roof, he was in full protection mode before anyone else had even registered what happened."

"Yeah, that's not the first time I had the feeling he was something besides a bartender. At the hospital, when we found the note he handled it like he knew what he was doing."

The EMTs were starting to roll her through the yard and out to the front, and Michael followed along beside her. "I'll see what I can find out about him."

"Thanks, Michael."

By that time everyone else had noticed that they were wheeling her away, and the crowd began following her to the ambulance with everyone talking at once.

The neighbors had to love them. They didn't have to go out and pay money for their entertainment, they just had to stay home, sit on their porches, and watch the crazy Wright family and all their drama. Ashley could see nosy old Mrs. Zimmer watching behind her curtains in her front window. Everyone else had come out and stood on their front lawns to watch the spectacle, but not her, she stayed inside and peeked out her curtains, the old dingbat. When they were kids they could never do anything that she thought was out of line in their own front yard, or she would be on the phone immediately ratting them out to their parents. They had all learned to keep away from the front yard and play at their friends' houses, or at least keep to their own back yard.

If anyone had seen who had thrown the firebombs, you could bet it was her. Ashley would have to make sure her dad or Michael questioned her about it.

The EMTs were attempting to put Ashley into the back of the ambulance and fighting off all the people trying to get close enough to give her well wishes or words of encouragement, which was making the job a little tougher. The EMTs were not having much luck, because she felt like she was riding the Tilt-O-Whirl again. She was being jostled from side to side and between her head and her stomach, she wasn't sure which felt worse. In the last couple of days, she had felt like someone experiencing the out-of-body thing way too many times. All the noise and excitement were starting to really wear on her nerves. She suddenly had the urge to start screaming again. The whole world was going crazy and she was stuck in the middle of the chaos. She wanted her boring, quiet life back. So what if she didn't have any social life, and heaven forbid a sex life, but at least no one was getting killed because of her and she wasn't making the hospital her home away from home.

Ashley was finally put into the back of the ambulance with some grunting from the EMTs, which really pissed her off. She was not exactly a four-hundred-pound woman they were loading, for goodness sake. She was glaring at them, trying not to piss her pants or puke from the pain in her head. She glanced up and out the back door of the ambulance right into the very intense eyes—make that the very intense and gorgeous eyes—of Derek. He was glaring like there was no tomorrow and she glared right back. He must have realized that he was staring a hole through her, and wiped the look off his face and replaced it with one of concern. Ashley wished they would unstrap her from this stupid gurney so she could talk to him and demand to know what the hell was going on with him. The female EMT was doing her fair share of looking at him also. The man was a huge babe magnet, that was for sure. Good God, her mom had even checked him out.

As she was lying there glaring at him, one of the EMT guys slammed the door and scared the heck out of her. She was so focused on Derek, she had forgotten for a second what was going on around her. The ambulance took off, siren blaring, through their once-quiet neighborhood, taking the corner on two wheels. Or at least sitting in the back that's what it felt like, strapped to a gurney like a mummy. She couldn't reach up to scratch her nose, or even her ass for that matter. Some things were just wrong and this was one of them. No one should feel so helpless. The female EMT riding in the back with her gave her a dirty look. Now, what the hell was that for? She must have assumed Derek belonged to her and gave her a look just for good measure. What else could she be mad at Ashley for? All she knew for sure was, she was tired of everyone glaring at her, giving her dirty looks and killing people on account of her. She was starting to get pissed off just thinking about it. She was the victim here! She, and those murdered women.

As they made their way to the hospital, she started making a plan for how she was going to handle things when she finally got through being bashed on the head for one reason or another, and could think straight. She was through sitting back and letting things keep happening around her without having an active part in it. She felt like a puppet and people kept pulling her strings, making her move around with no control at all.

Ashley looked around at all of the medical supplies, wondering if they had any happy juice to get her through the next few hours. She wondered if the grouchy-ass beside her would mind finding some and inserting it into her I.V. Ashley turned and noticed she was totally ignoring her. So much for concern for her welfare.

Wham! Suddenly they were flying around in the back of the ambulance. She had no idea what had just happened, but she thought someone must have hit them, because they were now lying on the side of the ambulance and it felt like they were being pushed along the road. Everything had fallen out of the cabinets and was flying everywhere. The grouchy-ass EMT was now lying half on top of Ashley, struggling to get a grip on something to brace herself. She was feeling around in the region of Ashley's left tit and she finally latched onto her arm as they both were being thrown around the back of the ambulance. Gee, if she had wanted to be felt up she would have asked Derek, Nick or Troy, not some *female* who was way not her type. Wow, did she have a female type? That thought scared the shit out of her.

They were still flopping around in the back like a couple of fish, as they were sliding across the road. The sound was horrible, metal screeching as they were being pushed along. At least that's what Ashley assumed was going on, because they would have come to a stop by now if they weren't. She could see out the back windows, but all she could make out were cars and buildings going by as they kept moving.

Suddenly there was a huge thud as they hit something hard. She had no idea what it was because they were both flung around the back again. The top of the ambulance was now crunched in

275

completely and had come down on both of them, pinning them in. Ashley could hear the EMT screaming, or at least she hoped it was her and not herself. Ashley was lying on her side, still strapped to the gurney; she could only see the EMT's leg, which was caught between her and the top of the ambulance and bent at an odd angle. Ashley could tell it was broken right below the knee.

Ashley was going to be sick. She tried to wiggle free, but that caused the EMT to scream in agony, so she stopped moving around and tried to get her bearings. She couldn't hear anything coming from outside, which was not a good sign. It was deathly quiet now and, after the horrible noise of the crash, it was eerie. She felt like her head was going to blow up and she could feel blood dripping into her eyes, but she couldn't tell if she was hurt anywhere else. She was having a hard time breathing and she wasn't sure if it was from having a body across her, the straps holding her to the gurney, or if she was hurt.

They were smashed together with all the medical equipment, in what seemed like maybe a foot or so of space. Whatever they had hit must have been solid because the whole top had been pushed in. If they had not already been turned sideways from the initial hit, they might have been hurt much worse than she thought they were.

Suddenly she could hear movement outside the ambulance; someone was here to help.

"Help! Someone help us, please."

No one responded and she yelled louder.

She could hear movement as someone got closer to them, and then she heard a voice. "You bitch, why don't you ever die?"

Ashley's blood ran cold and she frantically looked around for something to use as a weapon. Then she realized that even if she did find something, she couldn't get to it strapped like she was. She started breathing hard and she could feel the panic starting to take over her body. She was a sitting duck back here.

"Who are you? What do you want from me?" she asked.

"Your worst enemy and I want you to die."

"Why? What did I do to you? Please, there's been some mistake." She hated the fear she heard in her voice, but there was no way to stop it. It was running throughout her body at a fast pace.

"THERE'S NO MISTAKE, HOTSHOT COP!"

"What did I do? Why are you trying to kill me?" She could tell he was standing close to where her head was, because his voice sounded like it was right by her ear. She could hear other voices further away, yelling with excitement.

"Do you like all the women who died because of you? I thought you were Wonder Cop, and would have figured it all out by now; I guess you're not as smart as you thought you were. Maybe I should start leaving better clues on the next ones."

She could tell he must have been looking around, because his voice came and went.

"NO! Please don't kill anyone else. What do you want from me? Whatever you want, just ask me. I'll do whatever you want." The EMT was trying to remain quiet, so they could hear what he had to say, and she knew it had to be hard on her with as much pain as she had to be in.

"All I want is for you to die and then it will all…"

Ashley could hear him scrape against the side of the ambulance and then they heard footsteps as he ran away.

"What the hell did you do to piss him off?" whispered the paramedic.

"I have no idea," was her faint reply.

They could hear voices coming from outside as onlookers came to investigate the accident.

"Anyone in there?" someone asked.

"Yes! Please get us out of here." She lifted her head and instantly regretted it as she slammed her head into the rooftop; pain shot through both the front of her head and the back of it. She could tell that the doors were completely mangled and they were not going to be able to open them by themselves. Someone was trying, anyway, bless their souls. She could hear more and more people coming to help.

There was a voice suddenly at the same spot as *his* had been and she about jumped out of her skin. "How many are in there and how bad are you hurt?"

Ashley finally found her voice and answered, "Two of us and I'm doing okay so far, but the EMT has at least a broken leg. How are the drivers?"

"Both of them look to be okay. I only glanced at them as I rushed by."

As they were trying to pull the back doors open, the ambulance would jerk, and the paramedic would groan with pain.

"Wait, please stop. You're hurting her worse by jerking on the doors." She could hear sirens in the distance. "Could you please wait for the fire department? But thanks for trying to open them for us."

The voice beside her head startled her again. "Wow, this ambulance is toast. The guy who was driving the four-by-four must have been going about sixty when he hit you."

"Is he still out there?"

"No, there's no one in the pickup. He must have got scared and ran off."

"The other lady is hurting bad. How soon does it look like before we're out of here?"

"From the looks of things, it's going to be awhile if they have to cut it apart. The fire department and police are just pulling up. Is there anything I can do for you?"

"Just being here and keeping us informed helps a lot. Thanks."

"You bet. I wish there was more I could do to help. What's your name?"

"Ashley. What's yours?"

"Benjamin, but my friends call me Ben. What about the other lady? What's her name?" he asked.

Ashley could tell from his voice that he was an older gentleman, and that was soothing to her.

"Well, until this happened it had been Grouchy Ass, but I think she probably has a different one."

"Hey! I heard that," came a weak voice behind her. "My name's Rachel, not Grouchy Ass."

Ashley had found herself in some peculiar situations before but this had to be on the top of the list. She was lying here tipped on her side, her head bent at an angle, strapped to a gurney, with a woman's leg caught between the top of the ambulance and her, the EMT's crotch lying across her chest and the top of her body trapped somewhere behind Ashley. Ashley was just really thankful that nothing had happened to cause her to lose any bodily functions while they were both stuck in this position.

"See, I told you she probably had a different name." Ashley could hear a chuckle coming from the other side of the mangled roof. She was starting to feel a little claustrophobic with the metal just a few inches from her face. There was so much debris from the broken cabinets and all the medical equipment and supplies, that there was not an inch of space that wasn't cluttered with something. She didn't know where Rachel's head was, but she hoped she was doing a better job of breathing than Ashley was.

"Rachel, you hanging in back there?" Ashley got no answer and assumed she had passed out from the pain. She knew she was about to. She could smell blood and she knew she was still bleeding from the cut on her head, because it was running into her eyes. Her chest was wet, so maybe Rachel had peed her pants, but she didn't think so because she did not smell urine. Which meant she was bleeding from somewhere on her leg. That was not a pleasant thought for either of them.

"Hey, Ben? Could you tell them to speed it up out there? I think I lost Rachel for a while. She may be hurt worse than I originally thought."

"You bet. Let me go find someone. They're all on the other side and I'm back here wedged between the roof and the wall you guys hit."

"Ben, one more thing…"

"What's that?"

"Could you try and not touch anything around you?"

"Huh?"

"Try to not leave any fingerprints."

"Okay, whatever you say."

"And could you tell the firemen to do the same?"

"Sure thing. Be right back."

Ashley closed her eyes since they were starting to burn from the blood getting into them. She wanted to reach up and wipe it away, but couldn't with her arms still strapped down. She heard Rachel groan and she let out a sigh of relief. She didn't want any more people to die because of her. Two was two too many.

Ashley could hear the voices getting louder as people moved to the front of the vehicle, and movement at the top of the roof again.

"Ben, is that you?"

"Yes. Are you okay? You sound a little weak."

"Hanging in there. What's happening out there?"

"They are going to try and get the guys out of the front before they start working on cutting you two out."

"How bad are they hurt?"

"The one closest to the top looks to only have a broken arm and the one against the ground only has some cuts and scrapes. It's going to be a little tough getting him out. Guess they're going to have to go through the windshield. Have to tell you, it's not a pretty sight out here. You can't even tell this was once an ambulance."

"If you think it's bad out there, you should see it in here. Looks like World War Three."

Ashley could hear them trying to get to the drivers; there were faint moans among the breaking glass and metal being twisted. It seemed like she'd lain there forever before she heard Ben talking to someone. Their voices were muffled and she couldn't make out what they were saying, but she could hear them as they continued talking. Every once in a while she could make out a word or two but that was about all. Suddenly, a voice grew louder, "Ashley? She said her name was Ashley?"

"Hey wait! You're too big to get back there," she heard Ben call out.

"Ashley, is that you in there?"

"Nick?"

"Sweet Jesus, woman! What in the hell happened?"

Just hearing his somewhat familiar voice gave her instant relief. "I don't know, Nick! Get me out of here, okay?"

"Hang in there. Are you hurt?"

"I don't know, but the paramedic is. Hurry."

"They almost have the second guy out from the cab and then we're going to tackle getting you two out. Can you describe what it looks like in there, so we know where the best place to go in would be?"

Ashley told him where they were positioned and where she thought the best place to cut into the metal would be. "Nick, could you do me a favor?"

"Anything, babe."

Babe? He called her babe. Wow! The father of her children just called her babe. She started fantasizing about what their children

281

would look like: tall, really tall, boys with gorgeous wavy strawberry blonde hair, with the deepest blue eyes and the girls would be—

"Ashley? Are you still with me?"

Coming back to the present with a start, she tried to remember what they had been talking about.

"You wanted a favor, remember?"

"Oh yeah. Please don't call my family. I don't want them to see me like this."

"Were they going to meet you at the hospital?"

Groaning, she said, "Shit."

"I take it that means yes? They're going to figure it out when the ambulance never shows up, and then they're going to panic. Wouldn't it be better to hear it from someone they know?"

She sure in the hell didn't want to put them through any more drama than they already had been, but she didn't want them rushing here and freaking out when they saw the condition of the ambulance, either.

"All right, call them, but explain that I'm fine and ask them not to come here, just to wait for me there at the hospital."

"Do you know your family?"

"Yeah, you're right, but tell Michael that I asked personally for him to make sure they do it. You can call every so often and fill him in on the progress, can't you?"

"I'll try to persuade him. Be right back. You sure you're okay?"

"I'll be a hell of a lot better when you pry this tin box open and get us out of here. Um, did Ben ask you to be careful about not touching anything?"

"Yes, he did, and I assume you have a good reason for asking that. It's a little hard to rescue you and not touch anything, but I'll make sure everyone involved has gloves on."

"Thanks, Nick! I appreciate it." Ashley could hear him wiggle his big body out from in between the top and the wall. Now that he wasn't standing there talking to her, the other sounds came back into the picture. She could hear the voices in the front talking to the last guy still stuck behind the wheel.

Ashley couldn't help but worry about what her family must be going through now that the ambulance had not shown up. She wasn't sure how much time had gone by, but it was only a ten-minute trip to the hospital, and she knew they were way past that amount of time. Her brain was a little fuzzy and things were starting to blur. She had to keep things straight so she could relay what the killer had said. Thank God Rachel was awake at that time, because maybe she would be able to help her remember everything. Ashley closed her eyes so she could concentrate on replaying everything that was said between them. She couldn't stop the shudder that went through her at the thought that only a thin mangled piece of metal had separated her from a killer. This man was nuts. This was the third time he'd tried to kill her. Innocent people were being hurt and he didn't care. First, Michael, and now the ambulance crew, and who knows how many others before he was caught or he finally got his wish and killed her. Her family had been in the back yard when he had thrown the Molotov cocktails. The thought of dying scared her to death. There was so much she still wanted to do. She wanted to go to Hawaii and lie on the beach, and watch the waves wash across her body as she lay intertwined with her lover. She wanted to become a detective and be able to boss Malone around. She wanted the fairytale wedding and the kids and the whole bit. She wanted to do Nick, Derek and Troy. Maybe not all at once, but definitely wanted to do them all. Life was too short. Not that she was going to become a slut, but those three were definitely a must...

She must have dozed a little, because she was startled awake by Nick's voice again. "Ashley? Ash, answer me!"

"I'm here."

"God, woman, you scared me when you didn't answer me right away."

"Sorry. I must have dozed a little bit. Would it make you feel any better if I told you I dreamt about you and what you could do with that big tall body of yours?" she responded in a half-asleep voice.

Her comment was met with dead silence.

Hesitantly she asked, "Nick, you still out there?" She was mortified that she had said that out loud.

After a slight hesitation she heard, "Yeah, I'm here. A little concerned that you're delirious."

Oh God... "Um, Nick, about what I said, it must be the shock talking."

"Not sure if it's shock or what, but you sure had me going."

Ashley groaned and she heard him chuckle. His phone rang and she could hear him as he struggled to get to it. "Oh great, it's your brother. Should I tell him everything's fine?"

She listened to him as he moved out again and answered his phone. She could tell he was reassuring Michael by the tone of his voice. If she knew Michael, he was giving him the third degree and asking questions Nick had no answers for.

"Ashley, they're ready to start getting you out now, but they have to pull the pickup away from that side before we can get to it. You are going to hear a lot of noise. The two vehicles are meshed together pretty good. Is there any way for you two to cover your heads with anything?"

"Nick, I'm strapped down in here and I'm pretty sure Rachel is still out of it."

"That's okay. You may feel some sparks as we cut through the metal, but we have no other choice. Is Rachel stable? The metal may give when it's cut."

"I have no idea. All I can see is the top of this damn thing and a bunch of medical supplies, and I can't even *see* her, just her leg and crotch across my chest."

"Damn woman, do you know what kind of image that gives a man?"

"You men are all alike."

"I know. Isn't it great?"

He moved away again and she could hear all the commotion behind her as they started getting ready to separate the two vehicles. They were working at the end of the ambulance close to the rear doors, away from where she and Rachel were located.

"Hey Ashley. It's me, Ben. You still doing okay in there?"

"Hey. Where you been? I missed your voice."

"That giant of a fireman wedged himself in here and wouldn't budge. I take it you know him. They kept trying to get me to move away, but I told them you would need me again."

"Thanks, Ben, I do. It helps knowing I have someone to talk to. You're safe where you are, aren't you?"

"Yeah. They're cutting on the other side and I just have my head stuck in a little ways in case the car shifts. Don't want to get this gorgeous body squished, now do we?"

"Hell no! How am I supposed to take a squished gorgeous body to supper, to thank it for being there in my hour of need?"

"Really? I was here in your hour of need?"

"Ben, I can't thank you enough for staying here and talking me through this. It's been pretty scary for me and I might have lost it if you hadn't cared enough to stick around."

"You're welcome, little lady. My pleasure."

"Ben, do you have a piece of paper and a pen?"

"You bet. Why?"

"I want to give you my cell number. I expect things will get a little crazy when they bust us out of here and I may not get another chance. I want you to promise to call me in a couple days, okay?"

"I would be honored. I'm ready."

Ashley gave him her number and thanked him again for being there for her. "What's it like out there anyway?"

"Oh wow! This neighborhood hasn't seen this much action in a long time. There are about a zillion cop cars and fire trucks, plus all kinds of news vans and people everywhere."

"Where exactly are we?"

"You're on the corner of Cottonwood and First. It looks like you were hit down around Second Street and pushed along the whole block till he steered you into the side of the Dollar Store. There is debris strung along the whole block. Whoever was driving must have passed out or something to have pushed you that far without hitting the brakes."

Passed out, her ass! The bastard had hit the gas, not the brake. He must have watched them load her into the ambulance from her house, followed them and waited until he had a clear shot at them, then barreled into them going at an extremely fast rate to have caused this much damage. "Ben, how are the two drivers doing?"

"The one just had a nasty bump on the head; and the other guy was taken away in another meat wagon before I could see him, so I'm not sure about him."

They must have started winching the other vehicle away because the ambulance started rocking with the movement.

"Ben, move away!"

He never answered so she hoped he got out of the way before it rocked back again. Rachel let out a groan of pain as they continued to disengage the two masses of metal. Something must have given because suddenly Ashley's head was thrown up against the roof and she could feel fresh blood start pouring into her eyes again. She didn't think her head could take many more beatings; it was starting to feel like a bowl of mush. She was already covered in cuts and bruises and she hated to think what she looked like now. But, she was alive and that's all that was important. Cuts would heal; being dead was another story.

"Whew! That was a close one. Thought I was going to be Humpty Dumpty there for a minute."

Ashley could feel herself smiling but couldn't find the energy to answer. She was aware of the commotion as they continued to work. She heard the sound of the saw in the recesses of her brain, but it sounded like it was coming from a great distance away. She was vaguely aware of Ben calling her name, but as much as she wanted to answer, she couldn't seem to do it. Strange, it was like her mouth was moving but no sound was coming out. She could hear herself answering in her head, but nothing came out. She lay there with the blood dripping down her face, an unconscious woman lying across her body, and faded in and out of consciousness herself.

Ben kept talking, telling her how Nick was on the outside working like a madman, cutting into the side of the ambulance. They had to climb onto the top, which was actually the side, because it was too dangerous to go in from the bottom. They were concerned about the gas and the sparks that were flying around them all.

When Nick paused to get a different angle on the cut, he could hear the crazy old guy who had insisted on being left by the wall so he could continue to fill Ashley in on what was happening. The old fart began screaming Ashley's name, but Nick couldn't hear anything coming from inside. He felt panic racing through his body. Ever since he had seen Ashley during the shed fire, he couldn't get her out of his mind. She was a little spitfire who set his blood on fire, and all he could think about was getting to her fast.

After twenty minutes of cutting they were finally able to peel away a chunk of the metal to look inside. Someone passed a flashlight to Nick, who was lying down flat and took his first look inside. Just as he was doing it, Michael's head popped up from the rear doors. "How is she?"

Nick gave him a dirty look. "I thought your sister asked you to stay at the hospital?"

"Would you have, if it was your sister?" Michael answered.

Nick nodded to Michael, "Hell, no."

Michael crawled up onto the ambulance, being careful not to disturb anything. He reached the area where Nick was and they looked into each other's eyes for a soul-searching moment. "Is she…?"

Nick took a deep breath and answered, "I'm not sure. We haven't heard any noise from inside the ambulance for the last thirty minutes or so. We had to jerk the vehicles apart and who knows what that put them through."

Ashley didn't even try to respond; her lungs were on fire and she was having a hard time catching her breath. She saw the light through her closed eyelids as Nick switched on the flashlight and pointed the beam into the darkness.

"Holy mother of God," Nick whispered.

"Oh shit! I think I'm going to be sick." Michael pulled his head back from looking inside and started taking in huge gulps of air.

"Michael, you okay? You've turned a nasty shade of green."

"She's covered in so much blood."

"Michael, get a grip. You know how head wounds bleed."

"How do you explain the rest of the blood all over her body?"

"I can't."

"Jesus, what a mess. How are we going to get them out?"

"We're not. You're going to back off now and let somebody else up here that has some experience doing this."

"Bullshit! That's my sister down there."

"My point exactly. Now get your ass away from here so we can get her out and get her the medical help she needs."

Ashley could imagine Nick staring into Michael's eyes, waiting for him to argue or at the very least punch his lights out, but Michael surprised them and inched his way to the back of the vehicle, growling, "Get my sister out of there now, and I want a running commentary on everything that you're doing."

"You got it. Do me a favor and send Gomez up here and tell him to bring his supplies," Nick replied.

Once Michael was on the ground again, Nick yelled down to him from where he was still lying on the side of the ambulance. "Can you hear me, Michael?"

"Yes."

"I'm going to look back down into the hole and try to decide the best way to go about getting them out. This vehicle is smashed into a fraction of its original size, which makes it impossible to reach them, the way they're wedged together with not an inch of room to spare."

"Ashley, can you hear me?"

She was fighting to stay awake. She could hear them talking, she just couldn't find the breath to respond.

"Michael, she had a nasty cut along her hairline and it's bleeding at a good rate. I can't see much else of her, with the way the other woman is stretched across her. You're right, there's a lot of blood, but whose it is, is anyone's guess. If I can get the EMT awake I might be able to get her out and then figure out some way to get to Ashley. I'm going to inch my way in so that I'm hanging into the hole. I'm going to move stuff out of the way as I go until I can stretch out my hand and reach the EMT.

"Ashley, I don't know if you can hear me, but I'm going to keep talking so you and Michael know what's happening."

"Anyone know the EMT's name?" Nick asked up through the cut.

Ben yelled out from the side of the car, "It's Rachel."

"I'm going to touch her arm, give her a gentle shake," Nick said.

There was a moan from inside the ambulance, but Nick called up that he wasn't sure who it had come from. "I cannot get either woman to respond, but I'm going to try and get a better look around. Christ, this is impossible. Things are so tightly wedged in here, there's no room to move. We have to find another way to do this."

Nick shimmied back up through the hole they had cut in the side of the ambulance. As he was talking to everyone on the outside, tears fell from Ashley's eyes.

Gomez asked Nick, "How does it look?"

"Not good. Take a look for yourself."

Gomez stuck his head in the hole for a minute, before popping back out. "This is not going to work from this angle."

"That's what I came up with too."

They inched their way back down to the ground.

Michael growled, "What the hell are you doing coming down?"

"We're going to have to find another way to get them out," Nick answered.

"*Fuck.*"

Nick turned away to talk to his captain, while Michael stomped off in the opposite direction, and as he came around the side of the ambulance he ran right into Derek. "What the hell are you doing here?"

Derek said. "Helping."

"Fuck you! Get out of here. You have no business being here."

"I have every right to be here. Now stop being an asshole and tell me what's happening."

Michael reared back and punched Derek in the jaw. Derek's head whipped back, but he didn't go down.

Derek reached up and rubbed his jaw, turning back to look at Michael. "I'll let the sucker punch go, because I know that you're worried about your sister, but fair warning, I won't stand still for another one."

Michael was breathing hard, emotions racing through his body. Derek watched as the emotions flashed across his face. He knew this had to be hard on him and he was willing to wait him out. It took him several minutes to pull it all together, but he finally took a deep breath and seemed to settle down. Michael was rubbing his arm above where the cast ended as he stood there.

"You're right. I had no right to take my frustration out on you. Now, tell me who the hell you are, and don't even try telling me the bullshit bartender story."

"Michael, I owe you and your family an explanation, but I don't think this is the time or the place. Let's get your sister the help she needs and then we can all sit down and talk."

Michael took another few minutes and decided Derek was right. As the two of them were arguing, the firemen had made a new plan and were beginning to act on it.

Derek and Michael raced around to the front of the vehicle where the firemen were all gathered. They had started cutting away the rest of the windshield.

Someone explained that they were going to cut through the cab of the ambulance and try and pull them out that way. One of the firemen leaned through the hole on the top of the ambulance, holding a blanket in to protect Ashley and Rachel from the sparks and flying metal.

Michael, Derek and Ben stood and watched. Two were over six feet tall, both as broad as a tree, flanking a man of about five feet six inches and about a hundred years old.

Derek finally noticed Ben standing among them. "Who the hell are you?"

"Ben."

"So Ben, what's your story? Why haven't you been moved behind the police barricades?"

"I'm here for Ashley."

"What?" Derek asked.

Michael growled out, "Start explaining now, old man."

"Geez, you don't have to yell. I was the first one on the scene and talked to her through the top of the van until they started prying them apart."

"Is she okay?" they both asked at the same time.

"I think she was until that last jerk of the vehicle, and then I lost her. I tried to get her to answer but I got nothing."

Michael and Derek watched as the old man struggled not to let the tears in his eyes fall onto his weathered wrinkled cheeks.

"But you talked to her the rest of the time. Did she say anything else?"

"Of course she said stuff," Ben said, giving both men a look like they were daft or something. He turned his gaze back to the work in progress.

Derek and Michael looked at each over the man's head in amazement. They both stood there waiting for him to continue, but when Ben said nothing Michael barked out, "Old man, if you want to live to see a hundred and one you had better start talking *now.*"

Ben glared at both men, muttering under his breath about the younger generation and their disrespect for the elderly.

"Old man, you have no idea what kind of disrespect you are going to be seeing if you don't start telling me what my sister had to say."

"*Your sister?* Why the hell didn't you say so? She was fine when I first got to her, all spunky like, calling the other lady Grouchy Ass."

"That sounds like her," Michael replied.

"Anything else?"

"Yeah, it was kind of weird when she asked me not to touch anything and to make sure no one else left any fingerprints on that side of the vehicle."

Derek and Michael came to attention again at that information. "Did she say why?"

"Nope. Never got a chance to ask. Things started hopping after that. That big giant over there kept pushing me out, so he could talk to her."

Derek turned to look at who Ben was pointing to and noticed who was behind the mask doing the cutting. He made a low growling sound in the back of his throat, glaring at Nick as he watched him.

Michael watched as Derek kept scowling at Nick. "Well, it's obvious you have the hots for my little sister."

Derek tore his gaze away, turned to Michael with a go-to-hell look and answered, "That's none of your business."

"When it comes to my sister, IT. IS. MY. BUSINESS."

"Are you two going to start throwing punches again? 'Cause if so, warn me so I can move. I don't want to get caught in the middle of some macho fistfight while a poor girl is lying in there hurt," remarked Ben.

That sobered them both right up. They turned their attention back to where the firemen were almost through the metal behind the seat of the ambulance. As they watched, Nick was like a man possessed. Once they were done cutting, he threw the saw to the side and attacked the metal.

Snickering, Ben looked up at Derek and said, "I think you may have some competition on your hands, sonny."

Derek whipped his head down, asking, "What's that supposed to mean?"

"All I know is, she must be one dandy little lady to draw so much attention from two strapping young men like the two of you. But doesn't matter none. She's taking *me* out to dinner and not you."

"Bullshit, old man. You're crazy."

He held up the piece of paper with Ashley's cell phone number on it. "Do you have her cell number, sonny?"

"You two are pathetic. That's my sister you two are arguing over."

Nick had reached through the hole and was handing pieces of debris out to his fellow firefighters. They had a chain going with Gomez shouting out instructions as they went. They had a huge pile of medical stuff and plastic and metal parts that had broken apart from the cabinets lining the wall of the ambulance.

Nick was too big to get in and help extract the women, so Gomez was elected again to go in and try and work them free. He wiggled his body in through the hole and landed in a tiny space they had made.

Gomez shouted out, "Nick, I need you on top again. You're the only one big enough to be able to reach in and help get the women untangled. Put yourself back into the same position as you were before and help me by reaching in to stabilize the EMT, and hold her as I pull the gurney away from the top of the vehicle."

Rachel let out a groan, but she never came to as Gomez and Nick worked together to get a splint onto her leg and place a back brace behind her.

Ashley could barely open her eyes with all the blood, but she watched as Gomez placed a brace on Rachel's neck.

Gomez looked up to Nick. "I don't see any way to get her out without raising her up from where she is lying over the lady on the gurney. If you can help me raise her gently, I think I can reach around enough to get her strapped on."

Nick lowered himself down further into the ambulance and gently grabbed Rachel by the shoulders; between the two of them, they maneuvered her onto the back brace. She had made a gasping noise but otherwise remained unconscious.

Nick grabbed ahold of the brace by the handles in the side of it and started lifting her through the hole in the side of the ambulance. His muscles were bulging with the weight of Rachel, Gomez was helping lift and guide her through, being careful not to let her bang against anything as they worked.

Nick pulled Rachel through the gaping hole and passed her into the hands waiting to help get her down off the top of the ambulance.

As they carried Rachel past, Ben asked, "Is that her?"

Michael shook his head no.

Nick had gently dropped down into the hole once the EMT was gone, which caused Derek to growl again.

"Okay, Gomez, let's grab the gurney and turn it so that it's on its wheels again. On the count of three, let's go nice and slow. One, two, three, go."

Ashley could feel them turning her and thought the movement was going to make her pass out for sure.

"Nick, goddamn it. What's going on in there?" Michael shouted.

Nick took a deep breath, "We just turned her over, and I'm going to straddle the gurney because there is no room to do otherwise, and check to see what we've got going on. She has not moved since I dropped down here. Her breath is raspy; we need to move fast." He leaned over and moved her hair from where it was matted to her face with dried and fresh blood. She was pale from the loss of blood and her breathing was shallow. He took a quick pulse and yelled for Gomez to help him get her out of there. "She's lost a lot of blood and is in shock, and needs medical help soon."

They placed a cervical collar on her, slowly started moving her out through the hole they had cut behind the seat, and she moaned with pain.

"It's okay, Ashley, we're getting you out."

295

"Nick, I can't breathe," she whispered.

They set her down and yelled through the opening, and someone sent in an oxygen mask and tank. Nick gently placed it across her face, being careful not to move her head. They picked the gurney back up and proceeded to move her out through the waiting hole. He watched her face the whole time for any signs of distress. He winced with every flinch of pain that crossed her face. They finally emerged from the confines of the vehicle, and the crowd that had gathered let out a cheer as they moved her toward the back of another waiting ambulance.

Derek, Michael and Ben moved in as they carried her through the crowd of firefighters, cops and rescue workers.

She was aware of the movement and she thought she was going to die with every move they made. Her lungs were on fire and it felt like she had a semi sitting on her chest. She had managed to open her eyes again; she focused in on Ben's face and struggled to reach up and remove the mask, which wasn't easy since she was still strapped down. "Ben?" she managed to gasp out.

"Yes, ma'am."

Giving him her warmest smile she whispered, "Thank you and don't forget to call me."

"No way will I forget that! You get better real soon, okay?"

Ashley looked around and finally found Michael's face. "Dust the roof of the ambulance," she said, and then passed out.

CHAPTER EIGHTEEN

The ambulance roared off with Ashley in the back and Derek beside her. Michael chose to stay behind and call in the crime scene investigators to do as Ashley had asked, but called his family waiting at the hospital to tell them the latest developments first. He had been calling about every ten minutes throughout the excavation to let them know the progress of getting Ashley removed from the mangled mess of twisted metal. He had kept his information strictly about how the firemen were doing, not telling any of them how he had gotten a chance to peek into the interior of the ambulance and witness his sister covered in blood, unconscious. That was a detail that did not need to be shared with his worried family.

He still felt sick to his stomach when he thought of how she had looked, her hair matted to her head and her face pale and pasty looking. He had noticed that her breathing was shallow and she was struggling to catch her breath when they had finally pulled her free. He figured there was a good chance that she had some broken ribs and maybe a punctured lung, and he prayed there was nothing more seriously wrong. He had been on enough accident calls to realize that many people had internal injuries that were life threatening, and to think his sister was in that position right now scared the hell out of him. He really wanted to be there with her and the family, but knew it was just as important to try and catch the guy who was doing this. Besides, Ashley had plenty of people there to help her through this and they would keep him informed of any developments. Four patrol cars had escorted the ambulance as it made its way to the hospital, assuring Michael that there would be no more accidents.

"Michael, why did you let that piece of shit ride with your sister instead of you going with her?"

Chuckling under his breath, Michael turned to Nick. "I needed to stay here and take over the crime scene and I felt better knowing someone was with her, in case someone tries to kill her again."

"*What the hell do you mean, kill her?*" Nick shouted at Michael, and then moved closer to him when he realized people had stopped to stare at the two of them.

"I have a feeling this was no random accident. I called in the plates on the four-by-four while we were waiting for you to get her out, and they came back stolen. I think someone deliberately ran into her. She confirmed my suspicion when she told me to dust the ambulance."

Arching his left eyebrow, Nick said, "That's why she asked us all to not leave any fingerprints on it? But who would do something like that, knowing that she was already injured inside and with innocent victims with her?"

Rubbing the back of his neck with his good arm, Michael growled, "Some really sick fuck, if you ask me. The sick bastard tossed firebombs into our back yard earlier tonight. God knows who could have been hurt if they had landed close to any of my family. That's how Ashley got hurt again. Our hotshot bartender tackled her and covered her body with his when the first one hit. Then he jumped up and pulled a gun out of his pants and raced around front with Dad and me when we tried to catch the guy. I assume this asshole realized he missed Ashley and was pissed, so he decided to ram the ambulance on its way to the hospital. For some reason this guy really wants my sister hurt or even worse, dead."

"I don't even want to know why the bartender was at your place when all this happened; I assume he followed you all home this morning when you left the hospital. I knew I should not have gone to work today. Maybe if I had been there I could have been the one to protect her." Nick had a scowl on his face as he paced in front of Michael. "Wait, what do you mean he had a gun? Why would he have a gun?"

"Beats the shit out of me, but believe me, I'm going to find out what his story is, just as soon as I'm done here."

"Something's not right with that guy. I don't like the way he's always around your sister."

Michael stood and gave Nick a curious look.

"What?"

"Nothing, man. You just seem to be awful worried about my sister all of a sudden."

Nick looked up in surprise. "Ah...Michael...um..."

"Hey, don't sweat it, man. Just yanking your chain."

Nick gave Michael's shoulder a quick punch, staggering Michael with the force of the quick jab. "Keep me informed, will you? I'm on for another twelve hours."

"You got it. And thanks, Nick, for getting my sister out."

"No problem."

"You might want to see about those cuts on your hands."

Nick looked down in surprise.

"I must have cut them when I was prying the metal back. They're fine." The latex gloves covering his hands were ripped in several places and there was blood coming from several cuts on both hands.

"Hey man, whatever you say. Just don't contaminate my crime scene with any of your skanky blood."

"I'll show you skanky," he said and took a menacing step towards Michael.

Michael made a show of grabbing his injured arm and played the wounded sap routine. "Hey, I've already gone this route once; I don't think I'm up for it again."

Nick's captain motioned for him, so they separated and went their own ways. Nick went to help his buddies collect all the tools they had used to extract the victims, and Michael started talking to witnesses while he waited for the forensic team, Ben being his first. By the time he had questioned everyone who had seen the accident, he was no further ahead than he was before. No one had seen the driver of the four-by-four, only knew that it was a man, and he took off running behind the ambulance and was gone before they got to the scene. Everyone had been too far away to make out any details, and even Ben, who was the first on the scene, had not seen the driver. Michael got his number and promised to call him later to let him know how Ashley was doing.

His dad called him and reported that Ashley had made it to the hospital, but they had rushed her through the emergency entrance and straight back to triage. No one had even gotten to see her, which Michael was thankful for. They discussed security at the hospital, and then Michael told his dad about his theory and how Ashley had asked him to dust the ambulance for fingerprints.

"Why do you think she wanted that done?"

"I have a feeling the guy was around the ambulance. I can't wait to talk to Ashley so she can fill us in on what happened. No word on her condition?"

"None. Your mom is demanding to be let back so she can check on her, but they won't let her. You should hear her ranting and raving about being a member of this staff for over twenty years, and if it was one of their children she would let them back there. I feel sorry for Meg, who is working the emergency room desk."

Michael let out a sigh, glad he wasn't there at the hospital. His mom could be a real bear when she got her dander up. Hopefully she would be calmed down by the time he finished up here. "Hey, Dad? Is Derek still there?"

"Yeah, he is."

"What's his story?"

"When your sister's up to talking we'll tell the whole family, because you know she's going to be furious."

"So you know and you're keeping it from me? Dad, that's fucked up."

"*Michael!* Don't you dare take that tone with me! No matter what's going on, I'm still your father."

"Yeah, sorry, Dad. I'm just really frustrated with this whole mess."

There was a minute of silence as both men tried to get their emotions under control. "Michael, I know how you're feeling, but I only want to go over this once and my concern right now is your sister."

"You're right, Dad, I'm sorry."

They finished up the call right as the forensics team pulled up. Michael went over and told them what he wanted dusted. Between the stolen four-by-four and the ambulance, he was hoping to find something that would lead to the prick who was threatening his sister's life, and killing and hurting innocent people who got in his way. He watched as the team went about dusting all the areas that they thought might have been touched. He stood there, feeling helpless, rubbing his arm and wishing he could be more involved with the investigation. Luckily the captain had not pulled him completely off work, but let him stay on as an observer at least. He knew that even if he had been pulled, he would have been right in the middle of it anyway so it was better for everyone if he got paid for it.

As he watched, his phone rang with a text message, which was weird because he hardly ever got any. He hated to text. If someone wanted to talk to him, just pick up the phone and call him instead of all that stupid texting stuff. He retrieved the message and felt his blood run cold. Sprayed across the screen were the words, **_DO YOU THINK I'M STUPID ENOUGH TO LEAVE ANY PRINTS?_** His head whipped up and he frantically looked around, trying to see who could have sent the message. He couldn't believe the guy was close enough to be able to see that they were indeed doing exactly that. But even scarier was that the guy had his number. This phone was department issue, and even then only a few had the number. Everything else went through the police scanner in his car. Several people were still milling around watching the cleanup process, but no one seemed to be interested in what he was doing. But that didn't mean anything. The guy could be in any one of the businesses lining the street and watching him through a front window, and there was no way he would be able to spot him. Hell, he could have been in the crowd all along, watching. Michael may have even questioned him unknowingly. That would really get the guy's rocks off. Whoever this guy was, he had to have someone on the inside of the department giving him information, whether they were conscious of it or not. He had just a little bit too much knowledge of what was going on. First, he had known what hospital Ashley had been taken to after the first hit and run attempt, and felt comfortable enough to make himself right at home at the hospital, being able to leave the hunk of hair from the second murder victim on her food tray…and then to know where their parents lived, and to have access to a department-issued cell phone, meant someone was giving him information.

What really pissed Michael off was that he knew they were not going to find any prints left behind that might identify this guy. He felt like flinging his phone as far as he could but knew that the guy was probably still watching; he didn't want to give the guy the satisfaction of knowing that he had really pissed him off.

He had just clipped his phone to his belt when he got another message, but there was no way he was going to give the guy the satisfaction of seeing him answer it. He would wait till he was alone in his car before he checked it. He left it clipped to his belt and continued to talk to one of the guys who was dusting the four-by-four. After several minutes he got another message and then a few seconds later another one, both of which he ignored. Good. *It must be pissing him off that I'm not playing his little game*, Michael thought.

Michael stuck around for another fifteen minutes and then decided there was no reason to stay any longer, especially since he now knew they were not going to find anything useful. He wanted to get over to the hospital anyway and see what was going on with Ashley.

He climbed into his car, and after taking a few minutes to look around and make a mental note of the cars in the area, so he would be able spot someone who might follow him away from the scene, he put his car in gear and drove away. It took everything in him not to check his phone, but if the guy was watching him, he wanted to make sure he didn't see him check it.

He drove down First Street, heading in the direction of the hospital while keeping an eye on the cars behind him. None of the cars that had been in the immediate vicinity had pulled out behind him, but that didn't mean anything. The guy could have been on a side street, sitting in his car, watching the whole scene and staying a safe distance away. Michael had developed a knot in his stomach the second he had seen the car barreling towards Ashley days ago, and it was still there. Only now it had grown to the size of a bowling ball. Someone was out to kill his sister and neither he nor anyone in the department had the first clue as to who it was.

The scenes of the two murders had turned up absolutely no clues, which meant they were dealing with someone who took extreme precautions. No fibers, hairs, or DNA anywhere on either victim. It was like the guy had worn a plastic suit while he committed the gruesome murders. No sperm was found in either victim, which meant he had worn a condom. He had to have been covered in blood, as badly as he had hacked the victims up, but there had not been one drop of blood leading away from the crime scene. The guy must have stripped right there and bundled the clothes he was wearing so there would not be a trail. So far they had nothing to go on, no clues whatsoever.

Michael pulled out his phone and called the precinct, telling the captain about his text message, and asked them to run a trace on the incoming messages he had received. Then he checked the new ones he had ignored earlier.

YOU OR YOUR HOTSHOT COP SISTER WILL NEVER CATCH ME

This guy was definitely trying to push their buttons, and he was doing a damn fine job of it. Michael wanted to reach through the phone and pull the guy's jugular out through his asshole.

The next message read *DON'T IGNORE ME FUCKER* and the final one read *OKAY HOTSHOT YOU WILL PAY JUST LIKE YOUR SISTER.*

CHAPTER NINETEEN

Michael arrived at the hospital to find his family still gathered in the emergency waiting room. They all had worried looks on their faces, which caused the knot in his stomach to grow a little bigger.

"Any word yet?"

"The nurse came out a while ago and said they were taking her back to surgery. She has some busted ribs, a punctured lung and a nasty cut on her head, and probably a concussion. They are trying some new invasive laser treatment to try and seal her lung without having to open her up to repair the damage," Laura explained.

"They're using my sister as a guinea pig?" Michael was even angrier than he had been a few minutes ago.

"No, Michael. It's just a technique that's relatively new, and until they get her back into surgery they don't know if it will work on her injuries. Let's hope it does, because it will cut her recovery time in half." Laura looked up into his eyes and he could tell she was just about ready to lose it. Her eyes were red rimmed and she was just about as pale as Ashley had been in the back of the ambulance. He pulled her up and embraced her. She wrapped her arms around him and hung on for dear life. Over her head, Michael surveyed the room. His dad was leaning against the far wall talking on his cell phone, to the station or the captain, Michael assumed. Shannon was sitting in one of the chairs, along with Casey and Dan, both sets of grandparents and Derek. Michael turned his stare on Derek.

"You're still here?"

"I'm not going anywhere."

Michael was pleased to notice that Derek had a bruise forming along his jaw where he had punched him earlier. So what if it had been a sucker punch? It had felt good to wipe that smug look off his face. Michael had to give the guy some credit. He was definitely concerned about the welfare of his sister and if he hadn't gone around flashing a Glock, Michael might not be so worried about the whole deal. He kept his good arm around his mom and moved to help her sit in a chair. She looked like she was about ready to drop. She had been through more excitement in the last week than she had in her whole life. She had worked at this very hospital for over twenty years and dealt with this kind of trauma every day, but it had never involved her family before. The thought of someone trying to kill one of her kids was a little more than the average person could handle. Three members of her immediate family were in law enforcement and she had dealt with the everyday fears that went along with that, but none of them had ever been in any kind of real danger before. Leave it to his sister to dive head first into the kind of drama most cops never face in their whole police careers. She was somehow involved with the two murders, had three attempts on her own life, and now was back in surgery being a guinea pig, no matter what his mom said.

After placing Laura into one of the plastic chairs provided in the waiting room, Michael made his way to his dad. He was just finishing up the call and turned to Michael. "Derek explained what you've been doing. Let's hope something comes from it."

"I'm not putting much hope in it." Michael took out his phone, went to his message box and showed Dad what he had received as he was dusting the ambulance, and then went on to explain about the other three messages.

"*Son of a bitch!*" Harold growled, as he turned and smacked the wall with his fist.

Everyone in the room jumped, even Michael. They all stared in shock as Harold stomped from the room and headed down the hall. Laura had jumped up to follow him, but Michael grabbed her arm. "Let him go, Mom. He needs some time."

"Michael, what's going on? Why is your father so upset?"

"It's about the case. Nothing to worry about, Mom."

Derek's gaze became more intense at Michael's statement, and he got up and walked out of the waiting room. Michael watched him, wondering where he was headed off to. Everyone else had just sat by and listened to the exchange between Michael and his mom, but nobody had said a word. His mom went back to wringing her hands and looking up at the door every few seconds, waiting for someone to come with news about Ashley, while Shannon turned to Casey and they started talking in a hushed tone.

Michael waited a few minutes and then went to see if he could find where Derek and his dad had gone. Harold was coming out of the restroom and Derek was standing just outside the glass doors, talking on his cell phone. "Okay, Dad, it's time to put me in the loop on Derek's story."

"Let's wait till he's off his phone and then we'll go out so he can explain it to you." Dad passed a hand through his hair and turned back towards the nurses' station, looking to see if anyone was there who might have information on Ashley. Michael could see that Derek was done with his call and he was looking in at them, so he grabbed his dad's arm and went out through the glass doors, making sure they could keep both the nurses' station and the waiting room in their sights.

"Harold, how are you holding up?"

"Okay, son. I just wish we would hear something."

SON? Why the hell was his dad calling this gun-toting bartender, *son?*

Michael glared at Derek and Derek let out a sigh, knowing Michael was going to have a hard time with this, but not as much as his sister was, when Derek finally had to tell her.

Derek reached into his rear pocket, pulled out his badge and showed it to Michael.

"*FBI?* You're with the *goddamn FBI?*" Michael looked over at his dad for confirmation, and he nodded his head yes.

"What the hell are you pretending to be a bartender for? And why are you hanging around my sister? How long have you known about this, Dad? Does the captain know this?" Michael barked out the questions faster than they could answer, so they just stood back and waited for him to stop.

Michael was pacing around and finally stopped and glared at them. "Is someone going to answer me?"

"Are you done asking questions so we can?"

Michael wanted to punch him again, but refrained from doing so until he at least got his answers. His arm was throbbing and he couldn't believe he didn't realize sooner that Derek was some kind of cop.

As the three men talked, more and more of the family and lots of Ashley's friends had been making their way into the hospital. A few stopped to say hi but had quickly moved on when they realized that they were interrupting something serious.

"I'm undercover, following a serial killer. I took the job at the bar so I could be close to the station, have an ear open to the local gossip and be free during the days to follow up on leads. Your sister was just a girl I found attractive. That she became involved with the murders was totally unexpected. That's when I informed Harold."

"And you two didn't think I deserved to be told?"

"It wasn't a matter of deserving. We were going to tell you after dinner and everyone left your parents' house, but then all hell broke loose."

"So that still doesn't explain your sticking to my sister like glue. What does she have to do with this?"

"I've been on this case for two years, following this sick bastard through four states. So far eleven women have been murdered and we have very few clues. In each state the murders are all the same, all the victims look alike. The first state they were brunettes, the next state they were blondes, but in each state they could have been sisters. Then he moves on to the next set of victims. We just haven't been able to figure out why he picks that set of women and why he chooses the cities he does. We thought we had a lead, so I tried to get a jump on him. That's why I'm here. Then the first murder happened here and I knew I was on the right track, but when I found out about the notes your sister was getting and realized that it was the same M.O. as the previous murders, I was floored. His pattern was to always give notes to one of the victims, meanwhile killing several other victims, and then the woman who was receiving the notes ends up dead. It took us three states before we connected the links. That your sister happened to get the notes, and I knew her, was mere chance."

"Does she know any of this?"

Derek and Harold exchanged looks. "No, not yet."

"Oh, you are so dead meat. It almost makes it worthwhile that you kept me in the dark, because when she finds out that you've been on this case the whole time, she's going to kill you herself."

"Michael, Derek is here as a fellow professional, and I personally will take all the help we can get if it will help get this guy off the streets and stop him from trying to harm all of our family," Harold barked out, in a *this is no time to start with your macho stuff* voice.

309

"You're right, Dad, sorry. So does the FBI have any leads that we don't know about?"

"As soon as we know Ashley is out of the woods and settled into a highly guarded room, I've set it up with your captain to meet down at his office to go over everything we have, any new leads you might have collected from the ambulance scene and any forensics that your lab has been working on. Hopefully, we can get ahead of this guy and get him before he gets a chance to murder again, or make another attempt on Ashley's life."

"It's time we stopped pussy-footing around and get her into protective custody. We can set her up in one of our local safe houses," Michael commented as he paced around the small area in front of the emergency doors. Of the three of them, one was constantly looking through the glass, making sure there was no word on Ashley.

"She's not going to like that. I may not have known her very long, but I have come to the conclusion that she's the kind of woman who will hide away only while she feels she can be of some use to the investigation," Derek added. "I'm afraid if we take her away from the public eye, it will piss this guy off even more and then he will kill more innocent women who look like Ashley."

"We cannot use my sister as bait. This guy is determined to kill her and he doesn't care who gets in his way."

"I know, but I still think between you and me, we could keep her covered and the killer would never suspect a thing. He would just think I'm a new boyfriend and when I can't be there, you could take over and watch out for her. Plus, his behavior with Ashley is completely different than in the other cities. Never before has he taken a personal interest in his victims. As a matter of fact, the previous notes he left were not threatening, but more mysterious. And he killed *all* the victims up close and personal. These wild attacks on

310

Ashley's life, with no consideration for others, are completely out of character for him."

"Maybe it's not the same guy?" Michael asked.

Harold had been standing there listening but suddenly he took off for the doors, leaving Derek and Michael confused until they realized a scrub nurse had entered the lobby and was walking into the waiting room. They hustled in right behind him, following the nurse as she entered the room. Everyone had stood at the first sign of the nurse.

"Mary, how is she?" Laura asked as she grabbed one of her best friends' hands.

"Sit down please and I'll update you on Ashley's condition," she said as everyone took their previous seats. Everyone except Michael, Derek and Harold, who chose to stand. "Laura, she's stable, but she's pretty banged up. She lost a lot of blood, has several fractured ribs and her left lung was punctured."

Laura's face paled even more. "Did they use the new procedure?"

"Yes, and as far as we can tell, it worked. So as you know that means we did not have to cut her open to repair the lung, which in your daughter's case, was a good thing. She was very weak from the loss of blood and in shock, so the trauma of surgery might have been more than her body was up to. We gave her two transfusions, she has twenty-two stitches along her hairline and is covered in cuts and bruises and small burn marks."

"Is she in recovery now? Can I go see her?"

"We still have her back in I.C.U. and the surgeon is keeping her in a medicated coma to keep her absolutely still. He does not want her moving at all and feels keeping her back there will keep her quiet. I guess her doctor says her last stay was like a zoo around her, and warned that she needed to be kept completely away from any stress and excitement."

Laura turned to give everyone a look. Blank stares and raised eyebrows were pointed back at her. Many had guilty looks on their faces, and some even had a look of, "Who me?"

"I need to get back to her. Just as soon as the doctor says it's okay, I'll come back and get you, so *you* or *Harold* can go and see her. I'm afraid the rest of you will just have to get your updates from Laura or Harold." She gave Laura a pat on her folded hands and tried to give everyone else a reassuring look. Laura got up and they gave each other a hug, both knowing it was much harder when something like this involved one of their own kids.

Mary left the waiting room and everyone immediately started throwing questions at Laura.

"Laura, what does that mean?"

"How much pain is she in?"

"Will she get AIDS from all those blood thingies?" came from Grandma.

"Why is she in a coma? I don't understand," came from the other grandma.

"Why is she in I.C.U.?"

She tried her best to answer the questions, while Derek, Michael and Harold followed the nurse out into the hallway. She followed them with her eyes while she answered the questions, knowing something serious was going on. She couldn't wait to get her husband alone so she could find out what all the secret talks were about. This involved her daughter, and she wanted to know what the hell was going on.

Out in the hall, Michael explained to the nurse that there would be a policeman in Ashley's room at all times, Derek, his dad, or himself. She started to explain that they could not allow that back in the I.C.U., but after a couple of seconds, she knew she would have to go and get it approved, because these three men were not going to care about rules, they were going to do it whether it was approved or not. She didn't know what was going on, but if they felt Laura's daughter needed protection, she was going to make sure she got it. She told them to give her a couple of minutes and then she would be back to escort one of them to the I.C.U.

She changed direction and headed down another hallway. And they turned to each other, knowing it was going to be hard to decide who would take the first shift. It was decided Harold would take the first shift, since he and Laura were already the only ones allowed back there anyway, and then Michael would take the shift after that, with Derek coming in next. No one had gotten much sleep in the last few days, and they decided it was better to take shorter shifts tonight so they could try and get a few hours of rest. They did not want to jeopardize Ashley's life in any way, and knew they all needed to try to get as much sleep as possible.

Michael stepped away and made phone calls to both Ben and Nick as he waited for the scrub nurse to come back and lead his dad and mom back to the I.C.U. As he hung up, he received another text message, and he looked down with dread, wondering what the sick bastard would say this time.

CHAPTER TWENTY

Ashley woke slowly as a nurse was changing her I.V. bag. She lay with her eyes closed, trying to remember why her head and chest hurt so badly. She raised her hand and felt the huge bandage that was wrapped around her whole head.

"Hi, Ash. How are you feeling?" came a voice that sounded vaguely familiar.

Not opening her eyes, she said, "Like shit."

Ashley could hear movement to her left and then someone took her hand that she had put back down beside her hip on the bed. She could tell it was her dad's just by the way it engulfed hers. "Hi, Dad," she whispered.

"Hi honey. How did you know it was me without opening your eyes?"

"I always know when the best dad in the whole world is holding my hand. Is Mom here?"

"She's out in the waiting room, with about fifty other people, waiting for you to wake up."

"Ashley, don't move. It's very important that you stay perfectly still. I am going to give you some more medicine that will put you right back to sleep," another voice said.

"I don't want to sleep. I want to know what's going on. Oh God, everything hurts."

"I know, honey, but doctor's orders. I will give you something for pain also. Tell your dad goodnight, and you will see him in the morning."

"'Night, Dad. See you..."

"That must be some good stuff," Harold muttered, watching his daughter instantly fall asleep as the nurse injected something into her I.V.

"It is, but I'll have to make a note on her chart to give it to her a little more often throughout the night. We don't want her waking up at all. She is one stubborn woman, to have forced herself awake with all the drugs we are giving her," answered Tina, the nurse in charge of the I.C.U. tonight.

Tina had already been informed of the security that was going to be in the room throughout the night. She was secretly thrilled when she heard one of the guards was going to be Michael. She had been secretly in love with him ever since he had come in to visit his mom one day at the hospital and she had been introduced to him. He was polite, but had never shown any interest. How could she blame him? She had looked like some old hag that night. Her deep chestnut hair had been pulled back into a tight ponytail and she had been wearing her clown scrubs that night. She never wore makeup when she worked the graveyard shift because no one ever saw her. Why would any man, let alone a hot one, look at a nurse who looked like she was on her way to the circus?

When she had been informed earlier that Michael would be coming in next to relieve his dad, she went into the bathroom and took her hair out of the ponytail, glad she had at least curled it tonight before she had pulled it up. She put on some makeup and applied brown eye shadow and mascara, which she never wore to work, added some lipstick and a sexy gloss to her lips, and figured that was the best she could do under the circumstances. She was wearing a plain pink set of scrubs tonight that flattered her coloring and accented her breasts. She knew if any of the other nurses came into the I.C.U. tonight she would have a lot of explaining to do, but once they got a look at Michael they would understand the extra primping she had done. Thankfully everyone else on the night shift in this wing was already married; she did not want any competition for Michael's attention. Usually there were two I.C.U. nurses, but since there were only two patients, and they were short staffed, they had decided to pull the other nurse and put her in emergency.

Tina had a nervous little flutter in the pit of her stomach at the thought of spending a few hours in Michael's company. Both of her patients should sleep throughout the night and, other than checking on them every little bit and giving them their meds when needed, she should be able to visit with Michael and maybe they would get to know each other a little better. She would have to leave sometime to do her charts, but she could do that when the other cop came in and before the day shift came.

Harold used the phone at the nurses' station and called Laura out in the waiting room to fill her in on Ashley waking up for a few minutes, but reassured Laura she was asleep again, and that there was no way Ashley was going to wake again before morning. Laura insisted on knowing exactly what her daughter had done and said, word for word. It was killing her not to be allowed back in the I.C.U. to take care of her own flesh and blood. As far as she was concerned, there was no one more qualified to take care of Ashley than she was. She loved Tina to death but, when it came to her kids, she wanted to be involved. Laura had been back to see Ashley a little earlier; it was hard for her not being able to stay with her oldest daughter, but it was a little easier knowing that Harold was with Ashley. And if anything went wrong, she would know right away. Laura had cornered both Derek and Michael earlier and made both of them promise to call her no matter what time of night it was, if there was any change in Ashley's condition at all.

317

After Harold filled Laura in on all the details, they both decided that it was a good idea if she and everyone else in the waiting room headed home to get some rest. There was nothing they could do at the hospital, and that way they could come back tomorrow and maybe get the chance to see Ashley.

There was one other patient in the I.C.U., but he was on the other side of the room, so either patient's care would not disturb the other. Harold settled back into his chair, trying to get as comfortable as possible under the circumstances. Michael was due in an hour but Harold was reluctant to leave. Someone was trying to kill his daughter and he was having a hard time dealing with it. He had been involved with a few murders in his thirty years of police work, but he had never had to deal with anything that involved his family before. Oh sure, he had been called to his brother's bar a few times, for fights and the like, but that was as serious as it had gotten.

Captain Freeman had gone over the fact that no one was allowed back into I.C.U., hospital staff or visitors, without Harold's, Derek's, Michael's or Tina's permission. The police did not want anyone to come in to change dressings, give medicines, or anything. Since they had no idea who the killer was, they were not taking any chances that he could come in, dressed as hospital personnel and give her something in her I.V., or just plain shoot her when no one was looking. The killer had proven already that he could get into the hospital's core when he had left the hair on the tray.

The captain also posted a uniformed officer at the doors of the I.C.U., with the hopes that he alone would scare away any future threats. It hadn't helped this morning, but it was a little tighter security now than it had been earlier. Uniformed officers were patrolling the hospital and the parking area, along with a few unmarked cars as well. Hospital security was on full alert, with all the security cameras aimed at all the doors, recording everyone who entered.

Everything possible was being done to make sure she was kept as safe as possible.

When the captain met with Harold, Michael and Derek, they decided to hit the news with the possibility of a serial killer in the area targeting strawberry blonde women, and advise those who fit the description to take precautions. Alerting the public was the last thing they wanted to do with a maniac on the loose, or to give the killer the satisfaction of knowing he was making news, but they felt they had no choice. Derek had warned them that the killer had become much more aggressive than in the past. Before, he had done his killing quietly and then moved on before anyone was even aware of the danger. He usually was in and out of a city in a matter of days. He stalked his target, terrorized her with notes and then finally killed her. None of his targets had been police officers, either. The FBI had a task force busy trying to find a connection between how he chose his victims and why Ashley had been selected. Was it always a random thing, or did he plan his targets and then set up the kill? The fact that he had involved Michael proved he was getting braver and wanted to play a game now. He was out to show up the local police and was not afraid of anything. And if Michael was right, he had an inside source giving him information, or at least he had some police knowledge. That put them and Ashley in more danger, not knowing who they could trust and who they couldn't. All information was going through the captain, the FBI task force, and the three men who were going to stand guard over Ashley throughout the night. Everyone else was following orders, but not given the specifics. The FBI had taken over the investigation and all the lab work was being run through them rather than the local police. Everyone at the precinct had raised a fuss when informed of that development, but when the captain explained it was being done for Ashley's safety, they begrudgingly agreed. No one was notified of the suspicion of an informer. The less information leaked the better, for everyone involved.

While Harold was talking to Laura, Tina finished up taking Ashley's stats and checking her catheter. If that wasn't the most embarrassing thing, Ashley thought drowsily, to have some damn tube stuck up into her bladder, draining it at will. The idea of someone seeing her pee hanging on the side of the bed was not a pleasant thought but here she was, lying in a semi-coma state with no control over anything. Ashley didn't think things could have gotten any worse than they were right now; she was at her lowest, emotionally and physically. Her body was as battered as it had ever been and she didn't think she could take much more. She was at her breaking point and she knew it. Maybe after some sleep she would feel better, because she was pretty sure she had a long road ahead of her until this killer was found and put behind bars.

She could hear murmurs, then nothing, and then she was aware of noises around her again. She hated how she felt and she didn't understand why they felt they had to drug her. She wanted to be fully awake so she could defend herself from the madman who was stalking her. Lying here defenseless like this was driving her crazy. Ashley's mind was trying to absorb every noise in case he showed up. She was lying there like a sitting duck, waiting for some crazy to come in here and cut all her hair off from the top of her head to her pubic hair, and then carve violent words into her stomach. If she had wanted a Brazilian she would have gotten one from Troy. Oh, now there was a thought that could make a comatose woman smile! She had no idea if her dad was watching her, but she didn't care. The thought of Troy giving her a bikini wax was enough to make her squirm, even with the drugs. She could just imagine the care and attention he would give to that waxing. Ashley was pretty sure he was not licensed to give waxings, but she thought he would do a damn fine job.

"Tina, she seems to be really agitated. Are you sure you gave her enough of that stuff?"

"Some patients who are put in a drug-induced coma say that they have been able to hear and sense things going on around them. Maybe she's just reacting to that. She will not wake up again, I can assure you."

"I don't like the thought of her being like this. Is she in pain?"

"No, I just gave her something through her I.V., so she should be okay for three to four hours and then I'll give her more. She will be comfortable the rest of the night. Tomorrow when we take her out of the induced coma could be another story. She is going to be extremely sore. Broken ribs are the worst."

No shit, Sherlock. Ashley felt like every time she tried to take a breath, someone was stabbing her in the chest. She did her best to take small shallow breaths, but lying here like a zombie made things difficult. She could feel the drugs taking a better hold, because she was getting really sleepy; her tired little mind was going out.

CHAPTER TWENTY-ONE

Michael walked into the I.C.U. at two forty-five, and Tina's heart did a little cartwheel in her chest. *Wow, that man was good-looking.* He had auburn hair that was just a little long for the current style, but damn sexy, with a natural wave that just brushed his collar. He was wearing faded jeans that fit his ass like a second skin and a blue t-shirt under a button-down shirt that was left untucked. It was stretched over broad shoulders and she could imagine a very fine six-pack under that shirt.

He looked like maybe he had gone home and taken a little nap. His hair was messed up and he looked like he was still half asleep. Tina had visions of him looking like that after he had crawled out of *her* bed.

She had five hours to try to get him to notice her and, since his sister was going to be out, if he didn't at least give her some notice, he was either gay or already in a serious relationship. She didn't think so because Laura kept them advised on her kid's crazy antics.

Mary the surgical nurse had told Tina when she got to work tonight that Michael, his dad and some other guy were going to be taking turns sitting with Ashley. The whole hospital was abuzz with the rumors of some maniac out there killing innocent women, and that Ashley was a target. Tina could not blame her family and the cops for wanting her protected; she didn't want any killer sneaking in and trying to kill Ashley. She was thankful for Michael's presence in more ways than one. She had seen the news earlier; they kept showing the faces of the two murder victims and it was scary how much they looked like Ashley. Tina couldn't help but think if she had strawberry blonde hair, you can bet your ass she would already have been to the drugstore and dyed her hair coal black, no matter how bad it looked.

Tina watched as Michael approached his dad. The concern was evident on their faces. Ashley's appearance was pretty scary. Her head was wrapped in a bandage covering the stitches along her hairline, and she had cuts and bruises all over her face and arms, some old and some new. She had what appeared to be road rash in several places and her ribs were wrapped to help her breathe. She had an I.V. in one arm and the beginning of two black eyes. She looked pretty rough, and that was never easy on a family. But the laser treatment for the collapsed lung seemed to have been a success, so at least she had not had to undergo radical surgery to repair her lung. She was pale, but the transfusions were already bringing back a little color to her face.

Michael stood at the end of the bed, fury raging through him at the sight of his sister in a stark white hospital bed. She was so pale, and he could tell she was still in pain by the way her face was twisted in a scowl.

"Hey, Dad. How is she?"

"She woke up a little while ago but the nurse gave her something right away to put her back to sleep."

Michael glanced over in Tina's direction and then turned his attention back to Ashley.

"I got another text message as I was leaving the hospital earlier."

Harold gave Michael his full attention. "What did it say this time?"

Michael reached for his phone, scrolled down to the message and showed it to him. *SHE WILL DIE SHE WILL PAY.*

Harold sat there holding the phone as Michael stood at the foot of Ashley's bed. "What is her connection to this killer? Why does he want her dead? If Derek's connection is correct, Ashley must be the main target and the other women are just innocent victims who happen to look like your sister."

"I don't know, Dad. So far we have no leads as to why he is after her specifically. I have set up some meetings with Shannon, Casey, and her partner in the morgue to see if they can think of anyone who sis may have royally pissed off. If nothing comes from those, then I'll move on to anyone else I can think of that may have a clue. I'm going to go back as far as I have to, talking to every person she has ever come into contact with if necessary."

They spent the next few minutes going over the possibilities, but coming up with nothing. As far as they both knew, Ashley didn't have any enemies except Malone and as far as they could tell, it was purely innocent stuff, nothing serious enough to kill anyone over. Michael was not above questioning her though; she might know someone who may have something against his sister. They were desperate enough to grasp at any clue thrown at them at this point.

Michael said goodbye to his dad and watched as Harold stopped to talk to the pretty nurse as he left the I.C.U. She looked familiar, but Michael could not remember ever seeing her before. He took his time and checked her out while she was busy talking to his dad. She was about five foot five and had a nice shape as far as he could tell under her pale pink scrubs. She had gorgeous hair the color of rich mahogany wood, thick enough a man could run his hands through it. He could not see her face from here but the glance he had given her earlier had showed him enough to whet his interest.

Tonight could turn out very interesting. Very interesting indeed. He instantly felt guilty for letting his thoughts turn away from his sister and the situation she was in.

He dragged his attention back to his unfortunate sister, lying in a coma. He felt his gut twist as he watched her struggle for each breath, knowing she had to be in pain, no matter how many drugs they were giving her. He clenched his hands into fists and felt for the first time in his life like he could commit murder. If he was given the opportunity to be alone with the son of a bitch who had done this to his sister, he might not be able to stop himself from pulling his sidearm and blowing the guy's head off. He knew he was trained to keep a cool head in all situations, but he wasn't sure that covered someone trying to kill one of his family members.

Michael settled into the chair his dad had reluctantly given up just a few minutes ago. He leaned over and gently stroked his sister's hand, trying to give her the silent support she needed. He was close to his two sisters, even if he didn't show it on a daily basis. They were his world, along with his parents. Michael was not one for public displays of affection, but they all knew him and loved him just the way he was. He fought a tear as he stared long and hard at every wound that marred his beautiful sister's body, memorizing each and every one of them. He was going to make sure the bastard who put them there ended up with that many and more.

Being the older brother of two gorgeous sisters had been rough for him as they were growing up. Every time one of them had come home crying with a broken heart, Michael had seen to it personally that the guys who broke their hearts knew that he would not tolerate his sisters being hurt. He had given his fair share of bruised ribs in his days, protecting his sisters from the assholes of the world. It didn't take long for the guys who were only after one thing, to learn to stay away from the Wright sisters. Michael always figured if the guy was brave enough to ask one of his sisters on a date, knowing that if he treated them badly he had to answer to him, then he deserved a fair shot. His sisters might not have agreed with his philosophy if they knew, but he would have dealt with that problem if it ever had come up. Of course as they had grown older, they stopped being so open when they had been hurt by some jerk, so it had been years since he had to defend one of his sisters.

His sisters were like day and night, Ashley being more serious and tough, and Shannon being the lover of life, happy-go-lucky one. He loved them both, but had always had a soft spot for his tougher than nails middle sister. Ashley, being the middle child, always felt like she had to be the strong one. His little sister took whatever life threw at her and enjoyed the ride as she went, whereas Ashley always strived to control her life and in turn, was way more serious in general. Both had an amazing sense of humor and used it in their daily lives to make things better. He was the one who tended to be grim, inclining to look at life through the eyes of a cop at all times. He enjoyed spending time around them both, knowing by doing so he always walked away feeling better about things than he had before. He would never admit that to them, knowing full well that they would hold it against him for years. He could hear them now, calling him a big old softie or worse yet, a great big teddy bear.

Tina had finished her conversation with Mr. Wright and had gone back to her desk, pretending to look at her patients' charts, but in reality she was watching Michael as he sat by his sister's bedside with such a solemn look on his handsome face. She watched as the emotions crossed his face, and she marveled at how a man could feel so strongly about a family member. Tina was an only child of a single mother who never spent much time with her, preferring to chase after one man or another, so Tina was at a loss when it came to family caring for each other. She ached to find someone who felt the way Michael and his family felt about each other.

Watching this particular man had her stomach doing funny little flip-flops and her heart beating way too fast. She wanted him to look at her with love in his eyes, and touch her with such gentleness. The yearning was so strong it scared Tina. She had never felt like this around any other man and the feelings coursing throughout her body scared her. She jumped up, causing her chair to slide back and hit the wall, making Michael jump and look her way. She pretended not to notice and made her way over to check her other patient, keeping her back to Michael and his sister while she went about checking his vitals, making sure all of his tubes were clear and that he was as comfortable as she could make him in his serious state. Like Ashley, he had been in a car accident a few days ago, but he wasn't as lucky and had life-threatening injuries. He was in a coma and had undergone several surgeries in the last few days.

After seeing to his comfort, Tina went back to her desk to write down the latest numbers in her patient's chart and could feel Michael's eyes on her as she worked. Knowing that made her nervous but it was her own damn fault. If she hadn't been such a klutz before, his attention would still be focused on his sister and not her. She knew she was going to have to go over to Ashley's bedside soon, but had to get herself in control first before she made a complete fool of herself in front of the man she intended to marry. The thought brought a smile to her lips and she glanced up quickly to make sure Michael was not watching her. She sighed in relief to notice his focus was back on his sister.

Michael had jumped and gone for his gun when he heard the noise coming from the other side of the room. He had been so focused on Ashley that he had forgotten for a few minutes that they were not alone in the room. He was thankful that the pretty little nurse had not seen him go for his gun and had already turned her back to take care of the other patient. There were six beds in the I.C.U. and four were empty right now. He had gone to the far side of Ashley's bed so that he had his back to the wall and a clear view of the whole room, which also gave him a chance to watch the nurse as she went about taking care of the other patient. She moved around him, taking his vitals and tinkering with all the tubes that were coming out of the poor man. Michael didn't know what his status was, but he could tell the man was in much worse shape than his sister was. The nurse bent over to check the bag hanging on the side of the bed, which pointed her sexy little ass right at him. He could feel himself growing hard just looking at the way her cute butt moved back and forth as she went about doing whatever she was doing. He had to reach down and adjust himself before he made a complete fool of himself. If she came straight over to Ashley's bed, she would catch him with his pants tented, like he was a young adolescent getting his first boner. Luckily for him she went back to her desk, giving him time to get himself under control.

He was surprised at his reaction to her. He was not the kind of man who looked at every woman like she was nothing but a sex object, but was a man who appreciated a beautiful woman. Oh, he had his fair share of one-night stands in his younger years, but had outgrown the disappointment that they turned out to be. He always felt let down after he had sex with those women, knowing they wanted more and he was not the one to give it to them. He enjoyed sex just as well as the next guy, but as far as relationships went, he was looking for the real thing. He wanted what his parents had, and so far he just hadn't found any woman who stirred those feelings in him.

He had to admit the cute little brunette across the room was stirring some feelings he had never felt before. His eyes kept straying back to where she was sitting at her desk. The overhead light caused her hair to turn multiple shades of deep rich brown. When she tilted her head, the light would catch a particular color and make it blaze with a heat all its own. He was anxious for her to make her way over to his sister's bed, so he could get a better look at her than when he had come in earlier.

Michael tore his gaze away from the nurse and focused back on his sister. He pulled out his notepad and looked over the notes he had collected so far, which didn't amount to much. Both victims had been repeatedly savagely raped and sodomized before they were killed. The women suffered a lot of pain before the killer finally took their lives, which proved to Michael that the murderer was someone who had no feelings at all. Anyone who could do the things he had done to those women was a vicious bastard with no conscience. The fact that his sister was a target made him physically sick. Being a vice cop, Michael had seen his share of grisly things, but nothing compared to the brutality of these crimes.

Michael propped his feet up on the side of Ashley's bed and added the contents of the text messages to his notes. He was still waiting for a call from the FBI about whether they could trace where the calls had come from. Michael had brought the folders from the crime scenes and he opened them up as well, comparing them to see if something clicked that would help them catch this sick bastard. He laid his notebook on Ashley's legs, placed one folder on his lower legs and put the other one across his lap. He would stare at one picture for a long time and then move on to the next one. He did the same thing over and over again.

Tina had given up all pretense of acting like she was doing her charts. Michael was so engrossed in whatever he was doing that he had completely forgotten where he was. He had made Ashley's bed his desk and she was covered with papers and pictures. He was so intense it amazed Tina. He had a pen stuck behind his ear, and every once in a while he would reach up and take it out and jot down something on one of the papers or pictures, then stick it back where it came from. She didn't think he was even aware of his actions, they seemed like they were second nature to him.

Tina assumed he was working on the murders. The hospital was full of talk that Ashley's accident wasn't an accident at all, that someone had purposely rammed the ambulance going at an extremely fast rate, and then pushed them, accelerating until they had been slammed into the side of the Dollar Store. The news earlier had shown the scene, and Tina had been shocked that anyone had survived from that twisted piece of metal that had once been an ambulance. It had been so mangled that Tina couldn't help but say a prayer of thanks for all the victims that had been inside.

The three EMTs were all brought here to this hospital, which was one of the reasons Tina was working alone tonight. The E.R. was being slammed with not only that accident but several others as well. Rachel, who had been in the ambulance with Ashley, was a good friend, and she and Tina often went for breakfast after their shift ended.

Denise, who would normally have been helping Tina tonight, had gone to work in the E.R. She called her every hour or so and kept Tina updated on Rachel's condition. She was in surgery right now, where they were trying to put her leg back together. She had sustained multiple breaks and severe ligament damage along with a deep gash. Ted and Alan, who had been driving the ambulance, were treated and released with minor injuries. The front of the ambulance had missed colliding with the side of the building, so they had been spared that impact.

Tina knew she had no choice but to go over and interrupt Michael. It was time for her to check Ashley. It had been several hours since she had been given any medication and she was due. She hated to interfere with his concentration but her responsibility was to her patient. She was excited to finally get the chance to talk to Michael, since it looked like he was going to be working all night and not sitting idle beside Ashley's bed like she thought he might.

Grabbing Ashley's chart, she made her way to that side of the room, coming to a stop at the end of the bed. Michael was so engrossed in what he was doing that he didn't even notice her standing there. Tina watched him as he went about studying the pictures, watching the expressions flicker across his face as he would turn them and look at them from all different angles. He was so masculine and intense he set her blood on fire. Tina imagined that he tackled life with the same intensity as he was showing now. She let her gaze move from his face down the length of his body, at how his legs were solid masses of strength. Her gaze continued from his hand that was holding the picture to his arm that was flexed, and she marveled at how his biceps were chiseled like fine stone. She appreciated a well-kept body and this man kept his up real fine. Her hands ached to touch those muscles and the rest of his body. The desire was hot and fast. No other man had affected her like this one did. In a way it scared her, but on the other hand, she was no shrinking violet and was not afraid to go after what she wanted. And she decided in the few minutes that she had been standing there that she wanted this man, in every way there was. Her gaze fell to the picture he held in his hand and she let out a gasp of horror. Michael jumped, dropping the pictures and papers onto the floor as he stood up with lightning speed, drawing his gun, and turned and pointed it at Tina.

Tina's eyes went wide at the unexpected turn of events. She stood absolutely still, clutching Ashley's chart to her chest, not daring to move a muscle, until Michael realized she was no threat and he stopped pointing that huge gun at her. She had been holding her breath and suddenly let it out in a little gasp. Her eyes were glued to the gun pointed just a few inches from her face. She felt like she should say something, but with her heart still lodged in her throat, she couldn't utter a single sound.

Michael took in the situation in a matter of a few seconds and lowered his gun. "Jesus! Don't you know better than to sneak up on someone?" He turned and replaced his gun into the holster that was beneath his shirt, hidden from view.

Tina stood there a little in shock. She had never had a gun pointed at her before, especially by the man she was going to sleep with in the next few days if she had her way. She didn't like his tone, accusing her of sneaking around. This was her domain and no good-looking man was going to make her feel guilty for doing her job.

Finding her tongue, she said, "I did not sneak anywhere, Michael Wright! I have been standing here waiting to get your attention. Excuse me for being polite and not interrupting you while you were working, but you can bet, the next time, I'll make enough noise to wake the dead."

Michael glanced up sharply when the little spitfire started her tirade. Her eyes were flashing and her chest where she still clutched the chart was heaving up and down at an accelerated speed. His eyes were drawn to that and stayed there for several long seconds. She was amazing; her fire made his blood come alive and he wanted to see what else set this woman off. Her breasts were magnificent, solid and firm, where she had them squished up with the chart. He couldn't seem to tear his eyes away from them.

"Michael! Stop staring at my chest and move out of my way so I can check on your sister."

It took Michael a few more seconds to tear his eyes away and travel back up to her face. It had turned a pretty shade of pink and her eyes were the brightest green. He was mesmerized by their intensity. He couldn't help himself, his lips turned up at the corners in a slow smile of appreciation. He wanted this woman, and he wanted her now. She stirred things in him that no other woman had. He had to force himself to remember where they were and that throwing her down atop his comatose sister was not the best plan.

He bent over and gathered up the papers and pictures, never taking his eyes off of the pretty nurse. At this angle he could see cute little white shoes, along with her legs that were covered by the prettiest pink scrubs. He straightened back up and placed the pile on the end of the bed beside Ashley's feet. Then he stepped back, motioning for her to go to Ashley. He knew that by stepping back against the wall there was only a small space for her to pass by, but he was not going to move.

Tina looked at him and the small space he had left for her to pass, and saw the challenge in his eyes. Fine, she could play this game if he wanted. The thought of passing that close to him set her insides on fire. She walked to where he was standing and then turned so that she faced him, and moved her body between him and the edge of the bed. He was so close that his chest brushed against her hands where she still held the chart tight against her own chest. At the contact, she inhaled sharply at the electricity that surged up her arms and straight to her heart. Her eyes flashed up to meet his, watching the same reaction in them that was surely noticeable in hers. She stopped where she was, not moving the rest of the way to where Ashley lay in her bed.

Michael and Tina both stood exactly where they were, staring into each other's eyes, neither speaking.

Michael ached to reach out and touch her, but knew that if he did, he wouldn't be able to stop. The feelings were so strong that once he felt her soft skin, he knew the desire would take over any rational thought he had. So he took pleasure in watching her green eyes turn from a bright shade of emerald to a deep green as her own passion took hold of her. And she could deny it all she wanted, but it was there, just as strong as his was.

"Oh God! Would you two just kiss and get it over with so I can get some drugs in me?"

Michael and Tina both jumped at the sound of Ashley's hoarse whisper. Tina turned a bright shade of red and moved past Michael. Michael had the balls to look like a preening peacock, as she slid by him. He never took his eyes off Tina, even as Ashley chuckled softly.

"Michael, leave my nurse alone."

Tina was still red as she went about taking Ashley's stats, reminding her not to move as she did so.

"You don't have to worry about that. I couldn't move if I had to. How are the EMTs?"

"Good. The two drivers were released with mild injuries and Rachel just got out of surgery, and it looks good. Her leg was broken in three places and they had to do some repair work, but they say she should have a complete recovery."

Ashley closed her eyes in relief. "Thank God."

"Let me go get you some more pain medication, and I'm going to call and see about getting you something stronger to keep you asleep. You should not be waking up at all with the amount they are giving you now."

"You have some madman trying to kill you and let's see how well you would be sleeping. Really, I would prefer not to be knocked out." Ashley struggled to get the words out, stopping every few seconds to let her lungs rest. "Not that I don't trust my brother who was so diligently watching over me, but just the same I would like to have my wits about me."

Again Tina could tell it was taking everything Ashley had to say as much as she did. "Ashley, please relax and save your strength."

"You can tell the doctor I promise not to move the rest of the night. Besides, like I said before, there is no way I could, even if I wanted to. Between not being able to catch a deep breath and every bone in my body screaming in pain, I don't think it's a concern, at least not now anyway." Ashley closed her eyes after she finished her speech, lying perfectly still.

Tina and Michael both looked on with concern. She had become so still that they both glanced at her chest to make sure she was still breathing.

"God, you two, I'm not dead. You told me to relax, geez."

335

Tina muttered something about going to get her medication, and turned and ran smack dab into Michael. He had to reach out and grab her arms to keep her from tumbling onto Ashley's bed. He held on tight and slowly pulled her toward him until their bodies were flush against each other. Her head tilted back so that she could see into his eyes, and watched as he slowly lowered his head.

Tina watched in amazement as Michael lowered his head to within inches of hers. She caught and held her breath, anticipation running wild throughout her. Her eyes grew large as she focused on his lips and he drew even closer, his breath dusting her cheek as he drew near. She did not move a muscle in fear that he would stop, and oh sweet Jesus, she did not want him to stop.

As Michael drew nearer he could smell the sweet perfume she was wearing, and it went straight to his crotch, making him as hard as a rock. He knew she could feel it when her pretty green eyes grew even wider. He couldn't help but give her a knowing smirk at her reaction. He continued his downward descent toward her glossy, full lips, dewy where she had just licked them in nervous anticipation. Michael stopped just a hair's width away from her lips and stared into her shining green eyes. They had both started breathing heavily the minute that Michael took her by the arms. Neither seemed to be aware that they still were in the middle of the I.C.U. ward with patients, one being his sister, as they continued to hold each other.

Tina could not wait a second longer and pressed her lips to his, melting into his arms as she did so. *Oh God! It was better than she had even imagined.* His lips were soft but strong and they knew exactly what they were supposed to do. He seemed surprised for a split second that Tina had taken the initiative, but quickly recovered and took control. He wasted no time, taking over the kiss, not wanting to seem undecided.

The kiss started out gently, but within seconds it had taken on a passion all its own. Tina stretched up onto her tippy toes and put as much into it as Michael was. Time meant nothing to either of them as they became lost in one another.

Ashley had opened her eyes after she caught her breath, and watched in amazement as this adorable little nurse turned her big tough brother into mush. She smiled as she watched them turn an innocent kiss into one raging with passion. It felt good to know that her brother had some feelings deep down inside him. Shannon and Ashley had begun to think the man was made of stone. He never dated, that they knew of, and showed no interest in women when around them. Since a few high school flings, Michael had kept his private life just that, private. They always teased him about all the possible women they could fix him up with, which always sent him running in the other direction. Then all of a sudden, along comes a perky nurse with pretty green eyes and knocks Michael on his ass.

That he was standing here beside her bed, kissing the snot out of this poor woman, said it all. Michael did not do that—ever. He was going to be so pissed when he realized he lost his head and made out right there in front of her. Ashley was so going to have fun with this one.

As much as she enjoyed lying there watching her brother turn into putty, the pain was becoming too much to bear, and she knew she was going to have to break up their little passion fest.

Very gently, so as not to disturb anything that would cause her to have more pain, Ashley let her hand inch over to the nurse's butt and pinched it. She could have just said something, but that was too easy. She wanted to see the response that would bring.

Tina instantly let out a squeal and broke contact with Michael's lips. She reached back and rubbed her butt, giving Michael a glare. Ashley watched as Michael stood there completely baffled, wondering what had happened to make Tina pull away and then glare at him.

"What?"

"What do you mean what? You pinched my ass."

"Oh babe, if I was going to touch your ass, it would not be to pinch it, it would be to slowly start at the top and gently move it down and arou—"

"MICHAEL!" came from Tina, and weakly from Ashley.

"Oh for God's sake! I pinched it. Now would you two please wait until I'm passed out again before you start having sex?" Ashley managed to get out.

Michael tore his gaze away from Tina and finally looked at his sister. "Are you in pain, sis?"

"Probably the same as you are with that raging boner you have going."

Tina's hands flew to her cheeks and she mumbled something about going to get Ashley her pain shot. She pushed Michael out of the way in her rush to get by, almost knocking him onto the bed.

"Ash, I think you might have embarrassed her."

"Who?" she couldn't help asking.

"Um, good question. What is her name?"

"Michael. Adam. Wright."

"What?"

"You don't even know her name? That's pathetic."

He turned and watched as Tina went about getting Ashley's pain medication, never letting his eyes stray anywhere but where she moved. He liked the way she moved with confidence, and glanced his way every little bit. He was already thinking about the next kiss and maybe more, if he was lucky. He leaned against Ashley's bed, unaware his sister was watching him every minute.

Every word Ashley whispered sent agonizing pain through her lungs, but was worth it to tease her brother. "I'm telling Mom."

He never even looked her way. "Tell her what?"

"That you seduced my nurse as I lay in agony all night long."

He turned to glare at Ashley. "You wouldn't dare."

Raising her eyebrows over blackened eyes she answered, "Try me, dickhead."

"Who are you kidding? If you did that she would be all over you in a heartbeat! She would smother you with her care. So that's an empty threat. Is that the best you can do?"

Ashley hated that he was right, her mom was already going to be almost unbearable with her care as it was, let alone if she told some wild story like that.

"Fine, have it your way. I'll just talk to Tina's boyfriend instead." Ashley closed her eyes. She didn't have to see Michael to know what his reaction to that statement would be. She kept her eyes closed, just waiting. It wasn't long before Michael reacted.

Ashley could feel him stalk up to the head of her bed. If she wasn't hurting so much she could really enjoy playing with him all night, but the little bit of energy she had was all spent. She could really feel the pain now and all the talking had caused her to be short of breath. Her head was pounding, and she hated to admit it but the last few minutes of bantering had caused the stars to make a sudden return. She felt queasy and thought there was a good possibility that she was going to be sick. So much for trying to keep up with her brother; all she had accomplished was to make herself sick and maybe pull his chain a little.

"Ashley, open your damn eyes and tell me about this boyfriend."

"Nope, going to sleep now, hurt all over."

He stood there for a while trying to decide if she was playing with him, but after staring at her, he could see the evidence of pain around her mouth. He also noticed her breathing was getting weaker, and that her fists were clenched in the bed sheets.

Damn, here he was bending over the bed, demanding that she tell him about some boyfriend, and his sister was in severe pain. He glanced up to see Tina headed this way. At least he got her name out of his sister, even if it was in the same sentence as the fact that she had a boyfriend.

Tina walked around the end of the bed and instantly noticed Michael's glare. "What's wrong? Is it Ashley?"

"She's in a lot of pain," was Michael's answer. He continued to block Tina's way to Ashley's I.V., glaring at Tina.

"Then move."

He raised his eyebrows at that, but moved off to the side, giving Tina room to move in beside Ashley. She bent over Ashley as she slowly added the morphine to her I.V. tube, watching Ashley as she did so. "How is that? Any better yet?"

Peeking her eyes open, Ashley whispered for Tina to bend closer. Tina glanced at Michael who was watching like a hawk. Tina bent over the bed and put her ear to Ashley's mouth. "Told him you had a boyfriend. Sorry, couldn't help myself."

Tina smiled and understood the scowl that now covered Michael's handsome face. Wow! If the thought of a boyfriend could make him so grouchy, it must mean that he cared a little.

"That's okay. It looks like he needs to lighten up a little. Are you feeling better?"

"Yes. Going to go back to sleep now so you two can suck some more face. 'Night."

"'Night, Ash. Hit your button if you need anything at all, okay?"

Ashley was already feeling the effects of the morphine and drifting off to sleep as Tina asked the last question, so Tina straightened up and turned to face Michael.

"Michael, maybe this would be a good time to step out of the room for a few minutes."

He looked stunned. "I'm not leaving my sister's side."

Tina placed her hands on her hips and glared right back. "Listen, I understand your need to protect your sister, but there are a few things I need to attend to and she doesn't need the embarrassment of her big brother watching."

It took Michael a few minutes for the information to sink in, then his face turned pink; he spun around and muttered that he would be on the other side of the room, but that was as far as he was going.

Tina smiled, knowing he was embarrassed, but she was glad he had not fought her. She needed to check Ashley's catheter and didn't want to have her brother watching. She knew how some people were okay with that kind of thing, but Tina got the impression that Ashley would rather die than let her brother see her in such an embarrassing position.

Tina checked to make sure everything was good, took Ashley's stats again, checked her bandages and made sure she was comfortable. She noticed Michael's files lying on the end of the bed and remembered why she had let out a gasp earlier. The photos were shocking and more than Tina had been expecting. She had seen her share of horror working in the hospital, but it was different when it was photos of murdered women. It helped her to understand a little better what Michael and Ashley must be dealing with. The news channels of course had been broadcasting about the murders, but they had not gone into any details, and now she could see why.

She finished up with Ashley, picked up the file and the papers and went over to where Michael was leaning against her desk. She stopped in front of him, placing her hand on his arm and handing him the pile. "I thought you might like to have these over here." She looked up into his eyes and could feel the pain he was feeling for his sister. "She's tough; she'll be up and about in a few days, making your life hell just like she was before." Tina remembered what Ashley had whispered to her, and she couldn't bring herself to play along with the lie. Another time and place maybe, but Michael was going through enough, and he didn't need his sister and his future wife playing jokes on him. Tina smiled at the thought of being Michael's wife and how easily that thought had popped into her head.

He reached out and touched her hair. "Why are you smiling?"

"Sorry, Ashley told me what she said."

"Which part?" His heart accelerated at the thought that she was going to confirm that she had a boyfriend and she was off limits.

"The part about me having a boyfriend."

He held his breath, dreading what she was going to say next.

"She was teasing you, Michael."

He raised his eyebrows in question, afraid to say anything that might embarrass himself more than he already had tonight.

His fingers were still stroking a length of her hair, marveling at the softness of it and how he could smell her shampoo when he leaned in close.

"Michael, I don't have a boyfriend right now. Ashley was just trying to get to you, since she caught us kissing."

Tina could hear a low growl coming from deep within Michael's throat, and wasn't sure if it was because he was going to strangle his little sister when she was healthy, or for some other reason that had her heart racing.

He pulled her close just by yanking on her hair. He leaned his forehead against hers and whispered, "It really didn't matter, because after tonight he was going to be history anyway."

It was Tina's turn to raise her eyebrows. The cocky shit! Who did he think he was, thinking he could make her boyfriend disappear just like that? Just because she didn't have one didn't mean he was so magnificent that she would dump a boyfriend because the great Michael Wright wanted her to. Oh hell, who was she kidding? She would have dumped him in a heartbeat.

"Is that so? You're pretty sure of yourself, aren't you?"

"Babe, when it comes to you, no one is going to get in my way."

Tina could not believe it. Michael was laying a claim on her after just one kiss. What the hell would happen when she really turned up the heat?

"Then I suggest you hold on to your socks, cowboy, because this girl doesn't play around, if you're serious about this."

"Oh, I'm serious all right!"

CHAPTER TWENTY-TWO

Ashley woke up expecting to see Michael and Tina making out on the end of her bed or maybe the one beside her, but when she glanced over at the chair beside her bed, Derek was sitting there, staring off at the other side of the room.

So it looked like Derek, Michael and Dad were taking turns playing nursemaid to her. Yesterday this would have really made her mad, but after her ambulance ride yesterday and the maniac who was trying to kill her, she was grateful for the added protection they were providing. She was not some macho hero who thought she could take care of this guy all by herself; she knew this guy was way out of her league. He had proved after the first killing that he was not kidding around, and meant to cause her and anyone who got in his way bodily harm.

Ashley closed her eyes, not ready to deal with Derek's concern and intensity. She lay there remembering the events of last night and the horror of it all. Sometime during her hours of being trapped in the ambulance she must have passed out, because the last thing she remembered was Ben telling her that the rescue team was trying to find a way in to them. She had no idea how badly she was injured, but her lungs hurt like hell and her ribs were killing her. She felt like she had been a piñata at a kid's birthday party.

Her brain was fuzzy but she did remember Michael's make-out session with her nurse. Her blurry brain was having a hard time remembering what was said, but the look on his face was still pretty clear, and if she was right her brother had fallen hard. The fact that he didn't care if Ashley saw him kissing Tina was enough to tell her this woman was different than any others in his past. God, she hoped Tina was a sweetheart; he deserved to find someone who could love the big grouch. Anyone who hooked up with her brother was in for a rough ride; between the hours he put in at the station and being such a tough guy, any lady would have to have a lot of patience and love to make it work. She had visited with Tina a few times when she stopped in at the hospital to see her mom and had always liked her, and apparently so did her brother.

Ashley snuck a look at Derek and noticed he looked like death warmed over. If he'd had any sleep in the last two nights, it wasn't much. She knew for a fact that the night before, he only had a little nap while he was sitting in the chair beside her other hospital bed.

She was going to be paying this hospital bill for the next twenty years, as many trips as she had made here in the last few days. The department had good insurance, but she would still have to pay the deductible and her share of what wasn't covered. There went the new car she was saving up for. Maybe they had a frequent-stayers discount, she would definitely qualify for that program, plus maybe her mom would have some pull since she worked there. You would think they would write it all off, for anyone who made this many trips in just a couple of days deserved a break.

Besides, how was she supposed to keep Derek interested in her if the only way he got to see her was beaten up and lying in a hospital bed? She could just imagine how she must look. She remembered the blood dripping in her eyes and knew from how badly her head hurt that she must have a new injury. She wanted to reach up and feel around, but did not want to alert Derek that she was awake yet. She would just have to wait for a member of her family to show up and tell her how bad it really was. Michael said she looked like shit yesterday, so she was sure he would be more than happy to tell her how she looked today.

Each breath she took was sheer agony. She must have busted up a few ribs when the ambulance went crashing into the side of the building. She sure hoped someone took pictures so she could see what it looked like from the outside, because it sure was ugly from the inside.

Ashley vaguely remembered asking about the EMTs but she didn't remember what the answer was. She prayed that they all had escaped without too serious injuries. She didn't need anybody else's blood on her hands; two were enough. At the thought of the two women murdered, she couldn't hold in the emotions any longer and the tears started rolling out of her closed eyes. She could feel them sliding down the sides of her cheeks and the sobs were bound to follow. She had tried so hard not to alert Derek she was awake, but the emotions she had been trying to hide for the last few days just came pouring out. Maybe it was all the drugs that they were giving her that made her a sniveling whiney-butt.

Derek had been focused on the doors leading into the I.C.U. where an orderly had tried to enter a few minutes ago, but Tina had intercepted him before Derek could get out of his chair. She took the I.V. bags he delivered and sent him on his way, before he could even set foot in the door.

He had met Tina earlier when he relieved Michael from watching over Ashley. He wasn't sure what had happened before he arrived, but both Tina and Michael were flushed and nervous. Michael was his usual crabby self, but at least now he wasn't throwing insults Derek's way all the time. His attitude was at least respectful when it came to police talk, but Derek could tell Michael didn't like the idea that he was hanging around his sister. He made it known that he didn't buy the idea that he just happened to meet his sister by chance and then all of a sudden a deranged killer was after her. Hell,

347

he didn't blame him, he wouldn't buy it either, if it hadn't happened just like he had explained to Harold and Michael earlier. The fact that the killer was stalking Ashley and he was trying to catch him was just a coincidence. Derek didn't know if it was a good thing that he had a connection with Ashley or not. He could not let himself get personally involved with a victim, but who was he kidding! He was already in over his head when it came to Ashley. From the moment he spotted her among her friends that night in the bar, he knew she was special. He had watched her while she played darts and then when she had moved out onto the dance floor and started dancing with one of her friends. He didn't know what came over him, but before he knew what was happening he was out on the dance floor cutting in.

He had to do some fancy talking after the bar had closed that night when Gladys and Irwin had given him the third degree. Irwin was aware that he was with the FBI, and hadn't taken to the idea that Derek was showing interest in one of his favorite nieces.

He turned his head to look at the woman in question and instantly noticed the tears sliding down her bruised cheeks. In a heartbeat he was beside her, taking her hand in his and reaching out to wipe away the tears. It tore out his heart to see her crying. She had been so brave throughout this whole ordeal. Most women would have fallen apart when they realized a madman was stalking them, and killing innocent women in the meantime.

"Ash…?"

Ashley continued to lie with her eyes closed, letting the tears slowly escape, knowing Derek was holding her hand and gently touching her cheek, but she knew if she opened her eyes and saw the concern in his face, she would really lose it. She just needed a few minutes to let the emotions out and then she would be okay, or at least she hoped she would. Now that the tears had started she didn't know if she could get them to stop.

She lay there a few more minutes without saying a word. Derek never pressured her, he just stood there holding her hand and gently smoothing her face as the tears continued their path down her cheeks.

The tears stung the scratches along her cheek, but it felt good to let them go. She had to get her emotions under control if she was going to survive whatever happened next. One thing was for sure, she was done thinking this was just a bad dream and it would all just go away when she woke up. This was real and someone was trying to kill her. She wasn't sure what she was going to do, but she had to make sure no one else was hurt because of her.

"Derek, could you get me a drink of water?" Ashley asked, still not opening her eyes.

"Sure, I'll go ask Tina for you. Are you sure you're okay? Do you need something for pain?"

"I'm good, and no, no more drugs."

"Honey, you may think you're okay, but that's only because you *do* have drugs in you. Without them you would be singing a whole different song. Your unfortunate gorgeous body has been beat to shit and it needs the pain medicine to get you through the next few days."

Ashley thought over his words, knowing he was probably right, but she needed a clear head if she was going to help catch this lunatic. She was in quite a bit of pain, but she was not about to admit it to anyone. They were all being way too protective as it was, let alone if she told them she was hurting.

"Beat to shit, huh?"

"Yep, that pretty much sums it up. The doctor was in a little earlier and said your concussion was pretty serious and it'll take you several weeks to get over your injuries. I know you want to get out of here today and get to the station and be involved with this investigation, but Ashley, you're going to have to take it easy and trust us to take care of it."

She lay there for several seconds before his words sank in. "What the hell do you mean let *us* take care of it? Who are you? And no damn bartending story either."

"Oh God, Ashley, I didn't want to tell you like this. Let's just get you up and running around again and then we'll get into all this."

"Ain't going to happen, buddy. I knew there was more to you than you let on. And if anyone deserves to know what's going on around here, I do." She opened her eyes and gave Derek her most threatening look. Ashley wasn't sure how effective it was, lying here completely helpless and at the mercy of everyone around her. She could feel the despair settling into her and knew she could not fall into self-pity.

Derek raised his left eyebrow in a question, trying his hardest to hide the smile he was holding in.

"Damn it, I'm serious."

"Yeah babe, I can see that by the furious look on that beautiful face." He stood for several minutes just staring at her. He was beginning to make her really nervous with his intense look. That man could express a lot just by looking into someone's eyes.

"How did you get that bruise on your chin? I thought I was the one who was run over by a truck?"

He reached up and ran his hand along his jaw. "Someone needed to vent a little frustration, and I just happened to be in the wrong place at the wrong time."

"A little frustration, huh? Gee, I wonder if that would have been my father or my brother."

Suddenly he leaned over and slowly lowered his head closer and closer to hers. Her eyes widened a little with every inch he came within her face. She knew what he was going to do, and a part of her raced with excitement at the thought and another part was aware that he was avoiding the question. Shit! Who cared, at this point? She was in dire need of the comfort his lips would bring her.

Derek stopped within just a fraction of an inch of her lips.

"Oh, for God's sake, just kiss me already."

He lowered his lips the last little bit and the first touch stole her breath away. He started out gently, with the thought that he didn't want to hurt her, but as the seconds ticked by, he became more intense, the kiss becoming more than just a comforting touch. It suddenly was filled with a desire that neither of them could deny. Her arms were buried under the covers of the bed, so she was at his mercy. He held her head in the palms of his large hands, keeping it still. She knew even with the passion flying between them, he had her condition in the back of his mind.

He continued his onslaught for what seemed like hours, but was just minutes. He finally pulled back just enough to look into her eyes again. God, this man could turn her to mush with just his touch. Ashley thought if they ever took it to the next level, she would combust on contact.

She asked again, "Derek, stop stalling and tell me."

She could see him physically flinch. "The kiss wasn't enough to get your mind off of it, huh?"

"Oh, it took my mind off it, but I knew if I wanted to keep my-self from doing more bodily injury to myself, I needed to focus on something else besides that kiss."

Smiling like a baboon, he answered, "That good, huh?"

"You know damn well it was that good. I wasn't the only one doing some heavy breathing. So don't start acting like some macho caveman whose mere touch can melt a woman. It seems to me that this woman can do some melting of her own."

"Oh babe, if you only knew. There is a reason I'm still bent over this bed."

Her eyes immediately flew to where his crotch was leaning against the railing of her bed. Even with him pressed against it, she could tell he was swollen to a very impressive state.

It was her turn to raise her eyebrows into a question. Ashley couldn't help smiling.

"You think you're pretty funny, don't you?" he managed to growl out.

"Yep. I'm pretty damn proud of myself, actually."

"You wouldn't be feeling so cocky if you weren't in I.C.U., hooked up to all kinds of machines with tubes coming out of several places on your body, because then I would show you just exactly how good it really was. But then again, I'm not proud, if you want to give me your hand right now, I can still show you."

She glanced over to where Tina was still sitting at her desk, but she could tell by the look on her face, she had witnessed the kiss between them. Crap, now Ashley couldn't hold that over her and Michael anymore. She had given up a perfect way to torment her brother.

Glancing back at Derek, she could tell he was daring her to do something.

She slowly moved her hand from beneath the covers and put it between the bars of the railing, placing her palm against his still rock-hard penis. She knew from this angle Tina could not see what she had done.

Derek's eyes widened with shock and surprise.

"Umm, yes, I have to admit, quite impressive."

Derek jerked back and flopped down into the chair beside the bed, like he had been shot. "Good God, woman! Are you trying to make me explode in my pants?"

Ashley gave him a saucy look. "You started this."

"Jesus, woman! You're so going to pay for that little stunt." He looked up and gave a quick glance in Tina's direction, but she had made her way over to the man lying in the other bed. He reached down and made it no secret that he needed to adjust himself.

Ashley watched in amusement as he tried to make himself more comfortable. She had to admit that when she had so boldly touched Derek, a wave of pure desire had raced up her arm and went straight to her private parts. Thankfully he could not tell the effect her actions had done to her, or he would have tortured her with that knowledge.

They sat in silence for a few minutes, both of them trying to get themselves under control. She could not believe she had been so bold as to actually reach out and touch the front of Derek's jeans where they had been stretched tight with his bulging hard-on. Either all these murder attempts had made her braver than normal, or her brain was more rattled than she realized. But wow, was she happy she did. Just the thought of how good it felt was already making her feel better. Who needed drugs when Derek was around? Maybe she could ask the doctor if it was okay to just touch Derek's dick every so often instead of taking all the pain medication. She could easily imagine everyone's shock if she did ask that. She would send her mother into heart failure, her dad would be livid and she could just imagine what Michael would do. Derek might not complain too much though. She finally got brave enough to look over to where he was still sitting in the chair. He was leaning back now, so he must have gotten himself under control. He was watching her again with those gorgeous eyes of his. She didn't even want to know what he was thinking. She probably scared him off for good this time. Damn!

"Don't worry Ash, I'm not going anywhere."

Ashley looked at him in surprise, amazed that he was reading her mind again. He scared the snot out of her when he did that.

"Who said you were?"

He raised that beautiful eyebrow again, smiling as he did so. He got up again and leaned over the bed.

"Oh no you don't! I don't think my poor body can take any more of your assaults."

Instead of kissing her again, he placed both of his hands on her upper shoulders and held her firmly in place.

It was Ashley's turn to raise questioning eyes to his.

"I'm with the FBI."

She instantly started to rise up and she could feel him hold on to her firmer. "The FBI? You're with the goddamn *FBI*? I knew you were no candy-assed bartender. Why didn't you tell me that in the first place?"

"I was undercover and there was no reason to at first. Then when the first murder happened, and then the attempts on your life, things happened too fast."

"I think you could have found the time if you had really wanted to." She could not believe that he had kept something this important from her. She had suspected something was up, but never dreamed he was with the FBI.

"I had planned on telling your whole family that night after you were released from the hospital but, as you know things got a little crazy."

"Wait a minute. What are you undercover for?" She had a sinking feeling in the pit of her stomach that she was not going to like his answer.

Derek got a little paler and she noticed right away that he was thinking real hard about how to answer her question. "I have been tracking this same man for over two years, following him from city to city." Derek let that information sink in before he told her any more, knowing she was going to demand more, but not sure she was up for it right now. He looked up and caught Tina's eye, motioning with his head for her to come over.

Tina hurried over when she glanced up from her charts and noticed Derek trying to get her attention. She could tell Ashley was upset and by the look on Derek's face, she assumed she must be in pain. She moved to the opposite side of the bed from where Derek was standing. "Hey Ash, how are you doing?"

Ashley turned her head and looked into Tina's eyes. "I'll tell you how I'm doing: shitty, that's how I'm doing. First, some madman is going around killing women who look like me and then saying it's all my fault, and then he tries to kill me three times. Not once, but *three times!* Then, I find out from Mr. Hotshot Bartender here, that he's with the goddamn FBI. Did you know that? The FBI—shit! I bet everyone knows but me. I'll look like a complete fool in front of the whole department."

"Ashley, you need to try and calm down. The doctor still does not want you to move around. You could damage your lung," Tina explained as she started taking Ashley's blood pressure. She looked up and gave Derek a nasty look. "Maybe it would be better if you stood over on the other side of the room."

For just a second he considered refusing, but knew that Ashley needed to calm down and that as long as he was standing this close she wasn't going to. He hated that he had caused her to become so upset, but knew all along that when the truth came out, she would be furious. He hated that he had to tell her when she was lying defenseless in a hospital bed. If she had not been injured, he would probably be sporting a black eye to go along with the bruise on his chin. Hers would have been deserved, but not the one from Michael. He looked down at Ashley, seeing the hurt in her eyes, and he swore right then and there that he would never be the one to hurt her again.

CHAPTER TWENTY-THREE

Tina gave Ashley more pain medication, which made her drowsy, which Derek was thankful for. He was not ready to answer her questions and he knew she would have plenty. She deserved the truth, but he also knew how upset she would be when she found out that he had been working on the very same case that now had her beat to hell in this hospital bed.

He had discovered two things for sure: she was a tough cookie and she was full of surprises, which intrigued him. No woman had ever captured his interest like Ashley did. He was still a little in shock that she had called his bluff and actually reached out and touched him. The fire that raced through his body at the mere touch of her hand had just about caused him to lose it in his pants. Her brazenness was refreshing, not the same cat and mouse act most women played. He knew she was not someone who did these things on a daily basis, but for some reason, felt she could be herself with him. The thought made him smile and he hoped after he told her how involved he was with her case, she gave him more chances to see where their flirting would take them.

Michael had spent a great deal of time talking to Ben after the ambulance had left yesterday, drilling the poor old guy for anything Ashley might have said that would lead them to a clue as to who this madman was. Ben had not been much help, relaying the conversations he and Ashley had, but other than her asking him not to touch the ambulance, she had not given him a hint as to why.

Michael, Harold, Captain Freeman and Derek, along with a few other FBI agents, were scheduled to meet at ten here at the hospital to go over the facts they had so far, and see which direction they wanted to go with the investigation. He knew that the locals would probably have an attitude about the FBI's involvement, but that was just too damn bad. It had been their case first, plus he had put way too many man-hours in on this case to be pushed to the back now. They needed to all work together and use the resources that both departments had to come up with a suspect.

Whoever he was, his anger was intensifying. His rage this time was way more evident than in the past murders. He was either gaining confidence, or he really had something against Ashley and she wasn't just some random victim.

The two murders here had the same M.O. as in the other cities, but the killer had become more brutal and twisted in these last two. All the victims had been raped and sodomized, and he had carved words into each of their stomachs, but now he was raping them several times and beating them, while before it had seemed like he had performed the act and moved on quickly. He was bolder now and taking his time to torture the women. The police had not released this, but he had taken a souvenir from each of his victims. He had cut the victims' nipples off and had taken them with him. He took care when he did so, versus the hatchet job he did when he carved the obscene words into their bodies. That he shaved their pubic hair was also a puzzle. The M.E. had said that he did this postmortem, so they had assumed he was getting rid of any evidence that he may have left, but Derek wasn't so sure. He thought it was some sick fascination the murderer had.

Some psychologist probably would link it to a mother issue, but who didn't have a few of those in their closet?

Derek watched as Ashley rested. Her eyes were turning black, and the bruises were turning an ugly shade of purple. If he didn't know better, he would have thought she was a victim of abuse. There was a bump along with the cut in her hairline, and she had a bump and cut on her right cheek. She had scrapes and cuts everywhere, some from the attempted hit and run and others from the ambulance crash. Her breathing was better this morning than it had been when he had first seen her right after the surgery.

He was exhausted and knew he needed to get some rest soon or he would drop. He needed to be fresh so that he could tackle this with his complete brain, not like some sleep-deprived college kid. He was supposed to watch over Ashley until another detective came in to watch over her while he attended the meeting. None of them liked the idea of leaving Ashley in a stranger's care, but other than having the meeting here in the I.C.U., they didn't have a choice. Michael had assured him it was a trusted fellow officer, someone he could trust with his sister, and Derek had to take his word on that. Someone named Kelly was supposed to sit with her until Harold took the next shift, giving Derek a chance to get some much-needed rest. He knew he would only sleep a few hours, but it's all he would need.

He was anxious to meet with the task force and see if anyone had come up with anything new since he had been here at the hospital. He had talked to a few connections from the bureau and called in a few favors to see if they could run some ideas through the databases they had privileges to. This guy had to make a mistake somewhere and he was damn sure he was going to find it. He was strongly beginning to believe Ashley knew the killer, she just wasn't aware of it yet. When he finally got the chance to tell her he was working on her case and she calmed down enough to talk sensibly, he planned to drill her for any information she might have buried, not knowing it was connected to this madman.

The killer had never made any personal contact with the other victims before, and that he was enraged enough to try to kill Ashley several times meant he had a personal stake in this series of murders. Before, he killed the main victim in the same fashion as the look-alikes. The attempts on Ashley were so random. Maybe the others had just been practice, perfecting his skills, so that he would be ready for this one. He didn't know what Ashley could have done to piss someone off this bad, but that's the only explanation he could come up with.

Tina checked on Ashley one more time before she left for the day. It had been quite a night and she was both excited and exhausted. It was an added strain knowing that a killer could come bursting into the I.C.U. and start blasting away. She had already called security and asked to be escorted to her car. She was not going to take any chances if this guy was after people connected to Ashley; she was going to do everything she could to make sure she stayed safe. She had a new man to pursue and she was going to do everything in her power to make sure she was around to do it. Just the thought of Michael brought a smile to her lips.

"A penny for the thoughts that put such a pretty smile on your face?" Derek asked.

"Oh, sorry. Guess I was lost in thought there for a minute. I don't think you would want to waste a penny on it, though. How's she doing?"

"Seems to be in an easy sleep right now. She will need it in a few hours when her family is finally allowed to come back and visit her. Only her mom, sister, and of course Michael and Harold are allowed to visit."

At the mention of Michael's name, Tina turned a pretty shade of pink. She fluttered around Ashley, checking her vitals and making sure all the tubes were draining properly.

"So you got the hots for Michael, huh?"

Tina's head flew up and she looked at Derek in shock. "I most certainly do not. Where in the world would you come up with that idea?"

"He reads your mind," Ashley whispered.

Tina glanced down at Ashley, but her eyes were still closed, and if she didn't know better she would have sworn she imagined her having spoken. She looked back up at Derek, who had a smirk on his handsome face. Tina had been amazed when he entered earlier that morning to relieve Michael. Even as tired as they both looked, they were the two most gorgeous men she'd seen in a long time, and to have them both in the same room had caused her heart to race double time.

Tina answered, "Ashley, he does not, and besides, he's wrong."

"No, he's not. You were sucking each other's tonsils last night when I woke up. So I would say he nailed it right on the head, wouldn't you?" Ashley answered again without opening her eyes.

"Hey! Why am I getting picked on? As I seem to remember, I wasn't the only one doing some tonsil sucking."

"Yeah, but I *know* I have the hots for Ashley."

Ashley's eyes flew open and she and Tina turned towards Derek.

"You do?" came out of Tina and Ashley's mouths at the same time.

He looked into Ashley's eyes with that same intensity as before. "Yeah, I do."

Ashley looked back at Tina and they both mouthed "Wow" to each other. They could hear Derek snicker as he got up and stood beside the bed.

"Do I need to do some more tonsil sucking to prove it?"

"*NO*," came from Ashley.

"You two really need to take your act on the road. It's not often two women can say and think the same thing, at the same time, more than once, especially within a few minutes' time span."

Tina threw an empty bandage package at him and Ashley just grunted and closed her eyes again.

Ashley was secretly elated. It was nice to know that she wasn't the only one whose feelings were flying around unexpectedly. Of course, saying you were hot for someone was not exactly declaring your love, but from Derek, she would take that. He still had a lot of explaining to do, but she was too exhausted to try and figure it all out right now. She knew she would be stuck here in the hospital for several more days at least, so she had plenty of time to interrogate her bodyguard. Plus, she was sure she could get some information from dear old Dad when he came in a little later and relieved Derek from his shift. Now that she was becoming a little clearer headed, she needed to concentrate on remembering everything the killer had said to her when she was trapped in the ambulance. God, she prayed they had lifted a fingerprint from the top of the ambulance, where he had to have touched when he wedged himself between it and the brick wall to talk to her. It was the only lead they might be able to get on this guy. Whoever he was, he was a smart one when it came to covering his tracks. He was either a skilled killer or had some kind of police training, or maybe some military background.

Ashley was anxious to ask her dad if they had gotten anything from the notes that the madman had left on her car, or maybe they had tracked down where he had bought the rose. She needed to have them ask around her apartment building and the grocery store to see if anyone had witnessed him placing the items on her windshield. She doubted that anyone did, because the couple of times she had seen him, he had either had a baseball cap pulled down low over his face or the ski mask that covered his whole face. He probably wore some kind of disguise when he was out in public, on the chance that someone would spot him.

Ashley could hear Tina moving around the side of the bed and knew Derek was still watching her like a hawk, but she needed to collect her thoughts before she opened her eyes and had to deal with the intensity she always felt when looking into Derek's eyes.

"Ah crap…"

"What did you drop?"

"The roll of tape, so I can change Ashley's bandages," Tina muttered as she bent over to look under the bed.

"Can you reach it? It looks like it rolled up to the head of her bed," Derek asked.

"No, there is too much equipment on this side, can you get down here and reach it?"

Ashley heard Derek grunt as he lowered himself down and felt him bump the bed as he lay down on the floor. Ashley turned her head and all she could see was Tina's ass stuck up in the air on one side of her bed, and when she turned in the opposite direction, she couldn't see Derek at all. She could hear them both grunting as they tried to reach the roll of tape. The picture brought a huge smile to her face, until she looked up to the foot of her bed and witnessed the scowl on her brother's face.

"What the hell is going on here?"

Ashley felt two thumps as both Tina and Derek must have raised their heads at the sound of Michael's growl.

"Ouch! Damn it!"

Tina popped up from her side of the bed with a guilty look on her face. She glanced at Michael, back to Ashley and then to where Derek was just rising from under his side of the bed.

"I don't know, Michael. I was sleeping but I think those two were down there making out. Can you believe it? Here I was all comatose, and these two were wrestling around…"

"*Ashley!*" Tina cried.

"What? Why else would you two be grunting and panting like that?" she asked innocently.

Derek was rubbing the back of his head and looked like he was about ready to spit nails. "We were both trying to reach a roll of tape Tina dropped, and Ashley damn well knew that."

"Oh yeah, that must have slipped my rattled brain."

Michael glared at Derek, while Tina grabbed the roll of tape from Derek's outstretched hand. She shot Michael a dirty look and then she turned Ashley's way and started cutting away the bandage that was wrapped around her head. When she had cut through all of the gauze and started peeling away the bandage, Ashley watched as her tough-as-nails brother and the big tough FBI agent both started turning an ugly shade of green. Boy, it must really be ugly if those two couldn't handle it.

Michael shifted his gaze to Tina, preferring to watch her instead of the ugly wound on his beautiful sister's head. The anger that he had felt as he walked in on the scene of Tina and Derek under the bed only doubled at the thought that someone had purposely caused his sister bodily harm.

He had come back after getting only a few hours' sleep, but was hoping to be able to spend a little time with Tina when her shift was over and before the meeting to discuss the case. He had not bargained on finding his woman on the floor with another man, especially Derek. *Whoa! His woman?* He had never considered any woman *his woman* before. This lady had really captured his interest.

Tina was finishing up cleaning Ashley's wound and was rewrapping her head in gauze. He watched as she went about her business, being gentle and professional when she tended to his sister. The pride swelled in his chest as he watched her.

"Well, Tina, it's good to see the hotness runs both ways."

Tina glanced up from taping the gauze with a puzzled expression, then realized what Derek had been referring to, and shot a look at Michael. He had been watching her intently as she went about changing the dressing.

"What?" Michael looked from one face to the other, having no idea what was going on, but he had a pretty good suspicion that he was the brunt of some private joke.

Derek started to answer him but Tina interrupted, "Ashley, how are you feeling? Do you need anything for pain? Do I need to send these two to the other side of the room? Are they upsetting you?"

Ashley had watched the exchange with great amusement. Tina was so flustered it was amazing that she had been able to change the bandage as well as she had, and Derek was taking great pride in ruffling Michael's feathers for some reason.

"No, they're okay…and I'm good. No need for more pain medication yet. Besides, I know it's Dad's turn next to come sit with me, so I need to know why Michael is here already?" She looked from Derek to Michael, and knew something was up when they gave each other nervous looks, not saying a word.

Tina looked from one to the other with raised eyebrows. "Didn't anyone tell her you were having a meeting here at the hospital this morning?"

Derek and Michael made a hasty retreat to Tina's desk, leaving Tina to answer any questions they knew Ashley would have. Of course, she knew no more than what Michael had told her earlier. Michael and Derek had their backs turned towards her, knowing she would be trying to get their attention and demand some answers.

Fine, she could wait for her dad to get there. She knew he would never do that to her. She almost felt guilty, knowing that the minute he walked in he would be bombarded with her demands. The poor guy did not stand a chance.

Ashley watched as another nurse was escorted in by a uniformed officer, looking very nervous. She stopped dead in her tracks and just stared at Derek and Michael as they stood there in front of her desk. The uniformed officer said a few words to Michael and then left the room. The nurse looked from one to the other, not saying a word.

"Tina, you better go rescue your replacement. I think she's seriously thinking of bolting out the door, by the look on her face."

"Can't say as I blame her," Tina replied. "If I had walked in to work and encountered those two gorgeous men, I might have bolted too." She patted her hand, informed Ashley that she would see her again tonight and wished her well.

Ashley watched as she made her way over to the desk and took charge of the situation, introducing the new nurse to both Michael and Derek. She explained to her again what was going on in her I.C.U. even though she was pretty sure the woman had already been briefed on the situation. She looked to be about 50, with a hideous haircut dyed an ugly shade of red, and she stood at least six feet tall and weighed close to as much as either Derek or Michael. She nodded her head as Tina talked, finally relaxing enough to reach out and shake each of the men's hands. Ashley could have sworn Michael winced as she shook his hand up and down, holding on for several seconds longer than most women would have when shaking hands. She and Tina made their way over to the man in the other hospital bed, going over his chart together.

Ashley glanced back to where the two chicken-shits were standing, but both still had their backs angled towards her. Fine, they could hide all they wanted. She was too tired to worry about it now anyway. She would try and sleep a little more, so that when her dad showed up she would be ready.

CHAPTER TWENTY-FOUR

Ashley woke to the sound of the chair beside her bed scraping on the floor. She opened her eyes and watched as her dad stood up. Ashley glanced at the wall clock across from her bed and saw it was nine fifty. She reached out and grabbed his arm as he turned to go. He jumped and glanced sharply down at her.

Ashley felt guilty for scaring him, but there was no way she was going to let him sneak out to that meeting without talking to him first. She had slept through his coming into the room, and who knew where Derek and Michael were.

"Hi honey. How are you feeling this morning?"

"Hey, Dad. I'm doing better. Had a few rough patches last night, but the pain is much better now."

"You don't know how glad I am to hear that, and your mother will be ecstatic. She was in earlier, but left a little while ago to track down your doctor so that she could get the latest update. She should be back to sit with you in just a few minutes while I step out for a little while."

"Oh really? And where are you stepping out to?"

He glanced quickly toward the door, shifted his feet back and forth a few times, and did everything he could do avoid looking down at her.

"Dad...?"

"Nothing to worry yourself about, honey. I just need to take care of something, and then I will be right back."

"Take care of something, my ass."

"*Ashley Elizabeth!* Watch your mouth. You do not talk to your father like that."

"I do when my *father* stands there and lies to my face."

He turned a bright shade of red and had the good sense to not say anything more to incriminate himself.

"Dad, I know about the meeting and there is no way that I'm not going to be a part of it."

He looked at her in surprise. "Now Ashley, you are not up to taking part in this meeting. You need to get your rest. I will be back just as soon as I can."

"What is this meeting about?"

"Umm, just our next plan of action, what we have so far, that kind of thing. Nothing you need to worry about."

"Nothing for me to worry about? Dad, there is no way this meeting is going to happen without me involved."

"Honey, you are lying in the I.C.U."

"What's your point? You can either bring all those lugheads in here and conduct the meeting here, or I will wait until you leave and then get myself up and come and find where you all are. Which way do you want this to play out, Dad?"

"Ashley, you are not up to getting out of bed yet."

"Then I guess that answers that question, doesn't it?"

"Ashley, be sensible. We need to go over this stuff and you're in no shape to be a part of that."

Ashley looked into his eyes, then took his hand. "Dad, you of all people know I deserve to be involved the most in this discussion. I have not had a chance to even tell anyone what the killer said to me while I was trapped in that wreck. Don't you think that just might be something everyone would be interested in hearing? Plus, if any decisions are made, I want to be a part of them."

As she was talking, Harold's eyes had grown to about double their usual size. "He had the balls to talk to you?"

"Yes. That's why I had them dust for fingerprints. Dad, go get the rest of the team and bring them in here so we only have to go over this once. Find whatever hospital authority you need to get permission from so that they will let us conduct it here in the I.C.U."

"Michael and Derek are going to throw a fit."

"That's okay. I'm used to it by now." Ashley smiled at him, trying to reassure him that it was the only way this was going to play out.

He stood looking down at her for a few minutes and then, shaking his head in defeat, he made his way to the doors of the I.C.U. He glanced back and she almost felt guilty for bullying him into it, but damn it, this involved someone trying to *kill* her.

He was gone for a little longer than she had thought he would be, and then suddenly the doors opened and in came Phillip Kelly. He was ushered in by the uniformed officer who had been standing out in the hall the whole night. He stopped to check in at the nurses' station and then made his way over to the side of Ashley's bed. She was confused and embarrassed all at the same time. No one had said anything about Detective Kelly stopping by, and as far as she had understood things, it was only her dad, Michael and Derek who were in charge of standing guard over her beat-up body. She was horrified that the station hottie was going to see her at her worst. She still had not seen herself in the mirror, but she knew from everyone's reactions that she looked like hell. She knew she had numerous scrapes, cuts and bruises from the first run-in with the killer, and after the ambulance wreck, it had to be much worse.

Phillip walked to the far side of her bed. "Hey, Ashley. How are you doing this morning?"

She stared at him for several seconds, confused as to why he was there. "I'm doing better. Why are you here?"

Phillip laughed as he sat down in the chair Harold had vacated just a few minutes ago. "I can see they haven't knocked the fire out of you yet. That's good to know. I was asked to come and visit with you while your Dad and brother were busy for a little while this morning."

Ashley gave him a nasty look. "You can forget playing the innocent act. I know what they are busy with and they wasted your time by making you come all the way down here for nothing. I'm going to be part of that meeting, one way or the other."

He raised his eyebrows over those rich chocolate eyes of his, sat back and gave her his one-dimpled smile. "So, you found out about that, did you? I'm not surprised. I didn't think they would be able to pull that one off, but it was not a waste of my time, whichever way it goes."

She cocked her head at him in question. "Really? How so?"

"Now why would I pass up the chance to come see the hottest rookie on the force? But, if you tell your brother I said that, I'll have to pull some strings and make sure you get stuck down on morgue duty for a few more weeks instead of riding shotgun with yours truly."

"You wouldn't dare! I think I have been punished enough after the stunt Malone and Shaffer pulled last week, don't you? Besides, if you would try something like that, I would be forced to tell Malone that you think she's hot and want to take her out."

His eyebrows shot up again and she could have sworn he was turning an ugly shade of green. "Now who's being unfair? That is the meanest thing you could say, Ashley. That woman is a man-eater. She scares the shit out of me, the way she looks at me and tries to corner me every chance she gets. She tries to rub those silicone balls of hers against me every chance she gets, too."

Ashley had to grab her ribs as he was talking, because laughing hurt like hell. "Stop it! That hurts. Plus, that image makes the back of my eyes burn. I have to admit I'm surprised you haven't fallen under her spell like every other man that I know."

He looked at her for a few intense seconds. "No, Ashley, I would never fall for a woman like that. I go for real women, who don't play stupid games or use their bodies to try and trap a man."

"Oh," was all Ashley could seem to mutter as she sat there in amazement. Phillip was the first man, besides her brother, who had not shown any interest in Malone's ample charms. After over twenty years of watching that woman charm the pants off of every man she ever set her sights on, it was refreshing to know that not all men were attracted to her tricks.

"Well, well, Detective Kelly. I have to admit you just climbed the ladder in the male world. Anyone who can see through Malone has to be above average in my eyes."

"Oh Ashley, you underestimated me if you thought I could ever be attracted to the fake Barbie doll type. I'd go for a much more real woman who doesn't use her looks to hook a man, but rather uses her natural charm and personality. Someone who is made the brunt of a joke and knows how to give it right back, or is thrown into danger and keeps a cool head and doesn't go into hysterics. Someone like that is more likely to catch my attention."

He had stood up and moved to lean over the bed railing and, Ashley had to admit, the temperature felt like it had gone up twenty degrees as he had done so. He was looking over every cut, scrape and God knows what else that covered her body. She could see the anger as it took him over. His eyes became intense, his teeth and jaw were clenched and his hands were gripping the bedrail.

"Pretty ugly, isn't it?"

He tore his gaze from the bandage at the top of her head to meet her eyes. "No. 'Ugly' could never be used when it comes to you. But

I would like the chance to be alone with the guy who caused you so much pain."

"Ah, I bet you say that to all your best friends' little sisters."

He chuckled. "Nope. You're the only sister I would care enough about to feel that way."

Before she could react, Derek and Michael (both scowling their heads off), the captain, her dad, and two other men she didn't know, all walked in. The same uniformed officer who had led Phillip in followed, but stopped and blocked the door of the I.C.U. Harold stopped and talked to the nurse for a few minutes, and then they all made their way to Ashley's bed. The captain and the two strangers grabbed chairs from around the room and positioned them all around her bed. Harold pulled the curtain beside her bed, enclosing them in a wall of privacy.

Phillip had straightened up when they all walked in, but still kept his position beside her. Derek had not stopped glaring, but she could tell he now directed it at Phillip. He had moved past Phillip to stand closer to the head of the bed, making sure that by doing so, Phillip had no choice but to move a little further down. Phillip gave Derek a curious look, but made no move to fight him for space.

Phillip made eye contact with Michael. "I assume that my services are no longer needed. I guess this means that the meeting is to take place here instead of the conference room down the hall?"

Ashley looked at each one in turn, daring one of them to object to being here instead of down the hall. Derek and Michael both looked like they were about ready to explode, but she didn't care.

"Looks that way, but we would like you to stay and be a part of the discussion anyway," Michael answered.

"Good morning, gentlemen. I'm anxious to hear where we are in the investigation." Ashley looked at the two strangers, holding her hand out. "And you are?"

The first man reached out and shook her hand, trying to hide a smile as he did so. "Special Agent Clark with the FBI, ma'am." He stepped back and made room for the second man, who looked like he had a broom handle stuck up his ass. He looked down at her still outstretched hand with contempt. He made no move to take the hand. She raised her eyebrows and she could feel the anger building inside her.

"Well, it seems like there is always one in every group, doesn't there?" she couldn't help asking, never breaking eye contact with the rude son of a bitch standing at the foot of her bed.

The captain started choking and Harold looked horrified.

"Ashley, this is my boss, Special Agent in Charge Anthony Day," Derek answered.

Agent Day and Ashley glared at each other for a few more seconds before she could manage to respond. "I would like to thank most of you for including me in this very important meeting, but if Agent Day is not comfortable with this decision, he is more than welcome to wait outside. I am sure either Agent Clark or Agent Laws would be willing to fill him in later."

She watched as the man stood there glaring at her. No one said a word. Ashley swore to God she thought they could all hear the other patient breathing from across the room, the silence was so evident.

Michael quickly took over the uncomfortable situation. He sat down in the closest chair and pulled his notes out of his folder. "Derek, I think you should start, since you have been following this guy for years, and then we will move on to the case involving Ashley."

Everyone else quickly took the remaining chairs, except for Agent Day, who stood for a few more seconds before finally taking a seat. Derek and Phillip kept their positions beside her bed and Dad stood behind Michael.

Derek took out his notes and started explaining to everyone how he had been assigned to the case after the first set of murders. They had gathered facts at each murder, until they had some sort of pattern but basically no clues. The man was brilliant when it came to out-foxing the police at every turn. No evidence had ever been found at any of the murder scenes.

That had all changed when they had received a tip from the last city the killer had been in, from a motel clerk who said he had been watching a report of the murders on the TV when one of his guests came to the desk to check out. He reported that when he noticed the television on behind the clerk, the guest had become fixated on what was being said. The motel clerk had tried to talk to him, but the man was so zoned out, he never even noticed. The guest had stood and watched the whole report and then muttered under his breath, "The police are wasting their time and they'll never catch me."

Derek said the clerk had acted like he was busy getting the guest's bill ready, and when he turned toward the man, the man was watching him. The clerk played dumb and pretended he wasn't even aware of what had been playing on the TV. He tried chatting with the man, acting like he had not heard the report of the murders, but the man cut him short, paid his bill in cash and took off.

As soon as the man left, the clerk called the police who in turn called the FBI, Derek explained. They interviewed the motel clerk for hours, searched the guest's room for evidence, but found nothing leading to his identity. The room had been wiped clean, no trash or fingerprints anywhere. The only break they got was on the registration card; he had listed his home address here in Denver. It turned out to be a vacant lot, but they felt it was worth a chance to follow it up and see if he showed up here.

Derek cast a quick glance at Ashley to see how she was doing, but she was lying there listening patiently as he filled everyone in.

He glanced around the circle of men, noticing that they were all taking notes, but his boss had a scowl on his face. The man had always been a prick, and having Ashley insist they have the meeting here was enough to set him off. He didn't tolerate women much anyway, and in his words, *having some snot-nosed rookie making demands of the FBI was complete bullshit*. Derek had smoothed things over, stating the woman was the target, not just a rookie cop. It was a good thing neither Michael nor Harold had heard the comment Day made about Ashley, because both of them would have probably taken his head off, literally.

Derek jerked his thoughts back to the present when he realized everyone was still waiting for him to finish.

"Anyway, we decided the best action was for me to go under-cover and see if we could flush out something on this man, and who better to hear anything than a bartender." He gave Ashley a quick look that asked her to forgive him for his deception, and then looked up into Michael's eyes. He could tell that Michael was still pissed off that he had not been informed of all this earlier, but that was too damn bad. He would just have to get over it. He knew how things worked in the police department and he was just extra touchy since his sister was involved.

After Derek finished with his information, the captain started up with the details they had gathered from the two murders that had happened there. The FBI agents, Captain Freeman and Michael compared notes on those murders with the ones that had happened in the other cities, and everyone agreed that they all used the same M.O. The way he shaved his victims and cut off their nipples, and the fact that he had placed a .45 bullet in their vaginas, had never been disclosed to the public. He had repeated the same thing in the notes to each of the victims in each of the states he had been in.

Ashley listened to everyone going over the details of the murders and fought to ward off the tears that were threatening to spill out of her watery eyes. Everyone was busy looking at police photos and not paying any attention to her. How would it look if she started bawling like a baby after she had insisted on being involved with the meeting? She could see asshole Day smiling in satisfaction if she were to break down. That alone made her fight down her emotions and focus on what was being said. Her lungs were on fire and her head was throbbing. Her eyesight kept going double when she stared too hard; if she moved too quickly one way or another, she felt a wave of nausea come over her. She was not going to admit that to anyone other than her doctor and maybe her mom, because she would know anyway.

The details and photos of the murders were gruesome. Everyone had been passing around the photos of the prior murders, and when the one of the waitress came to Ashley, she couldn't help staring at the horror of it. How anyone could do those things to any woman was offensive. It was hard for anyone in their right mind to comprehend. But Ashley thought they had all decided they were not dealing with a sane person. The picture showed the woman lying between two dumpsters, naked. Her stomach had the word *slut* carved into it, and Ashley could tell she had been beaten severely. Her face was swollen so much her features were unrecognizable, and her nipples were both gone, blood running down her rib cage where he had sliced them off. Her head was turned to the side and she was lying on her back with her legs spread out. She was covered in bruises and abrasions. Ashley sat there in anguish, as she realized what this woman must have gone through. Ashley could feel the nausea climbing her throat and the hysteria threatening to overcome her body, no matter how hard she fought it. The photo in her hand was trembling as the panic set in. She couldn't tear her eyes away from the glazed look in the woman's eyes. Her look of death was overpowering, and Ashley could feel her hatred for the man who caused such pain deep within her soul. Panic and horror took a back seat to the overwhelming anger that came over her. She looked up and met Derek's eyes. He had stood by and let her go through the changing emotions, not interfering. He knew she needed to come to grips with this herself, without any prying from anyone else.

Derek gently took the picture from her hands, brushing his hand against hers as he did so, sending a gentle message that only the two of them understood. She took a deep breath and agony fired through her lung, and the pain that burned her ribs as she let the breath out caused her to grab her side. Again, no one noticed but Derek and Phillip. Phillip had been standing back against the wall, just listening and watching her with those deep brown eyes of his. She could not read what was behind them, but she was pretty sure that he missed nothing that was going on around him.

Everyone was through discussing the facts and was going over any physical evidence found involved with Ashley's case. The hair found on her car did indeed turn out to be from the first victim who was murdered on her way home from work, and since Ashley had not gotten a description of the vehicle that had raced away after he placed the hair on her car, there was no lead there. There had been no fingerprints or fibers on any of the notes left either on her car or on her hospital tray. The rose was also a dead end. He could have gotten the single rose anywhere, from a street vendor to any of the dozens of florists in the immediate area to any of the supermarket chains. They already knew that the car that had tried to run Michael and her over had been stolen, and no fingerprints or physical evidence was found there either. The hair on her hospital tray yesterday had belonged to the second victim, found behind the dumpster at Ashley's apartment; they were going through the hospital security cameras as they spoke, trying to see if they could catch a glimpse of the man entering the hospital. He had to have gotten into the kitchen somehow to have the chance to place the lock of hair and note on her tray, and to also know what room she was in. This meant the man knew how to move around without anyone suspecting him as not belonging in the hospital. The truck he had stolen to smash into her ambulance had belonged to a man who lived just around the corner from Ashley's parents' house. He had not been home at the time and the killer had smashed a window, then hotwired it while it was parked in the driveway. Of course no neighbors had seen anything; most of them had been gawking down at the Wrights' house, watching the excitement going on there.

The killer must have sat there waiting and watching the action after he had firebombed her parents' back yard. When he realized he had not finished her off, he had waited for the ambulance to leave and then followed them.

There had been no fingerprints in the pickup, no fibers or trace evidence of any kind other than the owner's, and the only fingerprints on the top of the ambulance had been Ben's and one set from Nick before he had put his gloves on.

"There is something else that I have not had a chance to report yet," Michael stated.

All eyes swung towards him.

"During the rescue attempt from the ambulance, I received several text messages from the killer."

Ashley's eyes grew large at his statement. Derek growled low in his throat. Thank God Michael had not heard that, and she could tell Derek was trying to keep a lid on the anger that raced throughout his body at the information.

"You don't think this was something that should have been brought to our attention right away?"

Michael turned his blue eyes towards Derek and gave him a cool look. "First of all, at the time I had no idea the FBI was involved, and then the protection of my sister became my top priority. Besides, I called the department immediately and put a trace on my phone, and started them tracing any incoming calls."

Agent Clark was brave enough to ask, "Any luck with that?"

"No. I just got a call right before I came in here from the station and the calls came from one of those pre-paid burner phones, found everywhere. I wish they would outlaw those things. They are a cop's worst nightmare."

Ashley still had not said a word, until now. "Michael, what did they say?"

Michael turned his head and looked her straight in the eyes. He reached into his folder and pulled out a sheet of paper. Stretching across the bed, he handed it to her.

The fact that he had done so without any hassle shocked her. Maybe he had finally come to terms with the fact that she deserved to be involved.

Ashley read the four messages. Her eyes were fighting to focus on the words on the paper, and she felt a chill sweep over her entire body. Her hands started shaking and she could feel the panic starting to take over. Derek gently tried taking the page from her hand, but it was clenched in a vise-like grip.

"Ashley, let go."

She turned her head and stared into his eyes, silently pleading for him to make this all go away. He reached up and with his other hand gently pried her fingers from the sheet of paper, never taking his eyes from hers. Ashley felt his silent strength as he held onto her hand a little longer than was necessary, and it gave her the courage to keep the panic at bay, for now at least.

She knew he was struggling to keep up a professional appearance in front of the other agents and his stick-up-the-ass boss, that there was nothing he wanted more than to gather her in his arms and give her the comfort he knew she needed.

He silently read the messages and then passed the piece of paper over to agent Clark, who read it and then passed it along. Derek looked at Michael. "This guy has your phone number and you didn't think it was important enough to let us know? This puts a whole new light on this thing."

"Listen, don't cop an attitude with me. I followed the correct procedure and put the right people on it, and like I said before..." Michael answered, his voice climbing a little as he spoke.

"The FBI has a better database and research team than you do here. You should have told us right away," Derek interrupted.

Michael stood up. "As I said before, I did not know you were even FBI, and—"

"STOP IT! Both of you!" Ashley said from where she had been lying, listening to their childish bickering. "Jesus Christ. You two are acting like a couple of first-graders out on the playground, staking your territory. I think it's time you both stopped bitching at each other, and we keep our focus on the facts of this case, and not who did what and when. We need both the FBI and the department's help in this if we are going to try to get ahead of this psycho. If you two can't control your macho attitudes, then I'm going to ask the captain and Agent Day to remove you from this case." Ashley was holding her side in pain as she finished her tirade.

She glared at each of them in turn and they both turned red. She wasn't sure if it was from embarrassment or anger, but at the moment, she didn't care. The room was quiet as they sat down, each taking some deep breaths, and that's when she looked around the circle of men surrounding her bed. Harold looked worried, Michael and Derek were both looking down at their notes, Agent Clark and Phillip had small smiles on their faces, and Mr. Dickwad was actually looking at her without his usual glare. She knew she had spent her energy and was going to pay for her outburst, but it just spilled out before she could stop it.

"So Michael, any guesses on how this maniac got your restricted phone number?" Harold asked, breaking the uncomfortable silence that had followed her explosion, which had caused her lungs to scream in pain. She knew she was just about done for, but wanted to try and make it through the meeting without having to ask for any pain medication. She gently placed her hand on her chest, trying to keep the pain away the best she could. She knew she had to be pale and her breathing was getting a little worse, and she prayed everyone was too busy to notice.

"Who knows? No one has it but the department and my immediate family. I guess anyone could call the station with some lame story and get it. He could have pretended to be another cop and I'm sure whoever answered the call would give it out." Michael had been watching the captain as he said all this, and Harold, Michael and Ashley could all tell he was not happy that the FBI would think that his department would make such a mistake. She was proud of him for keeping his cool and not questioning Michael's statement. They already had enough testosterone flying around the room without him adding to the fire.

Mr. Dickwad had not said a word this whole time. He glanced at Michael and then Derek. "If this is the same person as in the other murders, for some reason he has taken this to a whole new personal level. Before, he swooped in, did his killing and moved on. Now, it's like he is obsessed with both Officer and Detective Wright, and I have to sit here and wonder why. What do they have in common other than being brother and sister, and the fact that both of them are on the police force? I think we need to concentrate on that link. This guy has a real hard-on for these two. Agent Clark, I think we should dig into the other murders in the other cities to see if any of them were related or involved with the police department in their towns, especially the stalked women versus the look-alikes."

The captain cleared his throat. "Ashley, Harold said earlier that while you were trapped inside the ambulance, the killer talked to you. This information may give us a clue as to where this maniac is coming from."

All eyes swung in her direction again, some more intense than others. Ashley wished she had had the chance to tell this before her outburst and she had more lung strength, but knew she had to get through the story one way or another.

As she went over the details the best as she could remember, Ashley could sense the uneasiness in everyone surrounding her bed. She was thankful that they had only exchanged a few sentences, even if those few were the scariest she had ever encountered. She was not sure how much Phillip knew about the case, but was sure that he and Michael had gone over all this before he arrived here in her room this morning. He stood in the back against the wall, watching her as she relayed the story. He was thoughtful and she had a feeling that he was seeing something the rest were not.

After she finished, she looked around at their faces. Michael's and Derek's were about the same, anger and frustration evident in the scowls that they both wore, Harold's and the captain's were full of worry, and Agent Clark's was the only one that had a calm attentive look about it. She didn't give Agent Day's so much as a glance; she didn't really care what his looked like.

Phillip cleared his throat. "I can't help but notice that between Michael's text messages and the comments he made to Ashley, he has a real thing about referring to Ashley as a hotshot cop. He has used the phrase several times. He has also made comments about us never being able to catch him. It makes me think that since Ashley has only been out of the academy for a few short weeks and has had no chance to arrest anyone or piss anyone off, this has to be coming from somewhere else."

"So, what you're saying is that this had to have happened at the academy?" Michael asked.

"I think we need to look at who did not make the cut, both the ones who never even made the list to get in and then the ones who did not pass or were passed over."

"That makes a lot of sense. Ashley did kick a lot of guys' asses in all areas of the training and I could see how that would piss off a lot of guys. Passing both the written, physical and shooting with the highest scores in her class had to get under most of the men's skins," Harold answered.

Derek looked at Ashley with admiration. Ashley thought he was surprised at this information. Even Agent Day was looking at her with a little more respect than he had when he first walked into the I.C.U. Well, good. It was nice that they knew she was not just some female that got picked to graduate because the academy had a quota of females and minorities to meet the government's requirements. She deserved to be here and had worked hard to make sure she could hold her head up when other officers looked her way, unlike Malone who had slept her way through the academy.

Agent Day put in his second contribution to the conversation. "Clark, start looking into cadets who were either never picked for the programs or passed over in all the other cities where there were murders, and then match them up with the ones here. This might be just the area we need to be looking at. Maybe we will even get lucky and get a hit on the same person who tried to enter several different types of law enforcement and was rejected. Check everything, not just local levels. I would look into the fire department and any other agencies that he may have been turned down for."

Clark was busy writing down everything he was supposed to do, and Ashley could see that everyone else was starting to get a positive vibe on this lead.

"Ashley, is there anyone that jumps to your mind that you were in the academy with who fits this profile?" Derek asked as he leaned over the railing.

She knew he was getting in close because he was the closest one to her; he could probably read her mind and know that she was close to her breaking point. She was exhausted and was starting to really be in pain. She was hoping someone else would call an end to this meeting so she wouldn't have to.

"Not right offhand, but let me think on it awhile."

He searched her face and then leaned back up. "Well, gentlemen, I think we have enough to go on. Why don't we meet again later today and see what we've all come up with?"

Somehow, Ashley knew he would do this, and she was so grateful for once that he had the ability to read her thoughts.

Everyone stood and picked up the notes and files that had been laid around the edge of her hospital bed. They were talking among themselves, so she allowed herself to close her eyes for a few minutes of rest.

CHAPTER TWENTY-FIVE

When Ashley opened her eyes again, she realized that she must have been out for hours. She could see that the sun was setting through the one window high on the wall behind the nurses' station. It had to be close to eight o'clock at night and she was starving. She couldn't remember the last time she had eaten. It seemed like it had been days, when in all reality it was just last night in her parents' back yard, with her whole family around her. So much had happened in just a few short days, time was all out of sorts for her; she was used to her lazy days of sleeping all day and then sitting in a nice quiet morgue all night. She would give anything to have those days back again.

She looked over to her left, and her mom and Shannon were sitting there talking quietly. She glanced to her right and could see her dad standing at the door, talking to the uniformed officer in charge of guarding the door tonight.

Shannon was telling Laura about Grandma calling all her country club friends, claiming that her life was in danger and that some madman had tried to kill her with a firebomb.

"Well, someone actually just about did," Ashley muttered.

They both sprang out of their chairs and hurried to the side of her bed. "Honey, we didn't know when you were going to wake up. You had us all scared to death. What in the world got into you, insisting that they hold that meeting in your room? You should have known you were not up to all that activity, and I let Harold know just exactly what I thought of the whole idea. To be so stupid to allow all those cops in here while you were just a few hours out of surgery, was just..."

"Mom, take a breath, geez."

She suddenly stopped and looked from Ashley to Shannon.

"She's right, Mom. You could have been lying there beside Ash with all the air you were using. It was a wonder your lungs didn't give out after all that." Shannon turned to Ashley. "Hey, big sis...has anyone been brave enough to tell you that you look like total shit?"

"Asshole. Everyone was nice enough not to mention it, but I can always count on you to be brutally honest with me."

"Hey babe, I just call them like I see them. And to think all those hunky guys were here this morning seeing you in all your shining glory...both of them," she couldn't help adding.

Looking at her mom, Ashley asked, "Is it really that bad? Do you have a mirror on you?"

"Shannon Marie, I cannot believe you said that to your sister."

"Yes you can. You know I would never lie to her. Besides, I didn't tell her that to be mean, I just know *I* would want to know." Shannon looked back to Ashley and she could see the tears she was fighting hard to hide.

Laura looked at Shannon a few more seconds and then turned her attention to Ashley. "Honey, you have been through hell these last couple of days, so yes, you look like someone beat the shit out of you."

"*Mom!*" Shannon and Ashley both said at the same time.

She just smiled and laid her hand on Ashley's cheek. "You're beautiful no matter what some deranged maniac has done to you. Now tell me how you're feeling. How is your pain? Do you need anything?"

"My ribs and chest are still sore when I breathe or move and my head still feels like someone took a baseball bat to it. But my vision has returned to normal and I'm not as nauseous as I was this morning, but I'm starving. Is there any chance of getting something to eat?"

"I'm sure they still have you on a clear diet, but I'll go see what I can find out." She made her way to the nurses' station and Harold walked over to hear what was going on.

Shannon moved to where her mom had been standing. "So are you hanging in there?"

Ashley looked at her, fighting the tears she knew were bound to come. "I have never felt such fear as I do now. My mind cannot comprehend that someone is really trying to kill me. Did Dad and Michael fill you and Mom in on the newest developments?"

"They told us earlier, when we first got here. You have had about fifty visitors stop by and try to get in to see you. Casey and Dan are fit to be tied because they won't let them back here to see you. She has called my cell phone about twenty times today, getting updates. Bill's a nervous wreck and wants to be assigned to the case and off of morgue duty. And of course the whole crew has been by. The nurses finally put up a sign-in sheet by the doors, so you would know who had stopped by. That hunky fireman and Troy have both been by several times and some shriveled-up little old man has been out in the waiting room for hours."

Ashley's eyebrows drew together in confusion. "What little old man?"

"I don't know. He said something about being your rock in your time of need. I think he's some crazy old coot."

Smiling, Ashley remembered the voice outside the ambulance. "Hey, I'll have you know that he and I have a dinner date just as soon as they let me out of here. Will you do me a favor when Mom comes back? Will you go see if he is still out there and tell him I'm craving Mexican, so he better like it."

"Are you serious? You really want me to do that?"

"I have never been more serious in my life."

Shannon looked at Ashley like she was afraid Ashley had seriously damaged something when she hit her head for the hundredth time in just the last few days. Laura walked back over and told them they were going to bring her a tray shortly, but there wouldn't be much on it.

"Anything would be great...even green Jell-O sounds good right now. Shannon, would you run that errand for me now?"

Laura looked at her daughters and watched as Shannon shrugged her shoulders and said she would be right back.

Ashley waited until Shannon was gone. "Okay, Mom, tell me the truth. What's going on with me?"

Ashley knew she could count on her mom to tell it to her straight. "You have a cut along your hairline that took twenty-two stitches to close. You have a severe concussion, which is why you may have been experiencing the double vision and nausea. You must have hit your nose, because both of your eyes are solid black and you have several cuts and abrasions on your face, some from the other day and some fresh ones. They are minor and will not leave scars. You lost a lot of blood and they gave you a couple of transfusions. You broke several ribs, one puncturing your left lung. You broke a couple of fingers on your left hand, and you are covered with small burn marks, cuts and scrapes. But, other than that, you're great."

Ashley reached up and felt the bandage circling her head. "Will I have a huge scar?"

"Are you kidding? Doc made sure the best plastic surgeon was on hand. Plus, it's along your hairline, so after it heals you will hardly be able to notice it."

Tears filled her eyes. "Mom..."

She sat down on the edge of the bed, leaned over and held Ashley gently, stroking her hair. It was still stiff with the dried blood from the cut and Ashley knew it had to be really gross. Laura held her like that until Shannon came back in the room.

She was smiling ear to ear. "Hey Ash, not sure who that guy really is, but I know you just made his day. What a neat old guy! I think maybe I'll horn in on your date. Maybe he has a younger brother."

"What old guy? What are you two talking about?" asked Laura.

"He was at the accident site before any of the rescue guys showed up. He helped me get through those first terrifying moments. He talked to me and helped me understand what had just happened, and gave me the comfort I needed after going through that."

Laura looked at Shannon and then Ashley, the emotion in her face overwhelming. She stood up, patted Ashley's hand, reassuring her she would be right back. She got up and walked out of the I.C.U. Shannon and Ashley gave each other puzzled looks, with Shannon shrugging her shoulders. "Who knows? Mom works in mysterious ways. Is there anything I can do for you? Do you need me to get you some makeup or anything?"

Ashley raised her hand to touch her face. "You know, Shannon, at this point I don't even have the energy to care what I look like. I have never been in so much pain in my life and I literally don't have the slightest oomph to worry about how I look."

Ashley could tell that shocked her sister. She knew that several very hunky men would be coming back and forth through her room, and the fact that she didn't care what she looked like told her how much pain she was really in.

Ashley closed her eyes and fought back tears, scared by that fact also. The emotions were wearing her down. She wanted to lie here and cry like a baby, throw a fit, throw things across the room and scream at the top of her lungs, or at least as loud as her one healthy lung would let her.

Laura walked back in and Shannon and Ashley looked at her expectantly. She looked back and forth from one to the other. "What?"

"Don't 'what' us. Where did you rush off to?"

"I needed to meet this great old guy you both were talking about. I invited him over for dinner tomorrow."

Shannon and Ashley looked at each other and they started chuckling. "Mom, if you are trying to reward him for being there for Ashley, you might want to reconsider and take the poor man out for supper rather than punish him with one of your home-cooked meals."

Laura smacked Shannon on the forehead, which made her instantly stop laughing. "I can't believe you just struck me in a public place. You have always kept your beatings private," Shannon said as she rubbed her forehead.

Laura smiled. "I'll show you beatings."

The I.C.U. doors opened and a nurse's aide had her food tray in her hands. She glanced between the guard who opened the door and Harold to the nurse behind the desk. She stood there undecided on what she should do, and then they watched the nurse relieve the girl of the tray before her trembling hands dropped it. You could tell that the police presence in the hospital scared her to death. She wasn't the only one feeling that way.

The nurse who had taken over Tina's place last night brought the tray to Ashley, placing it on her tray table and scooting it over her bed. She lifted the tray lid, checking the contents, looking at each dish, to make sure nothing was hidden under them, making sure nothing looked tampered with. They all sat in silence as she went about her business, taking comfort in the fact that she did so. When she was satisfied everything passed inspection, she raised the head of the bed as far as was comfortable for Ashley, and with her mom's help scooted Ashley upright. After so many hours lying there, Ashley had shifted down to almost the bottom of the bed.

When they grabbed her under the arms and gently lifted her up, she couldn't help gasping in pain.

It took several seconds for her to catch her breath and for the pain to recede back to the dull ache it had been before they moved her.

The nurse moved back to her desk after she was sure Ashley was okay, and Laura and Shannon look worried. Ashley could see Harold out of the corner of her eyes and she knew he was just as concerned as they were.

Ashley concentrated on the contents of her tray. There was a bowl of beef broth, some green Jell-O, and a cup of hot water with the fixings for hot tea. She lifted a spoonful of broth to her mouth. She was so weak that she only got half of it to her mouth, the rest landing on the napkin the nurse had placed across her chest.

"Can I help you, babe?"

Ashley raised her eyes to her mom, tears forming again. Geez, she was such a crybaby. "Yes, thanks."

Laura sat back down on the side of the bed, taking the spoon from her hand and feeding her the soup and the Jell-O.

Shannon, sensing Ashley's discomfort, started talking up a storm. Her talk of course turned to all the handsome guys she had seen entering the room earlier this morning, wanting to know all about Phillip Kelley and the dashing FBI agent. She thought it was fascinating that Derek had turned out to be with the FBI, and thought it romantic that he was interested in her big sister. She filled Ashley in on who all had tried to come visit her. Her heart did a little flutter when she told her both Nick and Troy had been by and were upset when they were told they could not get in to see her.

Ashley's life had gone from "sleepy hollow" to full-blown out of control in a heartbeat, and she was ready for it to slide back into its boring nonexistence. Sure, she wouldn't mind a little male attention to fill the hours, but all of a sudden having anywhere from four to five guys show extreme interest was more than she was willing to take on. All she wanted at the moment was for her lungs to stop feeling like they were on fire with every breath she took, someone to find this crazed killer and put him behind bars forever, and her one true love to find his way to her. She did not think this was too much to ask for.

The beef broth tasted amazing and in no time she had finished off all of it, along with the Jell-O, and sat drinking her tea. She was so tired she was fighting to keep her eyes open long enough to finish the tea. Shannon had turned her attention to her mom and they were discussing what they would serve Ben when he came over for supper. They decided they would ask Grandpa and Grandma over so that Ben would have someone his own age to talk to. Ashley wasn't sure that was such a great idea. Why did Ben have to suffer through both her mom's cooking and Grandma's endless questions? She would be trying to fix him up with all her lady friends... Now, why would she just assume he was not married?

Ashley had finished her tea and placed her cup on her tray, listening to them both talk, hating to admit that she was ready for the visit to be over so that she could go back to sleep. She would never actually tell them that, but she was fighting off the urge to close her eyes.

"Um, I think our patient is ready to get some sleep, what do you two think?" Harold asked as he walked up to the side of her bed.

Ashley turned and reached for his hand, smiling and squeezing.

Laura turned a concerned look her way and she could tell she didn't want to leave her side, even for a minute, but knew that she was going to have to give in and let her get some rest. Ashley would be surprised if she left the hospital; she would likely head instead to the visitor's lounge. Laura stood, leaned over, and gently placed a kiss on her cheek. "Is there anything I can get you before I leave?"

"I'm good, Mom, but first thing in the morning I want to get up and take a shower. I can't stand this dried blood in my hair any longer. So, if you could bring everything I will need for that I would appreciate it."

"I'll pack you a bag tonight with all you will need and bring it first thing in the morning. If you need anything at all during the night, you let Tina know when she gets here in a few minutes. And you can always call me no matter what time it is, understood?"

"Yes, ma'am."

She and Shannon made their way to the doors, stopping to give Harold hugs as they left, and passing Tina as she made her way into the I.C.U.

Ashley watched as the four of them stood talking, sending sly glances her way every few minutes, but she really was not concerned, knowing they were talking about her condition. She was sure her mom was giving Tina her nurse's opinion on how Ashley was really doing, and making sure she would take good care of her throughout the night.

Michael walked in and joined their group. She couldn't help noticing that he chose to stand behind Tina. He was close enough to her for her to feel his heat. Ashley smiled, as she could imagine what having him stand that close was doing to Tina. In the time that he had joined them, she began fidgeting with the chart in her hands, and she kept sending small glances back over her shoulder. Everyone else in the group had no idea of the chemistry flying between the two of them. Ashley had not gotten a chance to mention the episode of last night between her brother and her nurse, but decided she would hold on to that information until a time when she needed to take some heat off of herself. She knew the days ahead of her were going to be filled with lots of caring and attention and that she would be ready to turn some of that away from herself. What better way than turn it towards her brother? He deserved some for a change. He had never been involved with a woman before so she knew the news would send her family into a tizzy. Just the thought of the chaos that would bring made her smile and settle a little more comfortably in her bed. She closed her eyes again, knowing her body needed the rest to recover from her injuries. Besides, she was not up to her brother's questions and knew she could escape in sleep.

CHAPTER TWENTY-SIX

When Ashley woke again, she could tell instantly that the pain was better. She lay with her eyes closed and breathing did not send searing pain into her lungs. The pain had receded to a dull ache but, then again, she had not moved yet. She could hear the machines connected to the guy across the room. Other than the noise they put off, she could not hear anything else in the large room. She knew for a fact that someone was sitting in the chair beside her bed, but she had no idea who. It could be any number of people from her brother, dad or Derek to her mom or sister. She lay perfectly still, trying to get a clue as to who it was so she would know what to expect when she opened her eyes. Nothing. No movement at all, no sound. Curiosity was getting the better of her and she was tempted to open her eyes to see who was sitting so still beside her bed. Maybe the person was sleeping and that was why it was so quiet. She had no idea what time it was, whether it was still night or early morning. She had been woken up several times throughout the night with Tina checking her vitals or her tubes or giving her medicine, but other than that she had no idea. Her guess was that it was morning, by the light coming through her closed eyelids.

Ashley slowly opened her eyes, turning her head toward the wall and the chair, expecting Derek to be sitting there with a knowing smirk on his face. But to her surprise no one was sitting there at all. She could not help feeling a rush of fear at the thought that she was a sitting duck lying in this hospital bed, with a gown on that barely covered her ass if she were to try to defend herself against a would-be attacker. She could see the headlines now: "Rookie Female Cop Shows Ass Fleeing Psycho Killer in Halls of Local Hospital." Ashley's heart had started a rapid pace as she made a quick surveillance of the I.C.U. and found that she and the man in the other bed were alone, as far as she could see. No one was sitting behind the nurses' station, no cop was posted at the door and there were no signs of any of her three wardens, her mother or sister. The panic took hold of her and made its way throughout her body. Wild thoughts were flying around in her mind, tripping over each other in her panic. She looked down and realized with dread that she was trapped in her hospital bed with the tubes still attached to her in several places, one of which she chose not to think about. She had no weapon within reach and no way to defend herself if someone should choose to enter the I.C.U. and kill her as she lay here. She glanced over at the machine that tracked her blood pressure and heart rate, and watched as both rose at an alarming rate.

Ashley knew she was being silly, but she could not help the anxiety that raced through her. As soon as one of those assholes who were supposed to be protecting her showed their slimy faces, she was going to demand that her firearm be brought to her, so that she could defend herself. She looked around for the call button, wanting to see if she could find whoever had taken Tina's place on the morning shift. She looked at the clock over the nurses' station to see that it was close to nine o'clock. She must have slept hard after her last vitals check. She had not heard anything for hours, not the nurses changing shifts or even her bodyguards doing the same. She knew she was exhausted but she was amazed that she had slept through it all. She finally found the call button, which was lying beside the breakfast tray on the hospital bed stand just out of her reach. She tried sticking her arm through the railing on her bed, scooting over to the edge and stretching her arm out as far as she could, wiggling her fingers within inches of the stand. There was no way she was going to reach it that way. She grabbed the remote that controlled the height of the bed and hit the down arrow so that she was lying flat, and then leaned over to the side, trying to find the lever to lower the railing. Leaning over had her breathing hard and she could feel the pain in her lungs and body. The lever was down on the bottom of the railing and she could just barely reach it. With a lot of effort, she finally managed to lower the railing. Scooting her body over to the edge again, she reached out with her right arm to try and snag the wayward cart. During her struggles, the covers had worked their way down to her knees and she could feel a breeze along her back; she knew she was probably shooting a moon to anyone who might walk in, but she was willing to take that chance. Ashley wiggled and squirmed but finally got a finger hooked under the stand and managed to pull it over to the edge of the bed. She rolled over and lay flat on her back, trying to catch her breath. God, she was a wreck. She needed to get out of this bed and regain her strength. She turned her head to the right and looked straight into the amused eyes of Derek. He was standing inside the swinging double doors of the I.C.U., his arms filled with Starbucks coffees and what looked like a bag of greasy food. The smell was amazing and she could hear her stomach growl.

"Ah babe, you're killing me with all these nice butt shots."

Ashley couldn't help but glance down at the fly of his jeans, which she could tell even from across the room were straining against the zipper. She could feel her cheeks burn. "Where the hell have you been? I could have been killed here in my bed while you were out God knows where."

He walked toward her, hooked the chair with his boot and slid it over; then he put the coffees and sandwiches on the tray beside the breakfast tray that was already there.

He took his time getting things all ready, reaching down and raising the railing back to where it belonged and then raising the bed so that she was sitting in an upright position again. He pushed the tray across the bed and took the lids off the coffees.

The whole time she lay there glaring at him, waiting for him to answer her. She knew her cheeks were still red, just knowing that he had seen her butt again. Why was it always him who caught her in all her glory and not one of her many family members, who always seemed to be absent when she needed them?

Ashley could tell he was just antagonizing her by not answering her, the asshole. She reached up and grabbed the nurse's call button, pushed it, never once looking at him. Within seconds the nurse was flying through the doors, carrying an armload of supplies that she threw down on her desk, and came to her side.

"What's the problem, Ashley? I was only gone for a few minutes and the policeman here said it would be fine if I ran to get the supplies I needed."

She looked from Derek to Ashley and gave them each a dirty look. Ashley scowled, and she didn't have to look to know Derek still had a shit-ass grin on his face. She also couldn't help but notice that he had conveniently placed his oversized crotch against the railing so that the bewildered nurse would not be able to witness his obvious reaction to her earlier display of her ass.

Never looking at Derek, Ashley answered, "Nothing urgent. It's not your job to guard me and I was wondering if I could get a fresh breakfast tray, since this one has gone cold."

She looked more annoyed than she had before, once again looking at Derek, then the food on the tray and back to Ashley. "Well, I guess you can, but you are NOT going to eat any of that food. It is strictly prohibited from your diet. You have been upgraded to a soft diet and are not allowed any solids at all." She gave the bag soaked in heavenly grease a nasty look and then turned her glare to Derek. "You were not planning on giving her any of that food, were you?" She was a short heavy-set woman who Ashley would guess to be in her mid-fifties, with a face that would scare little kids. That's probably why she was here in I.C.U. rather than in pediatrics. Most of the patients in here would not even be awake to see her. She wore an old-fashioned nurse's outfit with the little nurse's cap and everything. She wore white hose that were a good size too small, if the rolls visible through the starched white uniform were any indication. Her shoes were white with thick rubber soles that squeaked when she walked. Her hair was mousy brown and gray, and so frizzy it bunched up around the hat she had pinned on her head. She had no makeup except drawn-on eyebrows that were about two inches too long. She must have used a black eyebrow pencil rather than a softer toned one. The look was like she had been shocked by something and her face froze in that position. Either that or she used a round-shaped object as a pattern for drawing her eyebrows. Her scowl kind of lost its effect in the unnatural shape of her eyebrows.

Derek started to answer and Ashley interrupted him before he could say anything. "Of course I know I am on a strict soft diet. I couldn't possibly eat anything Mr. FBI brought in. By the way, do you know when my dad is expected to arrive?"

She glared for a time more before growling out, "Oh, he's already here! He's in the hall talking to your mom."

Ashley reached out and patted her chubby hand on the railing. "Would you mind going to get them? I would like to see them right away."

One last time she looked at Derek and then back at her again. "I will get him right away." She turned and made a hasty trip to the doors, glancing back to glare one more time.

"Ashley, you are…"

Ashley turned and shot him such a nasty look that he was taken aback and never finished his sentence. By the time he regained his composure, Laura and Harold were hustling over to her bed. Both seemed alarmed and it never occurred to her that her requesting them would cause them to worry.

"Honey, is everything all right?" Laura asked as she rushed to her side.

Ashley could see her dad giving Derek a curious look, but he never said a word. Ashley ignored Derek completely. "Everything is fine, Mom; I was just anxious to see you this morning."

Laura rose back to a standing position, her eyebrows making a deep V over concerned eyes. She looked between Derek and Ashley and put her hands on her hips. "Okay, what's going on between you two?"

"It all started as I walked in the door and—"

"Absolutely nothing is going on between us. I was really hungry and thought maybe you could make sure I get something to eat since I slept through my breakfast this morning."

"Ashley, I'm sorry. I forgot you were on a limited diet. I actually got some of this for you."

"I'm sure that what you brought is way too greasy for me, isn't that right, Mom?" Ashley looked up at her with what she was sure was an innocent look.

She lifted the lid of the tray that was still on the bedside table. They all looked at the lumpy oatmeal, and makings for hot tea that had long ago gone cold. She looked over at the sack of breakfast items that Derek had placed on the tray. "I think you better share that with Harold and I'll have a new breakfast tray sent up for Ashley. It looks like they still have her on a soft diet, and I'm pretty sure that whatever is in that sack would not be classified as light."

Ashley almost felt bad for him. He had thought he was doing a good thing by bringing her something that was a whole lot better than she was going to eventually eat and, truth be told, if she hadn't embarrassed herself flashing her ass to him yet again, she would have eaten every luscious bite before anyone could have stopped her. She was starving and the thought of oatmeal was enough to make her want to barf. Now that her embarrassment was a little less, she knew she had acted childish once again.

She reached over and placed her hand on his arm. Looking into his eyes she said, "Thanks for trying. I appreciate it and if you want to bring me something tonight that smells as good as that does, no matter what anyone says, I'm going to eat it."

He stared down for a few brief seconds, and then in the most innocent voice, responded, "I would be glad to bring in a fresh cinnamon roll from Hill's Café. I could even help you if you are too weak to eat it yourself."

The heat crept up her face at the memory of their last encounter with one of those cinnamon rolls. He knew exactly how his statement would affect her! She withdrew her hand from his arm. The shithead! So much for feeling guilty about the way she had acted. He had no shame bringing that up in front of her parents, who were no doubt bewildered.

Derek chuckled and then he and her dad moved over to an empty bed, put the delicious-smelling breakfast out on the tray, and dug in. Laura fussed with her pillows and made sure she was comfortable. Ashley shot Derek dirty little looks the whole time he was eating what should have been her breakfast. Damn.

After they had finished their breakfast, Ashley's doctor came in to check her out. Thankfully he had insisted that Derek and her dad step out of the room. After much prodding and poking, he claimed that everything looked good enough for the drain tubes to be removed, along with her catheter tube. He insisted she stay on a soft diet for at least one more day, along with the strict orders that she was not allowed to leave her bed without someone there to assist her in going to the restroom. He stated very strongly that he would have preferred her to stay in bed and use a bedpan, but both Laura and Ashley argued that apparently he had never had to use one of those things or he wouldn't even have suggested such a thing. He gave in and said he thought Ashley was improved enough to be moved to a private room so that she would have a bathroom close by. Although he was willing to move her to a private room, for at least the remainder of the day and most of tomorrow a bedside commode would be placed in her room, and she was to go no further than that to use the restroom.

Laura argued Ashley's case for needing a shower. He finally agreed to it, but it had to be later tonight after she had rested for several hours. He went over the plan for the next few days and assured her he would get her out of there as soon as was humanly possible, stating again that most of that was up to her, how well she followed directions and did what she was told. Ashley knew she wanted out badly enough that she would do whatever was asked of her without bitching or moaning.

After he left, the nurse set about removing the catheter first. Ashley had to admit the thought of having to get up and walk across the room to go to the bathroom was not a pleasant one. Just rolling around a few minutes ago trying to reach the remote had worn her out; actually walking was going to really take everything she had. This had to be one of the most humiliating things she had endured in a while. The nurse had Ashley lie with her knees bent up and her legs spread. Thank God she at least placed a sheet over her knees while she was getting ready. With her luck, as many times as Derek had walked in and caught her with her ass bare to the world, she definitely did not want him catching her lying there with all her womanly goods spread wide for his enjoyment. Just the thought sent a deep flush to her face and she couldn't help muttering, "Could you please hurry up before some jackass walks in here and sees me like this?"

Laura chuckled. With one sweet pull the nurse removed the nasty tube and replaced her legs to a more ladylike position. Ashley relaxed and watched as the nurse went to get a tray that she had placed on her nurses' station. It was covered in a small white sheet and Ashley couldn't help starting to feel a little anxious again. Jesus, now what? Was she going to perform some kind of surgery next? Maybe Ashley should have just left things the way they were. She could learn to adapt to a tube coming out of her side. Drain the little baggie thing filled with bloody discharge every once in a while. What would be the big deal with that? Not sure how it would do on the old love life but at the current time that wasn't something she had to worry about anyway.

When the nurse had all of her supplies ready she gruffly informed Ashley what to expect when she removed the tube coming out of her side. The nurse turned her on her good side, and before she could even think about it she had Ashley take a deep breath and said, "Now let it out, Ashley."

Holy shit! Ashley felt like she had ripped her whole insides out with the tube. She had been holding her mom's hand and the railing while the nurse had been getting her ready and Laura realized that she was squeezing so hard, it had to be killing her. The nurse completely ignored her pain and went on cleaning the area where the tube had been, then put a bandage on.

Ashley glanced over her shoulder to give the bitch a death look. She pretended she couldn't see Ashley glaring at her. Laura turned her head back in her direction. "Are you okay, Ash?"

"Sweet Jesus, Mom! Do you think you could have warned me that it was going to hurt that much?"

She patted the hand she was still holding. "Believe me, it would not have mattered. Sometimes it's just easier if the patient doesn't know what to expect. If we warn them, they tense up and it only hurts more. I'm sorry, honey, but you will feel so much better now that it's out. You will be able to move around more and the sooner we can get you up and going, the sooner you'll get to be released and come home to recover."

Ashley tried to catch her breath and relax her side, even though it felt like someone had stuck a red-hot poker in her. She gave her a weak frown and lay quietly as the nurse finished up and moved to pick up the tube and supplies she had used. The sight of the bloody tube and gauze was enough to make Ashley feel even queasier. She had broken out into a sweat as she had pulled the tube out. It had felt like the damn thing was anchored to her insides and when she had given it a hard yank, half of them had come out with it. Ashley turned her head quickly, not wanting to look too closely at the tube in case some of her insides *were* attached to it. Miss Happy Yanker was definitely on her least favorite nurses list.

Laura was busy fussing around her, trying to make her comfortable. Although it was good that the tubes were out, she was now as weak as a kitten again. She closed her eyes and let the emotion take over. All she knew was that they had better catch the son of a bitch who was doing this to her before she was turned into some sniveling crybaby who cried at the slightest little thing. She took a few deep breaths and let the anger of the situation take over again. There, that was more like it. She was imprinting every little ache and pain that he had inflicted on her deep into her memory, so that if she was around when he was finally taken down she could call upon it for strength to get her revenge. She wanted that man to suffer like she had. There weren't too many people who could claim to have been pushed down a street in the back of a turned-over ambulance at sixty miles an hour. The flashes of memory of that ride were racing through her mind. She recalled the impact on the side of the van, and flipping over. She could hear the scream of the EMT, the crunch of metal when they hit the side of the building, and she could feel herself starting to panic as the memories came rushing back to her. Ashley's breathing was increasing and her heart was starting to race.

"Ashley, what's wrong? Honey, you're scaring me. Are you in pain?" Laura signaled the nurse to get the guys back in there as she continued talking to her.

Ashley could hear and see her but the memories were too strong. She felt herself starting to shake and knew she was starting to lose it.

The nurse had stuck her head out into the hall and told Harold and Derek to come back in right away. All three of them rushed to her bed, fear evident on two of their faces and worry on the other one. The feelings were overwhelming and Ashley could not control them as they washed over her, one after another.

"Good Lord! What happened in here, Laura? What's wrong with her? I thought you guys were only going to remove the tubes. Should she be like this?" Harold's voice had risen with each word that had come out of his mouth.

"Don't you yell at me, Harold Wright! I have no idea what came over her. She was in pain from the tube removal but she should not be like this."

The nurse was busy taking Ashley's vitals and Derek was standing beside her mom with a worried look on his face. "Should I call for the doctor?"

Ashley had closed her eyes against the memories and could not make herself open them again. She was afraid that she couldn't handle the fear and panic that had overtaken her body.

Laura took over the situation. "Everyone calm down. She has been through a hell of a lot in the last few days and I believe it's finally caught up with her. She will be fine. Doris, give her some Lorazepam to help calm her down. Her mind and body have gone through a horrific battle and she has kept it at bay, trying to be strong. The shock of the pain from removing the tube may have just been enough to trigger the emotions she has fought so hard to keep away." She looked up at Harold, and her own emotions threatened to take over as well.

Harold took his wife into his arms, knowing she needed the comfort as much as his daughter did. He knew he could not comfort them both. "What the hell are you just standing there for? *See to my daughter!*" he yelled at Derek, who had been standing by helplessly, watching all the drama unfold before him.

Derek looked up in surprise at Harold. The man had just raised his voice at him and was glaring at him. Derek looked from him to Ashley and back again. He was frozen in place, not knowing what they wanted him to do. The nurse had given something to Ashley through her I.V. and she seemed to be calming down, but she was still deathly pale and he could see that she was still trembling beneath the sheet covering her black and blue body. He took the time to really look at all her injuries. She was one giant bruise, covered in cuts and abrasions. The wound on her head was still covered by a large gauze bandage and her—

"DEREK!"

Derek tore his eyes away from Ashley and swung them up to meet Harold's. "Yes, sir?"

"I have my hands a little full here, could you just sit down and talk to her in a comforting manner? She needs to know she is surrounded by people who care for her and are not out to harm her."

For the first time Derek noticed that Ashley's mom was crying softly in Harold's arms, with her face buried into his shoulder. His left arm was wrapped tightly around her and his right hand was softly stroking her hair while he whispered soothing words in her ear. He took in the tender scene and felt a pull somewhere near his heart. He was embarrassed to witness Ashley's mom's show of emotion. He had observed her over the last few days as she had dealt with one problem after another concerning her family, always strong and tackling anything they threw at her. She had not buckled once and he was a little surprised by her letdown now. Derek wasn't sure why he felt she was so levelheaded, but it was nice to know that she cared so deeply for her family. He was exposed to all kinds of situations in his line of work, and it was rare today to find a family that had strong moral standards and deep family roots.

He watched for a few seconds more then sat down beside Ashley, taking care not to sit on her or any of the cords and I.V.s that she was still attached to. He scooted closer to her, taking her hand in his. The emotions that came over him both shocked and pleased him. As he looked down at Ashley's battered face, a wave of protectiveness came over him, along with a few emotions he was afraid to face. The others in the room melted away as he watched her. He knew the medicine the nurse had given her was taking effect by the way she had calmed. She was awake but she had yet to open her eyes.

He leaned down within a few inches of her face. "Ash? Can you open your eyes for me?"

Ashley's thoughts were finally settling down. She knew Derek was sitting on the side of the bed, but wasn't sure she was up to any kind of talk. "I'm tired. I just need to rest."

"Are you sure that's what it is, or are you remembering what happened and your emotions are showing?"

Her eyes snapped open. "My emotions are just fine. And none of your business. Who do you think you are, telling me my emotions are showing? And so what if they are? I can show my emotions anywhere I want and you can't do a damn thing about it!"

Derek looked down at her, not smiling, not frowning, just sitting there. Ashley realized she had overreacted again. And he was only trying to help. She could see her parents from the corner of her eye and knew they were perplexed by her outburst.

Ashley looked into his eyes. "Sorry. I shouldn't have snapped at you."

For several seconds he rubbed his thumb slowly over the back of her hand, gently tracing small circles, lightly touching the cuts and scrapes that covered it, being careful not to disturb them. He knew she needed comfort and there was nothing he wanted more than to take her in his arms and hold on to her for dear life, but was also aware that her parents were both standing just a few feet away. His desire was so strong that he had to fight down his own emotions and take a few deep breaths. He looked up and was instantly aware that Ashley was giving him a quizzical look. He could read an emotion there that they were both feeling, but neither one had the slightest clue what it was.

Derek cleared his throat. "Ashley, it's okay to feel shaken up. You have been through more in the last week than most people ever do. No one will blame you if you let a few of those emotions out. It's probably not healthy to keep them all bottled up inside of you, anyway. Nothing is going to happen to you. We have taken every precaution we can think of to protect you."

As Derek talked, all she could think about was how good it felt to have him tenderly stroking her hand. All thoughts of her pain, the madman stalking her, the danger her family and she were in, everything just melted away as his words and his caress engulfed her. She knew it was probably not a good idea to let her defenses down, but between the drugs in her I.V. and the drug of Derek's words and touch, she really didn't care at the moment. She was just going to lie here and enjoy the peace while it lasted. The next hours would be another story.

CHAPTER TWENTY-SEVEN

Ashley woke again to complete silence. Glancing around, she noticed her dad was sitting over by another bed talking quietly on his cell phone. She did not like the look that was on his face. Whomever he was talking to was apparently not giving him news he wanted to hear. Laura and Derek were gone and Nurse Yanking Pants Doris was sitting behind the nurses' station, probably plotting her next act of pain for Ashley.

She could tell by the rumbling in her stomach that she had slept through lunch. She was for sure going to drop the five pounds she had put on while she had been stuck down in the morgue, eating junk food out of the vending machine and not getting the chance to exercise like she normally did.

Ashley took as deep a breath as she could; testing to see how much pain she was in. Although it still hurt like hell to take that deep of a breath, the pain was residing a little. As she lay there, the one thing she knew was that she had to pee like a racehorse and really didn't want to have to ask Doris for help. She sent a telepathic message to her sister and her mom, praying they would show up in the next few minutes so they could help her over to the little bathroom tucked behind the nurses' station. Doris guarded it like it was her very own private bath, giving anyone who asked to use it a look of pure death.

Harold finished his call and looked up to see that Ashley was watching the doors. He made his way over to her, stopping to watch her.

"Dad, you're making me a little nervous, standing there looking at me like that. Is Mom out in the hall?"

"No, honey. She and Shannon ran to the house to get you all the stuff you would need to take your shower. They said just as soon as you woke up again, they were going to move you up to your own room."

"That's good news. Dad, I hate to ask but I really need to go the bathroom."

He instantly turned a bright shade of red. Dad had never really gotten involved with any of the girlie things that went along with having two daughters, leaving those things up to his wife.

"Sorry. If you will just help me over to the bathroom, I can manage from there."

He looked around and spotted the wheelchair parked next to the bed beside hers. "I don't think they want you walking that far yet. How about I wheel you over there, and then you won't get so tired?"

"Sounds good, Dad. I would hate to embarrass myself by passing out halfway there and peeing all over Miss Grouchy Ass's clean floor."

"Ashley, that is not a very ladylike thing to say," Harold muttered under his breath.

"Who are you trying to kid? Neither one of your daughters are very ladylike. You have two tomboys at heart and you love it. You wouldn't know what to do with two sissified little girls who ran around in curls and prissy little dresses."

He chuckled as he wheeled the chair over and then took down the guardrail. Once that was out of the way, Ashley reached for his arm and swung her legs over the side of the bed. That instantly had her head spinning and she felt for a few seconds like she was going to pass out. She sat for several seconds, letting her sore, achy body adjust to the new position. Her ribs were on fire and she could feel all the aches that had been hidden while she was basically flat on her back for the last two days. Once she was sure she could handle standing up, she inched her feet to the floor and gingerly stood up.

Doris had made her way over to them, giving them her opinion that it was too soon to be up and moving around. She was just not a nice person and her attitude was really getting on Ashley's nerves. Just as she was about to let loose on Doris, Harold piped up with, "Unless you want to clean up the mess she is about to make on your clean white floor, I would stand aside and let us get her to the bathroom."

She stared at Harold in shock and muttered about how people were coming in and taking over her I.C.U., then she waddled back to her desk, turning to give them both dirty looks as she left.

"Ah, Dad, you really are my hero. Now help me into that chair or we are both going to be embarrassed in a few seconds."

He grabbed Ashley's arm, situated the chair so that it was under her butt and then lowered her into it.

"Holy shit! That's cold." For the few seconds that her bare ass had hit the cold material of the chair she forgot all about having to go to the bathroom.

Harold wheeled her over to the bathroom, Ashley hanging on to the I.V. pole, and then helped her to stand again. As she went into the little cubicle that served as the restroom for the I.C.U., Harold swung the chair around hard, bumping into Doris, who was watching them like a hawk. He just about knocked her off the little office chair she had planted her oversized body in. "Oh, sorry. Didn't realize you were that close to us."

As Ashley shut the door, she looked up and her dad winked at her. She could hear Doris through the door, muttering that she had not been in the way and she thought Harold had done that on purpose. She went on to say she had a good mind to put it in Ashley's chart that they were antagonizing her. Harold assured her that it had been a complete accident and he would never do something like that on purpose.

Thankfully, Ashley only had to take about two steps to reach the toilet, because between the pain and fighting off laughter, she didn't think she could have made it any further. It took her several minutes to empty her overfilled bladder and then several more to grab the handrail and get herself to a standing position again. She could hear her dad and Doris still discussing the accident as she washed her hands in cold water. Geez, couldn't this hospital afford some hot water? She looked up from washing her hands and got her first look at herself in the tiny mirror that hung over the sink. Oh sweet Jesus! It was way worse than she had imagined. The whole top half of her head was covered in this giant maxi pad, surrounded by a mile of gauze, wrapped around stiff hair coated with dried blood. She had a huge knot on her forehead, and the eyes looking back at her were surrounded by two circles of black, blue and a tint of green. Her left cheek looked like she had taken a digger on the asphalt in the parking lot, turning the side of her face into hamburger. It was covered by an oozing scab that was enough to make her stomach roll. There were scratches on the other cheek, her lower lip was split and also oozed something that looked like watered-down blood.

She took the time to actually look at the rest of her body as she leaned against the front of the sink. Her arms were covered in bruises, old and new, and scrapes and cuts. She pulled up her hospital gown and raised it as far as she could. Her legs looked like her arms, a huge nasty bruise covering just about her entire left thigh. There were three dime-size holes on her side and upper stomach where she assumed they did the laser procedure to repair her collapsed lung, along with a huge bruise covering most of her rib cage. She could also see the gauze pad that covered where the drain tube had been, but it was fairly small and nothing was oozing out of it. Dropping the gown back down, she began to feel like every scrape, cut and bruise was crying out in pain. If she wasn't depressed before, she sure as hell was now.

"Ashley? Are you okay in there?" Harold asked from the other side of the thin door.

She knew she could not let him know how she was feeling. He was worried enough about her as it was. "Yeah Dad, I'm just finishing." Ashley took one last look into the mirror, imprinting the image in her brain, so that when this was over and she was staring at the psychopath as she testified at his trial, she could pull up this image and have the guts to put him away for life.

Ashley managed to open the door and maneuver the I.V. pole out of the tight space without tripping or falling, and was grateful for the wheelchair Harold had waiting for her. She couldn't help glancing at Doris, who moved completely out of the way by going over to the only other occupant in the I.C.U., making herself busy with him as Harold wheeled Ashley back to her own bed. He helped her stand and get the pole back to where it had been parked before and eased her back to the edge of the bed. She sat there for several minutes enjoying the feeling of resting again. She was anxious for them to come move her to a private room, where she would have more freedom to move around and get her strength back. She wanted to get out of this hospital and back to her own place, where she had more control over what happened than she did here under the watchful eyes of Doris, and the swarm of police who were stationed not only in the hall but throughout the hospital. She knew she needed the police protection, but at her place they would be stationed out in the hall and maybe at the outer doors, not in the same room as she was.

Ashley was getting tired, so she swung her legs up onto the bed and leaned back in a semi-sitting position. As Harold was adjusting the covers back over her legs, the I.C.U. doors opened and several orderlies came in. Doris hustled over to them, checking name badges to a list she had on a very official-looking clipboard and checking the papers that they had handed her. She took several minutes to check them over before finally nodding her head and allowing them to pass her to Ashley's bed. Harold also checked their name tags with a list he had pulled from his jacket pocket, and once they were confirmed with his list, they said they were there to move her to her own room. Doris was busy transferring the I.V. to a pole attached to the gurney and taking her vitals one more time before she was out of her care. Everyone stood back as she finished up, making sure not to get in her way, the scowl on her face making it known she was still in charge.

Once Doris was finished, she finally moved out of the way so that they could swing the bed around and move toward the door. Harold led the way, pushing the doors open and checking the hall first to make sure it was clear. Ashley had to admit a rush of fear as they went through the doors and out into the brightly lit hallway. But the only one in sight was fellow rookie Officer Ryan Williams, who was standing right outside the double doors. He had been sitting in a wooden chair that looked like it could put your butt to sleep in a matter of minutes. He watched as Ashley was wheeled by, and by the look on his face, she knew he was a little shocked at her condition. He was the first one other than family, medical personnel and the FBI, who had actually seen her since word spread throughout the precinct that she had been the victim of a crazed killer. Ashley was hoping he would be a little discreet and not go blabbing to everyone about how bad she really looked. All she needed was for Malone to know that she looked worse than the roadkill she saw on her way to work.

Williams followed them to the elevators and they all piled in. The four of them surrounded her hospital bed, one of the orderlies punched the button for floor six and off they went. She lay there surrounded by men, but her heart was still racing in fear. She guessed she had felt more secure in the I.C.U. than she thought. She knew the odds of the killer being in the hospital were slim, but the man had proved he was not opposed to hurting anyone who got in his way when it came to killing her. Michael was still sporting a cast and sling, and several of Ashley's family members had been shaken up by the firebombs he had launched into their back yard. Her thoughts turned to the two murder victims and how they had been killed because they looked something like her. She was hoping that the news media were covering the story and were warning all women to be on the safe side. Hopefully, when he realized that she wasn't going to be an easy target, he would make a mistake and be caught before he could kill again.

They arrived at the sixth floor and when the elevator opened she looked out into the waiting room, an open area right off the elevator; it was filled with family and many of her friends. She groaned, "Dad, why didn't you tell me all these people were up here? I look like shit and will scare most of them away."

Harold looked around, worried, and whispered something to Williams and the orderlies. As they came out of the elevator, he headed to the waiting room. The orderlies and Williams took off at a fast clip, moving past the group of people who were unaware that they had just missed their chance to see Ashley. They were past them and through the doors leading into the sixth-floor hospital rooms before Harold had reached them. They continued down the hall and didn't slow until they were at her room, and even then, they wasted no time in getting her inside and closing the door behind them. Ashley smiled at the efficient way her dad had taken care of the situation and saved her a bunch of embarrassment. She had caught a glimpse of Nick among the faces as they had raced by. It was bad enough that Derek and Phillip had witnessed her in this pathetic state, but she really didn't want to scare off all her potential hotties. The orderlies maneuvered the bed from the I.C.U. up against the one already in the room and locked the brakes. She knew it was not going to be real ladylike when she moved from one bed to the other, and sent a glance at Williams. "Ryan, would you mind either stepping out in the hall or at least turning around so I don't have to humiliate myself twice today?"

He turned a cute shade of pink and mumbled something about waiting outside the door until her dad came back, then made a hasty retreat. When she smiled at his speedy exit, her lip cracked and she could feel it oozing again. Damn.

Ashley sat up in the bed and swung her feet over the edge, pleased that she was not nearly as dizzy as she had been just a short while ago. She waited until they had moved her I.V. to another portable stand. The clean white sheets looked inviting as she looked back at the crumpled mess she had been lying in before. One of the orderlies asked if she was ready to lie back and she informed him that she thought she would hit the restroom one more time before she settled in. He gave her a shy smile and stood off to the side as his companion finished getting the I.C.U. bed ready to take back down to where it belonged. As they were finishing, Harold and Laura both entered the room, moving aside so that they could get the bed past them.

Laura wasted no time rushing over to Ashley as soon as they were gone, setting a bag at the foot of the bed. "Hey, babe. How are you doing? Is the pain okay? Do you need something?"

"I want a shower, so probably should get some medication before I attempt that, but otherwise I'm doing fine. Who was out in the waiting room? It looked like half the family was out there."

"You know perfectly well the doctor wanted you to wait until after you had rested for a few hours before you attempt a shower, Ashley."

"I know, but I would just like to get it over with so that I can relax and not have to worry about someone else seeing me with all this dried blood on me. Besides, I'm starting to smell like something that was left outside in the garbage too long."

She gave Ashley a doubtful look, and then said she would go talk to the nurse who was assigned to her and get everything set up.

After she left the room, Harold looked at her. "You aren't going to overdo it, are you?"

"No worries there, Dad. I don't have the energy to overdo it. But come on, you have to admit that I really do need a shower. Now that I've seen the evidence for myself, there is no way I could relax, knowing I look this bad. I can't do anything about the cuts and bruises but at least with clean hair and body, I would feel a little better about myself."

He took the time to look at her from head to toe and for the first time, she thought he actually noticed the matted hair and the blood that was still evident in her hair and on the cuts and scrapes. He had been so busy protecting her and being involved in the investigation, he had not really looked at her in that way.

He smiled, "Yeah, you're right. You do stink."

"Dad! That was not really what I wanted to hear. Do I really?" she asked as she lifted her arm and sniffed her armpit. Making a face she lowered it again and said, "I hope Mom hurries up."

He chuckled and then his face got serious. Ashley could see that whatever had upset him earlier was back on his mind.

"What is it, Dad? Has something else happened?"

Ashley could tell he was struggling to find the words, but before he could say anything at all, Laura and a nurse came back into the room. The nurse had a stand with a computer on it in one hand and in the other she held the blood pressure cuff and the thermometer. She introduced herself as Lindsey and explained that she would be her nurse until the shift change at seven tonight. She took her blood pressure and temperature at the same time. Once she was finished with that, she sat down, pulled the computer up to her and started entering the data she had just compiled, then went on to ask a million questions. Ashley guessed they figured that while you are in I.C.U., you are exempt from having to answer all the mindless questions she was being asked now. Ashley sat patiently on the side of the bed answering them one at a time, knowing her strength was evaporating fast. Maybe she should have lain back on the bed, but she really didn't want to stain the sheets before she had a chance to take her shower. Laura had taken the bag into the bathroom and she could hear her moving around and getting everything ready. She finished and came to stand at the bathroom door, giving Ashley an intense stare. "Lindsey, could we finish this after we get her out of the shower? She is losing it fast and I know how she wants to get that accomplished this afternoon."

Lindsey seemed about to argue that maybe they should wait on the shower, but looking at her she must have decided if she were in Ashley's shoes, she would feel the same. She had given her a pill when she first entered the room and Ashley could feel the effects of it as it eased the pain away some, and she wanted to take full advantage of it. She knew without it, she would never be able to make it through the shower. Lindsey unplugged her from the I.V. pole, took a plastic bag she had stuck in her pocket, wrapped it around the I.V. site and taped it in place to keep the water out. She removed the bandage from around her head, then told both Laura and Ashley not to be overly happy with the water, that a quick hair wash and a quick rinse was about all they should attempt, making sure they tried to keep the water and soap away from the wound on her head. Lindsey asked Laura if she needed help, and after she assured her she could manage, Lindsey took the computer and blood pressure cuff and left the room, closing the door after her.

Looking at Harold, Ashley waited for him to go on with what he was going to say earlier. "Go take your shower. We can talk afterwards."

Ashley had a really bad feeling about it, but the thought of the shower overruled any lingering doubts she had. Laura was standing patiently by her side. She gave her husband a questioning look and then helped Ashley to her feet. Ashley took a few minutes to get her sea legs steady and then with her mom's help, moved into the bathroom a few feet away from her bed. Thankfully, it was fairly good sized and they both fit in there with no problem. Ashley told Laura she needed to use the toilet and she helped her sit down and then Laura went about turning on the water. Ashley had no problem having her mom in the room with her as she did her business. As they had grown up it was a common occurrence for either Shannon or her mom to come running into the bathroom, grabbing something they needed and then leaving again without giving any notice to her going pee.

Laura helped her remove the bloodstained gown she had been wearing. The shower was big and Laura had positioned the stool so that she was barely under the spray. She removed the hand-held showerhead and had Ashley tip her head back as far as was comfortable, and then she let the water run over her hair. Ashley let out a sigh of pure pleasure and could not help enjoying the warm water as it moved over her head, even if the rest of her body was getting a little cold. Her mom put the showerhead on pause and then went about lathering up her hair, being extra careful because of the bumps and bruises all over it. She washed and rinsed her hair twice before she handed Ashley a wash rag and let her lather up the parts of her body that weren't too sore to touch. She watched her and Ashley could tell she was having a hard time, seeing her daughter covered in the cuts and scrapes along with the bruises that would turn an ugly shade of green in a few days. Ashley didn't have to look

419

up to know her mom's face would wear a concerned look. "I'm okay, Mom," she told her as she finished up all the parts she could reach, and then Laura bent down and washed her lower legs and feet.

"I know you are, honey. That doesn't mean you didn't scare the shit out of me."

Ashley leaned her head up and looked at her. "Mom, such language coming from you! I have half a mind to tell Grandma you have turned into quite the potty-mouth."

"Go ahead. You think she'd be surprised? I remember many a time I got my mouth washed out with soap for saying the words my three older brothers had taught me earlier in the day."

"No, I bet you're right. I have heard a few coming from her over the years, too."

Laura turned the water back on and quickly rinsed the soap off of Ashley. She would have loved to just sit there letting the warm water run over her, but knew she had better call it quits. Laura turned off the water and grabbed a couple of towels. She handed Ashley one and then wrapped the other one gently around her head, took another one and started drying her back. After they were finished, she helped her into a clean gown, sitting her on the toilet so that she would not get too tired. Ashley was already feeling completely worn out. Laura took the wet plastic off her arm and then they moved back into the room where Harold was still sitting in the same chair, but Shannon had joined him and was sitting on the side of the bed. Ashley had to keep her arm tight across her ribs as she walked to help with the pain they were causing her.

"Holy cow! Your head must really hurt," she stated as she looked at Ashley's head wound now that it was unwrapped.

Ashley reached up and felt the cut where it was stitched together, wishing she had asked her mom to let her look at it when they were in the bathroom, but she was too tired to go back in and look now. "As a matter of fact, it does, along with every other inch of my body."

Laura hooked her back up to the I.V. while Shannon unwrapped her head from the towel and started gingerly combing her hair out. She started at the bottom and worked her way up, and Ashley could tell she didn't know what to do when she got close to the wound so she just stopped about an inch away.

"Would you mind putting it in a French braid, so that it will stay out of the way?"

She made fast work of putting it in a loose braid and then Laura redressed the wound with the supplies that Lindsey had left for them. This time it was more like a mini pad instead of the huge maxi pad that had been on it before. She only used a small amount of gauze to keep it in place, and then dabbed at the cuts and scrapes that were oozing after the water had soaked them. When they were both done, Ashley swung her legs up and settled under the covers. She had started to shiver now that she was out of the warm bathroom, so Laura sent Shannon out to the nurses' station to ask for a heated blanket.

She was back within a few minutes and Ashley was soon snuggled under a nice warm toasty blanket. The warmth seeped into her sore tired body. "Thanks. That's much better."

Harold had been sitting there watching the women, not saying a word. Ashley had been dreading what he had to tell them but knew she could not stall any longer. "Okay, Dad, what happened?"

Shannon and Laura looked at Harold with concern, not knowing what was going on.

He took several seconds before he cleared his throat and in a quiet tone answered, "I'm afraid there was another murder last night."

All three of them gasped in horror and surprise. "Oh God, Harold, when is this going to stop?" Laura asked as she took Ashley's hand, giving her the silent strength she knew she would need upon hearing this news.

Closing her eyes, Ashley let the information seep into her already weary body. From what Derek had said yesterday in the meeting, this was not his normal pattern. He had killed three women in five days with three attempts on her life in between. He was becoming more aggressive. His anger was building into something they could not understand.

"Dad, we need to step up the media coverage on this so that women fitting my description are aware of the danger they're in. They need to know that a sick man is out there targeting them for murder. It's past the point where we have to worry about public panic. They *should* be panicked."

"As I understand it, the FBI will be holding a press conference at five tonight and it should be covered by all the local media, along with several national syndications that have picked up the news on the wire." All four of them glanced up to the clock to see that it was four thirty-two.

"Mom, Shannon, can you give us a few minutes so Dad and I can discuss the details of the murder?"

"Ashley, I don't think you're up for this. Why don't you let your Dad and the rest of the team work on this, and you concentrate on getting yourself healthy again?" Laura pleaded as she looked from Harold to Ashley and back again.

Harold knew how important it was for Ashley to be familiar with everything that was going on in this case. She was hindered by the fact that she was stuck in this hospital, so she was reliant on everyone else to keep her informed of all of the facts. She would be getting out in a day or two and she did not want to play catch-up with this investigation.

"Ashley is right, Laura. We need a few minutes in private to go over the details. She has the right to know," Harold answered, while Laura glared at him.

He stood up and pried her hand from Ashley's. "I know this is hard on all of us, but it's the hardest for Ashley. You need to be strong for her and be understanding when it comes to the police side of this. First of all, she's our daughter and her safety is our number one priority, but second, she is a police officer. On top of all of that, she is a victim. I think she has enough on her mind. I don't think we need to add any family drama to her plate, do you?"

Laura looked at Harold with a little bit of anger and a whole lot of worry. She leaned down and gave Ashley a kiss on the forehead just above her right eye, being sure not to hit any of the tender spots. "We'll be right outside and we're only going to give you a few minutes. I don't care what your father says; you are physically not up for more than that. He may know police work, but I know medical, and I'm not going to let you get so weak that you have a setback. You just had surgery a day and a half ago, and you are so beat up that a normal person would still be in I.C.U." She gave Harold a warning look as she went to the door, Shannon following behind her. Shannon turned around once she was past her dad, and raised her eyebrows over her vivid green eyes to give Ashley a look like she was surprised their mom gave in at all.

"Gee, Dad. You sure know how to push Mom's buttons. She will make you pay for that for weeks to come." Ashley did not want to hear the details of the recent murder but knew they would only have a few minutes before both her mom and Shannon were right back in the room. "So how bad was it?"

Ashley could see the worry in her dad's eyes. He was not used to dealing with homicides of this magnitude, let alone three in such a short span. She could imagine what the precinct was going through. Most of the personnel probably had not experienced this kind of case. She was sure that the FBI had taken over the situation but it still had to have things buzzing. She was also sure that all other cases were put on the back burner until this madman was caught.

Harold interrupted her thoughts. "It was bad, honey. Worse than the last two, if that is possible. The victim was only twenty and was going to school down at Metro. She had a late class and was walking back to her apartment when she was killed. He must have pulled her into an alley and killed her behind some dumpsters that were there. Same M.O. as the last two, just more brutal."

"Were we lucky enough to get any DNA or evidence at all this time?"

"They're still processing the scene. The FBI has brought in some fancy new equipment that they are using to try and pick up anything that he may have left behind. The bad thing is he always picks a site that is covered in trash and debris, making it hard to know what he could have left and what was there for days, weeks or years. So far, they have not found anything on the victim. No hairs, fibers or DNA, but they are doing some high-tech sweep to see if they missed anything," he answered. He glanced at the hospital door, trying to gauge how long he had until Laura and Shannon came back into the room.

"We have officers scouring the neighborhoods trying to find any businesses that may have had a security camera directed along the likely path he took. There was only one way he could have entered the alley, so they are hoping that something shows up and we might get lucky and get a shot of him. We are interviewing anyone in the area who might have noticed either the victim or the killer to see if we can get a description that way. We are also checking security cameras around her apartment and the school in case he was stalking her and something shows up there. The best we can figure is that he had to have this planned in advance. There is no way he could pick three women who look so much like you on a whim. He had to have planned this way in advance, picked the victims, and then planned when and where he would kill them. So far there is no apparent pattern in where they are killed. The first victim was found on Kennedy, the second was dumped behind your apartment and the third was down on Sixth Avenue, miles from the others. There is no connection between the victims that we can find, other than they all were young and look enough like you to be scary."

Ashley watched him as he was giving her all the information and, for the first time, she noticed how exhausted he looked. "Dad, have you gotten any sleep the last three days?"

He smiled and patted her hand. "I grabbed a few hours last night at the station while we were waiting for the M.E. to finish with his autopsy. He was called in to handle the case himself, along with the FBI medical examiner from Virginia. She flew in first thing this morning and they have been working on the victim all day. Michael and Derek are at the command center set up in our conference room at the precinct now. I don't think either one of them have slept at all."

"Dad, you all need to get some rest. Having you exhausted is not going to help any of us. Why didn't Derek tell me about this?" The thought of him keeping things from her sent a fire racing through her.

Harold must have seen the look that passed over her face at that thought, because he was quick to assure her that neither Derek nor Michael knew about the murder until after they had spent time with her last night and this morning.

He had time to go over a few more details before Laura and Shannon stuck their heads back in the door. "Done?"

"Yes, honey. You guys can come back in now," Harold said as he resumed his place in the chair by the window. He kept one eye and ear on what was going on in the room while looking out the window with a view of the parking lot below.

They settled down in the available seating, Laura in the little office chair and Shannon on the ledge of the window. Laura turned the conversation away from the murders and went on to tell them about the visitors that had kept the waiting room full since she had been brought in almost two full days ago. She and Harold had filled out a list of approved visitors; the doctor said that starting tomorrow, Ashley was allowed one visitor at a time and she could only have three visitors over a four-hour period. He made sure to tell Laura that he was being way too generous with the visitors, but knew by the number of people still in the waiting room, he really had no choice if he didn't want a small riot on his hands. Each visitor was only allowed to stay ten minutes and was to be checked by both the guard at the door and with whoever was inside the room. The first thing Ashley wondered was if Derek would let either Troy or Nick into the room for a visit. Then again she doubted they were even on the approved list. She would assume it was grandparents, and a few of the closest aunts and uncles, along with Casey and Dan.

Her stomach growled, making everyone laugh. Laura promised that her food tray would be arriving shortly. She was so hungry that even the thought of broth sounded good. She had kept the breakfast down with no problems and had even passed a little gas, so that was a good sign.

The pill that Lindsey had given her was making her a little sleepy. Either that or just all the activity was. She lay in her bed, letting her mom and Shannon do all the talking. They were telling some story about how Grandma had latched onto Nick in the waiting room last night, and was trying to fix him up with one of her garden club ladies' granddaughter who was an accountant over at the bread factory. They said that Nick had sat there patiently, glancing up every few seconds, praying someone would save him. Casey finally took pity on him and had him go down to the cafeteria with her and Dan to get sodas for everyone.

Ashley had been listening but could not help but glance up at the clock every few minutes, watching as the time clicked closer and closer to five. She wanted to watch and see what they said about the murders and see who would be doing the talking. She was sure it would be Agent Stick-up-the-Ass himself, thinking he was the only one with enough clout to be able to do the news conference. Finally, Harold turned on the TV, and Laura and Shannon quieted down because they too wanted to hear what was said.

The murder was the front-running story, giving just the highlights before the anchor turned it over to the live broadcast that was being held on the courthouse steps. Ashley was right. Agent Day was standing dead center with both Agent Clark and Lieutenant Crane flanking him. She wasn't surprised Derek was nowhere to be seen, as he was supposed to be undercover. She wasn't sure if that was still possible since he was now guarding her on a regular basis. Anyone watching closely would probably figure out he was more than a local bartender or even a steady boyfriend. The police would not let just a boyfriend stand guard but, then again, unless the killer was actually in the hospital watching that close, he would have no way of knowing if Derek was actually in her room or out in the waiting room along with the dozens of others.

She turned her attention back to what Day was saying. Day went on to warn the public, especially strawberry blonde women ranging from the ages of 16 to 50, to be alert and cautious in going out alone. He advised them to be escorted to their cars and to do their errands in groups of two or more. They should be extra cautious in their homes, not answering the door unless it was a family member or a known close friend, to secure their windows and doors at all times. He asked the public's help in finding this killer and gave an eight hundred number to call with information. A reward was offered through Crime Stoppers for tips leading to an arrest.

Ashley sat in a state of numbness. This just could not be real. This happened in other cities, to other people, not to her. The sheer horror of it was finally starting to sink into her rattled brain. This man was out to kill her and anyone who stood in his way. She could only pray that he would not be able to get to any more women who looked like her, and with Ashley encased in a wall of security, she could only hope he got bored or frustrated enough to move on. She knew that was selfish of her but she didn't care. She wanted him out of her town, out of her life and to just go away.

"Dad, I want my revolver."

Laura and Shannon looked sharply from the TV to her. "Honey, I don't think that's necessary. You have a police officer at the door and someone in here with you at all times."

Harold looked at Ashley with his serious brown eyes. "I'll bring it over first thing in the morning."

"Harold, do you really think that's necessary? If the hospital found out she had a weapon, they would be very upset."

"Then I guess we won't tell them, will we? And yes, I think it's necessary. The way I look at it, better safe than sorry. We cannot predict what this man will do and to what extremes he will go. I'd feel much better if I knew that Ashley was not lying here completely defenseless. She can take care of herself in normal situations, but this is not normal and she has several handicaps to deal with as she lies in that damn hospital bed."

About that time a nurse's aide brought her supper tray to the door. They could tell she was really nervous as she handed the tray to Harold and made a hasty retreat, giving him an anxious glance. Ashley was pretty sure the police presence was not something the staff was used to seeing, and it had to make them all a little edgy. The police had conducted a meeting with all the personnel, covering what to expect and to be prepared to have IDs checked upon entering the hospital, her room especially.

Laura busied herself with getting her tray ready, with Shannon making faces at what lay on the tray. "Yuck...that looks boring. I almost feel guilty that we're going to go to Olive Garden when we leave here." She looked guilty, knowing Ashley was going to be annoyed that they were going to one of her favorite restaurants.

Although the thought of real food sounded good, she was too tired and sore to give it much thought at all. She reached for the spoon and dug into the chicken soup that was on the tray. She watched as Shannon raised her eyebrows at her mom, surprised that Ashley had not let them know she thought they all sucked for eating somewhere good without her. The seriousness of her situation was starting to weigh Ashley down and her mood was starting to hit rock bottom. She had kept things as light as she could, hoping and praying that he would be caught before she even had to face the facts. But with this last murder, there was no way to do that now. She kept her head bowed to the bowl, eating in silence as the TV went on to other local news, and then the weather came on. Laura was casting her nervous looks. Then she would look over at Harold and back to Shannon. She kept talking about anything and everything to try and keep things from settling into a complete funk. Ashley finished the soup and picked up the hot tea her mom had made for her. She pushed the tray aside and let the warmth of the cup seep into her hands, which had gone cold as she watched the broadcast.

The phone rang and everyone jumped. She slopped a little of the tea over onto her hand, and Harold stood and went to the phone. He looked at it, trying to decide what to do with it, then finally reached down and picked it up.

They all watched as his face turned an ugly shade of red and then he slammed the receiver down into the cradle. She knew at once it had been the killer. Fear and anger radiated from his body as he took deep breaths, trying to get control of his emotions.

"Dad...?"

"I need to go take care of something we apparently forgot to take care of earlier," he said as he made his way out the door without looking back.

"What did he mean by that?" Shannon asked in bewilderment.

"The phones," Laura and Ashley answered together.

"It was him, wasn't it?"

"I would make a good guess that it was." Someone had forgotten to make sure no calls were put directly through to her room. She bet someone was getting a royal ass-chewing about now. She, for one, was glad that her dad had answered the phone and not one of the women. It would have affected them much differently than it had him. Although he was afraid and pissed, he would take it in stride better than they would have.

They could hear him talking to someone out in the hall. Ashley would guess that he had made a call to the hospital switchboard, and then a call would be going to the precinct to fill them in on what had just happened. His voice had risen and she felt sorry for the person on the other end.

Ashley closed her eyes. She was close to losing it and took several deep breaths to try and steady the trembling that was threatening to take over her body. Only moments before, she thought she had things pretty much in control, but the phone call was enough to shake things up again.

"Mom, I'm really tired. The shower wore me out. I think I'm going to try and rest for a little while. Thanks for helping with my shower. I really appreciate it."

Before Laura could respond, Lindsey came back in with her two little friends on carts and started going about taking her vitals again; she wanted to finish up getting all the information entered into the computer before her shift ended in an hour or so.

"Shannon and I will wait for your father to come back and then we'll leave you alone so you can rest. That is the best thing you can do for your body as well as your mind. Honey, I'm so sorry this has happened to you, and I just want you to know that we're all right here for you and nothing is going to happen to you."

Ashley could feel the tears burning in the back of her eyes, and fought hard not to let them fall. "Thanks, Mom. Love you."

"Love you more, sweetheart. We'll see you first thing in the morning, but please call if you need anything at all. You know I won't be sleeping anyway and will be watching the clock for when I can come back over to the hospital. Your dad is insisting that I go home and try and get some rest."

"He's right, Mom. Take something and get some good rest, I'll be fine. I'm going to ask Lindsey here to give me something to knock me out for the night anyway." Ashley gave her a weak smile as she sat posed at the computer, waiting her turn to start asking questions.

"No problem at all. The doctor left orders for something that should do just that."

Harold had come back into the room. Laura and Shannon kissed her cheek, made their way over to tell Harold goodbye, and then they were gone.

CHAPTER TWENTY-EIGHT

Ashley woke early Sunday morning feeling rested, having slept through the night for the first time since this whole mess started. If they came in to do her vitals last night, she had slept through it, as well as Dad leaving and Michael taking over the watch. Her door was open and Michael and Derek were standing just outside, talking. Looking back at the clock she could see that it was indeed shift change for her guards. They were probably talking about any new developments on the latest murder.

She tested her lungs and ribs and took a deeper breath than usual; she felt pain, but not as bad as the last few days. She was getting antsy to get up and move around to try to get her strength back. The shower last night had zapped her pretty good. That along with the sleeping pill Lindsey had given her had done the trick for a good night's sleep. Now it was up to her to get healthy again. She needed to pee and wasn't sure she could wait until Derek made an appearance, and wasn't sure she wanted him helping her anyway. She hit the button to lower the guardrail and swung her legs over the side of the bed, sitting for several minutes to make sure she wasn't dizzy or weak. She looked at the commode and decided in one quick second there was no way she was going to let Derek catch her using that thing.

She stood and grabbed the I.V. pole, unplugging it so that she could take it with her. Glancing up, she noticed neither one of her guards was paying any attention to her. They were probably assuming she was still asleep. She took the few steps into the bathroom, closing the door behind her. Ashley could tell today was a much better day, with her ribs being the only thing really hurting her. She had a small headache, but since the first time she had hit her head on the pavement during the hit and run attempt, there had always been one nagging at the back of her head.

She finished up her business and stood at the mirror, washed her face and took out the French braid that had come loose throughout the night, then ran a brush through her hair. The braid had given it a nice wave, but that was about all she could say looked good on her. She looked like she'd had a run-in with a heavyweight boxer and had lost big time. But she was alive and that was more than she could say about those other three women. A wave of guilt hit her so strongly, it just about buckled her knees and she had to grab the sink to keep herself standing. She had to take several deep breaths, or as deep as her lungs and ribs would let her, to keep the emotions from overtaking her. She knew that all of this was no fault of hers and that she was just as much a victim as they were, but this did not make it any easier to handle. She squared her shoulders, fought down the gloom and replaced it with anger. She knew that was the only way she would get through this in one piece.

Turning away from the sink, she maneuvered the pole around so that she could get the door open and there, standing on the other side, was a very annoyed Derek.

"What the hell do you think you're doing? You're not supposed to be getting out of bed without someone there to help you. I had strict orders from not only the hospital staff but your mother that I would help you when you needed to get out of bed," Derek yelled at her.

She stood there holding her pole, letting the anger that had started to form in the bathroom build until she was about ready to explode by the time he was finished.

Without warning she reared back her hand, thankful that the I.V. was in her left arm, and punched him as hard as she could. She was breathing hard, gripping the pole till her knuckles were white. "Don't you dare come in here and start yelling at me, you son of a bitch. I couldn't help it you were not here when I NEEDED TO GET OUT OF BED. If you had been here instead of out in the hall, maybe I could have used your help, but since you weren't and there was no way I could wait, I managed on my own. Now get the hell out of my way and out of my room. I don't need some smart-ass FBI agent coming in here and yelling at me. Find someone else to guard me today," Ashley screamed at him. She pushed him out of her way and, making sure her gown was covering her ass, pushed past him.

Michael, who had been talking to Bill and Lindsey, came running when they had heard the screaming coming from Ashley's room.

All three stood just inside the door, a little bit in shock, as Ashley returned to the bed. Lindsey recovered first and leapt to help maneuver the pole back, and helped her in.

Ashley was so pissed she wouldn't even look at Derek, who was standing at the bathroom door, absently rubbing his chin where she had landed a pretty solid punch. He had not said a word and never took his eyes off her the whole time it took her to get back into bed. She was breathing hard from both the trip to the restroom and the fight with Derek. Her hands were shaking with emotion and it was taking everything she had not to completely lose it in front of them all.

Lindsey fussed with her sheets, blocking her view of Derek and the two standing at the door. She knew Michael was probably pleased at the little scene he had walked in on, and Bill was probably at a complete loss, having never seen her temper before. Ashley didn't lose her temper very often, but when she did you better stand back, because it was hard and fast.

The nerve of that asshole yelling at her, as if she didn't already know she wasn't supposed to be up on her own.

Michael cleared his throat. "Hey, I would stay and cover the rest of your shift, but I need to get down to the station. I have a suggestion...why don't Derek and Bill just trade places? You'll get the same double coverage, but this way we don't have to worry about one of you hurting the other one?"

When Lindsey moved over to get the portable unit she had left by the door so she could take her vitals, Ashley had a clear shot of Derek but she refused to look his way, though she could feel the intensity of his stare. She was still so pissed she would probably unload on him again. She was really madder at the situation than at him; he just happened to be in the wrong place at the wrong time and had pushed the wrong buttons on her, but she didn't care.

"If Bill doesn't mind, I think that would be a good idea," Ashley answered Michael.

Bill just stood there wringing his hat in his hands. He looked nervously from Ashley to Derek and back to her again. She didn't know if she could stand Bill's company for the whole day with the mood she was in.

"No, that's not what's going to happen. I was assigned to protect Ashley and that's just what I'm going to do. I apologize to her and to all of you for letting my anger get out of control and it will not happen again," Derek stated as he stood there in the same spot where she had shoved him.

Ashley turned and glared at him, wanting to punch him again, the arrogant good-looking bastard. She was too drained to fight anymore, and turned her attention to Lindsey as she went about her job, ignoring the tension that filled the room.

Lindsey was bent over the bed, taking her blood pressure, and when she was finished, she gave Ashley a look. "Um…I think I will come back right before I leave for the day and take this again. I don't think it's a true reading, or at least it's not one I want to record in your chart." She turned to address everyone in the room. "I'm not sure who was at fault in all of this, but I do know that it's my job to see to the wellbeing of my patient, and it's definitely not good for her to get this upset." Turning to her she said, "Ashley, if this situation happens again, hit your call button and one of us will come right away to assist you. And you gentlemen are under no circumstances going to upset Ashley. I don't care what she does, it's *not* okay to start yelling at her, is that understood?" She turned her glare toward Derek on that statement. Turning back to address all of the men she went on to say, "Because believe me, gentlemen, if you don't understand this, I will get the hospital administration involved, and we will come up with some other way to protect Ashley."

No one said a word. Michael raised his eyebrows with a look that said *I'm not pleased that I just got my butt chewed for something I had not even been involved with.* Bill still stood wringing his officer's hat, inching his way back to the safety of his seat in the hall next to the door.

Derek nodded his head at Lindsey. "Yes, ma'am. You have my word nothing like that will ever happen again. Again, I apologize for my behavior before."

Lindsey looked around the room, assured that everything was back to normal, then turned to her. "Ashley, are you okay with this situation? Because, if not, just say so and I will have it taken care of immediately."

Wow! Ashley kind of liked having a little pitbull in her corner. But even if she was still pissed at Derek for yelling at her, she knew that she was not stupid enough to cause a stink over it now that he had apologized, and she knew she needed the protection.

"It's fine. I'm sorry to have caused you to worry. I'll use my call button the next time I need help. I know you're here to help and I forget that fact. I'm just so used to taking care of my own needs."

She seemed satisfied and gave the guys another warning look before she gathered her equipment and left the room.

Bill used her exit as a way to make his own, following close behind her to plant himself back into his chair, face forward.

Michael's tired face still showed concern. "You two going to be okay if I leave, or do I need to pull in a roll-away and take my nap here?"

Neither Derek nor Ashley said a word, and Michael just snorted and pulled the door closed, but not before remarking, "You two play nice or I'll have to call Grandma and tell her to come and baby-sit you."

He left and the tension in the room could have been cut with a knife. Ashley grabbed up the remote and turned on the television that was anchored to the wall at the end of her bed. It was a thirty-six-inch flat screen, which she was sure her bill would be paying for, along with enough left over to buy one for every room in the hospital.

Ashley was half afraid that the morning news would be flashing a picture of the latest victim across the screen, but *Good Morning America* was interviewing Bruce Jenner. He was outfitted in a woman's dress and Ashley was confused, so she started flipping the channels, trying to find something to watch. She was not really interested in anything that was on, but she needed something to fill the quiet instead of just listening to Derek breathing.

Ashley settled on a rerun of a sitcom that she used to watch back before she joined the academy. Derek was still sitting in the chair, glaring at her, which she pretended to ignore.

A few minutes past seven, the day nurse and her aide came in and started doing their morning routine. Today's nurse was Jenny and her aide was Claire. Jenny was about six feet tall and couldn't have weighed more than one twenty, soaking wet, and her aide was five feet, if that, and weighed close to two fifty. Ashley couldn't help but smile as she watched them go about their jobs, complete opposites but working great as a team.

Ashley was informed that an x-ray tech would be coming sometime that morning to take her down for a follow-up x-ray and ultrasound, to make sure everything was healing right and that there were no complications. She was not looking forward to going down to the floor where they did all the x-rays and scans but preferred to have them come to her.

Jenny took her vitals, sending nervous glances at Derek. Once they were done with that, they helped her up into the other chair and proceeded to change her sheets, bring in new towels and straighten up the room. When Ashley was back into her clean, comfy bed, she was ready for a nap. She knew one thing; she was getting sick and tired of being laid up in hospital beds. She was not the kind of person who enjoyed lying around idle. She was more the "keep busy until she dropped" kind of girl. The aide brought in her breakfast tray and went about getting it ready for her to eat. Her stomach growled and she realized she was starving, the hospital fare looking better than normal. Mom must have had a talk with her doctor and the kitchen because she had scrambled eggs with cheese, bacon and toast along with a fruit cup and coffee. Ashley wasted no time and dug right in, pausing only now and then to glance up at the TV. Before she knew it, absolutely everything was gone from her plate, so she pushed the tray off to the side of her bed, lay back, and turned her attention to the television once more. It was a new sitcom that she had always hated so she hit the mute button and closed her eyes, hoping for a little catnap before the tech came to take her down to the pit. That's what her family had always called the basement level of the hospital where the lab and most outpatient tests were performed.

"Are you going to lay there and ignore me all day?"

Ashley thought about just ignoring him, but decided he would just keep nagging so she answered in a testy voice, "Yes, I am. So just sit there and be quiet." She had relaxed enough while they cleaned her room that she was a little afraid of how they were going to act around each other, now that everyone was gone and it was just the two of them. Deep down she knew Derek had only reacted out of concern for her welfare, but that didn't make it right for him to come in yelling at her like some furious husband or something. Gee, the thought of Derek as her husband was enough to thaw her anger. She thought she could handle coming home to him vacuuming in his boxer briefs. Now why did she automatically think of him in that choice of underwear? Maybe he was a tightie-whitie man, or just a plain old boxers man, but as far as she was concerned he could vacuum naked.

All of a sudden she was grabbed by the front of her hospital gown and gently raised up from the bed. Her eyes flew open in fear and she was looking into a very intense pair of hazel eyes. Before she could even comprehend what was going on, Derek's lips were crashing onto hers. The heat instantly exploded between them. She didn't even have time to register her shock, hell, she didn't have time to register anything at all except that she could feel the heat from his kiss clear down to her toes. She wasn't sure when it happened, but he was sitting on the side of the bed and she had her arms wrapped around his neck, pulling him in as tight as she could get him. Her hands started to move on their own, one busy running through the texture of his hair and the other one finding its way under the shirt that had suddenly come untucked from the tight jeans that covered one fine ass. His hands had moved from the front of her gown to her—

"ASHLEY ELIZABETH! What in God's name are you doing?"

Derek jumped back like he had been shot, running his hands through his hair as he turned to look into Ashley's mother's shocked face and her sister's very amused one. He started tucking his shirt in when he realized all three women had stopped talking and three sets of eyes were watching his hands as they tucked the shirt down the front of his jeans. He looked at each face and turned a deep shade of red. "If you will excuse me, I think I will just step out and check on Bill while you ladies visit."

He made a hasty retreat, squeezing between Laura and Shannon as they stood just inside the door of the room, neither one of them budging an inch. Ashley thought Shannon would have liked to reach out and squeeze his ass as he went by but resisted, as Laura turned her look on her.

"Hey, don't give me that look! You were probably thinking the same thing," Shannon shot at her mom as she turned and made her way to the side of Ashley's bed. "So big sis, what's it like to kiss a big hot FBI agent?"

Ashley was in a complete daze. The man had turned her anger into white-hot lust in the blink of an eye. She could still feel the tingling in areas she didn't think her mom and sister needed to know about. All she knew was she needed to get the hell out of this hospital bed, and someone had better find this crazed killer, so she would have time to seriously jump one hot-assed FBI agent before they both exploded.

As she thought about how delicious that would be, Shannon reached over and pinched her arm.

"Ouch! Damn it! That hurt."

"Then answer me, shithead."

Rubbing her arm, Ashley glared at her sister as she answered in a smug voice, "I don't have to answer some stick-thin, bimbo butt nosey ass."

"Well, am I a bimbo butt or a nosey ass?"

"In your case you're both."

Laura had gotten over the shock of walking in on Derek and Ashley as they were about to devour each other, and pinched both Shannon and Ashley on their arms.

"Ouch, damn it, Mom," they both yelped as she pushed Shannon out of the way, and reached down and gently kissed Ashley on the forehead.

"Hey! Why the hell does she get a kiss and I just got pinched?"

"She deserves it after getting someone that hot to lay a scorching kiss on her like that man was," Laura answered as she patted Ashley's hand, smiling like some half-witted idiot.

Ashley couldn't help but chuckle, "I think you both need to get laid soon and stay out of my love life."

The pat on her hand turned into a slap. "I'll have you know that I was *laid* last night," Laura answered with a chuckle in her voice.

"Oh gross, Mom, that is not something we really wanted to know. Just the thought of Dad bending you over the dining room table is enough..."

"Okay, stop. I'm not going to talk to you two about your father's and my sex life."

Shannon had moved over to the opposite side of the bed. "Well, that's a relief."

It was nice to be able to talk to her mom and Shannon without the strain of the situation coming into it. Ashley's thoughts had been in such a dark place for the last few days, it felt good to be able to joke around with her family. The tension was strung so tightly throughout her body that their teasing was doing a good job of relaxing both her body and mind.

They ignored the doctor's visiting rules, visiting for a couple of hours, telling her about the latest family dramas. Uncle Bruce had fallen off the hay stacker and injured his shoulder, but not enough to keep him from hopping right back on the tractor a few hours after he had fallen. Cousin Kyle in Texas had proposed to his girlfriend of five years while on a cruise, and the family had already started making plans for the big event.

They were just finishing up their visit when there was a timid knock on the door and Derek stuck his head in. "There's a lady out here who says she's your sister but she's not on the family list?" His face turned red as he looked from one set of eyes to the next.

"It's probably my twin sister, Casey. You can let her in."

Derek looked at Ashley, then turned his head and looked over his shoulder. "Um, that's what she said her name was, but I still don't have another sister down on my list. She doesn't look like your twin. As a matter of fact, she doesn't look anything like any of your family."

"That's because she was conceived the same day as I was, when Mom slept with the mailman after Dad left for work."

Derek's eyebrows went straight up high onto his forehead and he shot a startled look at Laura.

"Ashley, if you're going to tell our sordid family history, at least get the story right. It was the cable repairman, or at least I think it was," Laura answered, putting a finger to the side of her head like she was really trying to remember. "I never did figure out if it was him or that cute neighbor boy who used to mow our lawn until your dad threw him off the property." She wrinkled her nose up and made a V of her eyebrows in disgust.

Casey had been standing right behind Derek as Laura went on and on about her supposed *father*. She finally pushed past him, throwing her hands on her hips as she stopped just a few inches in front of Derek. "Mom, I told you it couldn't be the cable man, I absolutely hate to watch TV, but I love to run barefoot through the grass."

Derek stood there looking from one face to the other as they continued to pull his leg, finally settling on Ashley's. She could not suppress the laughter any longer, and was afraid if she left them to go on, things could get really ugly, knowing those two. "Derek, meet Casey, my best friend from kindergarten. She was at the bar the night we met. She had just gotten engaged to one of our best friends. She should be on the list because we all consider her part of the family."

They all watched as Casey turned around, and because she was standing so close to Derek, her head came to just about his armpits. They watched as she slowly moved her head up inch by inch until she finally settled on his face.

Derek looked down at her, giving her one of his to-die-for killer dimpled smiles, and Ashley thought Casey's knees actually gave a little.

Casey put her hand on his chest and purred, "Excuse me. I need to make a call to my fiancé and break off our engagement." She continued to run her hand up and down his chest as she was talking.

Derek gently grabbed her hand and looked over at Ashley, saying, "Oh she is definitely part of this family, all right. I will leave you to continue with whatever the hell you women do when left alone." He was still holding on to Casey's hand, and when he was finished speaking, he leaned down very slowly and kissed her on the cheek. "Congratulations on your engagement. He's a very lucky man."

Casey didn't miss a beat. She grabbed the front of his shirt and kept him close, planting a huge one on his shocked lips. When he managed to pull away, she once again purred, "Thank you. I'll be sure to let him know."

They watched as he made a hasty retreat, giving Laura and Shannon a nervous look, probably afraid they were going to jump his bones next.

Casey stood where she was till he had been gone for several seconds, before she finally turned and looked their way. "Oh my God, Shannon! Go get a fire hose. I think my crotch just caught fire."

"Casey Ann Carter! How dare you talk like that! You are an engaged woman now. Besides, he already had my daughter's on fire when we walked in here earlier. You should have seen the hussy with her hand under his shirt and his on her—"

"Okay, Mom! I think she gets the picture."

Casey's eyes had gone from dreamy to wide with shock. "What the hell? They ban me from seeing you since this fiasco started and now I learn I've been missing all kinds of smut. You all suck! Shannon, you should have been calling me and filling me in on Ashley's porn acts." She walked to the side of the bed and reached up and pinched Shannon's arm.

"Ouch! Dammit! I wish people would stop pinching me. Hell, who has time to call and report on Michael's and Ashley's lewd behavior? This hospital must bring out the lust in people with the way those two have been acting in here." She was rubbing her arm where Casey had pinched her and failed to see her mom's sharp look at the mention of Michael's name.

Uh-oh. She was in for it now. Ashley could tell her mom was ready to go in for the kill to get the information she wanted from Shannon. Casey and Ashley exchanged looks and before Laura had time to even start with the questions, Casey launched into some story about Dan and her trying to get in to see her last night. Casey said she had threatened the guard on duty with a lawsuit if he failed to let them in to visit, but he had just barred the door and told them they would have to take it up with his supervisor. Their names were

445

not on the list, and under no circumstances were they getting into Ashley's room.

Although she felt bad for Casey and Dan, she was pleased that the guard had taken his job so seriously. All the guys from her precinct were volunteering their off hours to help out the department so they would not be hit with a lot of overtime. Ashley had told her dad that she really preferred not to have Big Tits stand guard, and so far she had not seen her around. Ashley wasn't sure how her dad had managed to pull that off without causing a big stink, but whatever he did worked for her. The thought of Malone being in control of Ashley's safety was a damn scary thought. Plus, she did not want her anywhere near Derek or her brother if she could help it.

Laura and Shannon took off shortly after Casey arrived, giving them time to visit. Casey pushed her legs over to the side of the bed and plopped down at the end, facing her. She never said a word, just sat there.

"All right already! Stop with the staring thing. I know you have a hundred questions, so fire away."

"Nope, not a one, just waiting on you," she answered.

Ashley cocked her head a little and gave Casey the one raised eyebrow look. "Waiting on me for what?"

Casey sat for a few minutes, saying nothing. She was making Ashley nervous. This was not like her at all. Normally she couldn't wait to know all the details, and for her to sit there quietly was freaking Ashley out a little.

"Ash, it's me. Not your parents, or your boss, or some really hot FBI agent. Just me."

Ashley knew what she was getting at, but she was not sure she was up to going over everything that had happened or how she was really feeling. In the past she tended to keep her feelings to herself, but when and if she ever opened up, it was either to her sister or Casey.

446

Ashley was trying to decide how much she wanted to tell her best friend when they heard a commotion out in the hall. They could hear people yelling and what sounded like metal trays being banged around.

Derek stuck his head in the door. "Ash, there is something going on around the corner. I'm going to send Bill to check it out."

Ashley's heart accelerated at his words. Her eyes were searching his face to see if he was keeping something from her. He must have sensed her concern because he instantly reassured her by saying, "I'm sure it's nothing, Bill will investigate."

She gave him a weak smile and assured him they would be fine. Casey and Ashley watched as he talked to Bill, and then with a final look inside at her, Bill took off down the hall.

They could tell the noise was getting louder and closer. Derek stood in the doorframe, blocking the entrance to her room. He kept looking down the hall then glancing back into Ashley's room. "Ash, I'm going to call security and get someone up here. I can't see what's going on and I don't like the fact that Bill isn't coming back."

They watched him as he pulled out his phone and made the call. Ashley's heart rate was climbing as the yelling continued down the hall. It sounded like two or three men were arguing about who was the father of someone named Tiffany's baby. They heard a huge crash, and watched as nurses rushed down the hall past her door.

Derek had barely ended his call when his phone rang. Ashley watched the frown develop on his face as he listened to whatever was being said. He turned to look in at Ashley and then ended the call.

"What is it?" Ashley asked him.

"That was security. They got a frantic call from a woman in the E.R. saying they think a woman was killed in a downstairs bathroom."

"Derek, what if he's killed someone here in the hospital? I can't stand the thought that I might be responsible for someone else dying." Ashley's voice had risen with each word she spoke.

Casey was looking at her in alarm. Derek moved into the room and took hold of her hands.

"Ashley, this is not your fault. Try not to panic, we don't even know what's going on yet. I will call your dad and get them back over here so they can check it out."

"Derek, you can't wait for them to get back here, I need you to go. You might be able to catch him; we can't take the chance that he could get away again." Ashley was squeezing his hands hard, the fear overtaking her body.

"Ash, I can't leave you unprotected."

"Go get Bill and one of the security guys to watch me. Hell, get ten security guys; I just need to know for sure that he hasn't killed someone else because of me. I need you to go look for yourself, I don't trust anyone else to know what's going on," she pleaded.

He pulled out his phone, called her dad and told him what was going on, then took a second to search Ashley's face. He was so torn on what to do. On one hand he knew he needed to investigate the possible murder, but he was terrified to leave Ashley with anyone else but him.

"Derek, I'll be fine. Bill will be here and you can get more coverage for me from security, please go check on that woman."

Right then Bill came running up to the door; his face was flushed, his shirt was torn and he had a scratch on his left cheek.

Derek jumped up asking, "What the hell is going on down there?"

Ashley could tell Bill was a nervous wreck, his hands were shaking and when he tried to answer Derek his voice came out two levels higher than his normal voice would have been.

448

"There are three guys having a pushing shouting match about all of them being someone's baby daddy—"

"So this has nothing to do with Ashley," Derek interrupted.

"No, sir."

"Then I need you to take over watching Ashley, while I go see about a possible murder downstairs. I will send over two of the guards to watch the door while I'm gone."

Bill's head was swinging back and forth from Derek to Ashley. Derek had received another phone call and was on his way out the door.

Ashley watched as all the color drained from Bill's face. "Bill, it will be fine; we don't even know if there was a murder—"

Just as she was reassuring Bill, an orderly was at the door with a gurney, saying he was there to take her down to be x-rayed. He showed Bill his badge with his ID and then pushed his cart into the room. Bill's hands were shaking as he looked at the badge. He compared it to the list he had in his pocket and then moved out of the way.

The orderly was tall and well built, with long dark hair tied back into a thick ponytail and a close-shaved beard that was partly covered by the mask around his chin, mouth and nose; a surgical hat covered his black hair. His eyebrows were a little too thick for Ashley's taste and he wore glasses that were tinted. Ashley assumed they were prescription because of the tint, but they seemed to be pretty dark to be working indoors. She could not see the color of his eyes, but overall he was a good-looking man. He had stuck his ID badge into the pocket of his scrubs, which were a weird shade of orange, so she could not read his name. She had an eerie sense that she knew him but could not place his face. All of the Wright kids had spent so much time at the hospital over the years with their mom at one time or another that Ashley just assumed it was someone she had seen on one of those trips. Casey hopped up off the bed and moved to the other side, making room for him to maneuver.

"Good morning, Miss Wright. I'm here to take you down to the x-ray room so that you can have a few tests done."

His voice was low and soft and had a southern drawl to it, and he kept his head down while he went about adjusting the bed. Ashley swung her legs over the side while he transferred her I.V. bag over. She sat on the small gurney and waited for him to lift the head so she could lie down. He seemed to be struggling with the adjustment and when he finally snapped it into place, he glanced up to see her watching him. She couldn't help but be a little nervous, and he was not helping the situation.

He waited for her to turn and lie down and made no move to cover her with the blanket at the foot of the gurney. So Casey came around and helped cover her for the ride down to the pit.

Ashley kept glancing towards the door for Derek. "Shouldn't we wait for Derek?"

Casey stepped back. "I've nothing going on today and since I finally got through the Gestapo guarding you, I'll hang around here in your room until you get back so we can finally get our chance at a visit. I'll send either the security guys or Derek to catch up with you when they get here in a few minutes."

"That would be great. I'm sure it shouldn't take too long to do a few tests," Ashley answered as the tech swung the bed around towards the door, smacking the wall as he did so. She had to grab the sides of the narrow gurney so she wouldn't slide off of the stupid thing. She rolled her eyes at Casey as they passed her on the way out the door. She gave Bill a wave as they went on down the hall to the elevators.

Bill stood there, unsure about what he was supposed to do, deciding he better wait for the other security Derek was sending.

"So, how long have you worked for the hospital? My mom works here and your face looks familiar," Ashley asked the tech.

He took a few seconds to answer and when he did, it was still in the same soft voice. "Not long."

"Really? That's weird. Maybe you just have one of those faces that look like everyone else's."

He was pushing the gurney fairly fast and went right by the bank of elevators.

"Hey, you missed the elevators."

"We don't use those. We use the service elevators to transport patients, because they're bigger."

Ashley should have known that, but in the race down the hall, she guessed she forgot. They did not talk the rest of the way to the rear of the floor they were on. When they reached the elevators, another nurse was there waiting. She gave them a smile and when the doors opened on the elevator she held them open, waiting for the tech to push Ashley in. When he just stood there, Ashley and the nurse turned to look at him.

"Oh, sorry. You go ahead. I forgot to grab her chart. I need to go back and get it."

She gave him a puzzled look but stepped into the elevator alone and pushed a button as the doors closed.

He made no move to turn around and go get the chart. He stood there watching the lights of the elevator as it made its way down to one, and then when it did he punched the up arrow again.

"Don't you need the chart?"

He never bothered answering, just moved back to the head of the gurney, and Ashley could tell he was reaching around underneath. When she turned around to look at him again, she could see that he had a bottle in one hand and a cloth in the other. Before she even had time to register her alarm, he was moving in and placing the rag over her mouth and nose. She struggled for all she was worth, but in a few short seconds she was limp.

451

CHAPTER TWENTY-NINE

Derek was apprehensive that he had to leave Ashley's room and go investigate the call from downstairs. Didn't the hospital have their own security to handle these things? Or better yet, where were the extra personnel from her precinct? He wasn't sure Bill was the best officer to be guarding Ashley. He was just a rookie and gave Derek the impression that he was a nervous wreck. Derek would never have left Ashley's side if she hadn't been so upset and insisting he go investigate the possible murder.

As the elevators opened on the ground floor, two nurses were standing there along with two of the hospital security. Derek flashed his badge and asked, "So what's going on? Where is the restroom with the body in it?"

The taller and heavier-set of the two security guards stepped forward. "Well, I'm not sure what just happened, but we had an older woman enter the restroom back there and she started screaming."

Derek looked back and forth between them and when no one bothered to go on, he growled out, "And?"

"Well, I was busy trying to get an injured drunk to calm down when she started yelling, so I radioed for backup and that's when Tom here came from patrolling outside." He looked at the other security guard, who was nodding his head up and down in agreement to support his statement.

"Did either of you go check it out?"

Both security guards looked at each other with the same guilty look on their faces. "Um, yes sir," Tom answered. "I did."

Derek shook his head; getting the story from these two was going to take forever and he really needed to get back to Ashley. He pushed them aside and headed in the direction the guard had pointed to earlier. It was going to be faster if he just investigated it himself. The guards and nurses followed him, no one saying a word.

An older lady was being supported outside the restroom by another woman. She was probably around 80 years old and stood about four feet tall. Derek stopped and asked, "Are you the woman who found the body?"

She lifted her head up to look at Derek. "Well, yes and no."

Derek gave her a puzzled look and started to push open the door to the restroom.

"The body's not in there anymore," she said.

Derek was getting pissed that this was taking so long. "What the hell do you mean, it's not there anymore? Tell me what happened."

She took a deep breath. "Well, earlier I walked in here and there was a young girl laying half in a stall and half out. When I got close to her, she was lying face down and it looked like there was blood coming out from underneath her. I screamed and screamed."

The guard Tom spoke up: "That's when I showed up."

Derek shifted his attention to him. "Did you check the body?"

"I never got the chance. Before I even made it over to her, her phone rang. She lifted her head up, put the phone to her ear, listened for a few seconds, then got up and left."

"You let an injured woman leave? What the hell's wrong with you? You didn't try and stop her or talk to her?"

Tom looked from the other guard to Derek. "She didn't give me a chance, she hustled out of here in a hurry. It didn't look like she was hurt at all, and I don't think it was real blood on her. Believe me, I have seen a lot of blood around here and that did not look like blood."

Derek went into the restroom, taking in the scene in a glance. There was something smeared on the floor in the first stall. He bent down and ran his finger through it. He rubbed it between his fingers and then took a whiff of it. "Shit! You're right, this is watered-down ketchup. Did you try and follow her?"

Tom glanced at the older woman. "I was so rattled that I did not. We were in shock that she just jumped up like that and took off running."

Derek's mind had been racing with the thought that this was just a diversion to pull him away from Ashley. "One of you stay here and guard the scene; the other one come with me, I have to go back upstairs but I'll send a crime scene tech to go over the area."

Derek rushed out, running into Harold in the hall. "What's going on, why aren't you with Ashley?"

Derek didn't slow down, instead telling Harold what had happened as they headed to the elevators with the security guard following them the whole way. Derek asked Harold to call in their C.S.I. team. Once the elevator doors opened, Derek got in, pushing the button to Ashley's floor. He was starting to get a panicked feeling.

When the doors opened onto Ashley's floor, they quickly made their way around the corner and were instantly reassured at the sight of Bill sitting quietly in his chair. Derek hadn't realized his heart rate had spiked, but at the sight of Bill, he let out the breath he had been holding and went down the hall to her room.

Bill looked up, spotting Derek and Harold, and stood quickly. "What's going on? Is everything okay downstairs?"

"Yes. It turned out to be a false alarm. Casey still in visiting Ashley?"

"Well, Casey's still in there, but Ashley isn't. They came right after you left and took her down for x-rays."

Derek came to an instant stop. "What do you mean they came and got her? Who came, and why aren't you with her?" Derek's voice had risen with each word he had spoken. Bill's face turned completely white. Derek's voice had brought Casey from Ashley's room and Jenny from the patient's room next door.

Jenny was the first to ask, "Is there a problem?"

Derek never took his eyes off Bill. "You're goddamn right, there's a problem! I need you to call immediately down to x-ray and make sure Ashley is there and tell them I'm on my way down."

Jenny did not move. She just stood there, staring at Derek.

Derek tore his glare away from Bill, turning to look at Jenny. "Why are you not moving?"

Jenny started to tremble, her knees buckling so that Derek had to reach out and grab her. "Oh God..." was all she kept mumbling.

Derek's heart hit his toes. "Woman, what is it?"

A tear fell from her left eye and she managed to squeak out, "The lab called a few minutes ago and said they were backed up, and they weren't going to come get Ashley until after lunch."

Casey let out a shriek and Bill hit his chair with a bang as his knees collapsed. Derek reached down and grabbed Bill by his shirt-front, shaking him hard. "How long ago did they leave? What did the guy look like and which way did they go?" Jenny finally seemed to shake the shock off and went running for the nurses' station, and within a few seconds a code went out over the P.A. system. Derek was shaking Bill hard enough for him to be pulled off the chair before Casey had the sense to grab Derek's arm. "Stop it! You're wasting precious time."

Derek let go and Bill fell to the ground, landing in a pile. Derek took a deep breath, giving Casey a glance before he grabbed his phone and started running towards the nurses' station. It took

Casey just a split second to take off after Derek, leaving Bill sitting on the floor with his face in his hands. Harold reached down to help Bill up with shaking hands.

By the time they reached the station, Jenny was just getting off the phone, her face white, the tears streaming down. Derek did not wait to have her confirm what the lab had said. "Which way would he have taken her?"

Jenny took half a second and then she was racing down the hall. Her long legs were flying, with Derek right behind her. Casey had to put it in first gear to even stay remotely close to them. They all rounded the corner to the service elevator, Derek grabbing Jenny's hand before she could push the button. "I know it's a long shot, but we could get lucky and get a print off that button. I want you to go back and get the officer in front of Ashley's room—have him stand and guard this button until someone from the police station comes to dust for prints. Where are the stairs, and is there an exit at the bottom of this elevator?"

"There is the back entrance to the kitchen area, just right around the corner from where they open up." She pointed to the stairs and then went back down the hall to retrieve Bill.

"Casey, I need you to go back to Harold and tell him we didn't find them. Tell them I will call as soon as I can. I'm going to go down to the lab to make sure she's not laying around the hallway somewhere, waiting to be taken in for x-ray. Then I'll check out the area around the exit."

Casey was trembling and had a death grip on Derek's arm. "Oh God! This can't be happening. I was in the room when he came and got her and none of us thought a thing about it. He was dressed in scrubs and showed his badge to Bill in the hall, so we thought everything was okay."

"Casey, I will talk to you in detail, but right now I need to get moving. Wait for me in Ashley's room. I'll be back as soon as I can.

457

Hopefully, this was all just a misunderstanding and we are all panicking for nothing." He gently pried her fingers from his arm and took off running towards the stairs.

Casey took out her cell phone and punched in Michael's cell number as she slid along the wall to the floor.

CHAPTER THIRTY

Within minutes of Jenny's code over the P.A., the hospital went into complete lockdown and a state of panic for those who understood what the code had meant. Casey's call to Michael was the hardest she'd ever had to place. He didn't even ask any questions after she had said, "Oh, Michael...she's been taken." He had hung up the phone and was running to his car, placing a call to his dad and then one to his captain. He was at the hospital's front entrance within five minutes of Casey's call, arguing with the hospital's security to let him in. Finally someone realized that he was actually the police and let him enter. He pushed through the mass of people who were at the front desk, confused as to why they were not being allowed to leave the hospital. Michael made his way to Ashley's floor where he was again met by a security guard, demanding to see his identification. The thought ran through his mind that if the hospital had taken them seriously at the beginning of Ashley's stay, maybe all of this could have been prevented.

Bill was no longer sitting in the chair outside of Ashley's room, but as Michael entered the room he saw him and Casey both standing at the window. At the sound of his entrance, Casey turned with hope in her eyes, but at the sight of him her face instantly fell in despair. She flew into his arms, throwing both arms around his back, and held on for dear life. Michael absently patted her back, while demanding from Bill, "What the hell happened here, Bill?

How could this have happened? Where the hell is Derek and how did someone get past both of you?"

Bill stood trembling, his knees still threatening to give out. He tried to explain, but no words would come out. He cleared his throat several times but to no avail. His voice sounded like a squeaky fifteen-year-old's. Casey glanced back and could tell Bill was about to totally lose it, so she disengaged from Michael and set about filling him in on what had happened.

Fear had consumed Michael when Casey called him a few minutes ago, and it only intensified as she explained. As she was talking, both his dad and Captain Freeman entered the room, catching enough of her story to understand what had happened.

"Where is Derek now?"

Casey looked at Harold, seeing the fear in his eyes. "He went down to the basement to make sure it was not a mix-up, and then said something about checking the exit area down there."

The captain was on his walkie-talkie, relaying information to the dozens of police who were swarming the hospital and the immediate area around it.

"I'm going to the basement to see what's going on down there. Dad, why don't you wait here in case I miss Derek and he comes back here?" As he was about to leave, a call came over the walkie-talkie that a privately owned ambulance had been stolen earlier that morning.

Everyone in the room had no doubt who had stolen it, and why. Michael excused himself and made his way out of the room, along with Captain Freeman. Bill stood in the same spot he had been in for the last fifteen minutes, clearly at a loss. The man was holding on by a very thin thread, and Casey could tell it wouldn't take much to send him over the edge.

Harold finally seemed to notice that Bill had not said a word. He gently took his arm and led him to the chair beside the bed. "Bill, are you okay? Can you describe him to me?"

Bill's eyes seemed to come into focus and he looked at Harold. "Yes, sir. His name was Brian Street. His name matched the list I had of people approved to come into Ashley's room, so I let him in. They had said a tech would be coming up to get Ashley so we had been expecting him all morning." His chin was quivering and they could tell he was fighting very hard to be a professional and not turn into a blubbering idiot.

Harold looked at Casey and then Bill, running his hand through his hair. "We screwed up. We should have insisted on picture IDs along with those names. *Damn* it! Why didn't we think of that?" He proceeded to pace around the room, before he suddenly stopped and looked at Bill again. "What did he look like? We need to get that information out to everyone so they can be on the lookout for him."

Casey and Bill started talking at the same time, but then both stopped at once to look at each other. Harold looked from one to the other. "Bill, give me what you have. Then Casey, you can see if you have anything to add to that."

Bill's description was very detailed and Casey could not come up with any detail, except she had noticed a tattoo peeking out from the bottom of his right sleeve. She said it looked like an outline of something. She could only see a solid line that came down into a slight point. Harold had been busy writing everything down and then turned and talked into his radio, sending the description to everyone.

Captain Freeman came back into the room along with a man he introduced as the hospital administrator, a Mr. Negley. They informed Harold that Derek and Michael were organizing a complete hospital search, going floor by floor with a team of security and uniformed policemen. So far they had found nothing suspicious, and no sign of Ashley or the man who had taken her.

Casey swore she saw Harold age ten years right before her eyes. She knew that there had been three murders, but the news reports had been pretty tight lipped about any details. All she knew was that the three had looked enough like Ashley to be her twin, and that Ashley's life had been in grave danger since they found the first body five days ago.

Casey sank onto Ashley's bed, fear seeping into every pore of her body. Her mind was blank as people came and went from Ashley's room, reporting in and then heading back out again. She looked at the clock hanging on the wall and realized that forty minutes had passed since the man had come for Ashley. So far, there had been no sign of either Michael or Derek. She knew that with every minute that passed the chances of finding Ashley were slimmer and slimmer. The fear clogged her throat and she could not stop herself from letting out a choked sob as the emotions caught up with her.

Harold caught the sound and turned to notice that she was sitting on the side of the bed, her body shaking and tears streaming down her face as she stared at the clock. He glanced at the clock for the first time since entering his daughter's room and came to the same conclusion as Casey. Harold made his way to her, taking her slight body into his warm embrace as he sat down beside her on the bed. He gently laid his head down on the top of hers and tightened his hold on her. The minute she felt his arms go around her, all the feelings that had consumed her let loose into racking sobs that she had been holding at bay. Michael and Derek entered the room and immediately came to a stop, sensing the situation at a glance. Harold's eyes landed on each of them and he knew that Ashley had not been found.

Casey let out one last sob, and Harold reached into his jacket pocket and handed her his hankie. She wiped her eyes and nose, still in the safety of Harold's arms. She leaned back and gave him a watery smile, then turned to notice that Michael and Derek were there, her body becoming stiff.

Still no one had uttered a sound, respecting her need for comfort. Harold kept his arm around Casey. "Son…?"

Michael swallowed hard. "Dad, I'm so sorry…" he managed to get out before his own voice gave way to the emotion he had been fighting since Casey's call.

Derek stepped up and said in a quiet voice, "We found no sign of her anywhere in the hospital, sir. We combed every inch of it, from the basement to the roof, looking in every space that was big enough for a person to fit. The hospital security is pulling the security tapes now, and we came by to get you before we headed up to take a look at them."

Harold turned to Bill, who had been standing in the far corner of the room for the last hour or so. He was clearly in shock as his eyes darted from one person to the other. Harold called his name and he seemed not to hear, so Harold said in a louder voice, "BILL. I need you here."

Bill blinked a few times and turned his eyes to Harold, seeming to finally pull it together enough to focus, straightening his shoulders. "Sorry, sir. What can I do?"

"I need you to be here for Casey. I'm going to leave for a little while and I do not want her alone, is that understood?"

"Yes, sir. You can count on me." His voice quivered as the words left his mouth. He made his way to the side of the bed, placing his big beefy hand on Casey's shoulder.

Harold looked at her. "Are you going to be okay for a little bit? I really need to go with Michael."

She took a deep breath. "I'll be fine. You go do what you need to do."

Harold stood and looked down into her face, trying to read if she was really okay. This woman had been a part of their family for over twenty years and he thought of her as another daughter. He did not want to leave her if she was really not all right.

Casey attempted a smile. "It's okay, Harold. Bill is here and I know time is important. Please go and ..."

He leaned down and kissed her cheek. "I'll be back as soon as I can. While I'm gone I want you to talk and see if between you both, you can remember anything else that will help us find Ashley." He moved to where Derek and Michael were standing and with a look at the captain, they all moved out of the room, leaving Casey and Bill watching them with dread in their eyes.

"Do you think I should call Ashley's mom or sister?"

Bill tore his eyes from where they had been glued to the door, and looked down into Casey's questioning ones. "No. I think we should wait and let Detective Wright take care of that. I'm not sure they want this out yet."

"Yeah, you're probably right. They're both going to kill me for not calling them the minute it happened. Oh shit! I can't believe this has happened," Casey answered as she twisted her engagement ring around and around on her finger, fighting the tears that were threatening to spill again.

Bill still had his hand on her shoulder and gave it a reassuring squeeze. "I know. It's entirely my fault. I should never have let him into the room."

Casey quickly stood and faced Bill. "It's *not* your fault! He had the correct ID badge. Everyone underestimated how bad this guy wanted to actually take Ashley. Oh sweet Jesus! What is he going to do now that he has her?"

Bill knew she wasn't expecting an answer to her question, and his mind did not even want to think of the possibilities anyway. He had been in on the briefing of the second murder victim, so he knew the brutality of the crime and did not want to think of his partner in the hands of a man who could do the things he had. He had heard in the squad room that the following murder had been even worse. The killer was escalating in the violence of his murders and his rage was becoming more obvious with each one. To know that Ashley was at his mercy, that she had just had major surgery and was too weak to fight him, made his stomach pitch and bile rise in his throat.

While Bill and Casey were waiting anxiously in Ashley's hospital room, Harold and the rest of the team were just making their way into the security office where a white-faced man of around 60 was frantically lining up some disks on his control panel; his forehead was covered in beads of sweat and his hands were shaking. He glanced nervously over his shoulder. "I'm all ready for you, sir." Looking at the head of the hospital with dread in his eyes he said, "I have the front of the hospital in first, and then have them in order so that they show the exits. I figured that would be our best bet of spotting him. I went back to first thing this morning, not knowing when he might have entered the building."

Derek went to the desk, taking up the chair the man gave up for him. "I would like to start with the basement exit and go back from when Ashley went missing, if that is okay with you?"

The man jumped like someone had shot him. "Oh…that makes more sense, doesn't it? I'm sorry. I've never had this kind of thing happen so I'm not real sure how this all works," he answered. He shuffled through the disks on the control panel, finally finding the one he wanted, and replaced the one that was already in the machine. He hit rewind, looking at Derek to see how far back he wanted to go, and when Derek nodded he pushed play. They moved in closer so they all could see what was on the disk.

At first there was nothing to see except aides walking past with patients on gurneys, nurses and doctors heading to some unknown destination, and then all of a sudden Ashley's gurney came into view. She was lying flat with her eyes closed, making no movement at all. The man pushing the gurney had a surgical mask on and made a point to keep his face turned away from the camera. He stood beside the exit door, waiting until two nurses walked down the hall, and then he pushed Ashley through the door and was gone.

"Damn it! He must have drugged her," Michael swore as he stared at the screen.

"Could we see the disk of the exterior of that exit?" Harold asked.

The man shuffled through the disks once more, finding the one requested, and they all watched as the door opened. Ashley and the man came out the door and went to the back of the employee parking lot, passing several aides and nurses, who were on their way back into the building. Not one person paid any attention to the strange sight of a loaded gurney being pushed through the parking lot. The security camera was aimed to get as much of the area as possible, but as they watched, the man walked to the very back of the lot, where the camera only caught the very bottom of his legs when he stopped behind a white vehicle.

"What the hell? Can you zoom in on that vehicle?" Michael asked as he ran a hand through his hair, grabbing the back of the chair Derek was sitting in with a death grip.

"Oh God...no. It is stationary and that's as far as the camera picks up," the guard answered.

"Are there any more cameras posted at the back of the hospital?" Derek asked as he studied the picture of the vehicle where they had stopped the disk. "Look closer at this. I think we have the bottom half of the license plate. If we get this to the police lab they may be able to zoom in on this and get a better picture. I can't tell if it is an ambulance or a van. Can any of you?"

Everyone shook their heads in the negative and finally the captain muttered, "Give the disk to me, and I'll have an officer run it over right away so we can stay here to see if we can catch anything else on the other disks. In the meantime, I'll put an A.P.B. out on all white cargo vans and maybe we'll get lucky. Earlier, when we got word of the stolen ambulance, we put an A.P.B. out on any and all ambulances. Do you all realize how hard that is to do? We can't stop every one of them on the road when people's lives are at stake. My officers have orders to follow any ambulances to make sure they are proceeding to a scene or the hospital. It's the best I can do under the circumstances."

Derek handed the disk to the captain and began watching the next, to see if they could spot the van or ambulance from a different angle. "Harold, I think it would be a good idea to canvas the surrounding area and see if any of the other businesses around here have any security cameras. We may get lucky and catch something on one of those that the hospital security cameras missed."

Harold nodded and stepped out into the hallway, leaving the rest to pore over the remaining disks. He barely made it out to the hallway before his knees buckled and he had to grab the wall before he fell flat on his ass. He was shaking so bad that he leaned against the wall with his back flat so that it would support him. He took several deep breaths, trying to get his emotions under control, but gave up and slid down the wall, a sob escaping from deep within him. *Sweet Jesus, this couldn't be happening to one of his kids.* He sat there with his knees drawn up and his elbows perched on them, letting his hands support his head. The tears silently slid down his cheeks, making a wet spot on the dull white linoleum between his feet. He felt such a deep hatred for the sick bastard who had taken his daughter, it scared him. His mind kept flashing to the murder scenes of the three women who looked enough like Ashley that they could have been his own daughters. *What was she going through? She had to be terrified.* Wiping his face with the palms of his hands, he leaned his head back, closing his eyes and whispering over and over, "*Please God, keep my daughter safe and help us find her fast.*"

With every minute that passed, the dread was consuming him more and more. He also knew it was time to place a call to his wife, before some news hound picked up the news and reported it before he got the chance to tell her himself. His hand shook as he pulled his cell phone out of his pocket, hitting the speed dial for the house number.

In the security room, they discovered that none of the remaining cameras picked up any vehicle that could have been the one that had taken Ashley away.

"This man is very lucky or he is very, very smart. He knew where the cameras were and how much they picked up. We can check the cameras inside the hospital but I'm sure that we won't see anything different than we've already seen on this disk," Michael explained as they all rose from their hunched positions. "I wouldn't be surprised if the hair and eyebrows Casey described were fake, along with the glasses and southern accent."

Derek looked at Michael in agreement. "How the hell did he get a hospital ID and get past the security we had set up?"

"He definitely knows the ins and outs of security, or at least enough to make a fake ID and know when to avoid security cameras. I can't help but come to the conclusion that he has had some kind of police training. Forensics isn't coming up with any clues from any of the murder victims. A civilian would leave something behind, hair fibers or some kind of evidence."

Derek's phone rang and he stepped over to the corner to take the call. Michael watched his face as he was talking, and he was pretty sure that whatever was being said, he was not going to like it.

Derek finished the call and came to stand in front of the console once more. The security man and the head of the hospital had excused themselves when Derek's phone rang, sensing that their presence was no longer needed at this time. Derek paused for a minute or two before saying, "I think we should put together a list of everyone Ashley has had contact with since she decided to go into the police field. That includes anyone from the academy up to everyone at the station now."

Michael and the captain instantly stood straighter. Michael gave Derek a death look. "You want me to investigate my own squad? What the hell is wrong with you?"

Derek looked from one face to the other, taking his time as he scanned the faces of the men who were glaring at him. He knew what he was asking was going to be hard, but he had a gut feeling he was on the right track and that they were going to come to the same conclusion when they thought about it with calmer heads. He took a deep breath and rubbed his jaw. "I know what I'm asking you to do rubs you all the wrong way, but it makes the most sense. We've all agreed that this guy has some kind of police knowledge and has a very personal grudge against Ashley. So, who else would it be but someone from her past or present? Somewhere in her short career as a police officer, she pissed off one really deranged person. I'm not saying it couldn't be someone from her personal life, but from what you all have told me, there is no one who stands out as a suspect. No old boyfriends, acquaintances, or friends who even come close to hating her enough to do the things this man has done. It is rare for someone to be this violent if he was just randomly picking his victims. These last three murders have escalated into a rage we didn't see on any of the past victims. Those almost seem calm compared to what he has done here. Something triggered his rage and I am guessing Ashley is that trigger. We need to check everyone who has had contact with her in the last two years."

"Jesus! You want us to check everyone she has encountered in the last two years? You want my men to run background checks on themselves?" the captain asked in a barely controlled voice.

Derek gave him a patient look. "No, I don't expect you to do anything remotely like that. As a matter of fact, I don't even want you to tell anyone at the station that we are going to conduct that search. Agents Day and Clark are putting together a task force as we speak, to start the search." Looking at Michael, the captain and Harold, who had entered the room in time to hear most of the conversation, Derek went on to explain, "Look, I know this is tough but Ashley's life is at stake and I really do think this is the way we need to proceed. If your men are innocent, then what have we hurt? And if by some fluke it turns out it is one of them, do you really think the rest of them will care that we checked them out, if we catch this maniac?"

Michael and the captain looked like they were prepared to argue, but before either could speak, Harold stepped forward saying, "It sounds smart to me, Derek. Tell me where and when you want me and I will be glad to help out where I can. I'm sure if we need more manpower, I could call in a few favors and get some retired friends of mine to help out."

"Thanks, Harold. I'll keep that in mind. In the meantime, Agent Day has set up a conference room at the hotel where he's staying, which we can use to conduct that part of the investigation. So until we come up with a list of suspects, we will meet there. The fewer eyes to see where we are going with this, the better. Once we have completed and cleared everyone at the station, we can always move things back there. Captain, we will need copies of all the files you have already started, along with all of the crime scene photos of the three murders." He paused to give the captain time to accept the fact that his case was just basically taken over by the FBI. It was always a hard thing for most police departments to come to accept, when it happened to them. "And no, we are not pushing any of you or your team out of this case, just moving our location for Ashley's safety. We can still use your squad to conduct searches of any videos we may come across, along with anything else we deem useful."

The captain gave Harold a searching look and finally seemed satisfied. "Agent, you have our full cooperation. I may not like how this is happening but I'm not a fool. I know we are way out of our league here and appreciate all the help your team is giving us. I will send out a team to canvas the neighborhood to see if we can come up with anything that may be useful." He hesitated long enough to give Harold's shoulder a hard squeeze, and then left the room.

There was an awkward silence when the door closed behind him. Michael was still standing in the same spot since they had finished watching the disks. He was still scowling, but at least it was not at Derek anymore.

"Harold, I assume you told both your wife and Shannon that we are trying to keep Ashley's abduction as quiet as possible? It won't be long before the local news picks up on it, but the longer we have to work before it does, the better for all concerned."

A heavy sigh escaped Harold and his shoulders quivered a little before he managed to nod his head in the affirmative. "Yeah, I explained that to them, but I called my brother and his wife also, so they could come down and stay with them. I don't want them alone and I'm assuming Michael and I won't be going home much until Ashley's found." His voice broke down as he said Ashley's name.

Michael finally moved away from the console and went to his dad's side, taking him into a bear hug.

Derek was at a loss. The emotion was threatening to overpower him. Now that he had time to absorb the situation, an overwhelming fear raced through his body. His knees started to shake and his palms were sweating, and before he completely lost it, he mumbled, "I'll give you two a few minutes. I'll go check in with security and meet you back in Ashley's room." He quickly exited the room before either could look his way.

Derek took a few minutes right outside the door for a couple of deep breaths. He knew he was way too close to this case. Ashley had burrowed herself into his heart and he was afraid to look too closely at how he felt about that. Straightening his shoulders, he turned and made his way down the hall, where the head of security and the CEO of the hospital were standing. He knew they probably wouldn't find anything new here at the hospital, but he needed to leave a few instructions anyway.

A tall skinny security guard rushed up to the pair, talking and waving his hands, looking like he was about ready to explode from excitement. Derek's legs picked up speed as he traveled the last few feet to reach them and caught the middle of the man's sentence, "… down in the corner of the rear parking garage."

Without waiting to fill Derek in, they all turned as one and started running to the nearest elevator, the CEO making sure that Derek was following them. He did not miss a beat but quickened his pace to match theirs, knowing that stopping them for an explanation was a waste of time. He assumed from the little he had heard that something had been found somewhere in the parking garage. He could only hope to God that it was something that could point them in the right direction, because as of right now, they were at a complete loss as to where to start looking for Ashley.

As they entered the elevator, the guard hit the button for the basement and the CEO turned to Derek, explaining that someone had discovered a man tied up in the back seat of a car. Derek raised his eyebrows.

"Explain exactly how a man could be tied up in the back seat of a car and no one noticed a thing until now?" he growled.

Both security guards looked at their CEO, waiting for him to take the lead, neither wanting to tangle with a very pissed-off FBI agent. The CEO didn't miss a beat, apparently used to being under fire. "From what we have gathered in the few short minutes since we learned of this, someone walking through the garage heard a commotion in a car parked along the back wall, went over to investigate and found the man banging his feet against the back door, trying to get someone's attention. I'm sure when we all get down there you can question the man to find out what else you need to know."

Derek continued to scowl, but before he could ask anything else, the elevator doors opened and the skinny guard took off to the far back wall.

Derek pulled out his cell phone and punched in Michael's number; when he answered all Derek said was, "Get to the basement parking garage now," and hung up. He and the rest of the men went to the back wall, where about seven or eight people were gathered around a late model Ford car.

Derek wasted no time in pushing his way through the group, stopping in front of a man who was seated sideways in the backseat with his legs out of the car. Another security guard was removing some duct tape from around his ankles and an EMT was working on a head wound. The man was around 50, his brown hair just starting to turn gray around the ears, and overweight by about thirty pounds. He was in his tightie-whities and a muscle shirt that had turned a dingy off-white. As soon as the guy's ankles were free, Derek pushed the security guard aside and hunched down so that he was eye level with the man.

He took one look at Derek's stern face and blanched even whiter than he already was. He nervously looked around to the other men standing around behind Derek and then, taking a deep breath, he looked back into Derek's intense eyes.

Derek had given him a minute to realize who was the man in charge before he started blasting him with questions. He leaned in even closer and asked in a quiet voice, "Can you tell us who you are and what happened?"

The man visibly swallowed and then squared his shoulders, wincing as he did. "My name's Brian Street and I'm an x-ray tech here at the hospital."

Derek's eyebrows rose at that information and then, noticing that he was in his underwear: "What happened to you and when?"

The EMT was cleaning the wound on the back of the man's head where a pretty good-sized goose egg was beginning to form. Between her, Derek and the people crowded around them, things were beginning to feel a little tight, so Derek turned around and issued in a growl. "If you don't need to be here, I would appreciate it if you would give this man some space and privacy."

Everyone looked around at each other, not sure if that meant them or not. By that time Michael and Harold had joined the group, and it didn't take Michael long to narrow the group down to just the head of security, the CEO, his dad and him. The EMT finished cleaning the wound and turned to Derek. "As soon as you are finished asking your questions, he needs to be brought to the E.R. so that we can get some x-rays and get him stitched up."

Derek assured her that he would personally see to that, and watched as she and her partner gathered up their supplies and moved back towards the elevators.

Derek refocused on the man sitting there holding a bandage up to his head, his arm shaking.

Mr. Street cleared his throat and began talking. "I was coming to work here this afternoon and pulled in to park like I do every day. I got out of the car and opened the back door to get my lunch pail, when all of a sudden a man came up behind me and hit me over the head with something."

He looked around at the faces that were all staring at him expectantly. He had a sick feeling this was about something way more important than his just being hit over the head.

Derek was struggling not to grab him and shake him so he would speed up his story. "Did you get a look at the guy?"

Brian looked up into the eyes boring into his. "Yes, sir. I did."

Derek was tempted to coach the guy along to see if the man who assaulted him was the same man who had abducted Ashley, but before he said anything at all, the head of security asked him, "Did the guy have long black hair in a ponytail?"

Brian looked around, starting to shake his head in the negative. "No. It was dark hair but it was not in a ponytail. It was more of a military cut. I didn't get a great look at him, but I did notice that he was a well-built man, rather tall, and had one of those five o'clock shadow things going on."

Derek looked back at Michael, who had been listening closely. "Sounds like maybe our guy put on a wig to disguise himself."

Derek turned back around to Brian. "Can you think of any other features that stood out?"

Brian thought for a few seconds. "I seem to remember dark intense eyes under thick eyebrows, and I noticed a tattoo on his arm as he was tying my hands behind my back."

"Did you get a good look at it? Can you describe it or him to a sketch artist?"

"Yeah, I guess I could give it a try. I've never done anything like that before, so not sure how good I would be at it."

Derek noticed that the bandage Brian was holding to his head was becoming pretty blood soaked and he was starting to look even paler. He wanted to keep him here and question him some more, but knew he was pushing the guy already. He would not be any good to them if he passed out, so Derek motioned to the two orderlies, who had been standing back about ten feet from the car, to load the man onto the gurney.

"I'm going to send you to the E.R. so that they can get you patched up, and then I will have a police sketch artist waiting for you when you're ready. I want you to just relax and tell them anything you can remember, but before I do that, I have one more question…"

He was being helped to his feet by the orderlies, so he turned back to Derek.

"What happened to your clothes?"

He looked down in surprise and wonder. "I guess in all the excitement, I never noticed they were gone."

"So, it's a safe guess to say that the man who hit you took your clothes, too?"

"Yeah, I would guess so. After he hit me, I must have blacked out for a while, because when I came to, he was tying my hands behind my back and my ankles were already taped together. I was so dizzy I guess I never even realized that my clothes were gone."

"What were you wearing?"

The man turned a light shade of pink, which Derek guessed would have been a bright red if the man had not been so pale to start with. "I'm kind of known around the hospital for my unique scrubs. My wife and mom make me my own personal scrubs, dying them all kinds of weird shades. It gives the patients something to talk to me about and helps take their minds off the fact that I'm usually taking them to an unpleasant test of some sort. Today, I was wearing my tangerine orange ones."

Everyone heard Michael swear.

He was safely on the gurney then and he gave Michael a worried look. "I assume this man did something terrible or none of you would be down here worrying about a nobody tech?"

Derek thought about not answering for a half a second, but knew that the whole hospital probably knew what had happened by now, so what did it hurt to let this poor man know? "He kidnapped a patient who happens to be a police officer."

Brian turned even a paler shade of white at the news. "And he accomplished this by using my scrubs and ID, didn't he?"

"It's beginning to look that way. So, now you know how important it is for us to get a good description of this man as soon as we can?"

He got a serious look on his face. "You send the artist to me as soon as you can and I will do my best to get you that description, sir."

Derek felt a surge of hope at the man's words. "I will get someone here to the E.R. as soon as I can, and thank you, Brian, for all your help. The FBI and the local police appreciate all your help in this matter."

The orderlies whisked Brian off toward the elevators, leaving Derek, Michael, and Harold with the hospital CEO and head of security. Harold took a deep shaky breath and turned to Derek. "What's the next thing you want to do?"

"Can you line up your best sketch artist and get them here A.S.A.P? I think we've done just about everything we can do here at the hospital, so I think we need to get back to headquarters and start compiling lists of likely suspects, get reports back on any of the area surveillance cameras, along with any reports on whether the ambulance has been spotted."

Michael immediately got on his cell phone and was setting up the artist while they walked to the elevators. The CEO reassured Harold that they had the hospital's full cooperation in the matter, and that they would do whatever was needed to help the police apprehend the man who had taken a patient from their hospital. Derek shot the man a dirty look as the elevator door slid open. The CEO was kissing some royal ass, already guessing that once the press got hold of the story, the hospital was going to get raked over the coals for the sloppy way security let a man walk in and steal a patient right out of her room. They weren't going to be the only ones who came under the gun; the local police, along with the FBI, were just as guilty as anyone.

Once they reached the main floor, Derek, Michael and Harold quickly separated themselves from the hospital personnel, with Michael and Derek heading for the parking lot and Harold going back up to Ashley's room, where Casey was still waiting for some word about the status on Ashley. He wouldn't be surprised if his wife and daughter had made their way to the hospital by now and were waiting along with Casey.

CHAPTER THIRTY-ONE

Ashley slowly came awake and the minute she opened her eyes, her head exploded with pain and her stomach pitched dangerously close to the vomiting stage. She snapped her eyes closed again and started taking some deep, even breaths, hoping that she could calm down her stomach. After a few minutes things calmed down a little, with her headache settling into a constant steady pounding and her stomach going into a slow roll. As she lay there she could feel the movement of a vehicle, and as she thought about it, the few seconds she had her eyes open she recalled looking up at a white ceiling. She took a couple of deeper breaths and then barely opened her eyes enough so that she could look around. She was afraid to move her head, so she rolled her eyes as far as she could and realized in a very short time that she was once again in the back of an ambulance.

What the hell happened? Her head was so fuzzy; she was having a hard time putting her thoughts together. Random pictures flashed in her mind, but she was struggling to put any of them together to figure out why she was in the back of an ambulance again. She could tell by looking around that she was alone. No nurse was sitting on the small bench on the side of the ambulance, which was weird because there was always someone with a patient in the back.

She tried to lift her arm to rub her aching temples and discovered that both of her wrists were zip-tied to the railing, as were her

479

feet. Oh crap! The image of an orderly putting a cloth over her face flashed into her mind. It all came rushing back to her: the orderly coming to her room to take her to x-ray, the strange manner he was acting on the way to the elevator, and finally the smell of the rag as it came over her nose and mouth.

Fear sent blood pulsing through her veins. Panic made her strain at the ties on her arms and feet, pulling in vain till she was out of breath. It was no use. There was no way she would be able to get free.

Think, Ashley. Think.

She couldn't help remembering what he had done to the other victims. The man was a raving lunatic, and she knew that what he had planned for her was going to be even worse, since he had gone to all the trouble of kidnapping her right from under the noses of the local police and the almighty FBI. The other women had been brutalized, tortured and killed at the location where they were found, except the one who was dumped at her apartment building. She was terrified that he was going to make her death a long, drawn-out affair.

She started praying like she had never prayed before, going back to her Sunday school days and recalling every prayer Mrs. Turner had ever taught them. And she even changed the words to "Johnny Appleseed" to ones that would fit her situation. Her thoughts instantly jumped to Derek. Oh Lord, please help him find her. She knew between him, Michael and her dad they would be doing everything possible, but even she knew that they would have a hard time putting any clues together. Hell, she didn't even know where she was or where she was being taken. How they were going to figure it out was beyond her.

Ashley took a few minutes to calm back down and then she tried to lean up so that she could see out the back windows. She used the railing to help push herself up, but even then, she could just barely see out. She could see the tops of the trees as they flew by, which meant that they must be on a highway and not a residential street. Either that or he was busting balls down the streets, and she didn't think that he would take the chance of drawing attention to himself by doing that. She held herself in this awkward position for as long as her arms would last, but she was still too weak from her injuries to last long. Plus, she really couldn't see anything of any use anyway. She flopped back down and tried, once again, to get her arms free from the ties that were holding her prisoner to the gurney. She knew her chances of that were slim to nothing, especially since he had pulled them tight, not leaving any slack.

She looked up and could see the cabinets built into the side of the ambulance, and a shiny pair of scissors hanging there. A lot of good those would do her. Her wrists were already red and swollen and the ties were starting to cut into her skin where she had pulled and twisted them. She didn't want to give up the activity, knowing that without something to occupy her thoughts she would be forced to think about the horror of what must lie in front of her. Her emotions started to overtake her again and the tears were starting to form. She was afraid if she gave in to them, she wouldn't be able to stop. Once again the events of the last few days were catching up with her, and she knew she was about ready to give in to a pity-party. The only thing that kept her from crumbling was that she didn't know for sure how much further they would be driving, and she didn't want the asshole who had taken her to see her in a weakened state. All the classes at the academy that had covered this kind of scenario warned you not to show your weaknesses to your attacker. Yeah right! Who the hell did they think they were kidding? She bet none of those dickheads had ever been in this kind of situation before. That was the first thing she was going to do when she got out of this mess: go to the academy, walk in on one of those classes and tell everyone in there to go ahead and bawl their eyes out if they wanted to; even the big burly macho guys needed to know that it was perfectly fine to show some weakness. Because she knew for a fact that there wasn't a person alive who wouldn't want to bawl, scream or punch something in the same situation. As a matter of fact, she wanted to do all three, and since she did not want her kidnapper to see her in tears and with her hands tied down firmly to the gurney, she was left with only one choice...

At the top of her injured lungs she screamed as loud as she could, "YOU FUCKING ASSHOLE! LET ME OUT OF THIS DAMN AMBULANCE!" Oh hell, that hurt her lung, but she hoped he heard her. As often as she had been in one of these things in the last few days, she should know whether he could or not, but she didn't. She twisted her head around and tried to look behind her, but there was no window in this style of ambulance, so chances were he hadn't and all she accomplished was hurting her lung. She took as deep a breath as she could and knew that if nothing else, she felt better emotionally. She took the time to once again look around the ambulance and see if she could learn anything about the man who had taken her. She noticed the I.V. pole was still above her head, but it was not hooked up to her arm. He must have removed the needle when he put her into the back. She was pretty sure there was nothing hooked up to her except saline solution, but who really knew? It could have been something important that she needed to recover. This man was really starting to piss her off; playing doctor was pushing things a little too far.

On the small bench seat on her left was a scrub cap that looked like it had a wig attached to it. So, the ponytail she had noticed when he had first come into her room was a fake. She wondered how much else had been fake about his appearance. She tried to remember any details about him, and she still had a nagging feeling that he seemed familiar somehow. The look in his eyes before he covered her mouth and nose with the foul-smelling rag had been pure hatred. For the life of her, she couldn't think who would hate her so badly that he would kill women who looked like her twin, or brave kidnapping her from under so many watchful eyes. She remembered that Derek had said that he had been following this madman all over the country, so maybe it wasn't her personally; maybe she just happened to be the unlucky one who crossed his path when he was looking for his next set of victims. Either way it all sucked.

There was so much she still wanted to do with her life. She wanted to become a detective with a gold shield; she wanted to buy her own house, have some kids...OH GOD...she wanted to screw Derek's brains out, not just once but lots of times. And when he moved on maybe she would try out Troy or maybe Nick, or hell, maybe both, maybe even at the same time. Oh geez! She was freaking out if she was thinking about having a three-way. She might be with the times to a certain degree, but when she started thinking about having sex with two guys at once, she knew she was past rational thought. Although thinking about those three men did get her blood pressure up and kept her mind off of what was going to happen to her when this ambulance finally came to a stop. By just guessing, she would say that they had been on the road for at least half an hour since she had woken up. So that could put them in any of the suburbs surrounding the city, but not being able to see out the window she had no idea which direction they were heading. It was still early enough in the day that the sun had not begun to set, so that didn't help at all.

She noticed the ambulance started to slow, and she could tell that they were taking an off-ramp. They came to a stop and she once again rose to see where they were. Only the tops of the buildings were visible but she could see that the one to the left was a McDonalds. So, if she did manage to escape, she would communicate to them to come rescue her at one of the thousands of exit ramps that had a McDonalds on the corner. They turned right and she noticed that they were traveling in a business district. The buildings were large so they must be in some kind of warehouse district. Again, there were too many in the city and the surrounding suburbs to narrow down the area. Hopefully a building would have a sign on the top; at least then she might be able to narrow down where they were.

They continued down the same road for a mile or two before he slowed even further and turned right again. There were buildings on each side of the road but nothing that identified them. They were going slower now, so they must be closer to where he wanted to be. Her heart started pounding at a dangerous level as the thought of what that meant came rushing down on her.

All of a sudden, they made a sharp left and she watched as they passed through an old chain link fence. They were only going about fifteen miles an hour, circling the building. Another left and they must have entered a warehouse; it was darker and as they slowly moved forward, the entrance of the warehouse was evident through the back windows. He continued driving slowly while moving into the depths of the building. Too soon, he crawled to a stop and shut off the vehicle. Her heart was beating hard in her chest with fear once again spreading throughout her body. The ambulance shifted when he got out and then she felt and heard the door slam. She held her breath, waiting for the back doors to open. She strained to hear what was going on outside the vehicle, but all she could make out was her own harsh breathing.

In what seemed like hours but was in reality only minutes, she heard another vehicle approaching. She couldn't see anything but once again, she heard a door slam, and the motor was still running on the vehicle parked right beside the ambulance. She strained to hear what was going on and if someone else was out there or if it was just the one person. Deep down she was praying that it was only one person. She knew her chances of escaping one person versus two were much greater. She needed to stay alert and watch for her chance.

The sweat slid down the side of her face and between her breasts. The minute he had shut the ambulance off, the heat inside the back had risen about forty degrees, even inside the warehouse. If he chose to leave her here strapped down, it wouldn't take long for the temperature to play havoc on her already weakened body. Deep down she worried that even if she got the chance to escape, she wouldn't have the strength to get far. Being half naked and weak as a lamb didn't seem promising to her. If she was lucky, he would put her somewhere for a few days, leave her some food and water, and she could grow stronger before she took the chance to escape. But if, when he cut her loose from these railings, she could suddenly overpower him and take off at a dead run, she would. Surely someone would stop for a woman running down the street in a hospital gown with the back flapping open, showing her butt as she hobbled her way along.

The minutes ticked by and she couldn't tell what was going on outside the ambulance, but if she listened real hard she could hear movement somewhere on the right side near the back doors.

Suddenly the door was jerked open, and her eyes flew to the man standing there. Her eyes widened in confusion.

CHAPTER THIRTY-TWO

While the FBI task force was busy running background checks on the precinct personnel at the hotel, Derek sat at the oval table in the conference room of the metro police station, going through the files that were spread out in front of him. Officer Wood had compiled the names of all the cadets who had either quit or been tossed from the police academies in the area. Derek had taken the names for the state level, with Michael going over the list of the city academies for the state. It was a long shot, but it was the only lead they had.

They were going to check the academy that Ashley had attended first, hoping that a name would pop out at them, and then maybe they could cross-reference those names with names in the other states where murders had happened.

Harold was busy forming a task force to help with all the leads that were pouring in to the station. Within minutes of Ashley's abduction, the news stations had picked up the story and run with it. So far, they had not connected Ash's kidnapping with the other murders, but if they did, then all hell would break loose. Derek usually did not want the cases he was working on to be spread all over the news, but in this case he was willing for any leads they might get. Who knew what someone might know that would bust this case wide open. Every minute that went by with nothing to go on was putting Ashley in even greater danger.

Images of all the murdered women Derek had investigated in the last few years flashed through his mind, and his fear for Ashley's safety turned his blood cold. He of all people knew what this madman was capable of. The murders he had committed here were escalating to a dangerous level for everyone who came into contact with him. Each murder was grislier than the last and less time passed between each one. If he followed his M.O. from the other states, Ashley was his prime victim; he would kill her and then he would move on to another state and continue his murder spree.

Derek knew he had become too close to this case, but he had never met a victim before. He also knew it wasn't just that he had actually met someone; it was Ashley herself. He felt more for her than he had anyone in a really long time. When he was with her, he couldn't seem to stop the emotions and feelings. When she touched him or was throwing her sassy attitude at him, she made him crazy. The woman had more spunk than any woman he had ever met. If anyone could go toe to toe with this madman, it was Ashley. He hoped that she got the chance to use all the training she had received at the academy. She had finished at the top of her class in almost every category, so he knew she had the talent. The question was, would she get the chance to use it?

He thought back to his days at Quantico and how the lone woman in his class had struggled to complete the training. He had admired her for not giving in to the hassle the other cadets had given her or the sexual advances that had been a constant for her. She had passed but she had not excelled at any one thing, and thinking back on it, he wondered how he and his fellow cadets would have felt if she had exceeded them in the training. He hoped that he could have put his male pride aside and accepted it, but he knew for a fact that some in his class would not have handled it well.

Is that what had happened in Ashley's case? Had someone in her class not been able to accept that she had outdone almost all of them? She had to have pissed off more than one person in that class. Although she didn't have the kind of personality to rub it in their faces, it would still anger a lot of men.

The more he thought about it, the more it made sense to him. Is that what had happened in the other states? Had he flunked out or been kicked out of other academies and that's what had set off his murderous rages? Maybe after he once again failed, he turned to murdering a set of women he somehow associated with his failure. He had researched all the women in all the past murders, and none of them had been associated with any kind of law enforcement agencies. But maybe because Ashley had excelled on all her courses, he had targeted her instead of just a random woman who happened to be in the wrong place at the wrong time.

Derek pushed away the folders that he had half-assed looked at, went to where Michael was just sitting down to take a look at the folders that were stacked in front of him. He glanced up as Derek approached him, raising his eyebrows in question as Derek pulled out a chair and grabbed a folder.

"What? You miss me so much you want to share my folders instead of working on your own set?" Michael asked as he shot Derek a scowl.

Derek took a deep breath, knowing that Michael was just pissy because he was so worried about Ash, so he let the smart-ass remark slide and answered calmly, "I think we're on the right track, but I think it's more likely to be someone in Ashley's class, not some other fly-by-night loser who just happened to pick her at random. This case is just too personal compared to the ones in the past. He focused on her way more than any of his other victims. She's pissed this guy off, and since we have no other leads, my gut is saying go with this lead."

Michael stared at Derek for a few seconds and then handed him a handful of folders. "These are all of the dropouts and flunkouts of the academy that Ashley went to. So we can pull out the ones for the same period of time that Ashley was there, and then go from there."

They had only just started going through the folders when the chair beside Derek was pulled out and pushed right up beside his chair. He stopped long enough to cast a quick glance at the person who sat down in the chair that was almost touching his.

He couldn't help but give the busty woman a quick look up and down as she leaned over his arm and took up a folder. "Harold said you all might need some help going over these files, since I was in the same graduating class as our dear sweet Ashley."

Michael growled at her comment. "Malone, you can cut the sugary crap. We both know it's bullshit, but if you think you can impress Derek with that act, go right ahead."

Derek looked between the two and was afraid he was going to have to play referee for a few tense moments as they shot daggers at each other, but the she-cat sitting beside him decided that it wasn't worth it to waste her time on Michael, and turned her attention to him.

"We had a huge starting class, with several people not making it very far into the program at all, and then several who either left on their own accord or didn't even make it past the first few weeks of training. Then at the end several people made it through the academy, but there were too many of us who passed for the number of positions open, which left several without job offers. I remember several guys were unhappy about it and one guy was really pissed when it happened."

As she was telling the story, both Derek and Michael had pushed the files to the side and were listening to every word that Malone was saying. She seemed to realize that she had their full attention and leaned closer to Derek. By doing so she trapped his arm that had been stretched out over the table with her big double Ds. He glanced down as she continued to talk, seemingly unaware of the fact that she was resting her left breast on his arm, but he was pretty certain it had not been an innocent move. He was sure this woman knew exactly what she was doing at all times when it came to men. From the first time he had seen her in the back yard of Harold's house, he had pegged her as someone who used men for what she could get out of them and then tossed them aside as if they were garbage. He had also picked up on the undercurrent that had run between her and Ashley, and knew that there must be some bad blood between the two.

Derek glanced up at Michael, who noticed that his arm was pinned under Officer Malone's breast. Then he looked right into Derek's eyes with a *glad it's you she targeted and not me* smirk on his face. Derek scowled at Michael, purposely reached out for a folder on Michael's side of the table, and by doing so freed his arm from the breast trap it had been in. He made a pretense of glancing at the name on the folder, and then he made sure that his arm was close to his side and his hands were on the table directly in front of him.

Michael turned his attention back to what Malone was saying. "Do you remember the name of the man who was so mad about it?"

Malone tore her eyes away from Derek and gave Michael an *eat shit and die* look. She turned back to Derek and answered, "If I could see the list of the whole class I can tell you which names you need to concentrate on." She put her right hand on Derek's arm again and began gently rubbing it as she talked.

Michael was past the point of being irritated at her man-mauling antics and growled, "Why don't you stop pawing and rubbing your fake double Ds on Derek's arm and go talk to Officer Jones about compiling a list of those names for you? If I'm correct, Agent Laws does not have the time or desire to be a notch on your bedpost."

Malone's eyebrows drew together in a scowl, and for a second time Derek thought he might have to play referee between the two of them. He was a little surprised that Michael was taking the chance of getting a sexual harassment charge slapped on him, but if it was one of his sisters missing, who knows what he would be willing to chance? If Michael had not pressed the issue, how long would the officer have dragged out telling the story? He, for one, was glad Michael had spoken up or he might have been forced to remove himself from the table to escape her attention. He glanced back at her and could feel the anger radiating from her. He could also tell she was struggling to keep her temper in check, knowing that even if Michael had spoken out of line, he was still a decorated detective and if she responded to his comments in the very crowded room, she would be cutting her throat as a future police officer in this city. Derek had discovered early on when he had first been sent here to investigate this case that the Wright family were very highly respected, not only as police officers, but as all-around good people.

With the abduction of Ashley, the whole police department, along with all the neighboring departments, was focusing on this case as their number one priority. He guessed that Officer Malone was no dummy, and she would not do anything to jeopardize herself by saying something that would bring negative attention to her. She glared at Michael for a few more seconds and then turned her attention back to Derek. In less than a heartbeat, she changed from a glaring she-devil to a smoldering sexpot and informed Derek in a whispery, velvet voice that she would see about gathering the information and get back to him as soon as possible.

Derek watched as she made her way out of the room, noticing that several men looked up as she passed and watched her as she sashayed out of their line of vision. Turning his attention back to Michael he had to ask, "So what's her story?"

Michael had been running a hand through his mussed-up hair and he let out a deep sigh. "That woman has no business being in the department. Everyone knows that the only way she passed the academy was that she slept her way through. Rumor has it that there is an internal investigation into some of the instructors of the academy." He leaned over and whispered in a softer voice, "Besides, she has been causing heartache and turmoil for Ashley since they were in kindergarten together. She has made it her life goal to cause as much pain in Ashley's life as possible. From childhood pranks to mean and vicious acts, she has been a constant pain for our family. For that fact alone I have half a mind to blow off anything she may tell us, but I can't take the chance that she may actually have some useful information that can help us find the lunatic who took Ashley."

Derek heard the strain and hurt in Michael's voice when he said Ashley's name, and the seriousness of the situation came back to him in a heartbeat. The thoughts of what was really happening to Ashley as they sat here trying to find some break in this case flooded back into his mind, and he felt again the fear that made his guts clench into a ball.

"Well, we'll see what she has to offer and then we'll put her onto some meaningless task to keep her out of the way and to make sure she is not in any position to hinder this case. We don't want some old female cat fight to get in the way of Ashley's safety."

Derek's cell phone rang and Michael said he would go refill their coffee cups, leaving Derek some privacy. "Special Agent Laws," Derek answered.

"Special Agent Laws, this is Special Agent Billings from the field office here and I have some information for you. An abandoned ambulance was found in an old building in the warehouse district a few minutes ago, by some neighborhood kids who happened to stumble across it when they were cutting through the building after school. I have sent some local officers to investigate it, but I'm sure it's the ambulance that was reported stolen this morning."

Derek's pulse immediately skyrocketed. "I would like to be on scene. Do you have an address for me?"

After receiving the information from him, Derek rushed to where Michael was, adding sugar to his coffee. "We need to go. An abandoned ambulance has been found."

Michael dropped the spoon and left both cups on the counter beside the half-filled coffee pot. He turned toward Derek with a questioning look but didn't stop to ask questions. Instead he pulled his phone out to call his dad as he followed Derek through the room and out into the station. Neither stopped to talk to anyone, choosing to let Harold fill in the appropriate people.

They sprinted to Michael's car and as soon as they were inside, Michael hung up. He started the car up and left black marks as he made his way out of the parking lot.

Neither said much after Derek told Michael the address, both lost in thought, and praying that some kind of clue was left behind to aid them in their search.

Michael had passed on the information that Tiffany Malone had given them, and told his dad to assign a couple of the better task force people to investigate the names that she came up with. Between those and the found ambulance, maybe they would get lucky.

CHAPTER THIRTY-THREE

Ashley stared at the last man she ever expected to see as her abductor. Gone were the scrubs he had been wearing, and the ponytail and glasses were also missing. She could not wrap her mind around the idea that this man was capable of murder, and not just any murder, but ones so vicious that the normal mind could not even begin to understand it.

He glared at her with such hatred that for the first time since this horrible nightmare started, she truly feared for her life. No words were spoken. Her heart was beating so hard she was sure he could see her chest moving, and then she couldn't help but pray that he never even looked at her chest. The horrifying pictures of his last victims flashed through her mind and the fear raced through her. The whole time these images were going through her he never once took his eyes from hers. He must have guessed what was she was thinking, because the corner of his mouth rose slightly in a sneer.

Ashley knew from her training that she was not supposed to be showing that fear thing again, but fuck that shit, she was scared shitless! This man went to a lot of trouble to get her out from underneath not only the police but the freaking FBI. He had to have balls the size of King Kong's to have pulled off kidnapping a police officer right out from under the protection of so many police personnel.

She knew they had been staring at each other for only minutes, but it felt like hours. She finally tore her eyes away from his to look past him and try to figure out where they might be. She had been right; it looked like they were in some kind of abandoned warehouse. She could see windows up along the walls behind him, most of them broken out. Some of them had been boarded up at one time or another, but vandals had knocked out most of them. It was light enough to tell that there was not much in here but leftover debris from some long-ago business.

She brought her eyes back to his and he now had a full-blown smile on his face. All she could think about was how someone that handsome could be so evil.

"Ashley, Ashley, you know you are one hard girl to kill. But, I have to admit that out of all my past kills, you have turned out to be the most fun."

She could only stare at him in shock. *Fun?* He thought this was fun! Murdering helpless women and turning her into a frequent flyer at the hospital was his idea of fun.

He grabbed the railing and hopped up into the back of the ambulance, and she scooted back as far as the ties would allow. He chuckled as he watched her, stopping at the side of the gurney to reach down and very gently stroke her arm, with his forefinger starting at the ties and moving along the length of her arm.

She gritted her teeth but refused to pull away or show how disgusted she was by his touch. She raised her chin and met his stare full on. It was time to put on her game face and show this son of a bitch he was not going to intimidate her.

His finger kept moving up past her shoulder, dipping down to skim across the top of her left breast, and she could not help the shudder that went through her body.

Chuckling, he leaned down and whispered close to her ear, "Oh Ash, we are going to have so much fun together, but we really need to get a move on and finish this somewhere private. I'm pretty sure all your little FBI friends and that big hotshot dad and brother of yours are already hot on our trail."

He reached in his pocket and pulled out a nasty looking knife. It looked like something Grizzly Adams might have used. Before she even had a chance to react, he slipped it under the zip tie on her left hand and flipped her towards him. He slapped a set of handcuffs onto her wrist, and then snapped the other side of the cuffs on her right hand while it was still zipped to the other rail. Her hands were then handcuffed together along with being zip-tied to the gurney railing. He used the vicious-looking knife to slice the tie attaching her arm to the railing, quickly walked to the end of the gurney and grabbed her ankles, slicing through those ties and yanking her towards him.

Ashley was still getting over his quick maneuver of the handcuff trick, when she realized she was being slung over his shoulders like a side of beef. The minute she hit his shoulder she cried out with the pain that exploded through her. She was trying to catch her breath when he jumped down off the back of the ambulance, causing her to almost pass out. Oh sweet Jesus! She wasn't doing nearly as well as she thought she was. Just lying in a hospital bed was far different than being bounced around like a sack of potatoes. The pain in her ribs along with the damaged lung caused her to see blackness around the outer corners of her eyes. She was still fighting to catch her breath and not black out from pain.

Ashley was hanging upside down with her ass sticking up, bare as the day she was born, as he rounded the end of the ambulance and walked to the trunk of a brown car.

"Sorry, Ash. I'd love to have you sit up front with me but I don't think that would be a very good idea, do you?" He snickered as he dropped her into the trunk, and before she could even respond, he slammed it shut and enclosed her in almost total darkness.

Sweet Jesus! She wasn't sure if her body was up for any more abuse. She already felt like a pulverized piece of meat, but the rough handling he had just put her through was about to do her in.

There was just enough light shining through the cracks that she could make out the interior of the trunk. She was facing the rear of the car so she could see where the taillights were. All the training that she had heard about being kidnapped ran through her mind. You were supposed to kick out the taillight, stick a hand out and wave at the other motorists so they could see you. Wasn't sure how that was going to work out, starting with she had no idea how she could get her body turned so that her feet were in a position to kick anything, let alone there was no way to stick a hand out, as they were handcuffed together behind her back. The fact that she was barefoot didn't help the situation.

The car had started moving slowly as they left the warehouse and then gradually picked up speed. They made several turns and she assumed they were back on the freeway.

She was starting to panic. The chances of her getting out of this alive were starting to look pretty slim. Handcuffed in nothing but a hospital gown, in the trunk of a car headed God only knew where, was not exactly where she wanted to be.

She started sending telepathic messages to everyone she had ever met. She had no past history of this ability, but what did she have to lose? Maybe she could connect with some supernatural out there somewhere and they could get word to Michael or Derek.

Her only hope was that he was going to break his pattern with her. All the other murders had happened at the place that he had grabbed his victims, except the one left at her dumpster. If he decided to drag her death out, it gave her a slight chance of escaping or being found, but the thoughts of what he would be doing to her sent her back into panic mode again. Her mind flashed back to the bar in college when she had been nearly raped in the storage room,

498

and the trembling started. Where that guy had been a drunken ass-hole, this man was way past that. The things he had done to those other women were done by someone that was totally demented. The anger and hatred she had seen in those few minutes he had stared into her eyes had proved that this was personal to him.

Ashley tried to look around her, but it was so dark, with only a little light coming through where the taillights were, that she could not see anything in the trunk. She maneuvered herself so that she was facing the front of the car and could just barely make out the spare tire shoved up into the back of the trunk. Her hands were cuffed behind her, but she tried to feel around to see if she could find anything to break out the taillights with. She scooted up as far as she could and felt nothing. Then she scooted down as far as she could but it resulted in the same thing; there was nothing between her and the edge of the trunk. She wiggled as far to the front of the trunk as she could get, then turned over onto her back and rolled onto her left side so that she was now facing the rear of the car again. Her arms felt like they were going to break as she rolled over onto them. It was so hot in the trunk that sweat was rolling down the side of her face and her gown was starting to get wet. Rolling over had caused the gown to twist up beneath her, leaving her lower half uncovered. She was more panicked about being exposed than she was about finding something to defend herself with or break-ing out the taillights. She raised her side up and tried grabbing the gown with her cuffed hands and pulling it down. She did this sev-eral times until she managed to get her gown down enough to at least cover most of her. She lay there panting and trying to catch her breath. Just that little bit of maneuvering had exhausted her. She could feel the emotions again and there was no way she wanted that bastard to see her cry. She took a couple of deep breaths and lay there till she could breathe normally again.

As she had been turning herself over she had felt around the trunk as best as she could and found nothing. It was empty except for the spare tire and her. She assumed that the tire wrench must be under the spare, and he had made sure there was nothing in here that would help her.

She had no idea how long it had taken her to search the trunk, but she would have guessed at least a half hour had passed. They had not slowed down or made any turns, so her best guess was they were still on the freeway. She stared at the taillights and wondered how many cars were behind them with no idea that they were following a car with a handcuffed woman in the trunk. She didn't think she would ever follow another car again without wondering what was in the trunk.

The car started to slow down and shift slightly to the right, and she guessed they must be taking an off-ramp. The car came to a stop and she could hear and see the left blinker come on. They were stopped for a few seconds and she wondered, if she started screaming, whether someone would hear her, but before she could make a decision they were moving again. She could tell the car was not moving as fast as they had been, so they must be on a side street. He must be driving on a street with no stop signs or lights or was lucky enough to be hitting all the green lights, because they did not slow down. The car slowed again and she could tell they had turned right and must have turned onto a gravel or dirt road. She was bouncing around more and it was a much rougher ride than it had been. The road must not have been well maintained, because they were hitting potholes that made her cry out with pain at every jolt. They finally slowed down and turned to the right one more time, and moved slowly down some kind of road or trail. This one was even rougher than the last road had been, and she was developing bruises on top of bruises. If she got out of this mess she was going to have to lock herself into her apartment for a month before she was healed enough to be seen in public. A sigh escaped her dry lips at that thought. Here she was thinking about what she might look like, when more than likely she would be dead soon. Her thoughts went to her family and what they must be going through. This had to be so hard on all of them. Her dad and Michael would be feeling desperate, knowing what they did about this psycho who had her; her mom was a tough lady but she didn't think any mother could stand the thought that her daughter was with a madman who had killed who knows how many women.

She couldn't help herself, her body tensed up so tight with dread for what was about to happen that she started to shake all over. The car dipped as he opened the door and got out, and then the door slammed shut. She listened as a garage door was opened; he returned to the car, pulled it into the garage, and closed that door again. She waited for him to come to the trunk but she could hear him getting something from the back seat, then moving away from the car. She strained to hear what he was doing but all she heard was a door opening and then closing. He must have carried what-ever he had gotten from the back seat of the car into the house.

The heat in the car was horrible now that they had stopped moving. She was starting to hyperventilate, so she forced herself to take deep calming breaths. After several minutes, her body relaxed enough that the shaking stopped and she could breathe easier. It had been several minutes since he had gone into the house and she could hear nothing but the sounds of the car as it cooled down. How was she going to escape this mess she was in? The images of all the women he had killed over the years kept flashing through her mind, the vile things he had done to those women. The terror they must have felt when they realized that they were going to die had to be the same as she was feeling now.

The minutes ticked by and he still hadn't returned to take her out of the trunk. On one hand she was ecstatic that he had left her there, but on the other hand she was feeling the discomfort of being handcuffed in a trunk that had to be over a hundred degrees. She was sweating and growing weaker and hungrier by the minute. The stress since waking in the back of the ambulance was taking a toll on her, along with the abuse her injured body had taken when he had thrown her over his shoulder and then the rough ride in the trunk. Her eyes grew heavy, but she fought the sleep that her body so craved, afraid of what would happen if she should let herself give in to the exhaustion. She allowed herself to close her eyes for just a minute to rest, and with a tear sliding down across her nose and falling onto the carpet of the trunk, the last thought she had was that she really *really* needed to pee.

CHAPTER THIRTY-FOUR

Derek and Michael arrived at the warehouse where the local precinct had positioned a car across the driveway of the entrance, barring all other squad cars and the curious from getting any closer to the crime scene. Standing beside the car was a big brute who had to have stood six feet six inches and weighed in at two hundred eighty pounds of solid muscle. Off to his right was a group of kids who looked scared to death; none of them could be older than nine.

As Derek and Michael pulled in behind his car, the man walked to Michael's window, squatting down so that he could see into the vehicle. "Evening, gentlemen. May I see some identification?"

Derek could see Michael wanted to ram his vehicle out of the way so that he could get to the ambulance and start looking for clues, so Derek produced his wallet with his FBI identification, introducing himself along with Michael. The giant's massive chest had a name badge over the left pocket that read *L. Ford*. He immediately passed Derek's badge back and hustled to his car, moving it just enough so that they could move Michael's through the gap, and then he pulled forward, blocking the driveway once again. He motioned another uniform over to guard the entrance and raced ahead, showing Michael and Derek the door on the side of the warehouse where, about twenty yards in, sat an ambulance. Several men stood at the entrance, waiting for the crime scene techs to arrive and start processing the ambulance and the area around it. Michael positioned his car so that the headlights were angled to highlight the area until more lights could be brought in to make the scene workable. They knew not to approach and take the chance of contaminating whatever possible evidence there was to be found, but Derek could feel the tension rolling off of Michael as his eyes moved over the ambulance and its surroundings.

Neither of them knew what they would find in the back of that ambulance or in a dark corner of the warehouse. The thought of finding Ashley brutally murdered was enough for Derek's stomach to pitch violently. He took pride in the fact that he had never tossed his cookies at a crime scene but was afraid that if they did find Ashley's body, he very well could lose what little was in his stomach. He moved a few feet away from the car and squatted down, looking at the vehicle tracks in the dirt, noticing immediately that a set was leading to the back of the ambulance, and another from the side of the ambulance, crossing over that set and continuing through the dirt and out through the gate.

Looking over at Michael he stood back up. "He left in another vehicle, and I would say by the narrowness of the tires it was a car or another van."

Michael looked down and studied the tracks, coming to the same conclusion that Derek had, but the look in his eyes said it all: Was Ashley with him or was she left behind somewhere in this condemned warehouse?

A commotion at the gate drew their attention. The tech van was just pulling through the gate, along with several other vehicles. Derek and Michael rushed over to the tech van and started firing instructions as soon as the door opened. They stopped mid-sentence as a figure hopped down from the seat and landed at their feet. They looked down into the upturned face of a royally pissed-off woman. She couldn't have stood taller than four feet and a few inches, but the look she was directing towards them could have come from someone who stood seven feet tall. She had thick platinum blonde hair that reached to her waist and shined like the sun. Her eyes, the most startling shade of blue that either man had ever seen, were set in a strikingly beautiful face. Her features were delicate and reminded Derek of a porcelain doll his sister had once owned. She might have been small in stature but she had the body of a Playboy bunny. She was dressed in a sharp pantsuit, a deep shade of green, that accented her shape. She glared from one man to the other before she pushed between them and made her way to the back of the van, stripping off her jacket on the way. At the rear of the van she was met by her team and they immediately went to work, opening the doors and donning overalls and protective hats, gloves and booties. Derek and Michael stood in amazement, before they both recovered and made a dash to reconnect with her, as she had already found the tracks that they had been looking at just a few short minutes earlier, barking orders over her back to her crew.

Michael opened his mouth to give instructions but was interrupted by a lanky man on his way back to the van to get whatever equipment she had asked for. "Hey buddy, for what it's worth, I would give Inspector Mills her space. She runs a tight crime scene and doesn't appreciate interference from anyone telling her how to do her job."

At Michael's glare and Derek's astonishment the guy smiled slightly and said, "You guys are lucky you drew her. She's one of the best in the county, and if you leave her alone and let her do her job she will get you the answers you're looking for." He went to the van and grabbed three cameras, wrapping two around his neck and adjusting the other one as he trotted back to stand behind the woman who was still barking out orders to get lights set up, instructing different members of her team to handle different tasks (along with instructing one team member to move the assholes out of her crime area, glancing back at Derek and Michael, leaving no doubt in anyone's minds who she meant).

The men who had been standing at the warehouse opening had all taken about twenty giant steps back and were now hugging the fence line, giving the tiny tornado her space. Derek looked around and could already see that she and her team had found several grass stems in the tracks, so he thought it best if he guided Michael to a safe distance away before his frustration interfered with any clues they might find.

Connie Mills was four feet three inches tall, and she was used to not being taken seriously; people had always treated her like she was still 12 years old. Only her high school teachers and college professors knew what she hid in that small frame. She had been on her way to becoming a doctor when forensics became her calling. She could look past what everyone else saw and go one step further. She had the ability to scan a scene and her mind picked up the oddities in the picture. Her college professor, who discovered her talent, could never put a label on it, but was amazed and disappointed when she would not let him further test her abilities.

When Connie looked at a scene it was like taking a snapshot, then everything that was *not* supposed to be there stood out in her mind, like the cigarette ash partially hidden beneath a leaf, the smudge on a taillight, or a crystal bead off a victim's dress hidden in a crease along the floor. This ability had quickly brought her up through the ranks and landed her in the state's number one position at such a young age.

All eyes were on her as she removed a ladder from the back of the van and struggled with carrying it to the entrance of the warehouse. As Derek moved to help her, one of her team caught his eye and very subtly shook his head in the negative. Derek was caught with one foot six inches off the ground, stuck in limbo. Ms. Mills had situated her ladder where she wanted it and was climbing to the top when she glanced back at Derek in his state of suspension. Raising one very fine-shaped eyebrow over those startling eyes, she made it known that she could very well handle a ladder almost twice her size.

Michael stayed where he was, but dared to holler up to her and demand that she move to the van so that they could check to see if his sister was in the vehicle and in need of help. Ms. Mills ignored him and continued to direct her crew. Several men, along with the one who had warned them about her, were forming a semi-circle from where she had set up the ladder and began taking pictures of the dirt and tire tracks, placing markers at every spot that would later be looked at more closely. Others were following with evidence bags, and when requested they would photograph and then place an item in the bag. It looked like a group of army ants crawling at an ant's pace as they covered every inch of space. A man moved to the back of the van and removed a two by twelve by eight piece of wood that had been hinged together to form one sixteen-foot length of wood when unhinged. He carried it to the ladder and handed it up to Mills, who then slid it through one of the top rungs of the ladder, hooking the end to a device on the ladder that Derek and Michael had failed to see. She now had the piece of wood aimed at the ambulance, and with some pulley device on the side of the wood, unhinged it so that the far end gently settled on to the rough top of the ambulance. As her team continued their ant's pace of collecting outside evidence, Mills began making her way across the wood to the back of the van. She had her evidence-collecting tackle box in one hand and a camera in the other. She tight-roped her way over the heads of her team, to the rear doors of the ambulance, where she stopped about three feet short, placed her kit on the board, and lay stomach down on the board with her camera at the ready. She started snapping pictures at every angle and then finally leaned her body over the side of the board, using her foot to hook the outer edge and with the top half of her body completely off the board, looked into the ambulance's rear windows.

After several minutes of taking photos at all angles with different lighting and lenses, she turned to Michael and shook her head. Shouting just loud enough to be heard she said, "She's not in here, but she was."

Derek walked to where Michael was leaning on the side of his car, checking his phone for updates from the hospital and precinct. Michael glanced up at Mills and asked, "And how the hell can she possibly know my sister was in there by just taking a picture three feet away, hanging from a damn board like some kind of monkey?"

Derek looked back to where she had gone on to dusting for prints on the top of the ambulance doors. She had already signaled to her crew that she wanted all the vegetation that was found on or in the ambulance to be cross-referenced with what could be found at the hospital, and with what could be found in the surrounding area. She was telling them that this ambulance had been missing for over seven hours; he could have taken it to his hiding place and if they were lucky, some dried-up leaf could narrow down where she had been taken.

Derek turned back to look at Michael, raising his eyebrows just slightly. "I think this lady may just be the miracle we were praying for. I have been on more crime scenes than I can count but I have never seen one approached like this." She had now opened the ambulance doors and was back to hanging off the board, collecting evidence from the inside panel, never once disturbing the ground evidence that her crew were working up to. "Personally, I think the woman is amazing. I mean who would think to come in from that angle, at the same time as they are collecting on the ground? It cuts the collection time in half. The minute we get Ash safely back, I'm going to do everything in my power to get that woman signed up at Quantico."

Michael was still standing like a statue, not sure if finding out Ashley wasn't in the ambulance was good news or bad. He watched their "monkey" as she finished the doors and swung down into the inside of the ambulance, sweeping her head from side to side. From this distance it looked like a twelve-year-old girl was moving around in there. She stood for several minutes, looking over every inch of the interior. Then her camera was out and the flashes were so fast and furious it looked like a fireworks show bouncing from the back of the ambulance onto the dark warehouse walls. Her team had finished with the dirt area around the ambulance, and several were taking tire-track molds of the smaller vehicle tracks. The pictures had already been sent digitally to both the FBI and the local labs with the hope that those alone would be enough to identify the vehicle, but Mills was not taking any chances and wanted the molds to compare in case the vehicle was found. Mills was leaning over the gurney, dusting the rails and collecting items that they were too far away to see. She signaled to one of her crew, who approached her with some equipment. They met at the doors and within a few minutes the man was headed toward Derek and Michael.

"We have a positive match to your sister. Her fingerprints are all over the railing, and we collected blood samples along with hair and other bodily fluids; those are already being sent in to further identify she was here. The inspector wanted to pass on that her I.V. was disconnected, and she has already called and confirmed with the hospital administration that it was indeed the I.V. that was attached to our victim at the time of her kidnapping. There is no sign of any additional trauma other than what the hospital said she was already suffering from. There are bloodstains on the gurney, but small amounts consistent with her previous injuries. She was zip-tied to the railing and there is evidence that she struggled, trying to remove them and free herself, with blood smears on the railing where she cut her wrists in the process. The zips were removed with a very sharp instrument and left at the scene, along with some hair strands on the pillow. She was also drugged with chloroform on a rag found in the corner of the ambulance."

Derek was impressed. "You discovered this in just the few minutes that you have been processing the scene?"

The man smiled. "I told you she was the best. The woman absorbs more in a few minutes than it takes most to discover in an hour. It's like she sees the crime committed in her mind and she knows where to focus her attention, ignoring the unimportant things for later and concentrating on the things that matter. She also said to inform you that there is no reason to hang around here and waste your time. She has it covered and she will have a preliminary report within the hour for you, and a full one when she gets back to the lab and has time to input in all the information that has been collected. She did ask that copies of all other evidence collected at other sites be sent to her lab so that she has the complete picture as soon as possible."

"How can she possibly have anything that soon?"

Again he smiled. "Have you noticed officers coming and leaving in the last half hour? She has a few that she trusts with the evidence, so when she is working a crime scene where time is crucial, she sends evidence to the lab as she collects it so that her team back at the lab are already working it when she gets back, instead of collecting it all here and waiting until we are completely done before any tests are started. Like I said, the woman is the best. Every precinct in the state, along with many others, is fighting to entice her to join their divisions. Her conviction rates are out of this world. Plus, she has proven she is worth all the latest gadgets needed to get the job done in the shortest amount of time. Rumor has it she has had private contributions from the families of victims whose cases she has cleared, but all I know is she gets the job done right and I'm privileged to be on her team." With that he walked away.

Derek waited for Michael to come to the decision he had already reached. They were not needed here, but back at the task force, following up on leads and digging deeper into Ashley's past.

Michael looked long and hard at the scene and the ambulance, clearly torn between wanting to see the last place they knew Ashley had been and knowing he was needed elsewhere. Making his decision, he moved to his car, asking, "Are you ready? I think we should head back and see what's been discovered in our absence."

Derek glanced at the ambulance on his way to the car, making eye contact with Inspector Mills. The intensity of her stare sent a chill, as if she had spoken to him directly, reassuring him that she would discover the clues they needed to find Ashley. He dipped his head slightly and was rewarded with the hint of a smile before she turned back to gathering her evidence. Derek sat in the passenger seat, never taking his eyes from her as Michael maneuvered them out of the area. He had the strangest feeling that something had definitely passed between them, but knowing he did not believe in those abilities left him in a state of confusion.

Several miles down the road, Derek realized that Michael was talking to him and he had no idea about what. His mind was still on the sensation that he had felt with Mills. "...discovered a partial shot coming off the bus a few blocks from the hospital."

Looking at Michael like he was speaking from inside a glass bubble, Derek shook his head and asked Michael to repeat that last part.

Michael frowned at him but complied. "I said, they were working on the security camera from the bus stop a couple blocks from the hospital and may have found a person of interest. Ninety percent of the people who use that stop work at the hospital, which gave them the idea to get someone from both personnel and Human Resources to watch the video in slow motion, identifying the employees. After eliminating hospital personnel, that left only five people departing that bus who did not work at the hospital, in the time frame of when he attacked the man in the basement garage. He was smart and kept his head down and was wearing a baseball cap, but his reflection was caught in the bus door window. It's only a side view, but maybe with the help of the injured tech and the sketch he gave us, we will be closer to identifying a suspect."

"What about the other four suspects?"

"Two were women and the other two men did not even try to hide their identities."

Derek was on his phone texting someone. "I don't think we should rule them out for that reason alone. This guy has proven he thinks himself invisible already. Have the three suspects' pictures emailed to me, and I will forward them on to the FBI lab and have them run through all the databases we have access to. Maybe we'll get lucky and nail this guy."

They arrived at the hotel, where the task force was setting up in one of the conference rooms, and discovered what looked like total chaos. White boards were set up all around the room and several were already filled with information about the past murders. One had all the notes and items that the killer had left for Ashley, others were timelines showing when he had been in contact with her, and another was being filled with pictures of faces that they assumed were suspects from the academy or some other area of Ashley's past.

Harold was sitting at the table, going through copies of the notes that had been left on her car, trying to see if any of it made sense to him. They had passed a sketch artist who was working on the sketch of the man the injured tech had provided. Derek was impressed with the details that were already on the paper, and the officer was using his computer to fine-tune them.

Both men stood just inside the closed doors and watched as dozens of FBI personnel, along with Detective Kelly, Captain Freeman and Lieutenant Crane, were busy putting this task force together as fast as possible.

Michael was pleased that they had included his best friend Phillip Kelly in the task force, since he had known his family and had been his best friend for years. Phillip would put everything he had into helping find his sister.

Taking a deep breath, they both quickly moved into the room to see where they could be used the most.

CHAPTER THIRTY-FIVE

Ashley woke up to darkness, thinking she was still in the back of the trunk, but soon realized she was sitting up, strapped to a dining room captain's chair. It also didn't take her long to discover she was no longer wearing the hospital gown she had been in. Looking around, she could see faint light and hear noise coming from another room. Maybe it was the kitchen, by the banging of pots she could hear, which meant she was not alone like she was hoping.

Straining against the handcuffs was useless. He hadn't left any slack on her wrists and the wood that was holding her in place was a solid piece of oak, but he had failed to secure her feet to anything. If she could stand maybe she could sneak out of the house while he was busy in the other room. As she attempted to stand, the floor beneath her let out a loud squeak so she immediately sat back down, already sweating with just that small amount of movement. She was taking some deep breaths when she sensed that she was no longer alone. Looking up through her tangle of hair she could make out his silhouette in the doorway. He was quietly watching her, not moving or saying anything. The fact that she was naked was enough to send her into a panic, but there wasn't much she could do about it.

It was like he could sense what she was thinking, because she could hear him chuckling quietly. She knew that at the moment he really couldn't make out any of the details of her body, but he sure had when he had removed the gown and strapped her to this chair. Oh God, what else had he done to her? Horrible things that she would never know about. That thought was more terrifying than if he had done things while she was awake, because then she would have at least had the chance to defend herself. She was getting light-headed with the thought and a grayness was invading her outer eyesight; she knew there was a chance she was going to faint or pass out again.

She could hear him moving towards her but she was having a hard time focusing, when all of a sudden he slapped her hard across the face.

"Oh no you don't, you little bitch! You are not going to pass out on me now. Not when we have all this fun stuff planned," he said as he squatted down in front of her, spreading her legs apart and moving in close to the chair. He placed his hands on each of her thighs and gripped so hard she was afraid he was going to break her legs. Her instincts were to clench her legs closed so that he could not move in any closer to her, but the pain of his grip kept her from doing so, and he knew it. His pressure eased up to just a solid hold as he stared into her eyes. Ashley couldn't help but shiver at the coldness and evil looking back at her. He released her right thigh but squeezed harder on her left, while bringing his hand up to run his fingers down the side of her face. She drew her head back at his touch and he slapped her hard again, bringing stars to her eyes. "You always did think you were too good for the average guy, didn't you?"

Ashley was afraid to respond. She was pretty sure there was no right answer. He stared at her a few more seconds and then stood up and moved to the back of her chair, suddenly grabbing it by its seat and lifting it along with her, and moving out of the room. They went down the hall and into the kitchen, where he let the chair drop a few feet from an old scarred oak table. The impact sent pain shooting out from all over her body, causing her to gasp in surprise and pain, which seemed to give him great pleasure.

He moved to the stove, where he began to dish up some kind of goulash onto cracked and chipped plates. She looked around the kitchen. Its cupboards were barely hanging on the walls, with some missing their doors and others missing all the shelves. The walls were covered with a wallpaper of a faded yellow design of tea cups intertwined with rose vines, great chunks either missing or covered by stains that she was afraid to wonder about. The room was small, about ten feet by ten feet, with a door at the far corner from where she was sitting. It used to have a windowpane in the top half, but at some time in the past, someone had covered it with a sheet of plywood; same with the window that was to her right.

He was cooking on some kind of camp stove and the only light in the room was a camping lantern sitting on the table. Ashley had no sense of time. It could still be the day he had taken her from the hospital or it could be the next day. He had changed out of the orange scrubs he had been wearing into jeans and a shirt with the Under Armour logo on the left pocket. He was wearing heavy-duty hiking boots and a baseball cap that also had the logo on it.

He turned around and brought two plates over to the table, dropping them side by side, slopping half of her plate's contents onto the greasy, dirty table. He grinned as he pulled a three-legged chair up and sat down beside her. He pulled out his nasty Grizzly Adams knife and started scooping mouthfuls up and devouring them, all the while knowing there was no way she could eat with her hands handcuffed to the chair back. The hot mess had splashed onto her naked chest, burning a spot on her left breast. Her stomach growled and he smiled around a mouthful, but it didn't slow him down at all. Ashley looked away while he finished his plate. He belched and leaned back as far as the three legs would allow, stretching his arm above his head and then bringing it down around her shoulder, with the knife grazing her cheek.

She sat still, her eyes closed, as he slid the knifepoint along her cheek, breaking the skin in one spot. A single drop of blood ran down her cheek and he leaned over and licked it off. He continued moving the knife down her neck with just enough pressure to not break the skin. Moving across her chest, to circle her right nipple several times, pressing a little harder with each swipe until he broke the skin and drew a drop of blood. Her eyes flew open with the fear that he was going to lick that drop off also.

He watched as the blood slid down the underside of her breast before he brought the knife back to the table, scooped up some of the food that had spilt and brought it to her mouth, waiting for her to open it. The thought of eating that food off that disgusting table made her stomach flip, but she knew she had no choice if she was to gain any of her strength back. She opened it as far as she dared, fearing he would stick the point of the knife in and stab her in the back of the throat, severing her head from her body in one swift move. But he dumped the food in and removed the knife, watching to make sure she chewed up what he had put in her mouth before he brought up another knife-full. Neither of them had spoken a word since he had hauled her into the kitchen, and she prayed that it would stay that way. She was terrified he would start talking, telling her about the other women he had killed or how he was going to kill her next. But he continued feeding her, not saying a word. He just stared with those cold, lifeless black eyes of his.

As she chewed she couldn't help remembering the only time she had met him. She had thought he was mysterious and attractive. He was tall but slim-built with solid muscles from hard work, not body building. He had classical movie star good looks, looks that turned women's heads as he passed. His dreamy eyes and brown hair most women would be envious of. But she didn't realize what lay beneath those dark eyes, the madness that was evident by the way he looked at her now.

By now, the food was gone and he went over to the corner of the kitchen where there was a cooler she had missed on her inspection; he reached in and pulled out a bottle of water, downing all but a small part of it before bringing it over to her. Grabbing her hair and pulling her head back, he poured it down her throat. She couldn't help but choke as the water hit the back of her throat. She could have drunk the whole bottle, but had to do with the little that managed to make it down. His grip loosened but he was still holding her hair in his fist.

He leaned down next to her ear and whispered, "How is our little Wonder Woman holding up? Gaining some of that strength back yet?"

She could only move her eyes to look at him since he was still holding her head back at an awkward angle. And no, she wasn't any stronger, the stupid ass! She had been dragged out of her hospital bed, removed from whatever drugs they had been giving her and fed some kind of slop off of a table that had not been cleaned in years. That should really help out the old digestive system. Plus, the plush ride in the trunk had really helped out the cuts, bruises, collapsed lung and other injuries she had endured at his hands, she thought as she stared up into his face, but she said not one word.

Letting her hair go and shoving her head forward was his reaction to her silence. Grabbing the wood that was holding her handcuffed hands behind her, he lifted the chair, forcing her to almost fall out as he started dragging it into the other room, barely giving her a chance to get her feet under her enough to follow along. Her arms were wrenched up at an awkward angle and a shooting pain ran down them. They moved back down the hall they had come from earlier, but this time he stopped at a smaller door and it was pitch black in the room. He turned her and unlocked one of the cuffs, causing her to drop to her knees without the chair to hold her up, but as soon as he dropped the chair he grabbed up the arm he had un-cuffed and pushed her into the dark room. The smell alone gave her a clue as to what the room was, and once her eyes adjusted she could tell it was a bathroom at one time. The tub was filled with God only knew what and the toilet and sink were missing. Instead a five-gallon bucket was sitting over the drain of the toilet; the smell was enough to make her stomach want to rid itself of its contents.

"Here you go, Wonder. It's your only chance to use the facilities."

Ashley looked around at her choices, the disgusting tub or the bucket! Well, there was no way she was going near that tub, so it looked like copping a squat over the bucket was her only choice. She turned to him, waiting for him to step out of the room, but he just smirked in the dark, crossed his arms and leaned against the doorframe.

There was no way pride was going to get in the way. She had to go now or mess herself soon. She spread her legs as far as she could and then squatted over the bucket, hoping she was over the center of it, and let go. The humiliation she was feeling was worse than walking around nude in front of him. She was lucky there was nothing much in her system more than fluids and the little bit of food he had just given her, or things would have been even more humiliating. There was no paper so she squatted there as long as possible, dripping dry, her knees shaking with the effort before standing again. He immediately grabbed her arm and closed the empty cuff onto his arm.

She was surprised by the move and then disgusted when he moved to the bucket and started unzipping with the hand that was attached to hers. She tried pulling her hand away but he just pulled it back, hard enough that her hand hit his penis. This time she pulled her hand back and up as far as the cuff would allow, keeping it out of the way of his urine. Turning her head away was not smart, because she did not trust him or what he would do next, so she concentrated on his chest, hoping that would give her time to react if he tried anything else disgusting.

When he was finished they moved back out into the hall, where he stopped and moved her back against the wall with his body, putting just enough pressure on hers so that she could feel his arousal against her hip. He leaned his head down next to her ear and ran his tongue all around it, whispering, "You ready for this?"

Ashley's insides turned to jelly, and if he hadn't been leaning into her she would have hit the floor as her knees buckled. Sweat broke out along her upper lip and she knew that all her training was no good to her now; she was too weak, injured and terrified. Her only hope was that he would stop at the rape and not kill her. She couldn't stop the tear that slid out of her eye with the realization that she was in a situation so bad she was praying for only a rape.

He pulled her down the hall and into a room that was once a bedroom, where an old mattress sat in the middle of the floor with a new sleeping bag rolled up on top. He bent over and started taking it out of its bag with no regard to being cuffed to her. He acted like she was not attached to him, and she soon started anticipating his next move to save her arm from being pulled out of its socket. He unzipped the bag and flung it over the disgusting mattress, plopped down on the edge, which brought her to her knees beside him. He began untying his boots and flung them to the end of the bed. He removed the knife from where it had been stuck at the small of his back and stood again. She remained on her knees and watched in horror as he unbuckled his belt and slid his pants and boxers down, never removing his eyes from hers.

With their cuffed hands he started rubbing his crotch, while holding the knife in the other hand and running it along her face again. When she tried to close her eyes he pricked her with the tip of the knife, causing her eyes to fly open. By this time, he was fully aroused and was right in front of her face. It took everything in her power to not bite the damn thing off. She swore to God, if he planned on sticking that ugly thing in her mouth, she would tear it off with her teeth even if he did stab her to death. But all he did was rub it against her cheek, watching her with a look of pure hatred and lust. It took everything she had not to gag.

He grabbed her cuffed wrist and threw her onto the sleeping bag. He lay down beside her, unbuttoned his shirt, took it off his arm and let it hang on the wrist that was cuffed. He was on his back, which pulled her arm across his chest, but when she tried to pull it back towards her, he stopped the movement and pulled their hands back to his crotch, while he began finishing what he had started earlier.

The disgust she felt after he had finished ejaculating was mixed with relief that he had satisfied himself and had not turned to her. Her emotions were in turmoil, not knowing what to expect from this psycho. Was this what he had done with his other victims, and then moved them to the area where he had viciously raped and murdered them, or was this just a new game for her alone?

Ashley was starting to shiver with cold or shock, the room in complete darkness, with cold air seeping in around the broken window on the side of the mattress she was on. He was still holding the knife in his un-cuffed hand, but had relaxed and acted like he was going to go to sleep. Maybe if he fell asleep she could get the knife…and what? Could she really stab a man to death in his sleep, and then what, drag his body over to his jeans and pray that the cuff keys were there and not lying on the kitchen counter or God knows where, and what of the car keys? She was naked, cuffed to a brutal killer, in a condemned house that she was sure was in the middle of nowhere. They had to be out in the country somewhere, because no lights or sounds were coming from outside, meaning there was no one near enough to hear her screams. Her only chance would have to come when and if he ever un-cuffed her.

She felt the mattress dip as he turned towards her. "I can hear your Wonder Cop mind spinning out of control, but you can forget it. I'm a real light sleeper, so if you think you can get this knife," which was all of sudden flashing in front of her face, "you can forget it. You so much as move and I'll be on you before you can even take another breath, and I promise you that this time I will be ready to have you join in the fun." He ran his hand and the knife down over her breast, squeezing hard, and then moved down and placed the knife between her legs, letting the cold steel rest there while he chuckled and turned over onto his back again.

Ashley had sucked in her breath when he started talking and was still holding it, even though she felt lightheaded. Her body was so tense she felt like she was going to break; the hysteria was threatening to take over at any minute. She could not stop the silent tears from escaping and rolling down the sides of her face. She had to take some deep breaths and make her body relax, because she could not let him know the extent of her panic.

By the time she had calmed herself down he was snoring softly beside her, as relaxed as if this was something he did every day. Ashley could feel exhaustion seep through her, but she was too afraid to let go and fall sleep. She knew her body and mind needed to rest so that she would be better equipped to handle whatever the new day would bring her.

CHAPTER THIRTY-SIX

The task force was still in full panic mode and Derek had never felt so helpless in his life. They had compiled a list of all of Ashley's classmates in the academy, along with a list from Casey of people from school and college that she felt might have held a grudge, but even with those they had so many unknowns. When Casey told him about the guy who had attacked Ashley at the bar and almost raped her, Derek had seen red, and they had no idea who the man even was. How many others out there had a fixation on her that no one even knew about?

A couple of agents were following up on the whereabouts of all the academy wannabees, along with the ones who had graduated, taking no chances with who it could be. Others were following up on the names that Casey had supplied, and Michael was following up on leads from cameras and eyewitnesses who had seen the ambulance that was stolen. That left him waiting for the sketch artist to finish fine-tuning the sketch the x-ray technician had provided, and for that initial report from Inspector Mills on the ambulance evidence. He would give her about ten more minutes and then he was going to her lab to get the answers he needed.

Time was running out for Ashley and they all knew it. If she was still alive it was only because he had broken his pattern with her. That he had made so many half-assed attempts on her life was already going against all the patterns that he had followed in the other cities. Derek couldn't help but wonder if the man who took Ashley was a different man than the one he had been hunting for months. This series of murders just felt different than the others, even if they had started out with the same pattern that led up to his signature kill. The cat and mouse games with the firebombs and vehicle accidents were new to the killer's M.O., and meant that the other murders were all just practice for this one, or Derek was way off base about this being the same serial killer.

The door opened and the sketch artist brought in his finished drawing, stopping just inside the door, not knowing who he should approach, his boss or one of the many FBI in the room. Derek made the decision for him by jumping up and making his way to him. "How did he do? Did he seem like a reliable witness?"

The man did not hesitate. "Yes, sir. I believe we can trust this man. I don't know if it's his medical background that made him aware of the little details or if that is just his personality, but I had to do very little guiding. He only got a glance when he was being tied up but it was apparently a good look. I think we got lucky on this one, sir."

Derek finally turned his eyes to the drawing and then the computer-generated likeness. With today's technology, most sketch artists still sat down with the witnesses and had them describe the suspect, just like they had been doing for years, erasing and changing when and where they told them to. Then once they were confident they had as close a drawing as they were going to get, they switched to this new computer program and had the witness start all over again. It took more time, but nine times out of ten they came up with almost an identical match, and the computer program created more of a photograph than a drawing.

Derek was looking at an all-American football captain on any college team. A man with striking looks, what women would classify as handsome, with strong features and eyes that looked right into the soul. He had dark hair, brown eyes and a slightly crooked nose that had probably been broken somewhere along the line.

Derek had no idea where to start. Should he show it to Ashley's fellow officers, and her friends and family, or take it straight to the media? He didn't have the time for each group to spend countless minutes or hours looking at it with no results. He found Michael, who was still following up on sightings of the ambulance. He stopped talking on the phone and looked up as Derek approached. "That him?"

Derek didn't waste time with words but just handed the copies to him. He looked from one to the other, and the hope that had been in his eyes disappeared instantly. "I don't know him. I was hoping that when we finally did get a description I would instantly know who it was and we would be on our way to rescuing Ash. This guy could be anyone. It doesn't help us find her any faster."

He handed the copies back and resumed his phone conversation. Derek moved over to Harold and Detective Kelly, looking for any connection they could come up with. Derek handed the sketches to Harold and watched as he took in every inch of the man's face. Derek could feel Harold's exhaustion as he had the same reaction Michael had. He passed them to Kelly and raised tired, bloodshot eyes to Derek. "We're no closer with these than we were an hour ago."

Derek was not going to lie to him. "No, sir. I think we need to get this to the media and see if we can get lucky..."

Before Derek could finish his sentence Kelly had jumped up, knocking his chair over, and was running to another table. Every single person in the room stopped what they were doing and either followed him with their eyes or with their bodies. He started going through the cadet folders, taking a look at one, then tossing it aside, not caring where or how it landed. He was like a madman, glancing at the picture in the corner of the information sheet and then moving on. He was halfway through the stack when he stopped, and looked back and forth between the sketch and the picture on the jacket of one of the academy failures.

Derek, Michael and Harold pushed their way to the front of the group. "Phillip, what is it? Do you know who this man is?"

Kelly pushed folders out of the way and laid down the sketch and the picture he found. "Michael, look at these two men. It's not the same man, but I'll bet you my pension that they are brothers, or at least related."

Everyone who could see the two pictures looked back and forth between them, trying to decide if they agreed. It only took Michael ten seconds before he was yelling out orders. "I want this man's whereabouts immediately. Crane, you find his family history. Turner, you find someone who was close to him in the academy and get him over here now." He picked up the two pictures and held them side by side. "Phillip, how did you make the connection?"

Phillip had a dazed look in his eyes. "Michael, I really don't know. I had been studying the folders earlier and was paying special attention to the ones who had done well at the academy but were passed over due to lack of positions available at the precinct, because I knew how I would have felt if that had happened to me. Some of these guys have wanted to be in law enforcement their whole lives and some just went to the academy on a whim. Can you imagine the disappointment of finally achieving your dream and then being passed over at the last minute because of lack of openings? I know your sister finished at the top of her class but that would be hard for a lot of men to swallow. To have a woman outshoot you, finish the course faster and score higher on the exams, it takes a strong man to accept that or one who really didn't give a rat's ass if he made it or not. I think this man was in the first category."

One of the FBI agents approached the group. The look on his face did not bode well. "Gentlemen, I just got off the phone with

Justin Carver's mom. She informed me that a week after her son was passed over at the academy, he took his late father's service revolver and blew his brains out at his father's gravesite. His father was killed in the line of duty and it was her son's only desire to follow in his father's footsteps and serve in the police force. Her son had moved across the state to go to college here and get his degree in criminal justice. She said when he was passed over, her son went into a complete depression. Getting accepted into a police department was his only goal, and no matter how hard she tried to make him see he could still do it in another city or even another state, the depression had already taken hold and he could or would not see it that way."

There was not a sound in the room. Every man and woman felt the pain this family had been through. One man's life taken too soon in the line of duty, something they all feared every day of their lives, and the tragic events that led to his son taking his own life.

The agent looked around at their faces. "Gentlemen, Mr. Carver had an older brother."

Twenty voices immediately started asking questions, one right after the other, but the agent just looked at all of them.

"EVERYONE SHUT THE HELL UP!" Derek yelled. When things had quieted down, he turned to the agent and asked calmly, "Do you have any other information on this brother?"

"She said that both boys grew up following their dad around, learning everything they could about being a *cop*. Her husband would spend hours teaching the boys about collecting evidence, looking for clues, everything it took to become a good cop. Justin's interest continued till the day he died, but Jason lost interest in his early teens. The mother said he was considered the black sheep of the family. He had always been in trouble. Nothing serious, just enough to cause his dad and family embarrassment. After graduating from high school he took off, and they had not seen or heard anything from him until he showed up at his brother's funeral. She said he would not speak to anyone and was really pissed. He took off right after the service and she has not heard from him since."

"All right, let's get some info on this guy. I want a full background check. I want everything on this man from the minute he graduated, to now. Where he was, where he worked, who he hung out with, who he slept with, I want it all and I want it ten minutes ago. Davis, I want his last known address and vehicle, now!"

"Michael, as soon as we have confirmed that these are the same two men, I think we need to hit the media with it. It may be our only chance to get to Ashley in time. He thinks his brother's suicide is your sister's fault. His twisted mind has picked her out as the reason his brother was passed over for a position in the department. His father's death, along with his brother's suicide, had to have messed this guy up pretty bad." Derek was trying to put a timeline together with the murders in the other cities, but until he knew where this man had been over the last five years, he was wasting his time.

Jason Carver had just jumped to the top of the list of suspects. Derek looked around, and every single person in the room was either on a phone or in front of a computer. It shouldn't take them long to have a complete history on this man, but that wouldn't guarantee they would find where he was holding Ashley. The family was not from around here, so there were no local ties to a certain property. If the only reason he was in the area was to avenge his brother's death, he could be anywhere. Their only real hope was that he was using his own car and they'd be lucky enough that someone had spotted it. Since Ashley's body had not been discovered in an alley somewhere, he might have special plans for her. That meant he would not be in an apartment building or in a busy neighborhood. They needed to be looking at abandoned buildings, remote areas where he would not have to worry about being discovered or interrupted.

"Michael, is there any way you can get a list of condemned buildings? Any place that he would feel comfortable taking her and not afraid of being discovered? I know I am not waiting to confirm this guy's identity, but my gut says this is the right guy and we should roll with it. You may want to get the word out to your neighboring sheriffs and have them be on the lookout for any activity in old farmhouses, barns and the like. I don't think this guy had the patience to go far. He would be too anxious to start his plan."

Michael turned a shade paler than he already was. Derek looked up and noticed the effect his words had on him. "Sorry, man. That was insensitive of me. I just want you to know that I'm just as worried as you are about Ashley. She means…" Derek pulled his hands through his hair. "Hell, I don't know what she means to me at this point. I just know she wormed her way into my feelings and we haven't had time to sort them out yet."

Michael just nodded and took off to find the nearest available computer. Derek called the local agency and told them what they had, and what he needed from them A.S.A.P.

CHAPTER THIRTY-SEVEN

Ashley woke slowly, disoriented and confused. Opening her eyes, she saw a cracked ceiling with an old glass ceiling light. She was cold, and looked down to see that she was naked except for a man's shirt across her chest, doing little to ward off the cold of the room. It didn't take long for the memories to come flooding back; fear and complete terror overtook her. She could hear the man snoring beside her and she dared to glance over with her eyes, trying not to move at all. He was lying flat on his back with his cuffed hand between them and the other hand holding the knife on his chest. She must have pulled his shirt over herself sometime throughout the night, but now that she was awake the thought of it on her made her skin crawl. There was no way she could move it aside without waking him, and that was the last thing she wanted to do, knowing that when he woke, her world was going to become very difficult.

Now that she'd had some rest she knew he had something special in mind for her, otherwise he would have raped and killed her last night. She had recognized him right away when she saw him at the back of the ambulance. She had met him the weekend after she and her fellow cadets were finished with the academy, waiting for test scores to be announced, and a few of the cadets had gone out for beers. Ashley couldn't remember his name but she remembered his brother was Justin. Justin had been in the top half of the class, but his skills on the firing range had hurt him. He was still a hell of a lot better than Malone was, so several of the cadets were really upset when she had received a position in the department and he had been passed over.

The night that the brothers had come in, Ashley remembered, all the women in the bar had taken notice of them. They were both very handsome. Justin had been quiet but he seemed like a nice guy. His brother though, had given her a bad vibe. It was his eyes. When he looked at her, it was like looking into death. He hadn't stuck around long and she remembered being relieved when he had left. She had not given either of them another thought when they had all gone their own ways after the academy.

Why? What did this man want with her and why now? She had never even spoken to him that night. Justin had introduced him but that was it. This made no sense. He had to have mistaken her for someone else. Surely, when he woke up, she could make him see his mistake. But she couldn't help feeling that he knew who she was and for some reason wanted to see her dead. If he had been doing all the firebombs and car accidents, then this was not a mistake but a calculated plan.

The hope drained out of her as she realized that there was no way that anyone was going to be able to connect this man to her kidnapping. They would be looking at old boyfriends and jilted lovers. This would be a dead end for them. She only had one enemy, and she was probably right in the middle, trying to help with those big tits of hers. If Ashley was going to get out of this she was going to have to do it on her own.

Ashley took some deep breaths and her lung felt better. It was no longer a sharp pain. But then again, she was lying down and not exerting herself at all. It would probably be a whole lot worse when she was up and moving again. She would just have to outsmart him rather than try to overpower him. Her mind flashed back to the

534

pictures she had seen of his last victim; her stomach heaved and she couldn't stifle the gag that escaped her mouth.

The sound instantly had him up and over her with the knife pressed to her throat. Her eyes went wide and she lay there, not moving a muscle. He was breathing hard and had rolled over so that he was half lying on top of her. His weight was making her body scream with pain. She couldn't catch her breath, her forehead broke out into a sweat, and she was beginning to feel the hysteria taking over.

He eased the pressure of the knife away from her neck a fraction of an inch, and she could feel where he had sliced her neck with the pressure he had applied. His eyes had a crazed look in them and she wasn't sure he even knew she was there. He blinked a few times and seemed to realize she was lying still, making no threat to him. He rolled off her and sat at the edge of the mattress, raking his right hand through his hair, still holding the knife, their hands still linked by the straining cuffs. Ashley's body was trembling from the shock of the suddenness of his actions. There was no flash of her life passing before her eyes, just the shock and fear of the knife at her throat and the terror that it was going to slice her open from ear to ear.

He seemed to collect himself and pulled at her arm, indicating he wanted her to get up. The way he was pulling, it was either do what he wanted or he was going to tear her arm out of its socket. Once she was up he went to the so-called bathroom, using the bucket. She averted her eyes, knowing she was going to have to make use of the disgusting thing again, but the thought of doing so in the light of day made her so sick to her stomach she was sure she was going to vomit. He didn't even seem to notice that they were both naked, just glared at her with those cold eyes and moved aside so that she could use the bucket. The smell was so rank, and now that she could see it she was horrified. Thank God she had straddled it last night and she was going to make sure she did this time too. She dreaded what would happen if she was given more solid food and she would have to use the bucket for other uses. As she was squatting she saw the huge dark bruises where he had grabbed her thighs yesterday. They were stark against the purple, yellow and green ones that ran all the way down her body. The cuts and scrapes were beginning to heal, but she still was one ugly mess. She had finished peeing and was waiting to drip dry, but he had had enough and yanked her up, almost causing her to fall. She caught herself against the bathroom wall, and barely had enough time to get her feet under her before he was off and moving towards the bedroom again. He reached down and grabbed his boxers, pulling them up with both hands, which caused her to bend and follow along. For a second she met his eyes, and she could see he was trying to decide if a repeat performance of last night was warranted or maybe something worse.

The whole time Ashley had been with him he had only spoken to her a few times. She could feel his anger but he was keeping it to himself for the time being. She wanted so badly to ask him why he was doing this, but was afraid that if he were made to think about the reasons, he would act on them, so for once in her life she kept her big mouth shut.

His eyes had gone darker and he was now looking at her in a whole different way. He moved closer and she couldn't help moving back, which he stopped in a heartbeat with one yank of her cuffed wrist.

"What's the matter, Wonder Cop? Too good for the likes of me? Only spread those legs for the boys in blue?"

At the mention of the boys in blue his eyes went from sexual to pure hatred. It happened so fast, Ashley wasn't sure she had even seen the change, and before she knew it he had thrown her back down on the mattress and had the knife out again, pressing it under her left breast. He made a slicing motion, bringing it up and over, leaving a trail of blood as he did so. He followed the blood drops with his tongue, pulling back enough to see the terror in her eyes.

There was no way to hide it; it was in every fiber of her being. As he looked back down to see where the knife was headed, she could feel anger replacing the terror. She had done nothing to this man and did not deserve what he had planned for her. He obviously hated cops and for some reason kept calling her Wonder Cop. If she didn't stop this now, he was going to rape her.

So she either had to try and win him over or outsmart him, and there was no way to win him over when she didn't even know what was wrong.

"Why do you keep calling me by that name?"

He glanced up with surprise in his eyes, but that lasted only a split second before the surprise was gone and the hate was back. "Well, I guess the answer is because you think you *are* Wonder Cop." The knife had stopped moving down away from her breast and was now just pressed into her stomach, circling the incision where they had repaired her lung.

She had distracted him; he was now thinking about the name instead of cutting parts of her body off with that knife, and that had been her goal.

"As a matter of fact that's why you're here. I need to see firsthand what a hotshot you really are. It's not every day that you get to witness Ms. Wonder Woman in action."

By now Ashley was really confused. Since their only connection was his brother and her attending the academy together, it had to be related to that somehow. He had rolled off her again and was getting into his jeans and boots, leaving her half on the mattress and half across his lap as he used his cuffed hand to tie his boots. He untwisted his shirt and pulled it up over his shoulders, leaving it unbuttoned. He dragged her down the hallway and into the kitchen, where, in the daylight, things looked even worse than they had in the darkness last night.

He removed the cuff key from his pocket, unlocked the one on his wrist and placed it on her other wrist, but at least they were in front of her and not through the chair this time. He took the knife out of his waistband and placed it under her chin, raising her head so she had no choice but to look up into his eyes. Again he applied just enough pressure to break the skin. "You so much as move a muscle from that chair and I will gut you like a deer and send your body parts, one at a time, to that mightier-than-God family of yours."

He removed two bottles of water and a sack of apples along with a couple of granola bars from the cooler, tossing her one of each. She struggled to catch them because of the cuffs but managed, placing them on the disgusting table. Her mouth started watering with just the thought of something to drink. She took slow, easy drinks so her stomach had time to adjust to having something in it besides the few bites he had given her last night.

He was leaning against the counter, watching her as he devoured his apple and granola bar. Ashley was afraid he would finish his and want hers like he had last night, so she took a bite out of each, hoping that would lay claim to them. Her jaw hurt when she chewed but it was worth the pain. She finished the granola bar and decided after a few bites of apple that her stomach had had enough. She finished the water though, knowing that her body needed it.

"Why?"

The minute she asked the question, she knew she had made a mistake. His body went from relaxed to tense and she could feel the hate radiate off his body. He lunged for her and she involuntarily let out a squeal as she reared back in the chair to try and avoid him, but he had a handful of her hair in a flash, yanking her up and out of the chair and bringing his face within inches of hers. "YOU BITCH! YOU FUCKING KNOW WHY."

Ashley was trying to keep him from yanking all her hair out, but decided it was time to try and figure this psycho out. "*No, I don't!* I know that you are Justin's brother, but I have no idea why you have kidnapped me and tried to kill me several times. Justin would not want you to do this."

At the mention of his brother, an explosion seemed to go off inside of him. He grabbed her shoulders and threw her up and over the table, and she landed hard on the floor beside the counter. Before she could even catch her breath he was on her. He yanked her up and out the door, entered the garage and stopped at the car, all while holding her arm in a death grip. She used her other arm to try and protect her ribs. She couldn't stop the tears from falling, the pain was excruciating. He opened the glove box and pulled out some pictures, then dragged her back inside and shoved her into the chair. As she sat there trying to catch her breath, he placed a picture in front of her. It was a picture of a headstone with what looked like something out of a horror story next to it. He grabbed her by the back of her neck and shoved her face down so that her nose was almost touching the picture.

"That's why! Because of you, my brother had nothing to live for and decided this was the answer to his problems."

Ashley recoiled in horror, slapping her hands to her mouth, but there was no stopping the bile from escaping. She barely had time to turn her head before everything she had just put in her stomach came hurling out, landing on the table and the floor beside it.

He grabbed Ashley by the neck again and yanked her back up and out of the chair, moving her towards the kitchen door that she had seen last night. He shoved her out and down the couple of steps, letting go so she fell to her hands and knees. Her stomach was still heaving but there was nothing left in it to come up, so she knelt there letting the sobs rack her body.

She turned pleading eyes to him. "I…was that Justin? Oh God." Her body was still trying to heave contents that weren't there.

He reared back and kicked her left hip, sending her rolling in the dry dusty dirt. She came to rest on her back and lay there, her body numb with pain, the emotions racking her into a sobbing, hiccupping mess. "Why? Why would he have done that? He had so much going for him." Ashley sobbed out. She never gave a thought to how those questions might cause her more pain, she spoke before she could think.

He had advanced and was standing over her, the anger so strong that spittle flew from his mouth as he shouted out each word like it was torn out of his soul. "Because of you, Wonder Woman. He wanted what you had, and couldn't stand the thought of life without wearing the blue. His whole life he idolized our policeman father, and when Dad was gunned down by a pack of gang punks the desire was even stronger, but you took away that dream and in his mind, the only way he could be with our dad was to go to his grave and blow his brains out!"

"NO! No, it wasn't my fault! I knew nothing about any of this. Your brother could have applied at a different precinct. He didn't need to do this."

"Well, it's a little late to get that message through now, isn't it? He should have had a spot in the openings that year. No woman should have finished top of the class. *No woman could*, unless she was sleeping her way there, and my brother should not have been punished because you fucking sluts spread your legs and get whatever you want in life. Well, not this time. Your family is going to know what it's like to lose someone because of your whoring action. Maybe when I'm finished with you I'll move on to that cute little sister of yours."

Ashley had no idea what he had planned for her, but she knew it had to end with him and her. There was no way she could let this man continue torturing her family for something he mistakenly thought was her fault. She knew nothing she said would convince him that she had nothing to do with how his brother finished in the academy. He didn't even come in second. He was just an average guy, and with a little practice and help he would have passed the tests easily the next time around. But his grieving brother did not want to hear that. In his eyes Justin had been number one, and there was nothing that could change that fact.

CHAPTER THIRTY-EIGHT

Within an hour Derek had Jason Carver's last ten years in his hands, along with a driver's license picture confirming he was the man who had assaulted Mr. Street in the hospital basement.

Michael was running his D.M.V. info through the system, hoping that he was still driving the 2008 Chevrolet Monte Carlo that was listed as his last known vehicle. The agents and officers who had pored over the surveillance videos of the area surrounding where the ambulance was found were now going over them again, looking for any sign that he had left the warehouse driving that car and in which direction he had been going. They had already sent the vehicle information over to Mills at the lab so that she could compare the tracks found at the site to that make and model.

An agent had already been sent to the mother's house in Chicago to interview her, and go through Jason's belongings or personal property he may have left in the family home, providing clues to where he might be headed or holed up. Every person who had attended the academy was also being interviewed, especially anyone who had been close to Justin or who had talked to him about his brother.

Officer Wynn and a team of officers were passing the two photos of the suspect around at the hospital. One was his current driver's license photo and the other was computer-generated, adding the ponytail and scrubs and cap, hoping someone at the hospital had seen something that might help them.

Everyone was afraid to admit it, but now that they had a suspect and had something to go on, they were praying that they were not too late and Ashley was still alive.

They were compiling all the facts as they became available, trying to assemble the specifics so that they could make some kind of sense of where this man was and what he might have planned. The room was filled with an urgency that had tensions at the breaking point. They all knew how the recent murders had shown a man who was not above doing something to Ashley that they could not accept. It was also known that every hour that went by without finding Ashley, her chances of surviving were getting slimmer and slimmer.

The doors to the task force conference room swung open and the tiny tornado herself entered, carrying a folder. Derek was once again amazed by the woman's charisma, her coloring so striking she took your breath away. Now that she was not scowling at him, he could appreciate her beauty, not that she would welcome it. She gave off a certain vibe he could sense from clear across the room, one he assumed she had developed at a very early age. People were cruel when it came to things they did not understand and Derek was sure that Ms. Mills was a very complex package; her size, her beauty and her brains made people uneasy.

She joined Derek and Michael. "Gentlemen, do you mind if we sit, so that I don't have to address your stomachs?"

Michael raised an eyebrow and started to pull out a chair for her, but she was already seated and had her report open, ready to deliver it, glancing up to see what the holdup was. Both men quickly sat opposite her and waited for her to begin.

"First off, we confirmed the maker of the tires from the scene as Goodyear, compatible with your Monte Carlo, but that is not what brought me over here. We did not find anything on the ambulance itself that would help in your search, but in those tire tracks we found plenty. The tread on the tires was relatively new, so that meant plenty of soil was up in the tread, and when the vehicle was pulled into the warehouse, it went up and over onto the concrete, causing dirt and debris to fall out of that tread. We were able to collect not only dirt samples, but leaf and weed fragments. The dirt sample was compared to the local area and we discovered right away that it contained nutrients that are not found within the city limits. They would only be found in an area that was commercially fertilized at some point, and not recently either. The nutrients were weak like the land had not been used in years. From the chemicals and nutrients, I would be fairly certain that you are looking at a corn crop. I would imagine that should narrow down your search area, to the east of town, it being the only area surrounding the city with the right kind of soil to produce corn."

Michael started to get up from the table and she leveled those startling blue eyes on him, making him sink back down into the chair without a word. "As I was saying, along with the soil sample we found evidence of glyphosate-resistant weeds like lamb's-quarters and mare's tail, and although those weeds are found throughout the state, after some research we discovered a particular county was hit hard with it several years ago. Farmers in the area had battled hail damage, flooding, drought and finally these vicious weeds over a ten-year period, with many choosing to abandon their farms and move away. County records show that five such farms have never been resold."

Derek looked at Michael, hoping he understood what she was talking about. He remembered Ashley telling him some of their family were farmers, but Michael seemed to have a blank look on his face also.

545

Mills looked from one to the other, shaking her head. "The evidence shows that your suspect has driven through one of these farms within a few days of driving into that warehouse. Locate that farm and I'll bet you find your suspect," she turned to Michael, "and your sister."

Michael was up and out of his chair, knocking it over in his haste, turning to rush over to where his dad was working on a computer. He made it halfway before stopping suddenly and rushing back to Mills. "Sorry, I'm not acting very professional right now. Do you happen to have that list of farms and their locations?"

She had been holding out a collection of papers, which Michael took, nodding his thanks as he rushed back to his dad.

Derek's heart had started doing double time the minute she said they'd find Ashley. He stood up, reached down, grabbed Inspector Mills under her armpits and lifted her out of her chair, and planted a big kiss on her cherry red lips, causing her to squeal. He twirled her around and then sat her down very gently in her chair. "Thank you! I knew you were the miracle we needed for this case. You may have just saved Ashley's life."

Her shock turned to pleasure and she smiled up at him. "Go find that poor woman. Oh! I didn't get a chance to tell Detective Wright, but if I had to guess by the soil samples, I'd try the area marked in orange first."

Derek hurried over to where Michael was already forming a search party.

The search area covered over fifty miles, but Mills had enlarged each farm so that it showed where the house was located on each property. They had no proof that he had her in any one of those locations, but it was as good as they had at the moment. Three of the farms were in one county and two were in a neighboring one.

Michael directed two of his detectives to call the counties' sheriffs and start them on the search, since they were closer to the locations.

Derek had placed a call while he was waiting for Michael to finish, and then grabbed his arm. "Michael, I think you, your dad and I should take the site that is highlighted in orange, Inspector Mills believes that is our best chance according to the evidence. An FBI helicopter is landing on the roof as we speak. We can have the local sheriff's department meet us a few miles away and we can approach from land. Bringing in a helicopter could force him to do something rash. I have requested a satellite to pass over and take some aerial shots that may help us determine if he is there, and if not, they are instructed to do the same for each area. I should have those shots sent to my phone before we take off."

CHAPTER THIRTY-NINE

Jason left Ashley lying in the dirt while he walked to the garage door. She couldn't see him from where she was lying, but she heard the car door open and then a few seconds later close again. He came around the end of the car holding a Glock pistol, a standard police-issue weapon.

Stopping before her, he kneeled down. "All right, hotshot, let's see how good you really are. You're going to perform three tests, and how well you do will decide how much I torture you before I shoot you in the head like my brother."

Ashley stared up at him in shock, having no idea what the tests would be, but knowing that in her weakened condition she would fail them all. If he expected her to fire that gun after just having had surgery, well, there was no way that she could. She turned her head and glanced around the area, taking in the lopsided barn, and off to the side a makeshift obstacle course. He had strung some old tires together and then dug a trench and filled it with water that was now full of a slimy green mud. Beyond that were rows of barbed wire strung about eighteen inches apart. He had placed stakes about every two feet in a zigzag pattern, running the barbed wire along the ground and then again at the top of the stakes, which she assumed she was supposed to crawl between. After that, she could see one of those big square bales of hay, so old and moldy it was more green than brown, and who knows what was beyond that.

Ashley was having a hard time taking a deep breath. Between her lung and broken ribs, the abuse he had dealt by throwing her around was causing what little strength she had regained to evaporate at a fast pace. She placed her left arm along her ribs with a light pressure, hoping that would help her deal with the pain. In the dirt- and weed-filled yard, the grass that apparently was there years ago was long gone. Stickers and rocks poked her hip and leg, which were already cut up and so bruised that she had a hard time lying there. She wanted to roll onto her back, but was afraid that it would put her in a more vulnerable position. Now that they were out in the daylight, his eyes had taken on a more lustful sheen when he gazed down at her. He had basically stopped looking at her face but instead kept his gaze on her body. There was no way to hide from his leering, and she wasn't going to give him the satisfaction of trying.

He had a shit-eating grin on his face, knowing she was not going to pass any of his stupid tests. She was so weak she was fighting to stay conscious, let alone do anything more vigorous.

"All right, Wonder Woman, which test would you like to do first? The hundred-yard dash, the obstacle course or the firing range? Now remember, if you fail a test, you will receive the punishment right then and there, before you go on to your next test. And don't think for a minute that you can just decide to pass on them all and just let me shoot you in the head, because that would be no fun at all."

He knew that was what she had been thinking, because he burst out laughing. The man was completely unhinged.

He squatted down beside her, running the gun up and down her leg. He started at her knee and scraped it up the outside of her thigh, applying more pressure to the bruises, then moved it to the inside of her thigh and down again. Her legs automatically tensed and squeezed together when he had moved the gun to her inner thigh. He repeated the move again, this time making sure the gun moved between her legs, and kept the end pushed up against her.

Ashley had sucked in her breath when he had placed the gun in between her legs and was afraid to let it out. Her whole body was so tense and her teeth were clenched together so hard that she could feel the pressure causing her head to throb with renewed pain.

With his other hand he started rubbing his crotch as he slowly moved the gun back and forth between her closely clenched legs. She could feel the gun's sight scratching her inner thigh and knew that she was causing herself more pain, but there was no way she could make herself relax.

She looked up into his eyes and felt such fear that she started to tremble. His eyes were alight with a look of pure evil and lust. Ashley knew she needed to do something fast before he raped her right here in the middle of the yard.

In a quick move she relaxed her legs, grabbed his arm and moved it away from her vagina, rolling away from him and coming to her feet in an unsteady move. She stood bent at the waist, her legs shaking so badly she wasn't sure they would hold her in a standing position. She was afraid to look up. She knew that anger and lust would be evident in his eyes.

Before she could give it any more thought he grabbed her hair, jerked her head up, and pulled her up against his body. The gun was still in his hand and it was pressing down into the top of her head. With his other hand he grabbed her hand and pressed it against his crotch, where she could feel his enlarged penis. "You feel this, bitch? By the time this day is over you will be praying that it was the gun that was between your legs again instead of what I have planned for you. You think what I did to those other women was bad, you'll be wishing that's all that had been done to you. I had nothing against any of those other women in all those towns. It was just a game I liked to play to amuse myself. But after all the conversations I had with my brother about how he had let me and our dad down by failing to get into a police force, I knew that I needed to come here and turn my little game into one that would avenge my brother. If I could have figured out a way to bring that big-titted bitch into it, I would have. Guess I'll just blow her brains out on my way out of town. She's not my type, but hey, I know a gang down in L.A. that would show her a good time. You two like to spread your legs so much, they'll make sure they are spread until everyone has had several turns at her."

He was standing so close she could feel the heat and anger rolling off of him. With every word his hatred became a living thing. Ashley had been in such terror since she woke up in the back of that ambulance that she had not let herself think of how this was going to end. But standing flush against his body, it was hard to fight off the utter despair she was feeling.

That this madman had made his brother's suicide somehow her fault showed how demented his mind was. His brother must have mentioned Malone and her graduating during one of their discussions, and he fixated on that as being the reason for his suicide. Ashley having finished at the top of their class in several categories really had no effect on his brother not being chosen for a spot in their precinct. But what she couldn't understand was why Justin didn't apply for other positions anywhere else in the state. There was no reason to commit suicide, but maybe his mind was messed up in some way. His brother's sure was.

He had let go of her hair, but was still standing with his body pressed against hers. She had been trying to pull her hand away from his crotch but he had her wrist in a death grip. She had been so busy thinking about his brother that she hadn't realized how much he was hurting her. Her broken fingers were pushed against his crotch and were causing her to feel the pain all the way up to her shoulder. She finally stopped fighting him and let her body relax, realizing that he was getting off more in her fighting him than the actual act of her hand touching him. He enjoyed her disgust and fear more than anything else.

He looked at her for a second and then burst out laughing. "Ah, Ashley, you are a smart woman; none of the others ever figured that part out. But your bravery will not last; I'll see the fear back in your eyes very soon. Now where were we? Oh yes, you were trying to decide what you wanted to do first. Your choice, Wonder Cop."

Raising her chin, she looked him in the eyes. "You can't make me perform your senseless tests! This is stupid; I had nothing to do with your brother not getting a job. What do you think this will accomplish?"

"This will prove that you are not the hotshot you think you are. Out here there are no horny instructors for you to sleep with. Just you and the tests. We'll we see how well you do when you can't spread your legs to get a passing score."

She stood in defiance. She was not going to be a part of this. What could he do to her to make her participate? She was already so beaten up that she could hardly stand.

He started chuckling again, shaking his head at her. "I was so right about you, I knew you would need a little incentive, so I slipped a little something extra into your goulash to make sure you slept like the dead throughout the night. I snuck out early this morning while you were still sleeping like a baby and brought something that I think will make you try a little harder."

She thought her grogginess this morning had been from exhaustion and stress, not from being drugged. The thought that he had left her alone with the chance to escape sent her even deeper into despair. He left her in the middle of the yard and walked to the old barn, not worrying about her trying to escape. He knew that as weak as she was, handcuffed and naked, she could go nowhere.

He came out of the barn just a few minutes later, dragging a naked Casey behind him. She was kicking and fighting as he stomped back to Ashley, and he was laughing at her horror. She scrambled to find enough energy and started running towards him, making him stop and bring up the Glock and aim it at Casey's head. "Really think this through, Ashley. I can just blow her head off right now, or you can complete the tests and she walks away, or at least hangs in the barn until they find your dead body and whatever is left of hers, depending on how long it takes someone to stumble across this old abandoned farm. Her fate is in your hands and those of the almighty police force, but then you know how much faith I have in them."

Ashley's eyes sought out Casey's, trying to take in her condition. He had her hands zip-tied behind her and gray duct tape across her mouth, but otherwise it didn't look like she was hurt.

Casey was trying to act brave but Ashley could see the fear in her eyes. She had to think this through. Could she really do any of these tests he had come up with? Glancing at his bizarre obstacle course and the barbed wire that was strung out everywhere, she knew her chances of finishing that without doing serious harm to herself were slim. She had no idea what kind of torture he had in mind, but whatever it was her body could not take anything else.

"If I pass a test, do I still get tortured?"

Casey's eyes went wild and she started kicking and struggling again. He took the butt of the Glock and gave her a light tap on the forehead, enough to get her attention, but not enough to knock her down. She stopped kicking but was struggling to make eye contact with Ashley.

"Now you know the rules. You get no free passes, just like my brother didn't. The severity of your punishment will depend on how well you finish the test. If you don't finish the tests, well then, maybe Casey here will have to do them. How well do you think she'll do? She's pretty damn puny. I can't see her tossing that hay bale over, do you? Oh, no doubt she could run fast, but I think I would have to shoot her in the leg to make sure she didn't just keep right on running. Ah damn, I gave away one of the tortures, now you know what to look forward to."

His eyes kept straying to Casey's body and Ashley didn't like the look in them. She needed to hurry this up, before he decided to forget the tests and just rape and kill them both. She had the best shot at the shooting range and, if she was lucky, maybe someone would hear the shots and call the authorities.

Ashley stood as straight as she could and reached for the Glock. "Silly woman! You don't get to hold the gun till you're ready to shoot." He released Casey and pointed for both of them to move towards the barn. Ashley took off walking, knowing Casey had no choice but to follow. Two naked, restrained women and a psycho with a gun was not something she ever thought she would be a part of, but here they were.

"Casey, I'm so sorry. I never…"

"SHUT UP! I never gave you two permission to talk." He motioned them around to the back of the barn, where he had spray-painted a bull's-eye on the back wall. He indicated they should follow an old tire rut that led away from the back of the barn.

He had drawn lines in the ruts at what Ashley would assume to be seven, fifteen and twenty-five yards. "You get three shots at each mark, that's nine shots. For every one you miss you will get a little prodding." He reached back behind his back and pulled out a cattle prod from under his shirt. "Now, I'm feeling real generous, so Casey here can take up to half of your prods if you want. And just in case you were feeling real lucky and think you're good enough to shoot me, I'll be standing right behind you with a little more incentive to do well." He pulled out the vicious knife and held it up under Casey's throat, pushing tight enough that the blade left a bloody nick.

"You need to leave Casey out of this. She had nothing to do with this. You should have brought Malone; she's the one you hate."

"Now that makes no sense at all. You would have shot her first and then tried shooting me. I know how you feel about her and what fun would that have been? Now when it comes to little Casey here, you would do anything to ensure her safety and wellbeing, now wouldn't you?"

As was talking he had been rubbing the gun up and down Casey's body, lingering on her breasts, and then moving down to rub the gun along her thigh before moving it back up to her breasts again. He never took his eyes from Ashley, chuckling softly at her distress.

Casey stood trembling as he played his little game. Her eyes were huge and Ashley could see them fill with tears. Ashley's heart was breaking at her pain and fear; it was bad enough that she was feeling those things, but that her best friend in the whole world was being forced to endure the same things was beyond her comprehension. Looking her in the eyes, Ashley gave a slight tilt of her head. All through school they had developed this private way to communicate. Taking a deep breath, Casey gave her a slight smile and tilted her head to the right.

Whatever happened, Ashley knew she needed to make sure that Casey got out of this in one piece.

Looking from Casey to Jason, she turned and slowly walked to the last mark in the dusty lane with the others following, moving behind her as she turned and faced the target.

Sticking her hands out she asked, "Are you going to un-handcuff me?"

"Not for this one, Wonder Cop. You're so good, you can do this handcuffed and blindfolded."

He looked at her for several minutes, and then removed the gun from where it was rubbing against Casey's body and handed it around to her. "Remember, your little friend's life is in your hands. Any funny business and she is dead before you even get turned around."

He stood behind her and Ashley could feel Casey squirming against his hold. When she had turned towards the target, he must have been afraid Ashley would try something because he had moved and pressed Casey into her left side and back, while he was still pressing the knife into her throat. She was standing perfectly still while Ashley prepared to shoot and Ashley leaned into her, using her as a support to keep herself steady.

Ashley took hold of the gun and tried maneuvering it around in her grip to account for the handcuffs and the splints on the fingers that were broken, using her left hand to help steady her right. Her arm was weak and she could feel the pull on her broken ribs. Holding her arm up for nine shots and the little bit of recoil would be torture on her body. She looked down at the barn wall and tried to focus on the target. Her head was hurting so bad that she had a hard time focusing. She squinted and raised her arm, took as deep a breath as she could and fired off three rapid rounds.

She could feel him jump, not expecting her to fire all three rounds at once. Her arm instantly fell to her side, giving in to the weakness. She looked down at the target and could tell that two of her shots were dead center of the bull's-eye, and the third was just barely touching the inside of the painted circle he had drawn on the back of the barn. She did not turn around and look at him, but just waited to see how he scored the third shot.

Ashley glanced over her shoulder and was met with his glare, his hatred for her so obvious that he was pushing the knife deeper into Casey's neck without realizing it. Ashley knew she had to draw his attention so that he would release the pressure, so she started walking up to the next line drawn in the dirt. He had no choice but to hurry after her, or take the chance that she would turn and put a bullet between his eyes. Having the gun in her hand gave her the hope that maybe she would be able to get them both out of this mess. She stopped and waited to catch her breath. She knew that even though she was closer to the target, sometimes shooting from this distance was harder than farther away, and getting weaker instead of stronger would not help on this one.

He had not said a word after the first round and she was guessing he was furious with her, hating to admit that maybe she was not going to give him the satisfaction of torturing either of them. Not that it really mattered, because he was not going to leave either one of them alive when this was all said and done. In his twisted mind he blamed Ashley for his brother's suicide, but Casey had nothing to do with any of this except being her friend. Ashley wondered if anyone had noticed Casey missing from her work. Sometimes she went straight into a research room, or had a court appearance, so it might be hours before she was discovered missing. Dan might have tried calling but he would not be alarmed yet. It was up to them to get out of this mess. Maybe if Ashley could talk Jason into letting her rest between these tests he had come up with, she would get a chance to talk to Casey and work something out.

Ashley had been thinking this out and forgot he was waiting for her to shoot again. He grabbed her hair and pulled her head back, leaning over her. "Get on with it. If you're stalling, thinking someone is going to come to your rescue, you can forget it. There's no one for miles in any direction and even if they did hear the shots, they would just think it was a bunch of kids out target practicing." He released her hair and pushed her for good measure, causing her to stumble and almost go down.

Ashley was not going to have any hair left if he kept grabbing it. Her head was already so sore, her headache was starting to become severe enough, that she was afraid it would turn into a migraine. She was so drained, and along with all the other pain her body was feeling, she just wanted to sink to the ground and bawl. It took everything in her power to shake off the self-pity and concentrate on completing this test.

She positioned herself once more and was praying he would shove Casey back up against her again, to give Ashley the extra support she needed to hit the bull's-eye.

He was standing close but was still an inch or so away, so she shifted her body like she was getting ready to shoot and leaned into Casey. She must have realized what Ashley was doing because she stiffened up her body where they were touching to give her additional support. Ashley raised her arms, realizing they were shaking more than they had been just a little while ago, but she steadied them the best she could and fired the first round, knowing she was not strong enough to do all three at once. The bullet hit just on the outer edge of the circle he had drawn for the bull's-eye, just barely touching the paint line.

She could feel Casey tense even more, both of them waiting to see how he scored it.

"Well, Wonder, you had better do better than that on the next one, because I won't be so generous."

Ashley's knees were getting weak, whether from the stress, pain or hunger, she wasn't sure, but she was barely going to make it through this, let alone any of the other tests he had planned.

Casey and Ashley leaned into each other again, praying he wouldn't realize what they were doing, and she lifted the gun. She swore the thing was starting to feel like it weighed fifty pounds. She fired again and this time she missed the target by an inch.

Casey groaned behind her tape and he let out a cry in triumph. "Sweet Jesus! I knew you were no Wonder Woman. You had to have slept your way out of that academy. Okay, bitch, who gets the cattle prod, you or your little friend here? Remember that you still have four more shots to make."

Ashley spun around. "Me. I'll take it. Casey has nothing to do with this."

Casey was screaming behind her gag, bumping him over and over again.

He laughed and pulled the prod from behind him where he had stuck it in his pants, "My, my my, who would have thought both of you would be so eager to volunteer?" He started swinging the cattle prod back and forth between them. "Eenie meenie minie MOE!" He stuck the prod on Casey's right breast and pressed the button, before either of them had time to react. She jerked straight up and her eyes got enormous, sweat instantly forming on her upper lip.

He started laughing hysterically at her reaction. "How did it feel, little one? I always wanted to do that to someone."

He still held Casey firmly against him with the knife under her chin. It was a good thing he had moved the knife away when he had pulled the trigger on the prod, or her reaction might have caused her to cut herself on the sharp blade. He was staring at the mark the prod had left on her breast. He replaced the prod behind his back and then reached out and started rubbing her breast.

"Now, see what you made me do, Wonder? This is just too nice of a breast to have any ugly old mark on it. He reached down and started kissing it, never taking his eyes off of Ashley. She could see that Casey had stiffened even more when he started kissing her breast. Ashley's stomach did a violent pitch and she was afraid she was going to be sick all over again. Before she could even think, she was lifting the gun and pointing it at his head.

He leaned up and pressed the knife against Casey's throat with more pressure than before. He was still standing behind her, but at this range Ashley could blow his brains out before he even blinked. She glanced back into Casey's eyes, and terror was staring back at her. Her body was trembling, whether from the effects of the prod or just the situation, but whichever it was didn't matter, because what she was going through was Ashley's fault. She could not put Casey through Ashley shooting him at point-blank range, splattering his brains all over her. Plus, Ashley couldn't be sure that he wouldn't do severe damage with the knife when his body reacted to the bullet entering his head. She couldn't take the chance with Casey's life, so she lowered the gun, the hatred pouring out of her. Before he could do anything more she swung around and walked to the next line, lifted the gun, and fired three times before he had the chance to move Casey in behind her again. She only gave the target a glance and knew that she had placed all three shots, dead center of the bull's-eye. She swung around with all the confidence that had been instilled in her by her upbringing, the preparation from Michael, and the training she had received at the academy.

"You don't scare me anymore. You can run me through all the tests you want to and it won't change the fact that your brother chose to take his own life. HE made that decision, not you or me. Killing us will not bring him back or change the facts. You're the sick one, killing all those innocent women all over the country."

He advanced on Ashley, dragging Casey beside him, the knife still pressed to her throat. Ashley didn't think he was even aware that he still had his arm wrapped around her neck or that she was tugging at his arm, trying to pull the knife away before he cut her throat in his haste to reach Ashley.

He stopped within a foot of where Ashley was standing, swinging out and backhanding her before she could see it coming. She stumbled but did not go down. She reached up with the gun still in one hand, and wiped the blood from her already split lip.

They glared at each other, neither backing off.

CHAPTER FORTY

The helicopter had landed as close to the deserted farm as they felt they could. While they had been in flight headed to the first farm, Derek received satellite photos of three of the farms in question, and the one they were heading to showed a farmhouse with an attached garage, along with two figures in the yard between the house and the barn. The other two looked completely abandoned. They had no idea for sure if the figures were those of Ashley and her kidnapper since the photos were taken from such a great distance, but they had nothing else to go on and had decided to take the chance that it was them. While in the air, Michael had been coordinating with the local sheriff's department to meet them at the farm, where they could then move closer to the site where they believed Carver was holding Ashley. The sheriff believed that they could drive through an old cornfield and be hidden from view to within a few hundred feet. He had his undersheriff and deputies coming in from other angles, so that they would have the place boxed in from all sides. The only road in to the farm was blocked off a few miles down the road. They were all wired with headsets so that they could communicate once they were in position. The helicopter pilot was also wired so that if Carver heard them coming and took off, he was prepared to follow in his chopper.

Harold stopped Derek and Michael before they both took off. "Listen you two, I don't need to tell you how serious this situation is. We are dealing with a maniac who has no regard for women." His voice broke with the emotion that had been consuming him for the last few days. He ran a shaky hand through his ruffled hair and fought to maintain control of himself. He knew he needed to step aside and let these two younger men take charge of this situation, but this was his daughter they were dealing with. He had promised Laura that he would bring her daughter home to her and he meant to do just that.

Michael once again took his father into his arms, squeezing tight. "We understand, Dad, and I promise you that I will get her back. But we need to remember that he's had her for almost twenty-four hours and we have no idea what he has done to her. Keep that in mind, Dad. We need to be ready to handle this, no matter what we find when we get there, okay?"

Derek heard the anguish in both of their voices and he could not imagine how they were feeling. He knew how he felt, and he had only known Ashley for a very short time. She had the kind of personality that took over everything and everyone around her. As the hours had gone by he couldn't help but fear what was happening to her. He had been following this sick bastard for years and had seen the damage he had done to his victims. To think that Ashley was enduring any of that made Derek want to vomit.

They all took a minute to deal with their emotions, and then turned to the sheriff to put this rescue operation into motion. He informed them that his deputies had maneuvered into position around the farm. They stayed far enough back, waiting for them to arrive for word to move forward. On the satellite picture he had drawn out where he thought they should begin the approach. They went over the plan one more time, making sure everyone was on the same page. They wanted no mistakes made. Michael had brought along a sniper rifle and he took off with a deputy towards a hill between the house and the barn, hoping to get into a location where he could see the whole area.

Derek, Harold and the sheriff spread out and were going to come up on the other three sides of the farm, advancing through the decayed cornfields. They had all put on flak jackets, and tested their headsets to make sure everything worked before taking off.

They were moving into position when suddenly they heard three shots fired in rapid succession.

Everyone stopped in his tracks. "Michael, can you see where those shots came from?"

"No. I'm a few yards away from the hill, give me a few more minutes to get into position and I'll report on what I can see."

Everyone's heart rate had jumped to triple time at the sound of those shots.

Michael and the deputy moved to the back side of the hill and inched their way up to the top. They were about a hundred yards away from the farm; not knowing what they would find and afraid they'd be spotted, they looked cautiously over the hill. Michael raised the rifle up over the edge of rise and slowly crawled up so that he could look through the scope. He focused in below and scanned over to the house where the satellite photos had shown the two figures before. He could see no one and he broke out into a sweat, fearing that the shots they had heard meant they were too late. His pulse and heart rate were racing out of control. He slowly moved the scope over the area surrounding the house and focused on the garage. He could make out the car that was parked there. He had memorized the suspect's license plate and could see that it was indeed the car they were looking for.

He keyed his mike. "The suspect's car is in the garage. We have the right place. I see no sign of them yet, but have just started looking."

Derek looked over to where Harold was crouched down, where they were moving through the cornfield. Harold had stopped when Michael started talking and Derek watched as he took a deep breath, then bowed his head in what Derek assumed was a prayer.

Michael swept the scope across the yard, focusing on the barn now. The doors were open but it was too dark inside to see if anyone was in there. He continued on and suddenly noticed movement behind the barn. It took him a few seconds to realize that he was indeed looking at his sister and Carver. He sucked in a breath and held it as he continued looking through the scope. He kept the scope trained on his sister, taking in her condition. Michael's anger grew beyond anything he thought imaginable. Her hair was a tangled mess, her face was covered in new bruises and she was bleeding from several cuts in her lips. He moved the scope down her body and could see that she had endured a lot more abuse since her abduction. His hands started shaking as he witnessed the condition she was in. He took a deep breath and tried to calm his nerves before he moved to check out the situation with Carver.

"Dad, she's alive. I've spotted them. They are on the north side of the barn. I can see them standing on what looks like an old dirt trail."

Derek could hear what Michael was not putting into words. The situation must be bad. He could recognize the strain in Michael's voice. He shifted his position and started moving closer to Harold now that they knew where Ashley was. He moved within fifty yards of Harold and they picked up their pace.

Michael's voice came over the line, filled with anger, "Guys, she's handcuffed and he's stripped her naked. It looks like they're arguing... Wait, he just moved; he has someone else held up to his body. Oh shit! It's Casey. He has Casey! He has her stripped too and it looks like she's gagged and has her hands zipped together. Did you copy? There are two hostages!"

Michael was in shock. When had he snatched up Casey? This had to have put Ashley in a worse situation than she had been when it was just her. He knew his sister well enough to know that she would now only be concerned about saving Casey's life, with no regard to her own.

"We copy. We are closing in fast. What is our best strategy?"

"He has a huge bowie knife to Casey's throat, using her to control Ashley, I would assume. Our hands are tied as long as he's holding her like that. Stand down until I can see where this is headed. Ashley won't do anything to jeopardize Casey's life. Ashley looks like she's in pretty rough shape. We need to take the first opportunity we get to end this. I don't see a gun, so I'm not sure where the shots came from, just the knife at Casey's neck."

Derek's heart skipped a beat at the news of Ashley's condition. "Michael, is there a way I can get behind him and signal Ashley that we're here?"

"No. It's an open pasture behind him, but I'm a little behind and to the side of his position so let me see if I can work it out. I'm afraid if I stand up, he'll see the movement."

Michael was watching through the rifle scope, and could see that Ashley's situation was coming to a climax. Whatever they were discussing was causing Carver to become very agitated. Michael glanced up to the sun and back at Ashley. He crawled over about twenty feet and angled the rifle up so that the sun hit the end of the scope, and kept angling it so that the reflection would shine on the side of Carver's arm. He moved the rifle up and down slowly so the reflection moved only about two inches or so. Then he shifted it away and brought it back, over and over again, hoping Ashley would realize what it was, or at least glance around and investigate the source of the light.

Derek had raced across the yard and moved to the front of the barn, with Harold and the sheriff moving in from the other side.

Derek could see Michael from his angle, but was afraid to look around the side in fear that he would be spotted. He watched as Michael moved his rifle up and down, not sure what his intent was. He was too close to communicate through the headsets, so watched and waited for a signal from Michael.

Derek hated that he was not able to see what was happening. He had followed this case and knew that Carver had reached his climax. His gut told him that Carver had no regard whether he lived or died, his only goal was to kill Ashley. His deranged mind had somehow blamed Ashley for his brother's suicide. Derek wondered if Ashley knew yet why she was a victim in the situation. She had to be going through hell, dealing with a man who had lost all rational thoughts. He could only pray that whatever Michael was planning was good enough to get Ashley and Casey out of a very dangerous position.

CHAPTER FORTY-ONE

Ashley stood in front of Jason, realizing that she had really enraged him. He was glaring at her with so much hatred that she knew it was only a matter of minutes before he killed them both, forgetting that he wanted to torment her with his stupid tests. She still held the gun at her side, and he had apparently forgotten that she had it, but it was still no use to her while Casey had a knife held to her throat. As Jason and Ashley stood glaring, she noticed a reflection on his sleeve. At first she thought a piece of equipment was reflecting the sun, but after a few seconds of watching, it would disappear and then reappear. The wind was not blowing at all, not even a breeze, and the sun was beating down on all of them. She allowed her eyes to move off him for a split second, looking for the source of the reflection. There was no equipment, just a pasture with a hill to the side of it. She looked back at him and noticed the reflection was back but was now moving side to side, not up and down. Her heart leapt to her throat and excitement raced through her; she shifted her eyes once more to the hill and noticed an arm extend from it for a split second and then disappear again.

Looking instantly back at him so that he would not turn to investigate, she started talking again so that he was distracted and wouldn't look around. "I'm sorry. So, so sorry that your brother is gone. It was my fault and you're right to want me dead."

Casey looked at Ashley, startled. She met Casey's eyes and blinked rapidly several times, then shifted her eyes to the right. Casey seemed confused, and then her eyes widened in understanding and she blinked back.

Ashley knew she only had a few seconds to make this happen. She needed to get the knife away from Casey's neck. Nothing would work as long as there was a chance she could be hurt. Ashley's mind raced with different scenarios, all sounding crazy in her rattled brain.

In the few seconds she was debating what to do, a red dot appeared suddenly on the side of Jason's head, above his right ear. It moved a fraction of an inch up and down, then disappeared, only to be back a second later.

Time was up; she had to do something. She switched the gun to her left hand and lifted her arm like she was handing it back to him, but then dropped it in the dirt instead. His eyes flew to where it had landed, giving her the split second she needed. Ashley grabbed his left arm with her right and pulled it away from Casey's neck, and at the same time she jerked Casey down, falling on top of her. A shot rang out and Ashley watched out of the corner of her eye as Carver stood for a split second, and then crumpled to his side, falling behind them.

Casey tried to turn her head to see what had happened, but Ashley held her in place, preventing her from seeing his sightless eyes and his head, partially exploded when the bullet had entered his right ear.

Before she even had time to move there was activity all around them. Men poured from the fields and from around the barn. Ashley's head was still tucked in close to Casey, when suddenly a shirt was placed around her and arms lifted her away, holding her tightly as they ran for cover around the end of the barn. She didn't have to look to know who held her. The strength in those arms told